'D‸   s.
He turned to look at the fat butcher tied to the stake like a
grub about to be roasted. He asked the crowd: Why should
this man die?

'The crowd told him: He is Chaos. Destroy him!' – *from*
Hatred *by Ben Chessell*

'YOU SEE THIS?' the witch hunter, Obediah Cain, said in a
wild voice, brandishing a parchment. 'This contract holds
the keys to the greatest magical mysteries of the age. Its
clauses have been set down in the name of the
unchallenged master of magic, Lord Tzeentch himself. Aid
me now and sorceries beyond your wildest imaginations
shall be yours to command!' – *from* **The Chaos Beneath** *by
Mark Brendan*

IN THE DARK and gothic world of Warhammer, the ravaging
armies of the Ruinous Powers sweep down from the savage
north to assail the lands of men. REALM OF CHAOS is a
᠁᠁᠁ collection of a dozen all-action fantasy short
᠁᠁᠁᠁᠁᠁ desperate times, showcasing the very
᠁᠁᠁ azine.

Also from the Black Library

GOTREK & FELIX: TROLLSLAYER
by William King

GOTREK & FELIX: SKAVENSLAYER
by William King

GOTREK & FELIX: DAEMONSLAYER
by William King

SPACE WOLF
by William King

GAUNT'S GHOSTS: FIRST & ONLY
by Dan Abnett

EYE OF TERROR
by Barrington J. Bayley

INTO THE MAELSTROM
edited by Marc Gascoigne & Andy Jones

WARHAMMER FANTASY STORIES

REALM OF CHAOS

Edited by Marc Gascoigne
& Andy Jones

A BLACK LIBRARY PUBLICATION

Games Workshop Publishing
Willow Road, Lenton,
Nottingham, NG7 2WS, UK

First US edition, August 2000

10 9 8 7 6 5 4 3 2 1

Disitributed by Simon & Schuster
1230 Avenue of the Americas
New York, NY 10020

Cover illustration by Martin Hanford

ISBN 0-671-78405-6

Set in ITC Giovanni

Printed and bound in Great Britain by
Omnia Ltd, Glasgow, UK

See the Black Library on the Internet at
http://www.blacklibrary.co.uk

Find out more about Games Workshop
and the world of Warhammer at
http://www.games-workshop.com

CONTENTS

BIRTH OF A LEGEND

Gav Thorpe

'GRUGNI'S BEARD, I wish they'd quieten down! I've got one hell of a hangover!' King Kurgan spat derisively at the burly green-skin watching over them.

The four dwarfs were tied to stakes, their hands and ankles bound with crude rope. A huge bonfire raged not far off and the orcs were celebrating their victory. The air was filled with the sound of beating drums and the woods reverberated with the constant pounding. As the night passed, they broke open huge barrels of their foul intoxicating brew to wash down the hunks of charred dwarf flesh they had eaten earlier. The flames of the fire leapt higher and higher and the orcs shouted louder and louder.

Kurgan's blood boiled. He strained at his bonds with all his strength. It was to no avail; the knots remained as tight as ever. He was condemned to look on despondently while the foul creatures made a banquet of his household. Over to his left, Snorri slumped semi-conscious against his pole. The others, Borris and Thurgan, seemed similarly dazed. The king's gruff voice cut across the laughter and shouts of the orcs.

'Snorri! Hey, Snorri! A curse upon us for being captured rather than killed, wouldn't you say?'

The venerable advisor groaned and looked up at his king, one eye screwed shut with pain, the lids stuck together with congealed blood from a cut on his brow.

'Aye, a pox on the green devils for not ending it honourably, sire. I'll see them all rotting in hell 'fore I'm for the pot! Mark my words!'

Despite their predicament, Kurgan was heartened by Snorri's defiant words and he grinned to himself. Out beyond the fire he could see the orcs smashing open the barrel of ale he had been taking with him to his cousin in the Grey Mountains. A tear glistened in Kurgan's eye as he thought of that fine brew, made over five hundred years ago and matured in oak casks stored in Karak Eight Peaks, wasted in stunted orc throats. What he had paid for that small keg could have trained and equipped an army for a month. The potent ale had seemed like a good investment at the time, but when the orcs had poured from their hiding places yelling their shrieking war cries, he had realised that perhaps the money should have been spent on an army after all.

Kurgan pushed aside thoughts of ale and studied the orc camp, trying to figure out a plan of escape. Most of the orcs – he wasn't sure how many there were – sat in small groups, dicing, squabbling or just sprawling, bloated. The smaller goblins scurried to and fro, fetching and carrying for their bigger cousins, who would occasionally kick or punch one of them for raucous entertainment. A particularly inventive black orc used his spear to elicit a yelping noise which the orcs found amusing.

Kurgan could see that most of the dwarfs' stolen weapons, armour and treasure was piled all over the camp, with no plan or order. In one part of the clearing, Kurgan's mighty field tent had been crudely erected for the orc leader, although the sides of the massive marquee had not been unfurled. Inside, gold and gems were piled high, but Kurgan was looking for the magical weapons and armour that had been stripped from him and his Longbeard retainers. Across the darkness Kurgan could make out the massive warlord, sitting on a fur-backed throne at one end of the tent while his drinking cronies squatted around him. A mass of glittering treasure was spilled around them. They laughed heartily at some brutal jest. Perhaps the warlord felt Kurgan's gaze lingering on him, for the orc slowly turned his heavy head to fix the dwarf king with evil red eyes. That malevolent glance fastened Kurgan to the wooden stake as surely as the ropes which bound him. For a short moment he stopped struggling.

Kurgan regained his composure, scowling at the dark savage with what he hoped was his most frightening glare. The warlord back-handed one of his subordinates for some misdemeanour, sending the orc sprawling in a spray of teeth. The huge brute stood up abruptly, shouting something to his subordinates, his bosses. He grabbed a passing goblin and tossed the unfortunate creature into the blazing campfire. As the warlord's comrades laughed at this jest, the huge orc began stomping towards Kurgan. His glowing eyes never left the dwarf for a moment. The milling throng of orcs and goblins parted effortlessly before the stride of the mighty warlord, closing in behind their leader as he marched towards his most prized captives.

The orc warlord was dressed in heavy black mail and studded plates, and even Kurgan found himself thinking that he presented a fearsome sight. At his belt hung a string of grisly trophies: severed heads, hands, feet and ears dangled from a chain looped around a thick leather strap. The warlord's skin was dark green in colour, almost black, and slab-like muscles rippled beneath the surface. The orc's bucket-jawed head thrust forward from between two chain-bedecked shoulder pads, his red eyes burning with fierce power. They were pinpoints of pure hatred, smouldering with a barely-repressed violence that made Kurgan tremble with fearful anticipation. Switching his gaze before he betrayed any weakness to the advancing orc, he looked at the huge column of smoke pouring into the sky, lifting burning fragments of his comrades' clothes into the chill night air.

ACROSS THE WOODS, other eyes had seen the smoke. Now they moved silently through the forest towards its source.

Ansgar turned to the youth leading the hunting party and asked the question which had been nagging him.

'Are you sure this is a good idea? We've got no clue as to what's out there!'

The burly young man simply turned to him and winked, before pressing forward along the rough track. Ansgar sighed and beckoned the rest of the party to follow, swapping worried glances with a couple of the older members, veterans of no few battles. Eginolf passed by and Ansgar fell into step with his twin brother.

'I don't like this at all, Eginolf. He's a fine lad, but he's not ready for something like this. Headstrong, if you ask me.'

'I didn't,' came the grunted reply.

Ansgar shrugged and padded along the game trail in silence, his hand holding his sword to his thigh to stop it making any noise. The hunting party included warriors of all ages, from veterans in their thirties like Eginolf and himself, to seasoned warriors in their early twenties and untried boys who had seen only a dozen summers.

Their leader, perhaps surprisingly, fell nearer that end of the scale. The youth was a fine-looking young man. Only fifteen, he was already over six feet tall and his well-muscled body put any man to shame. It wasn't only his physical prowess that impressed Ansgar, though. The hunt lord was clever and canny, with an experience of hunting and battle that belied his age. The lad had a toughness inside too, a resolute stubbornness to overcome any problem.

Ansgar fondly recalled a time, maybe five years ago, when a party had gone to the river to catch fish. The group had been confronted by a massive bear, there for the same purpose. Everybody else had frozen, but the young lord had strode forward, hands on hips, until he was a few paces from the huge beast. 'These are our waters, fish somewhere else!' he stated in a level voice. Ansgar had expected the bear to swipe the boy's head off, but instead it had looked at the youngster's unwavering stare and had turned and lumbered into the woods without a growl.

From that day, the young lord had become known as Steeleye, and his reputation had done nothing but grow. He was a good leader, generous to those who served him well, swift to act against the enemies of the tribe. He was very much like his father and when that great man was eventually ushered into the halls of the dead, his successor would bring a time of equal prosperity. But that was for the future. All that mattered now was finding out who was trespassing on their lands.

The warriors of the hunting band were dressed for the cold night, their brightly patterned woollen breeches and fur-lined leather jerkins protecting them from the biting north wind. Most of the men wore their hair in one or two long braids down their back, woven with bright ribbons and beads to match their chequered leggings.

As the lord's hunting party, they were equipped with the finest weapons forged from sturdy metal mined in the south-eastern foothills. Each of the men also had a short hunting bow, carved from the horns of mountain cattle. The warriors of the tribe were taught how to use the bows from the time they were able to lift one, and even in the darkest night they rarely missed their mark. Ansgar was proud to carry the champion's bow, edged with gold and silver thread, which he had won four times in the last six years. Whatever his words of caution, Ansgar was as eager for a fight as any of them, looking forward to the promise of more glory in battle. If there was some fighting to be done this night, he would be ready for it.

The party moved on in silence, the forest around them in almost total darkness as the cloudy sky obscured the twin moons. Now that they had dropped into the dale the distant flicker of fire could no longer be seen, but the scouts had taken their bearings well and they were headed almost straight to the north to investigate the intrusion. Soon they would find out just who it was who thought they could camp within their borders.

BY THE TIME the warlord was stood in front of his dwarf captives, most of his warriors were behind him. His head cocked to one side with concentration, the large orc looked at each of them in turn, assessing their remaining strength. Noticing Snorri's injury, the massive black orc's mouth twisted in a cruel smile and he stepped forward for a closer look.

It was just the opportunity Snorri had been waiting for. Lashing forward with his head, the old dwarf delivered a smashing butt to the bridge of the orc's nose, sending a spatter of green blood spilling through the night air. The mumbling throng behind him fell silent except for a few gurgling gasps of horror and the clatter of the odd weapon or cup dropped in stunned disbelief. As the chieftain shook his head to clear the dizziness, one of his lieutenants stepped forward, a bared scimitar lifted above his head. His intent was clear. Angrily, the chieftain pushed the orc back into the mob and grinned evilly at Snorri. Wiping away the mixture of blood and mucus dripping down his long top lip with the back of his gnarled, scarred hand, the battle-hardened orc chuckled. 'I likes dis wun – 'e's gorra lorra spirit, hur hur!'

When the stunned silence continued, the warlord slowly turned on his heel to glare at his warriors. Under his hostile gaze, the mob broke into howls of sycophantic laughter. Satisfied with this display, their leader turned back to the dwarfs, his attention now firmly fixed on Kurgan.

'Wotcha, stunties! Are we cumfurtabble? Do yooze knows what I'm gonna do wiv yooze lot? Dere's lots of fings we can do togevver, and it'll be a lorra fun. We 'ad a lorra fun wiv yer mates!'

To illustrate his point, the warlord let rip with an enormous belch, spattering Kurgan with spittle. The stench of charred dwarf flesh and fungus beer was nauseating and the dwarf king felt his stomach lurch uncontrollably. With some effort, Kurgan quelled the bile rising in his throat and grimaced at the warlord.

'Course, we woz 'ungry den, so we 'ad to be pretty quick wiv da butcherin'. Yooze fellas, we's gonna take our time over, ain't we lads?'

The warlord turned to his ragtag army, his cavernous mouth yawning open to display an impressive set of yellowing, cracked fangs in what Kurgan assumed was the orc equivalent of a grin. This time the mob cheered on cue, laughing heartily. Kurgan tried once more to loosen his bonds, without success.

'Da furst fing we's gonna do is put yer feet inna fire. Dat'll warm yer up fer sure. Den we can stick fings in yer eyes, so's you don't see no more. Den we's gonna chop off yer fingas and toes and ears and noses and hack off yer luvverly beards. I fink yer king's beard will go well wiv me uvver mates.'

The orc stretched and grabbed a handful of Kurgan's hair, dragging his head forward until it was level with the vile decaying decorations on the orc's belt. The stench of rotting blood and filth emanating from the warlord's unwashed fur leggings made Kurgan want to retch, and he had to muster every ounce of self control not to heave up his breakfast. The warlord released his grip and continued.

'Den I fink we'll start boilin' bits of yer inna pot, and we'll feed 'em to yer so's yer don't go 'ungry. Yooze stunties are tough 'uns, no mistake, and I reckon dere'll still be plenty of life left in yer after dat. So den we start peelin' yer skin off an' feedin' it to da boarz. Da last fing we's gonna do is cut out yer tongues, cos by dat time yer'll be screamin' really loud and musical, beggin' us ta stop 'avin so much fun.'

Kurgan spat again, and raised his head to stare straight at the old orc. Clearing his throat of smoke and ash, the dwarf king's voice rang clearly out over the camp.

'You have plagued us for many years, Vagraz Head-Stomper, and we have never been afraid of you. You don't frighten us now! You will never get me to beg anything from you, you worthless dung-head! I'd bite off my tongue before I would give you that pleasure. You can torture us, but you'll never break our spirits.'

The warlord frowned at the interruption. With a non-committal grunt, the orc delivered a short punch to Kurgan's jaw, smashing his head back against the post and splitting his lip.

'You mite not fink I'm very smart, but I knows a few fings about yooze stunties. F'rinstance, I knows dat da worst fing for you is gonna be to watch yer mates gettin' it furst.' Gazing at the roaring fire and then back to the dwarfs, Vagraz gave an evil chuckle. 'Enough words. Let's get started!'

With that he spun and delivered a mighty kick to Snorri's midriff. The ancient counsellor fell to his knees, doubled up with pain. Another kick from the iron-capped boots knocked Snorri sideways, spiralling down the pole until he was left choking in the mud. Eager to regain his lost standing, the burly orc with the scimitar pushed forwards again, two swift hacks severing through the ropes binding Snorri. As a goblin darted forward to wind more cord around the dwarf's wrists, the orc subordinate leant down and snarled into Snorri's ear.

'Lucky you, da boss wants yer furst!'

THE MOONS BROKE from the cloud and the party halted briefly by a swift-running brook. The men sat down in the undergrowth along the bank, splashing the cold water onto their faces, swallowing a few gulps of the cool, refreshing liquid and chewing on the odd meat twist or fruit they had brought along. Soon they were moving again. Slipping silently into the darkness, disturbing the bushes and branches less than the touch of a breeze, the scouts ran off ahead. Soon the first of them returned, melting back from the shadowy darkness. They gathered around the hunt lord to report. The oldest of them, Lando, spoke first.

'It's an orc camp, lord. It's difficult to say how many, they keep moving around, but by my reckoning it's odds of at least four to one in their favour. They've got a few guards, but they're all drunk. We could slit their throats without any problems. From the trails they seem to be heading westward, from the mountains.'

Frodewin carved a picture of the scene in the dirt. 'The most sheltered approach is from the west. We can circle round the Korburg and move up Aelfric's Vale to attack. The moons are almost set; soon it'll be completely dark. With that massive fire they've got burning, their night vision is going to be worthless. We should be able to pick off half of them before they realise there's anything amiss.'

The blond curly hair of Ringolf bobbed up and down with excitement as the young lad pushed his way to the front to add his news.

'They've captured somebody, but I couldn't get close enough to find out who.' The young man gulped a breath. 'There's a whole horde of them. Maybe we should wait for the others to arrive.'

Steel-eye sighed and looked at each of his men. Without a word, he turned and started off towards the orc camp at a run. The others exchanged confused glances and then followed without protest. The going was easy, following a deer track to the west through the ferns that studded the base of the mound known as Korburg. The scouts slipped ahead once more, spreading out to silence the slumbering sentries they had located. The main party continued around the tor, breaking to the north when it reached a small stream which splashed down the steep slope from a high spring.

Quickly and carefully, the hunters passed through the woods without a sound. The twin moons dipped out of sight and the forest was plunged into blackness. Steel-eye signalled a stop and then moved forward, tapping Ansgar and Eginolf to indicate they should accompany him. They half crouched, half ran towards the clearing. Ansgar could hear the drums and the chants of the orcs quite clearly now – and smell the stench of burning flesh on the breeze. The old huntsman uttered a whispered curse and Eginolf placed a warning finger to his lips. He pointed towards a small thicket where a dozing orc leant against a tree, its crude club lying next to it.

Without a sound, Eginolf drew his long hunting knife and slipped into the trees. A moment later he was rising out of the bushes behind the orc. His hand clamped around its long jaw and the knife flashed down in one swift stroke. Eginolf laid his prey down carefully before rejoining his fellow huntsmen who lay in a clump of ferns at the edge of the clearing. From here they could clearly see four dwarf prisoners tied to stakes, two of them pretty badly wounded. As they watched, an immense black orc walked over to the dwarfs, followed by almost the entirety of his warband. There was a brief exchange, during which the chieftain was knocked sprawling by a head butt from one of the captives. All three of the humans grinned in appreciation of this act of defiance, and both Eginolf and Ansgar nodded when their lord started to string his bow and gestured for them to fetch the other warriors. Before long, the whole war party was hiding along the western face of the clearing. In the centre of their line, Ansgar and Eginolf flanked the hunt lord. One of the dwarfs was being dragged from his post and they watched as he started to fight with his captors before being savagely beaten into acquiescence.

Ansgar spat and whispered another curse, before shooting an inquiring look at his master.

'As much as it riles me to see such creatures on our lands,' he whispered urgently, 'why should we risk ourselves for the stunted beardlings? They've never offered a hand to us.'

Steel-eye spoke for the first time that evening. His voice was strong but quiet. It had an authoritative ring to it which forestalled any quarrel.

'I don't like orcs. Any being, man or dwarf, who can still put up a fight when bound certainly earns my respect.'

He pulled an arrow from his quiver and rose to one knee.

SNORRI WAS HAULED roughly to his feet. As the orcs jostled him towards their leader, the venerable dwarf lashed out with his foot, smashing the knee of one of his guards. As the other orcs grabbed him, Snorri stamped on the fallen orc's neck, producing an audible crack. He was bundled to the ground, the orcs kicking him and jabbing him with the butts of their spears.

Throughout the cruel, mocking laughter of the warlord cackled out over the roar of the fire. Bloodied, smeared with mud and half-fainting from pain, Snorri was dragged across the camp towards the fire. The orc mob gathered around, whooping and cheering, eager for blood.

The air was suddenly thick with black-feathered arrows, each picking out a separate target with lethal accuracy. The orcs had no time to scream before they were dead. Even as the others in the camp looked around with dumbfounded disbelief, a second hail of shafts picked off another swathe of greenskins. The air was filled with startled, raucous cries. The drunken orcs fumbled to get their weapons ready, stumbling over their dead companions and tripping over the stashes of loot that littered the clearing. Another deadly volley poured from the dark trees, followed by a series of whooping cries as a band of humans broke from their cover, dropping their bows and drawing long knives and swords from their belts.

Kurgan strained again at his bonds, then looked up at Thorin's yell.

'This is our chance, uncle! Let's try to get out of here while the greenskins are diverted by these primitives.'

A glance to his right confirmed to Kurgan that Borris was still unconscious, hanging from the ropes like a tattered rag doll. The massive bruise on Borris's head was as dark as coal and dried blood stained the whole side of his face. Escape didn't look very likely, but Kurgan was not one to look a gift pony in the mouth. He clenched his teeth and wrenched at the ropes once again.

The orcs had now recovered from their initial surprise and had started to organise themselves. Compared to the mass of greenskins, Kurgan thought the humans looked pitifully few. Gnashing his teeth in frustration, he strained at his bonds until his arms went numb, but there was no give in the ropes. Despite their lack of numbers, the humans were taking a heavy toll of the stunned, drunken orcs. One young man in particular was cutting a bloody path through the horde, slaying another orc with every swing of his sword. The greenskins were beginning to surround their attackers though, and Kurgan feared the reprieve from the orcs' bloody attentions would be short-lived.

* * *

ANSGAR WAS GRINNING with the rush of battle, even as he parried another serrated orc sword. Lunging forward with his left hand he buried his hunting knife in the savage's midriff. As the orc dropped gurgling to the floor another stepped forward, only to be felled by a blow from Eginolf, who fought to his brother's right. The twins looked around for more foes. Their hunt lord was surrounded by a throng of greenskins, but even if they'd been sober the orcs would have been poor match for the mighty human lord. Although covered in a dozen light scratches and bruises, he paid no heed to his wounds and fought with the ferocity of a bear. Roaring the tribe's battle cry, he plunged his sword through the neck of a goblin and, with a backhand blow of his knife, disembowelled another.

Most of the goblins were dead or fleeing into the welcoming darkness of the forest, and no few orcs too. Nevertheless, Ansgar could see that the surprise attack would peter out unless they could break the main orc horde. Suddenly his attention was drawn to Steel-eye. Screaming in anger, the youth leapt over the heads of his attackers to come crashing down in the middle of their impromptu shield-wall. Ansgar lost sight of him behind a wall of green bodies and flailing swords.

Concerned for his lord, Ansgar shouted for his trusted veterans to follow him. He set off through the throng, hacking his way towards the youth. Ansgar's worry was short-lived. The muscled young man burst into view, rearing up from a tangle of corpses to hack at the exposed backs of his would-be attackers. Breaking in panic, the orcs tried to run, only to be cut down as Ansgar and Eginolf led their seasoned fighters to support their leader. There was an open route to the captives now, and Ansgar directed some of the men to act as a rearguard while the rest followed Steel-eye as he hurried towards the dwarf prisoners.

KURGAN COULDN'T HELP but be awed by the fighting prowess of the young human, obviously their leader from the way the savages clustered around him. Even as the dwarf king watched, the youngster effortlessly dodged a clumsy spear thrust, before stunning his attacker with the pommel of his sword. Ducking beneath a wild axe swing to slash the hamstrings of another greenskin, the youth stabbed upwards with his knife, showering himself in a fountain of orc blood. Kurgan almost felt like

a spectator at some macabre dance, watching carefully choreo-
graphed moves executed with grim precision. The young man
was constantly moving, weaving between the blows of his
adversaries while his own weapons bit deep with every strike. A
powerful kick to the spine sent a black orc crumpling to the
ground, while the lad headbutted another adversary, snapping
the orc's spiked helmet back with a jarring crack.

Kurgan noted that the other humans weren't faring badly
either. A few had fallen, but nowhere near as many as the orcs.
The lithe huntsmen darted through the throng in pairs and
trios, singling out a foe to gang up on. After dispatching one
individual they would find another, and so on, moving
through the orc camp with ruthless efficiency. For all their primal savagery, the humans were brave fighters.

Kurgan heard Thorin spit a curse and he turned to see his
nephew glaring angrily at the approaching humans.

'What's wrong, lad?'

'Those damned pinkskin humans. They're fighting over us
with the orcs. I don't know which of them is worse. With orcs
you know they're a bunch of cut-throat scum, but these
humans are all falsehoods and backstabbing. They've probably
come to cart us off to whatever foul pit they call a home. And
they'll take the treasure too, I'll warrant.'

'Mayhap, lad. Whatever their reasons, as long as they're
killing greenskins I've no quarrel with them. I'll give them their
dues, they know how to swing a sword when the going gets
tough. Quit bellyaching and try to get free!'

Kurgan turned his attention back to the battle. Some of the
humans had broken through the orc line and their leader now
led a small group of their oldest warriors towards the dwarf
king. Seeing their painted faces, foam-flecked lips and wild,
bloodthirsty eyes, Kurgan was unsure he wanted to be the
object of their attentions. Still, these stupid humans might
unwittingly provide him and the others with some chance of
getting away. Without a word, one of the youngest warriors ran
behind the posts and Kurgan winced as he anticipated a dagger
thrust to his kidneys.

It never came. Instead, Kurgan felt the rasping of a knife
against his ropes. They were wound loosely around the pole
itself, looped many times over and the lad was having difficulty
cutting through them as they slipped and slithered up and

down the rain-slicked pole. Kurgan exerted all his strength in one last mighty effort. With a snap the ropes parted and he pitched forward into the mud. In another few moments his legs were free and he looked up to see how the battle was progressing.

A quick glance showed Kurgan all he needed to know. Despite the casualties inflicted on the orcs, things still looked grim. Skill and speed was one thing, but in this battle raw muscles and numbers counted for more and the pressure was beginning to tell on the men. Almost half the humans had fallen; now only the toughest and most skilful fighters remained. Hoarse war-cries were drowned out by the clash of metal on metal and the screams of the wounded and dying. Foot by foot, the humans were being pushed back.

Thorin was free now, but the humans were having trouble cutting loose the bonds on the unconscious Borris. With a snarl, their blood-drenched leader sheathed his sword and grabbed the stake itself. He heaved upwards, muscles bulging under the pressure. His legs were slowly straightening, even while his booted feet sank into the mud. Kurgan looked on in astonishment as the top of the pole begin to rock from side to side, first only a few inches, and then a foot, and then it was swaying wildly. With a grunt and a twist, the stake came free and toppled to the ground. A tall human with plaited hair and a drooping moustache stepped forward, slipped off the ropes holding Borris to the stake and draped the inert dwarf over one shoulder.

The young human leader was about to start back towards the fight, but Kurgan grabbed his cloak. He formed the unfamiliar words of the human language with difficulty, speaking in a thick accent.

'You not hold them off by your own. Thorin and I can help. Ancient dwarf weapons here, lots of runes. Magic. Understand me?'

The young man stepped back in astonishment, then grinned widely. Kurgan was surprised by the calm strength in his voice, even though his chest was rising and falling rapidly from his recent exertions.

'You've got magic weapons here? Why are we standing talking? Let's go get them!'

They set off at a run towards the warlord's ramshackle tent, even as the human line began to falter under the constant onslaught of the orcs. A few of the greenskins broke through and raced across the muddy clearing, eager to intercept the freed prisoners. Kurgan and Thorin both looked around for something to fight with, stopping to grab a couple of axes and shields from the piles of loot left over from the orcs' ambush.

By now the main fight was raging around the part of the camp given over to the warlord, and the humans were being pressed back to within an arm's reach of the tent. Vagraz wasn't about to give up the treasure and prisoners he had already fought for once that day. The humans around Kurgan shouted their battle-cry once more and charged into the fray. The human leader was leaping amongst the orcs, sweat gleaming off his rippling muscles in the flickering firelight. He moved with a grace rarely found in one of his size, darting through the crowd and hacking down a mountain of foes.

Now Vagraz himself led the greenskins, a mob of black orcs around him. They were fearsome foes and the heavily armoured orcs smashed into the humans with terrible ferocity. The warlord cleaved through a handful of humans with a single blow from his massive axe. Vagraz's backswing beheaded another unfortunate before the orc strode forward to deal more death. The humans fell back before him.

Having gained the warlord's tent, Kurgan and Thorin rummaged through the treasures stolen by the orcs, searching frantically for their ancient weapons and armour. Nothing else would hold back the tide of greenskins now. Beside them lay the still form of Borris, whose deathly pallor did little to cheer Kurgan. Looking up briefly, he saw the orc warlord crush the face of a hunter with a mighty punch, before swinging his axe round in a deadly arc that left three more fighters dismembered. Cursing his befuddled head and aching limbs, the dwarf king redoubled his search.

BEFORE THE TENT, Ansgar and Eginolf fought back to back, surrounded by a crowd of orcs whose blows rose and fell with relentless ferocity. Each of them was marked by a dozen light cuts, but the pile of bodies around them testified that each drop of blood had been drawn at a heavy price.

As Ansgar gutted one orc and stepped back to avoid the swipe of a sword, he felt Eginolf stumble behind him. Hacking wildly at his foes to push them back momentarily, Ansgar glanced over his shoulder. Eginolf, his twin brother, was on his knees. A spear had punched through his stomach; its barbed point now jutted from his back. Eginolf still swung his sword and screamed at the orcs.

'It'll take more than a green scum twig like this to end me. I'm going to bathe in your blood, you cowardly wretches!'

Time slowed for Ansgar as he saw a black orc push forward from the throng, a mighty cleaver in each hand. Even as Eginolf weakly fended off one blow, the other arm swept down with unstoppable force. Helpless to intervene, Ansgar watched with horror as the head of his twin tumbled to the ground.

Something inside Ansgar snapped. Yelling incoherently with pure rage, he threw himself at the orcs with renewed vigour. He was berserk, giving no thought for his own life, as he hacked and slashed, stabbed and jabbed with his sword. Startled by this unexpected fury, the orcs fell back.

Ignorant of everything except his raging hatred of his brother's murderers, Ansgar pressed on wildly, each step taking him further from the sanctuary of his comrades. As he shouldered one foe aside, Ansgar's blade was knocked from his grasp and was lost beneath the orcs' stamping feet. Ansgar tossed his knife from his left to his right hand and ducked his head down. In the press, the orcs' heavy weapons were useless. Ansgar's hunting knife was far more deadly; opening arteries, severing windpipes, ripping tendons and puncturing vital organs.

DESPITE THE veteran's frenzied counter-attack, Kurgan thought the humans looked close to fleeing. The dwarf king was hastily hauling on his rune-encrusted armour, feeling its ancient plates fold over him like an old lover's embrace. Thorin was busy strapping on his studded gauntlets when he gave a cry of dismay. Turning, Kurgan watched in horror as Vagraz burst through the ranks of humans. The orc's massive axe glittered with dark magic, black flames playing along its edges. A few foolhardy men tried to interpose themselves between the awesome killing machine and the dwarfs, but in a few swift heartbeats they were dead, their blood seeping into the forest floor to mix with the gore of a hundred other warriors, orc and human.

Then the humans' youthful leader was there, leaping over the axes and swords of the orcs to attack their warlord. The young warrior stood with his legs slightly apart, ready to face the oncoming butcher. Still staring at the approaching orc, the human shouted to Kurgan.

'Where's your magic, beardling? I think now would be a good time to see it!'

Bellowing his wrath, Vagraz charged. Rolling beneath a wild swing of the warlord's baleful axe, the human youth dived to one side, then swung his long sword down at the orc's neck with his whole weight. The blade shattered on the enchanted armour of the warlord, who turned slowly and grinned at his would-be killer. Without hesitation the hunt lord flung the shattered stump of his sword into the orcs' face and leapt, his feet thudding into the warlord's jaw with a sickening crunch. The orc was knocked sprawling by the unexpected blow.

Allowing the hulking brute no time to recover, young Steel-eye moved behind Vagraz and started raining punches into the back of his thick neck. Roaring in anger, the orc spun around, smashing a plate-sized fist into the lord's chin, hurling him to the ground. Shaking his head to clear it, Vagraz lifted an immense booted foot to stamp on the young warrior, but he was too slow and the hunter rolled to his feet with fluid grace. The young man delivered a sweeping kick that made the warlord buckle at the knees.

Kurgan was cursing constantly now, throwing heaps of gold and gems aside in his frantic quest for his ancient weapon.

'Where the hell are you?' he spat, but even as he spoke his hand fell upon sturdy stitching wound around cold steel. With a yelp, he pulled the rune-forged warhammer from the concealing pile of glittering treasure. Kurgan fervently prayed he wasn't too late.

He span around to see the beleaguered human leader slip on the slick of mud and blood that covered the ground. As the orc chieftain lifted his massive axe above his head, its blade shining with unearthly energies, Kurgan flung his hammer to the young man. It arced across the campsite, spinning slowly, its head flashing in the glow of the bonfire. The youth's long arm snapped up to grab it, his fingers closing round the hilt. As Vagraz's dark axe swept down, the barbarian leader brought up the rune hammer to meet it. The weapons clashed with a shower of black and blue sparks and the two fighters were locked together.

The orc had the advantage and pressed down with all his weight, bringing the sorcerous axe blade ever closer to the young man's throat. The youth's arms trembled with the strain, sweat poured across his body and his face was purple with effort. His huge muscles twitched and veins stood out like cords across his neck and shoulders. With a scream Steel-eye thrust the orc back with all his remaining strength, swinging the hammer to one side to knock the warlord off balance. Howling, the hunter leapt to his feet and the two adversaries stood facing each other again. The human was grinning wolfishly, his eyes ablaze. The orc's hand constantly clenched and unclenched on the haft of his massive axe in agitated anticipation. Gauging each other carefully, the two leaders circled slowly.

'Your axe is very pretty, scum, but this hammer will be your doom. Even unarmed I was besting you and now I have this, you have only a heartbeat left to live! Enjoy your last moments, greenskin offal!'

'Keep talkin', pretty boy! Froat Biter hasn't finished wiv yer yet. Perhaps yer voice won't be so dainty once I've cut yer froat from ear ta ear!'

'I'll bathe in your blood and count the heads of your friends before that clumsy lump of pig iron touches my skin!'

'Let's see if yer muscles are as big as yer mouf!'

As one, both combatants swung. Their mighty weapons rang against each other with an explosion of magical energy. Steel-eye ducked Vagraz's swing and brought the warhammer around in a mighty blow that smashed off one of the warlord's shoulder pads. Amazed that his magical armour had been penetrated, the warlord was thrown off-guard. Vagraz barely had time to throw a hasty parry as the warhammer swung upwards again, knocking the orc backwards. Without pause, the young human leapt forward to sustain his attack, raining blow after blow against the orc.

Vagraz was not going to fall easily. A wild swing opened up a gaping cut in the hunter's side, but left the orc leader's defences open. With a defiant yell, the young man ignored his injury and swung again, the head of the hammer sweeping Vagraz off his feet with an audible cracking of bones. A second blow snapped the orc's head backwards and sent his axe tumbling from his grasp. Somehow the orc still clung to life. With a grunt it raised itself to its shattered knees and held up a hand. Confused and suspecting treachery, the hunt lord checked his next blow, staring distrustfully down at the broken creature on the ground before him.

To Steel-eye's surprise, the warlord started laughing, a dull chuckling that rose to a guttural thunder. Vagraz snorted contemptuously, spitting several teeth into the mud, and he raised a hand to form one final, vulgar gesture.

His patience gone, the hunt lord stepped forward. 'Was that really the best you could do?' Steel-eye taunted, stepping on the orc's other hand with a crunching of bones, as it stretched towards the fallen axe. Steel-eye steadied himself and swung one final blow. As the body slumped to the ground, the hunter stepped absent-mindedly to one side to avoid a rivulet of green, viscous fluid that drained towards the trees. He was staring intently at the body, as if suspecting it still presented some danger.

After a moment's pause, Steel-eye turned to look around him. Kurgan strode up, laughing heartily. The dwarf king tugged hard on the hunter's ragged, bloodstained cloak, stopping him as he took a stride towards the fight. The lad turned quickly to glare at the dwarf, his wide, battle-crazed eyes full of questions, the hammer in his hand half-raised to attack.

'Woah there, it's only me! You're a fine fighter, lad, and no mistake. Perhaps you pinkskins aren't so bad as we thought.'

Steel-eye looked down at the dwarf and held out the hammer, haft first. When he spoke, his words came in panting gasps, his breath carving misty shadows in the cold air.

'Thank you for… your weapon… Talk later… orcs to kill… Take it back… I'm sure I can find… something else.'

The dwarf king shook his noble head. Stroking the tangles out of his long beard, he looked up at the human with a wry smile on his face and a mischievous glint in his eye. Kurgan took the proffered warhammer and patted its rune-encrusted head. With a short chuckle, he handed it back to the surprised youth.

'I think he likes you better than me. Keep him. His name is Ghal Maraz, or Skull Splitter. You've done us a great service today. A small gift hardly compares to the life of a dwarf king, now does it?'

The youngster nodded his thanks and turned to rejoin the fight. The remaining orcs were falling back into the woods, all thoughts of battle gone now their warlord was dead. Kurgan laid a hand on the hunt lord's arm and halted him again.

'This day will be recorded in our annals with joy. What's your name lad, that we might honour you?'

Steel-eye hefted the hammer in his hand, his eyes straying towards the fleeing orcs. He looked at the dwarf king again, his eyes smouldering with energy. The rest of his face was in darkness and as the flames flickered in those intense grey eyes, they took on an eerie light. Even the baleful gaze of the orc warlord hadn't exuded the raw power of the youth's stare. His reply was short and simple.

'Sigmar.'

THE HOUNDS OF WINTER

Jonathan Green

RUNNING. HE HAD to keep running. The snow flew up in flurries around his feet as the peasant raced on through the night. The biting cold forgotten and the bundle of firewood he had been carrying now discarded, his only thoughts were of the hounds baying behind him. Above the choking, tearing rasp of his breath in his ice-seared throat, he could hear them panting and barking. Muffled by the snow and trees, their howls took on an echoing, almost ethereal quality. He dared not turn to snatch a fleeting glance of his pursuers for fear of what he might see if he did. He did not know what they were or where they came from, and he did not care. He only knew that he could not let them catch him.

Through the dark silhouettes of tall pines he saw the dim lantern light shining in the window of his hovel. Then his foot snagged in an exposed tree-root hidden under the snow. A searing pain blazed in his ankle and he fell. In panic, the man tried to scramble to his feet but as he did so his torn ankle all but screamed out in protest. Terror helping him to ignore the pain, he staggered on. With every limping step, shelter from the cruel winter night and the dark horrors it held came ever closer. Only another sixty yards and he would

27

be safe. But with every desperate step the snarling of the hounds got nearer.

He had not realised how near, until he was suddenly tugged backwards with a fierce jerk as the first of them sank its claws into the calf of his leg. Crying out, he landed spread-eagled in the freezing snow, the breath knocked out of him. The rest of the pack were upon him before he could spit the snow from his mouth to draw another frozen breath. In a few moments of snarling savagery it was over.

As quickly as they had fallen on the man, the hounds tossed the body aside and bounded off again into the night. The pack was closely followed by the masters of the hunt. Flaming hooves and iron-shod feet trampled the corpse into the hard ground, white turning to crimson with a hiss of steam as the man's hot blood soaked into the sullied snow.

The Hounds of Winter were abroad once more.

WITH A CRASH, the inn door was flung open and a chill gust of wind drove the warmth from the room.

'Shut the door!' a gruff voice shouted from a table of hard-bitten adventuring types. Midwinter's Eve on the fringes of the Northern Wastes was as bitterly cold as any of the Weather Sages of Erengrad could predict and outside was where the inn's clientele wanted it kept that night. With a resounding boom, the portal was sealed again by a second gust of wind and the air inside the snug was still once more.

Everything about the inn told its age. Huge oak beams the size of whole trees formed a bracing structure, which supported the centuries-old, filth-coated rafters; around the beams, walls thick enough to withstand a besieging army had been built. Something about the huge stones gave the impression that they had been here long before mortal men had decided to build an inn in this inhospitable place. The bar took up most of one wall and on the opposite side of the hall-like room a fire blazed in the vast stone fireplace. Between the bar and the fireplace were tables, benches and stools, most of which were occupied by a combination of local villagers, enjoying a warmer atmosphere than that which they could find at home, Kislevite soldiers having completed their patrols of these dangerous lands, and hired swords making the most of the money they had earned and always on the look-out to make some more.

'We haven't a moment to lose! Barricade the doors and windows! Arm yourselves!' the newcomer shouted above the hubbub.

Casuall, with feigned disinterest, the party of adventurers seated in the centre of the bar turned to see who had disturbed their quiet drink in the warm. Standing just over the threshold was an old man, his age-lined face testimony to a life of hardship but also of great inner strength. A thick mane of white hair fell back from his forehead and his wide jaw was buried beneath a luxurious beard. He gripped a staff like a tree-branch in one great hand, and around his broad shoulders rested the hide of some unfortunate bear, its claws now pinned by a clasp about the stranger's neck.

'They're coming I tell you! We must prepare for battle!'

'Calm yourself, old man, calm yourself,' black-haired Torben Badenov said, rising from the table of adventurers, his huge frame blocking the old man's view of the fireplace. 'Why don't you have a drink and let us get on with ours?'

'There is no time for that! Do you not know what night it is?'

'Of course we do,' Torben retorted. 'Not all of us are suffering from dementia as yet. It's Midwinter's Eve.'

'But not just any Midwinter's Eve. Tonight is also the Conjunction of the Two Moons!'

Oran Scarfen, a gaunt, toothy warrior whose rodent-like features and spiky moustache almost belied any human heritage, fumed and sneered in the vague direction of the newcomer. 'What's he ranting about now?'

'The Conjunction of the Two Moons only happens once every three hundred years – when both Moon and Dark Moon are directly opposed to each other, on Midwinter's Eve, dead on midnight, their fell powers pulling equally upon this world.'

'So what does that have to do with us?' Torben asked flippantly.

'It is upon us tonight! Do you not know the legend?'

'What legend?'

'Oh!' the stranger wailed, despair cracking his voice. 'Too many have forgotten! Is it really so long?'

Torben strolled over to the bar and leaned back against it casually 'Do you know this character?' he whispered through the side of his mouth to the rotund landlord, as the old man paced about the bar.

'I don't know his real name,' the chubby, red-faced barman replied as he tried to buff up a dull pewter tankard with a filthy rag, 'but everyone around here calls him Old Man Mountain. He's an odd fellow. He's been around for as long as anyone here can remember. People sometimes tell of seeing him striding through the snowdrifts up beyond the tree-line but they always steer clear of him. He's never actually come down into the village before, though – I'd be careful not to anger him if I were you,' the barman warned.

'Don't worry, he doesn't frighten me. I've dealt with his type before.'

In truth, Torben Badenov had indeed encountered many strange old men in his time as a mercenary on the borders of Kislev, and the obscure pronouncements of this addled mountain-dweller troubled him about as much as a goblin did a dragon. Yet despite the stranger's obvious great age, Torben noticed that there was a certain bearing about him. He held himself tall and proud, looking every bit a man of thought as well as action and Torben was sure that his great bear-skin cloak hid powerfully muscled arms.

Moving back to his table, Torben motioned to the enigmatic character with his tankard. 'Come then, tell us your story, old man. Make it a good one and we might just buy you a drink for your troubles.'

The stranger stopped pacing and turned his piercing amber eyes on the mercenary and his companions. 'We have little time, so listen well,' he said, coldly determined, 'and I will tell you of the Hounds of Winter.'

Oran Scarfen rose from his stool and swept his hand to it sarcastically, but the old man refused to sit and kept pacing with nervous energy.

'It was a night much like this, when people gather around their campfires to tell each other stories that make the blood run cold. It was a time when the tide of Chaos was rising in the land. It was Midwinter's Eve–'

'Get on with it. I thought time was short!' Scarfen jeered. All but the old man laughed.

'An Imperial patrol was escorting a wagon train from Talabheim to Kislev. Three days into the journey, a Chaos warband attacked!' The old man's earnest voice held the attention of the assembled warriors – perhaps this was to be a fine tale after all.

'Outnumbered, the patrol was routed. Many brave men were killed by beastmen and Chaos warriors that night. The soldiers thought themselves all doomed.'

The old man paused, coughed to clear his throat and gestured for a tankard. Badenov passed over Scarfen's, stopping the latter's complaint with a wicked grin. The stranger supped a few mouthfuls before continuing. 'Then, from out of the wilds came a being who seemed to be as much beast as man. He wielded deadly, sorcerous powers, and fought against the Chaos vermin. 'Twas a wizard, come to aid the soldiers in their fight.'

By now, Old Man Mountain had quite an audience, his story gripping even the most hard bitten adventurers in the bar. 'But the foul enemy was too strong, and in the end there was nothing for it but flight, to spread word of the coming of Chaos to Kislev and maybe the Empire beyond.'

'Hurry it along, old timer,' Oran interrupted. 'Cut to the chase.'

'Listen!' the old man reproached his heckler. 'Every detail is important. You must hear it all!'

'Very well, mountain man,' Torben said, ignoring his glare. 'Tell us everything, but get on with it!'

'The Winter King, champion of Chaos, led this warband. His infamous acts of cruelty had carved him a reputation as bloody as his crimes.' He paused a moment. 'As the survivors of the wagon train fled from his clutches, the Winter King called on his Dark Gods for help, and from the red mist of battle his vile, Chaos-spawned powers shaped the dread forms of daemonic hounds.' The old man sniffed the air dramatically. 'Picking up the scent of the fleeing survivors, the abhorrent beasts bounded off into the night in pursuit of their human prey.'

The old man shot his audience a glance to make sure that he now had their full attention. Satisfied that this was so, he went on.

'Though it appeared that the wild man's arrival had been a stroke of good fortune, this wizard had in fact been trailing the warband for some time. The Winter King had stolen a magical crown from an ancient burial mound, a crown imbued with the power to command the forces of Chaos. The wizard knew that if Khorne's champion reached the Empire, he might unite the twisted creatures of the Dark Gods dwelling within the

Forest of Shadows into an unstoppable army. The warband had to be stopped before it reached the Empire's gates!'

'Where did the survivors make their stand then?' Torben interrupted.

'I was just getting to that!' the old man snapped, taking a moment to compose himself again before resuming the story.

'The wizard led the few survivors to a circle of standing stones carved with powerful, ancient runes and sigils. By accident or design, it was a fitting place for their last stand. The brave soldiers fought beyond their measure, but died one by one, until only the wizard remained.

'Even in death, however, their energies combined with the magic of the place to imbue him with a terrible power. With the roar of a beast, the wild sorcerer shed his last vestiges of humanity and took on the aspect of a mighty bear. Raging and clawing, he drove off the servants of Chaos, though suffering terrible wounds himself.'

The old man's words were so vivid, and so heartfelt, that all who listened were held entranced.

'Trapped and beaten, the Winter King slunk away into the darkness to die, cursing the wizard. He vowed that though the wizard had won the battle, the war would continue in death and beyond. He would return.'

The old man looked up, his story done. 'That is the saga of the Winter King.'

A HEADY SILENCE hung over the bar. At last Torben spoke: 'Well, you've earned your drink – that was quite some tale.'

'But it's not just a tale, it's real, I tell you! Now is the time! The moons are in conjunction and the battle will be fought again!'

A thunderclap shattered the night, shaking the inn and causing every lantern to flicker. Above the winter gale could be heard the savage baying of hounds. All eyes turned to face the stranger in disbelief.

'They're here,' he said.

Torben's hand moved instinctively to the hilt of his sword. As the inn's customers listened they could also make out the sound of harness jangling, the snorting of steeds and the clink of armour.

'It is time, old man!' came an icy voice from beyond the door, heavy with damned resignation and full of menace. 'Are you within?'

'I am!' the old man called back, his voice strong and unwavering.

'And are you ready to die again?'

'We will see.'

'Then prepare to defend yourself!'

An order was shouted – and it was as if all hell had been unleashed. The first of the dogs assailed the inn, shutters splintering under their claws and muzzles as the monstrous creatures tried to batter their way inside.

'Now this is just too much!' Torben exclaimed, rising to his feet, sword already in his hand. 'One old lunatic I can just about stomach, but this is going too far. Are you with me, lads?' There was a growl of agreement from the mercenary's companions and they jumped to their feet, weapons at the ready.

'Ah, at last. The brave warriors remember their part in all this,' the white-maned stranger said enigmatically. 'Together we will drive the evil from this place!'

Ignoring the old man, the mercenary adjusted his armoured jerkin and continued to urge his band of fighters on. 'Come on, lads! Let's give these deviants a taste of cold steel. That'll soon calm their appetite for destruction!'

By now the rest of the inn's customers were also preparing to fight – it was plain that their only chance of survival depended on it.

'Follow me!' the bear-cloaked stranger shouted above the blood-curdling howls of the hounds, the war-cries of Chaos warriors and the braying of beastmen. Flinging open the great oak door of the inn, the old man stood silhouetted for a moment in the flickering light of the torches carried by the warband, snow plastering to his hair and beard. 'Stay within the light cast by the inn!' he offered as a parting piece of advice, then leapt out into the night. The defenders followed unhesitatingly, as if the old man held greater sway over them than they realised.

Once outside the inn, it appeared to Torben as though all hell had broken loose. The great dogs that assailed them were no creatures born of the material plane but blood-red monsters with slavering jaws and scaly hides. The vile flesh hounds were possessed of an unbridled fury and hurled themselves at the humans, trying to clamp an arm or a leg in their teeth, to rend their victim limb from limb. Beyond the vanguard formed by the daemonic creatures pressed a rabble of brutish beastmen and spike-armoured warriors, their faces hidden by huge, horned helmets.

As Torben fought on, swinging blow after powerful blow at the mutants and hounds about him, he could not help noticing that at the heart of the warband there fought others whose faces were visible and of a deathly pallor. At the back of the serried lines of mutants and madmen, a shadowy, almost spectral figure appeared to be directing them all.

A spear glowing with orange flame streaked through the swirling snow, hurled by the old man. The missile exploded among a mass of beastmen, the foul stench of scorched fur filling Torben's nostrils.

So the old man has some magic at his disposal too, Torben thought to himself. There was a lot more to him than first appeared.

Something else was happening as well. As he fought, it felt to Torben as if his body was being invigorated by some renewing power that sent new strength surging through his arms and legs, stimulating muscles that should have become tired from the constant exertion and giving him the stamina to keep battling on. From the curious expression on the faces of his fellows the same thing was plainly happening to them as well.

Through the swirling storm, Morrslieb's light began to dim as the time of the Conjunction neared. Torben had lost track of how long the battle had been raging. The ragged collection of defenders were greatly outnumbered and although they fought with their vigour increased, they were horrified to see those that they struck down rise up again as shadowy wraiths and rejoin the fray.

The battle raged on, Torben fending off the blows of his enemies, his thrusts and parries given extra impetus thanks to the inexplicable invigorating energy affecting him. As he fought, he almost felt like some energy was guiding his hand. It was like no other conflict he had ever taken part in before, and there had been many. It seemed to the mercenary that he had fought this battle before, although not in this lifetime.

One by one, despite their efforts, Torben's companions were being struck down by these otherworldly Chaos fiends. Shooting anxious glances around him he saw their bodies lying motionless in the trampled snow – but there was no sign of any blood or wounds of any sort. With an abruptly silenced cry of surprise, Oran fell to a wraith's sword.

'Do not be concerned for your friends,' the white-haired wizard's reassuring tones came through the snow flurries. 'It is almost time. We must hold them but a little longer.'

The Chaos horde, and particularly their leader, appeared to be becoming more and more agitated at their failure to break through the defenders' line and assail the inn. The beastmen and warriors were driven by some overwhelming need unknown to Torben and the others. Their shadowy leader screamed orders to the rabble, his desperation adding an intensity to their attack – and making the defenders' struggle to hold them off seem all the more important.

At last the heavenly bodies completed their movements and an all-encompassing darkness fell over the battlefield. Now the only illumination came from the horde's torches and the interior of the inn.

'Now it is time,' the old man hissed with satisfaction. 'Retreat into the inn!' At his command, the few survivors hurried back towards the welcoming glow of the great stone portal, dragging the chill bodies of their fallen comrades with them. As Torben dragged Oran's body over the threshold, he could see not a mark on him, yet he had himself seen him struck down with a ghostly blade.

When all were safely back inside, the door was barred and the defenders prepared to meet their end.

'Where's the old man?' Torben exclaimed suddenly, looking around.

'He must still be outside,' the landlord realised with horror. 'He'll never survive out there alone.'

'But will we survive in here together?' a haggard local lamented.

With a chilling clarity that cut through the howls of the Chaos hounds, the defenders heard the temple bells start to chime midnight down in the valley. As the last chime tolled, the great roar of a raging beast drowned out the barking of the terrible hounds. Curiosity driving them, Torben and the others leapt to the shuttered windows and tried to peer through the cracks to see what was going on, but all was black as pitch. They could see nothing, but they could certainly hear the slaughter that was taking place beyond the walls of the inn all too clearly.

The defenders remained transfixed, listening to the wailing of the Chaos horde, and were chilled to the marrow by the bellowing of the monster that had suddenly appeared amid the carnage.

At last the sounds died, the cries of those apparently still able to flee fading into the distance. Even then the humans did not dare move from the protection of the inn, for fear of what they might find outside.

DAWN CAME, and with it the confidence to leave the inn. Unbarring the great door, Torben cautiously ventured out into the crisp, cold morning.

The snowy ground was littered with the foul bodies of vast, bestial hounds, rapidly decaying in the grey light. Here and there lay the corpse of a beastman or iron-clad warrior, but there were far too few to account for the sounds of slaughter that they had all heard at midnight. Of the bodies of the Chaos lord and his awful retinue there was no sign. Neither was there any trace of the old stranger, dead or otherwise, or any monstrous beast.

Where had they all gone? Torben wondered. The old man could not have survived the onslaught of the entire warband and the midnight monster. He peered in alarm at a set of clawed, bear-like footprints that lead away through the snow towards the mountains. There were no matching prints leading towards the scene.

'Mercenary!' the landlord's bewildered, astonished voice called from inside the inn. 'Your companions are returning to life.'

Torben hurried back inside. On the floor where his body had been laid, Oran was sitting up, rubbing his head and looking around him dazedly. The others who had also fallen to the wraith-like fiends were similarly stirring, as if waking from a deep sleep.

'How can this be?' Torben asked in amazement, kneeling down beside his friend. 'What happened to you?'

'When I was struck by the wraith it felt as if something chill and evil had struck me,' Oran said vaguely 'I was consumed with the most agonising death throes which ill-matched the wound I thought I had received. It was as if I was reliving the heroic demise of someone else from another time. Then I blacked out.'

Torben stood up, rubbing his head with both hands, as if that would somehow help him to make sense of the night's bizarre events.

At last he spoke again: 'Ho, landlord, I think opening time has come early today. Crack open that cask of Bugman's XXXXXX I know you've been keeping back. I think we've all earned it!'

The mercenary looked back through the open doorway at the battlefield. What exactly had taken place during the Conjunction of the Two Moons? The sun had struggled through the snow-choked clouds, casting its wan light onto the portal. On one of the ancient cornerstones of the inn, it picked out a number of age-worn markings etched into the stone. Stepping over to the threshold to take a closer look, Torben ran his fingers over the carved symbols.

The stone was huge, apparently set deep into the ground. Something told Torben that it had lain there a long time, longer even than this old inn had stood here. The building had no doubt been made from local stone; despite having borne the weathering of the elements for centuries the markings were plainly ancient symbols. The adventurer traced the shape of an arrow under the lichen. His curiosity satisfied, he gave a shrug and returned to the bar and the hopeful expectation of a quiet drink at last.

As the solid oak door closed behind him, the rusted inn-sign creaked in the breeze, its picture of a rampant bear almost faded now beyond all recognition.

HATRED

Ben Chessell

I am hatred. I am revulsion. If you know me and do not hate me, you are evil. I have enough hate for myself.

THE GIBBET in Kurtbad was unoccupied. Swinging in the gentle breeze, the empty loop of rope regarded the village like a macabre eye. The people of Kurtbad slept, though they had gone to bed afraid. The two guards posted outside the barn which served as meeting hall slumped against the wooden door, blankets wrapped around them like shrouds. Their pitch-forks lay discarded on the black Averland soil. If the humble wind which shook the noose had been so bold as to sniff the breath of these men, it would have smelt wine, much wine.

The midnight watch in the midst of an Averland witch hunt was not a duty to face unfortified. The small stocks of wine, kept in Kurtbad for Taal's Day of Spring-return, had been cracked open and distributed to all the villagers. When that day came, and it would be soon, everyone but the children would understand.

Now all that mattered was that a man had been killed.

* * *

GUNTER PULLED his woollen cloak tighter about his shoulders and made enough noise to wake the form in the bed he had recently left – but got no response. The thin moonlight didn't help Gunter see whether she really was asleep. He buckled on his sword, his since his father had died on a frosty night early in the winter, and drew back the bolt on the door of the house which had come to him the same way. Ice on the stone step cracked under his militiaman's boots and the breeze blew away the last cobwebs of sleep. Gunter found much solace in his duty, the sole permanent militiaman in the village of Kurtbad, responsible for more than a hundred men, women and children. He straightened his back and headed for the barn to see how his new recruits were doing.

Anja waited for the door to close behind him before sitting up and lighting the candle from the last coals which winked like dying stars in the ashen sky of the hearth. She returned to bed via the door, where she drew the bolt again. Gunter's side of the bed was warm but cooling quickly. She crawled back to the corner where she had curled like a cat on the night when Gunter fetched her from her family, telling her mother that she would be safer with him. It was probably even true. How could her mother, older now than most women in the village, tell the militiaman, tall as a bear, he could not take her only daughter. It was for Anja's protection, after all.

Anja and Gunter were not married, and had he not been arguably the most important man in Kurtbad, action would have been taken. As it was, many people in the village muttered after she passed by and looked at her as if to see some sign of her sin worn openly on her garments.

Anja curled up and thought about these things, looking at the candle flame and how the beeswax melted and ran down the stem like tears. The candle cried itself to death.

OUTSIDE THE VILLAGE, on the road to Nuln, the night was shredded by a startled cry and a flash of blades. A man leapt from the back of a horse and stumbled in the mud at the side of the road. Another man rolled on the ground, the winter leaves sticking to his face, his wrist in his mouth. The struggle was as bloody and quick as a dogfight. When it was over, the inadequate moon lit only naked skin and cooling blood.

The victor of the battle rode through the forest toward Kurtbad, searching for something.

OTTO THE BUTCHER slept well that night, despite a nagging feeling of guilt. He was used to that.

KURTBAD NESTLED on the edge of the Reiksbanks Forest in central Averland, four days' ride from Nuln. It sat beside an old trading route which led from that great city of commerce and industry to a dwarf outpost at Hammergrim Pass in the Black Mountains. There, for centuries, the dwarfs had sucked lead and iron from the guts of the fat mountains. The ore was loaded onto oxen carts and passed through Kurtbad on its way to the markets at Nuln, and thence by river to whatever Empire foundry was prepared to pay the best price: gold for steel. Kurtbad had seen some business in those days.

The greed of the dwarfs eventually exceeded their skill and the bounty of the Black Mountains and the ore dried up like a staunched wound. Hammergrim Pass was abandoned and the dwarfs returned to fight the Goblin Wars or whatever dwarfs do. Kurtbad became a ghost town overnight. The inn was closed and its keeper, who was a business-man, left for Nuln with a girl from Kurtbad he had married. She later returned to the village with a young child, no money and a brand on her arm. The inn was knocked down. Perhaps it was anger or perhaps the people of Kurtbad needed the wood for their sheep pens, living in wolf country as they did.

Nevertheless, in the space of a generation, the village had purged itself of the influence of the dwarfs and merchants, and grass had grown on the road to Hammergrim Pass.

Into this small village, a single black stitch on the great embroidered map which hangs in the commerce hall of the Merchant's Guild in the city of Nuln, came a black horse with hooves of silver. On its back was a tall man clad in dark cloth. He wore a hat the colour of coal, with a plume which must have been dyed because no one knew of any bird with feathers like that. He wore a sword and a knife, in the manner of a gentleman, and his boots were of soft leather, also stained the colour of moonless night. His arms were scarred and scratched, from old battles and new, and he grasped the reins with his left hand as if the right was unequal to the task.

He sat on his horse for some time, surveying the village and
its people as they stirred in the dawn grey. He sat there long
enough for Wilhelm, chastened for being asleep on duty at the
barn, to ring the huge bronze bell. This bell was the last remnant of the dwarf mining days, except for the occasional
brightly painted rail which kept the sheep in. It had originally
been used to warn the wagons as they left the mountain trail
that the road was too muddy for reliable passage and they
should wait for a drier day. Now the bell, which bore the
crossed hammer and axe stamp of the miners, was struck with
a mallet to summon the villagers to the common, the steam
mechanism long since decayed.

*I am a snake. I am a worm. There is poison in my blood. I can never
die a peaceful death. I am burning now as I will burn then.*

GUNTER HEARD the bell as he stared for the fifth time at the place
where Gregor's body had been found. There were signs to read
here, he knew that, answers written in the ground as clear as
any illuminated manuscript.

Just as he couldn't read the scratchings in ink which adorned
the pages of his father's books, so he couldn't comprehend the
signs in the mud which had hardened and cracked since
Gregor's violent death two days ago. He had found the pieces
of clay from the shattered bottle, but they only served to con-
fuse things further. The only marks he could read reliably were
his own deep boot prints, four sets.

He turned away and straightened himself as he made his way
to face whatever disaster had befallen Kurtbad now.

ANJA LOOKED OUT between the curtains of Gunter's cottage. The
man sat silently on his horse like a sculpture cast in black
leather. She thought he didn't look well. He had the balance of
a drunkard, and as she watched he shut his eyes and swayed
like a young tree in a breeze. Anja pulled on the shoes which
Gunter had bought for her on one of his trips to Nuln and
unbolted the door.

She was the first of the villagers to approach the man and she
straightened her hair as she walked carefully towards him. He
made no sign of having seen her, so she moved around to the
front of his horse. The big brown eyes of the stallion regarded

her critically but the man's head remained slumped. There was a stain of dried blood, Anja knew it by its colour, on the man's right wrist, above his black leather glove. Anja could see he was alive; his chest rose and fell slowly.

She summoned up the courage to address him without considering that she didn't know how one should properly address a witch hunter.

GUNTER DREW BREATH and held the air in until all the goodness had been taken from it. A witch hunter. Just what we don't need.

He sized the man up. Anja had helped the man from his horse, which was now grazing contentedly on the lush grass of the Kurtbad common, before Gunter had banished her inside. Foolish girl. These witch hunters had no purpose but the discovery and destruction of Chaos, he knew that, and although there was a dangerous killer on the loose, perhaps even a monster of some kind, the man in black might be just as dangerous. Didn't she know that? Of course she did.

Even now she watched proceedings from the window and heated water on the stove for the man. Anything to make contact with the world outside Kurtbad, that was what Anja wanted. Why can she not be content with me? Gunter knew that it was likely only his training and foreign postings with the Empire army had brought Anja to his home in the first place, and that was a fragile bargain he was determined to protect.

He turned his attention to the witch hunter. The man sat slumped against the wall of his house like a wilted flower, except that he knew no blooms that were the colour of Death. Gunter addressed him formally, welcoming him to Kurtbad and asking his business.

When the man spoke it was in a voice which sounded like it was squeezed through a throat too small to let the words pass, and he shut his eyes in pain. His name was Dagmar, he was indeed a witch hunter, and he knew about the troubles in Kurtbad. Gunter had no choice but to offer him the hospitality of his cottage.

DAGMAR LAY in the strange bed and contemplated the rafters. They were oaken and old. Like strong ribs which held the thatched skin of the roof from collapsing, they met at a huge beam, a great rounded trunk which still bore bark in some places. A crossbow hung from one end of it, he noticed, well oiled and maintained. The other held cooking pots and bundles of roots and spices.

Dagmar shifted in the bed and turned his head to watch the girl who stirred the pot. A whip-crack of pain shot through his ribs when he turned his body to the side, so he contented himself with the briefest of glances and returned to looking at the thatching. Grey sunlight filtered between the straw; it lay across him like gashes.

He had allowed the girl to remove his boots but otherwise he was clad as he had been when he arrived, in ill-fitting witch hunter's clothes. The fight in the forest last night had almost been his last and only the overconfidence of his opponent had saved him. Dagmar waited patiently for the girl to return with the stew she was making and wondered if his luck might be changing.

Anja had to feed the man as he couldn't easily sit up. Gunter had not told her his name, saying that he thought it was better if she didn't know such things. He had gone now, to attend to the horse or get wood or something.

She fed the man patiently, noting that he was most polite. He told her his name in an attempt to learn hers. She learnt that he was called Dagmar and freely named herself. What was the danger in that? From what she knew of witch hunters, they were good folk who hunted monsters throughout the Empire. She had never seen one but Gunter had occasionally mentioned them in one of his many travel stories. If he had come here to catch Gregor's murderer then wasn't that a good thing?

She looked at the man's mud-spattered and blood-stained clothes. Normally she would have undressed him and washed his clothes for him. He was clearly wounded beneath the expensive garb. Gunter had not protested when the man had climbed into his bed fully clothed but Anja had seen his face. She did not want to anger him further. Not now.

I am evil and it is consuming me. There is no place in me but hate. There is no place in me but disease. Do not touch me.

GUNTER CUT WOOD as if each log was the head of an enemy. He saw many faces beneath the wedge as he drove it deeply into the chopping block – goblins, Bretonnians, men who he had slain or almost slain. Most of all, he saw what he imagined was the face of the monster who must have killed Gregor: scaled, with tusks and fangs. The creature's head split with a satisfying snap but there was nothing inside. He lifted his axe for the coup de grace but the face he saw became that of his guest and he held the stroke.

Angry with himself for unworthy and inhospitable thoughts, Gunter reasoned, as he gathered the wood, that the witch hunter had done nothing to earn his enmity. Perhaps he could bring resources to bear on the problem that would enable them to catch the killer. He determined to consult with this Dagmar, after they had all eaten, and returned to the house in a better mood.

What he saw as he came through the low door destroyed his good nature as surely as if a daemon-wizard had banished it to another realm.

ANJA MOPPED Dagmar's brow with one of Gunter's kerchiefs and sat by him as he dozed. When Gunter returned with the wood she was cleaning the cut on the man's right arm. The wound was not very deep but had bled a great deal and had ragged edges like a newly ploughed track. She tried to take off his leather glove but he clenched his fist; the pain was obviously too great.

She bathed his arm and wrist but did not ask to take off the glove again. There was clearly something wrong with the arm, which had a bulge in it where hers did not. He had talked of a fight in the forest. Perhaps he had broken a bone then. When Gunter suggested she should return to her mother while the stranger stayed in his house, she shrugged him off. Gunter might be a great soldier but he had no idea how to look after a sick man. When he tried to order her, she responded by reminding him that they had taken no vows and that she only need take orders from her mother until such a time as they did.

Things became more heated and Anja was forced to stop stitching her sling and stand up to face him.

Dagmar got out of bed at this point and made excuses about needing to perform his ablutions.

Anja's pointed comment about the stranger's good manners did nothing to pacify Gunter.

* * *

WHEN HE RETURNED, she had gone and Gunter sat by the soup pot. Dagmar could not be sure whether the man or the fire glowed more hotly.

The two men found they could talk easily enough and Dagmar imagined that he might have more in common with this lonely man than he thought.

For his own part, Gunter was surprised to find himself trusting the engaging witch hunter, and rethinking what he knew about their kind. This man, Dagmar, although very knowledgeable about mutant creatures of Chaos, was unlike any witch hunter he had ever heard of.

Dagmar talked with Gunter for several hours, making various suggestions for the defence of the village. He suggested, and this is just one example of his useful ideas, that some mutants have thick, strong necks, and might survive a hanging. Dagmar proposed the building of a pyre, with a stake set into it, so that the criminal, when captured, could be burned.

He also said that the mutant was quite possibly living in the village and promised to hunt the man down. Dagmar asked many keen questions about the habits of the villagers of Kurtbad, and Gunter told him who was reliable and who perhaps was not. Then Gunter took a deep breath and told Dagmar his suspicions.

I am unclean. How can you not smell it on my breath? The rot of my body, the decay of my heart. We are so much the same, and so different.

OTTO FLEISCHER was a very fat man. He was not a nice man. If the villagers knew everything there was to know about Otto, instead of just suspecting it, they would never have let him be their butcher, let alone their undertaker. When Otto had buried Gregor he had made no secret that he would not grieve for the man.

ANJA THOUGHT that the cottage looked like Gunter had been carousing all night with one of his mercenary friends who occasionally came to Kurtbad, most likely to hide from the law, and not like the place where a sick man had been quartered. There were two empty clay bottles next to the fire and Gunter was snoring loudly. He had obviously slept on the hearthstone and his face was covered with a thin layer of ash which lifted in tiny clouds with each snore. The veins on his cheeks were red like a fox and his moustache curled upward on one side.

Anja looked at this man, her lover, as a farmer might appraise a new-born lamb, and turned as if to compare his visage with Dagmar's. The bed was empty.

Anja put the steaming breakfast she had brought onto the scarred table and walked outside.

DAGMAR EASED the glove off his right hand and washed both in the stream. The small stream ran down from the Black Mountains beside the road from Hammergrim Pass and beneath the stone bridge at the north of the village. The small graveyard for the people of Kurtbad lay on the top of the oppo-site bank. The water was like knives of ice but the hand was mostly numb anyway. He stared at it in disgust.

He unbuckled his belt and took off his boots. The touch of the water on his feet was agony but he forced himself to stand, unsteady on the slippery rocks beneath the shallow flow. He watched the dirt and blood billow and mingle with the water, quickly lost in the enthusiastic stream. He imagined a purify-ing experience.

He heard the girl approaching just in time to get the glove back onto his hand.

OTTO SCUTTLED from behind Gregor's gravestone and picked up his sack. He knew what he had seen. He took the long way back to the village.

GUNTER PINCHED the skin above his eyes, his hand clasping together at the bridge of his sharp nose. He shook the ash from his clothes and, wiping his eyes again, looked around the cot-tage. Breakfast. No Anja. No Dagmar. He took a knife from the roof beam and began to eat the spiced tomatoes. He tried to remember the conversation of the previous evening. Had he gone so far as to mention Otto's name? That was unworthy.

Gunter had long disliked the butcher and declined to eat his meat, preferring to kill and smoke his own, but he had no evi-dence that the man was a murderer. What had possessed him to tell a witch hunter? Dagmar had been talking about muta-tions caused by exposure to Chaos he had had experience with and had mentioned that such a man might become extremely fat but otherwise remain normal. That did fit Otto's description.

Gunter had to admit that the Tilean wine was mostly to blame for the liberties he had taken. It was not fair to his guest, who seemed to be a decent man, to burden him with wild suspicions.

Gunter lurched to his feet like a becalmed ship which suddenly finds the wind, and went off in search of Dagmar.

ANJA SAT ON a dry rock in the stream and listened intently to Dagmar's story. The man was charming, there was no doubt of that, and appeared to be well recovered, almost impossibly so, from his illness of the previous day. There was colour in his cheeks and his beard seemed to have grown overnight.

Dagmar was standing solemnly on the bank of the stream in mock concentration as he related an apocryphal tale about an acolyte of the Temple of Verena in Nuln. The story was convoluted but Dagmar told it faithfully and well, keeping his face serious until the punch-line, which made them both laugh.

Dagmar bent double, exaggerating his laughter and slipped on the muddy bank. He fell heavily on his right arm and his face screwed up in pain. Anja pounced across onto the bank and helped him to sit. Her face was a flag of concern. A great deal of blood stained the sling she had made and she could see bone sticking through the skin below the elbow. He held her away with his good arm, which was surprisingly strong, like a man shielding himself from the sun.

Eventually she calmed him down and they both sat together on the bank. When she went to put her head on his good shoulder, he let her.

GUNTER STOOD on the bridge and gouged the moss of the low stone rail with his knuckles. He felt the water flow beneath his feet and felt the blood flow through his body. He made himself breathe the air as he watched them. Gunter remembered how he felt when he saw Anja dance with other men on Taal's Day. He stood there for some time.

When he finally managed to uproot himself from the bridge and make his way down through the trees to the stream he walked noisily, so they might hear him and untwine by the time he reached them. Gunter completely forgot his purpose in seeking Dagmar.

Anja met him as he emerged from the trees, smoothing her dress and pulling leaves from her hair. She matched his gaze and her eyes danced.

Dagmar stared into the stream and cradled his right arm like a babe. Gunter could have sworn he was talking to it.

When Anja had gone, the two men looked at each other for a moment, the kind of moment which might be the prelude to anything. As it was, Gunter suggested that they go together to examine the tracks at the place where Gregor was killed.

OTTO KNOCKED on the door again. He was sure someone was in there. This was the one time he had ever been desperate enough to call on the help of the militiaman. He was dismayed when the door was opened not by Gunter, but by his harlot.

DAGMAR STOOD behind Gunter as he crouched over the tracks, pointing at various features which he had indicated with muddy sticks in the turf. They stood like a blighted forest, marking the last steps taken by the man called Gregor.

Gunter was trying to understand how Gregor could have been ambushed by the mutant in such an open area as, apparently, he was always a careful man.

Gunter did not suggest that Gregor might have been very drunk on that night. Perhaps the bottle he had found did not fit the fiction of the man's death which Gunter was trying to write in muddy characters on the killing ground.

Dagmar suggested that perhaps Gregor had been the attacker and the mutant had merely tried to defend himself. Gunter was vehemently opposed to the suggestion.

Dagmar explained to Gunter his own version of the tracks. He moved some of Gunter's markers with his good arm, showing exactly where the mutant had been surprised, where Gregor had picked up a stick, and where the broken halves of the stick now lay, stained with the mutant's blood. He finished by showing where the mutant had finally fought back and where the body had fallen.

Gunter concluded that Gregor must have been drunk to be so foolhardy.

* * *

I am trying to tell you. I am amongst you. I am Chaos. Destroy me.

ANJA SAT ON Gunter's bed and stared into the fire. She had heard
what the butcher had had to say, heard his testimony about the
scaled hand of the witch hunter. She had asked him what business he had had in the graveyard but Otto had pressed his case.
The man, apparently, had red-green scales on his right hand
below the wrist – a sure mark of Chaos. The fat butcher had
pointed out how badly the man's clothes fitted him, how he
was clearly not a natural rider of that perfect stallion.

Anja had listened to all of this and she saw that it might be
true. She promised Otto she would fetch Gunter, and told him
to retire to his cottage and wait for them. Then she sat in the
dark and tried to recall the taste of the man's breath, as it had
been on the bank of the stream.

She tried to remember the taste of decay, of corruption, but
she could remember nothing but the sound of the stream and
the look in his eyes.

GUNTER CAME slowly back to the house as the burning galleon
of the sun sank behind the Grey Mountains. He thought about
what Dagmar had said, how he had shown him a different way
of looking at the signs in the mud. How he had forced him to
see the truth which had all the time been set before his eyes.

More than ever, Gunter felt he was in a great library, like the
one he had seen in Middenheim, where all the knowledge of
the world was kept and yet he could not read a word of it. He
walked past the waiting pyre and smelt the oil. A small group
of Kurtbad residents stood about it, like birds of prey who
anticipate a kill. Gunter felt it too and began to trot back to his
cottage.

Anja was waiting at the open door for him, a sight which
grasped his heart. She brought him inside and after looking to
see that he was alone, she closed the door. She told him: *I have
found the killer.*

DAGMAR STOOD on the slope above the village in the struggling light. He looked at the cottages and their hearth-fires
which sent up vines of smoke from holes in the thatch. He
imagined the meals being prepared. There would perhaps be
children, certainly animals, underfoot. There would be both

happiness and unhappiness in those cottages. He hated them, every one.

I am hatred.

Except her. He thought of her by the stream. Reflected sunlight splashing her face, cooling her eyes. He thought of the way their faces had touched.

How can you not smell it on my breath?

He shattered the picture with the mallet of his hatred.

How dare she?

Do not touch me.

Doesn't she know what she's done to me?

He pulled off his right glove and shook his arm free of the sling. As he flexed it he felt blood course through it and the cuts at his wrist opened again and bled freely.

There is poison in my blood.

How dare she? I am a killer.

I am Chaos.

I will show her.

He drew the witch hunter's sword from the witch hunter's belt and strode down the hill.

I have changed my mind. I will not die. I will live as I am and I am as I will.

GUNTER SURVEYED the assembled crowd. Fifteen or so men and boys had gathered in the gloom. Each carried a weapon of some kind, many carried torches which they lit from the coals of Gunter's fire.

Anja sat on the bed and said nothing.

Gunter gave his last instructions and the group moved out. Gunter led them. He was the only man with military training and although they felt they knew their quarry, who could tell what strength the curse of Chaos could lend to a man? They were not scared – there were too many of them for that – but there was a thrill which ran through them as they moved closer. They spoke of revenge and justice, though not one was thinking of Gregor.

Gunter gripped his sword and strained his eyes in the dark. He thanked Sigmar that Anja was safe, having come so close to danger. Images of the library returned to him but Gunter no longer needed to read.

* * *

ANJA HEARD him coming. He was walking loudly and didn't seem to know anything about the mob. She stood behind the door and cancelled her breath while he tried the handle.

Dagmar staggered into the room and she saw that his left hand held a sword. His right hand hung at his side, the fingers moving, almost as if he was not aware of it. It looked as if the first two and second two fingers were in the process of fusing and they did not move independently. Perhaps that was why he no longer wore the glove.

'Dagmar?'

He turned on her like a cornered boar and she saw his face contorted by pain and rage. She brought the iron firestick down on his left hand and the sword bounced off the flagstones.

He moaned, *No*, growled in pain and sank to the floor. He looked at her. Tears of black blood streamed from his eyes.

GUNTER GAVE the signal and the mob moved forward. They had trapped the murderer in the house and all that remained was to apprehend him. As far as they knew, he was alone. Hardly surprising. By all accounts, Chaos carried a stench that was enough to make a soldier cry.

Gunter steadied himself and kicked the door with his mercenary's boot. It gave way easily and he almost fell into the room. The sole inhabitant of the cottage leapt up in shock, banging his head on one of the butcher's tools which hung from the central beam. The mob piled in behind Gunter, pressing him forward.

Otto cowered away from them, but some spark of unworthy courage flared and he grabbed a cleaver. He wore no shirt and Gunter stared in disgust at the rolls of fat which hung over his linen breeches. The skin was pasty and white and the whole cottage smelt of dead flesh. Gunter disarmed the man with a chopping stroke to his right wrist. The mob grabbed him and silenced his protests.

ANJA MET THEM at the pyre. She held fresh torches in her hands. She watched without flinching as the unconscious Otto was lashed to the stake. It had been easy enough to convince Gunter. He had seen Otto many times with the blood of pigs on his hands. Such a man could kill. There was little distance between the butcher of Kurtbad and the Butcher of Kurtbad.

Otto was a hateful man and Anja told herself that the village would be better off without him.

Gunter was calling for the matter to be settled and judgement to be passed. The eyes of the crowd, hungry and violent, turned to where she stood, supporting Dagmar with her shoulder. His right arm was back in its sling and the hand was tightly bound with linen bandage.

She nudged him forward. Dagmar stepped into the torchlight. He smelled the oil. He looked at the circle of people, death in their faces. He turned to look at the fat butcher tied to the stake like a grub about to be roasted. He thought of the dead, drunk man, buried by the butcher in the graveyard. He thought of the witch hunter, stiffening beneath a pile of forest leaves. He thought of the militiaman, who surely knew and wondered why he stood there amongst the ignorant, blood-driven rabble.

He thought mostly of Anja, of what she had said to him, of how she had looked at him, of what she must have seen when she did, and of how she had again brought him back to himself. He tried to imagine what might happen after this night was over. Someone was forcing a torch into his left hand.

He spread his damaged fingers apart and held the wood as if in a claw, between thumb and forefinger. He hesitated. He asked the crowd: *Why should this man die?*

The crowd told him: *He is Chaos. Destroy him.*

Dagmar's right arm twitched and stretched against the fabric of the sling. Anja touched him gently with her fingers, a reassuring squeeze. The sling tore and scales backhanded her away.

Dagmar leapt onto the pile of oil-slicked logs. He looked at the men and women with their torches and their murderous fear.

We are so much the same, and so different.

The butcher tried to lift his head. Dagmar thrust the torch into the logs and a forest of flames sprang up. Otto screamed and Dagmar howled. He embraced the fat man and locked his claw hands around the back of the stake.

The people of Kurtbad drew back from the thick, fetid smoke and the stench of decay. All except Anja, who stood in the glow of the flames and wept gently, her tears mingling with blood from a cut on her cheek.

Gunter dragged her away, put himself between her and the flames.

Dagmar's body melted like a candle as if the blaze inside him was hotter than the fire of oil and sticks. It took longer for the butcher to die.

I am burning now as I will burn then.

THOUGH KURTBAD remained a single stitch on the merchant's map it was never the same town. Some believed that they could always smell the stench of the mutant on the common. Chaos had touched them, they said, and that was the reason the crops were poor. The lonely gibbet was demolished and the wood used to make a new sheep pen.

Gunter tried to resign his post but he was forced to stay by the people who said that now they truly understood the gravity of the threat. He tried to learn to read. Anja left the town on the black stallion with the silver hooves, which she was said to have sold for a fair price in the market at Nuln. She never returned to Kurtbad, either with a child or a brand on her arm.

GRUNSONN'S MARAUDERS

Andy Jones

'GENTLEMEN, the deal is done. Your honour, sorry, *our* honour is at stake!'

The young man stood defiantly in front of the rough wooden table, around which three travel-worn characters played cards and drank from battered tankards. Two tankards were full of frothy ale in which suspicious shapes surfaced now and then. The other held a liquid golden glitter, which the owner refilled from a delicate bottle every so often.

'Raise yer ten, and throw in me spare dagger of wotsit slaying.' The gruff voice was that of a dwarf of indeterminate age and very few teeth. His black beard was streaked with silver grey (and gravy stains), his face a mass of scars from old wounds, weather-beaten and rugged. His armour was dented and scratched, and two fingers were missing from his left hand. A huge, rune-encrusted axe leaned against the table next to him. Unlike everything else about the dwarf, the axe gleamed and shone, even in the fuggy gloom of Ye Broken Bones Inne. Grimcrag Grunsonn peered at his cards through beady black eyes.

'Ach, Grimcrak, ven to admit Defeat! Dat Kard is nozzink bot a Seven.' The heavily-accented growl came from the lips of a wolfish barbarian sitting opposite the dwarf. Heavily muscled, with a bearskin draped across his broad shoulders, the barbarian glanced at Johan Anstein and grinned, showing white teeth. 'I got 'im now, ja?'

Johan threw his eyes heavenwards and tapped an impatient foot on the worn floorboards. 'Look, we've been sitting around for weeks now. So I've sorted us a job out, and–'

'What sort of a job, lad? More wet-nursing ladies on the way to court? You know what happened last time! Hah! Wet-nurses!' Jiriki the elf laughed quietly, a knowing look shining in his eyes.

Keanu the Reaver, the fur-clad barbarian, emitted something halfway between a belch and a throaty guffaw. 'Vet-nurse! Ha! Zome joke dat, eh, Grimcrak?'

The dwarf stared stony-faced at his cards. 'Weren't no fault of mine. Should've had good dwarf buckets 'stead of them shoddy things.'

Johan winced at the memory, but pressed on bravely. 'No, a proper job. You know, underground – with monsters and danger and stuff, a real quest.' The young would-be hero looked dreamily across the bar, already envisaging the many brave and daring deeds awaiting them.

The others ignored him. They'd heard it all before; Johan's pipe-dreams rarely came to anything.

'Okey-dokey, Grimcrak, da dagger it is.' The Reaver held his cards to his massive chest in a conspiratorial fashion.

'It's a wizard, see, lives here in town, wants us to find a long-lost magical item.'

'They all do, lad, they all do,' Grimcrag muttered. 'Let's see you, then.'

'Funf tenz!' proclaimed the barbarian.

'Damn!'

'Ja!' Keanu grinned viciously. 'I vin! I vin! Da dagger, if ya pleez…'

Johan drew in a deep breath and threw a sizeable bag down on the table. It clinked with an instantly recognisable metallic sound. 'He's given me a down-payment.'

Expecting a row for dubious tactics, Keanu was more than a little surprised when Grimcrag handed over the dagger, but the Barbarian did notice that a familiar glazed look had come over the dwarf's craggy features. Even as Grimcrag's left hand passed over the weapon, his right sidled of its own accord towards the bag, giving it a nudge. The bag jingled again.

'It's–' Johan began.

'Shush now, lad, I knows what this is.' Grimcrag's features had taken on a look of rapturous awe. 'Bretonnian gold, brought back from the new lands of Luscitara.'

'Lustria actually,' Jiriki corrected. 'And you only had to ask; we've known about the humid, swampy, jungle infested place for…'

'Never mind that. Their gold is second to none.' Grimcrag felt the bag again. After a few more investigative pokes, a secretive, greedy look came over the dwarf's craggy face, and he paused, before continuing in a disappointed tone.

'Actually, on second thoughts, I'm wrong y'know.' He dragged the bag towards him across the table.

'Vot meanink?' Keanu asked, his razor-sharp intuition picking up the change in the dwarf's manner.

'He's gone all goldsome on us. They all go like that,' the elf sighed. 'He'll be alright in a minute or two.'

'Can we get on with it? The wizard is waiting.' Johan was getting more exasperated by the second. 'You've got… sorry, we've got the gold. It's just a down-payment; we've got to meet him at his tower within the hour.'

Grimcrag shook his head, a sly look in his eye. Jiriki gave a short barking laugh and drew his dagger. From past experience, the elf knew what was about to happen.

'You've bin done, lad,' the dwarf said, peering inside the bag. 'Yup, just as I thought: brass and copper, brass and copper – just enough to pay back what you owes me for the sword and stuff I gave you.' Tutting disappointedly to himself, Grimcrag made to put the bag into his pack, moving with startling speed – but the elf and barbarian proved faster.

Keanu held Grimcrag's wrist while Jiriki split the bag open with one lightning-swift stroke of his dagger. Gold coins spilled across the table, glinting and gleaming in the light.

'Koppa?'

'Brass my–' Jiriki began.

'Sorcery!' exclaimed the dwarf, looking sheepish, 'It was all brass a moment ago, I swear.' Johan could have sworn that the dwarf was shaking, and had tears in his eyes, but he put it down to the smoke which filled the air of the gloomy inn.

The young man drew a deep breath and gave it one more try. He was one of the Marauders now, so they had to listen to him. Johan tried to look stern and authoritative, copying a look he'd seen Grimcrag use to good effect a number of times – usually when confronting ogres or trolls and addressing them as if they were naughty children who deserved spanking.

'Ahem!' Johan frowned for effect. 'AHEM!'

Keanu shot the ex-Imperial envoy a glance and involuntarily spat beer across the table.

'Vot's up, jung 'un? Konstipatid?'

Grimcrag was dabbing his eyes with a dirty cloth, whilst trying to regain his composure. Jiriki was putting the last coin away in his pack to be shared out later, but he looked up and grinned at Johan's posturing.

'Not bad, lad, not bad – now, what's the story again?'

Seizing his chance, Johan closed his eyes and took a very deep breath, before rattling off as many of the details as he could remember of his chance encounter with the cowled wizard with the twinkling eyes.

'Err… He wants us to rescue a magic item of some sort from the clutches of the monsters – that's undead and suchlike – from some caves under the Grey Mountains. He's been after it for years, and it's all he wants. He has lots of gold and treasure, and the bag is a down-payment. He lives in the big tower on the outskirts of town, and says that if we bring the artefact back, we can keep all the other loot from the dungeon – all he wants is the thing itself!' Panting, Johan finished his monologue and opened his eyes, proud of his powers of recall.

He was sitting on his own at the table. A few regulars stared at him as if he was mad, or had the plague perhaps.

Flushing a bright red, Johan picked up his pack and stumbled for the door, making his excuses as he fled. 'Damn them all to hell!' he muttered, buckling on his sword belt and setting off after his companions. He could just make out Grimcrag's stumpy figure running off at the end of the street.

'Wait for me, you callous bunch of thugs!'

Johan set off in hot pursuit. Well, he knew where they going. As he tore round the corner, he heard the unmistakable voice of an enraged innkeeper.

'Wretched Marauders! Who's payin' for all this beer?'

Johan Anstein wasn't stopping. This was his quest, and he was going to be in on it whether the others liked it or not.

THE GREY-COWLED wizard had obviously been expecting them, since he was waiting by the door to his tower. It was a run-down building, perhaps a hundred feet high and little more than twenty feet in diameter. Weeds grew in thick clumps around its base, and ivy crawled up the lichen-encrusted brick-work. No windows looked out any lower than a good thirty feet up the walls, giving the tower obvious defensive capabilities.

From the top, Johan imagined, you could see for miles and miles, at least as far as the Grey Mountains, far off to the north. He also noticed that although the tower looked decrepit in places, the front door was very impressive indeed. Ten feet tall, five feet broad, its dark black timbers and heavy iron surround suggested indomitable strength and near indestructibility. It had so many locks and bolts that in places it was hard to see the wood at all.

'Spose that's magic-locked too?' Grimcrag had asked with grudging admiration.

'Not at all, not all,' the twinkly-eyed wizard beamed from deep inside his grey hood. 'You can't beat a good set of locks and a strong door. In my experience, ostentatious displays of magic just seem to make the wrong sort… inquisitive, if you know what I mean.' With that, and the jangling of a hefty bunch of keys, they were in.

The tower was gloomy and dusty inside, betraying the fact that it had not really been occupied for some time now. Most of the doors up to the fifth floor were boarded over and nailed shut, and Johan couldn't help being intrigued and curious. He'd never been in a wizard's den before, not a real one.

Keanu had stayed outside 'To be keeping Guard' but Johan knew that, for all his muscles, the hulking barbarian didn't much trust the powers of magic, and stayed well clear unless he couldn't help it. If the stories were to be believed, the only way Keanu liked to deal with wizards was with a sharp blade. However, gold was gold, a job was a job, so the Reaver was 'Votchink for Troubles' outside.

'A wizard's tower, eh, Grimcrag, Jiriki?' Johan's voice was a muted, awe-struck whisper.

'Poor decor, very dusty, not much of a colour scheme,' the elf muttered, mostly to himself.

'Badly built, needs repointing, I've knocked down better,' Grimcrag added from up ahead. 'Hold on a minute – how come Keanu had five tens anyway?'

'Yes, but still… oh, never mind!'

Eventually they had reached the top level and emerged breathless into the wizard's chamber. There, seated amidst the bubbling vats, stuffed animals, astrolabes, ancient books and all the other accoutrements of his trade, the wizard had explained the mission.

It seemed that he had spent his whole life searching for the Finger of Life, a powerful magical artefact, crafted when the world was young and death but a dream.

'Read that somewhere,' Grimcrag interjected at that point. 'Go on.'

The wizard explained that this item was a power to heal, to restore, and unspecified Dark Forces had conspired for years to keep it from his grasp. Now he had pinpointed where it rested, yet he was too old to go and wrest it from the powers of darkness. He needed heroes, mighty warriors of great renown, to go and retrieve the Finger of Life for him. He had heard of the great deeds of Grunsonn's Marauders, and knew that it was Fate which had brought them to this small backwater, south of the Grey Mountains.

'The way will be hard, but think of the greater good! Think of the children to be healed, the starving to be fed!'

'It's really that good, is it?' Jiriki inquired languidly as he peered out of the window in the tower. 'Hey, Grimcrag, I can see into young Miss Epstan's boudoir from here.'

'That good and better, young man!' exclaimed the kindly old wizard, ignoring the elf and concentrating on Johan. 'You see these boxes?' He threw a stout chest open, so that sunlight glinted on the contents within. Johan gasped: he'd never seen so much gold all in one place. The wizard noticed his shock and grinned. 'All as nothing compared to the Finger of Life, believe me.'

Grimcrag coughed and tried to maintain his composure, but when he spoke his voice shook a little. 'Take it off your hands if you like, I can see it's, erm, cluttering the place, and filling all your nice boxes too. If you like, that is…' His voice trailed off as the wizard flung open another chest containing a myriad assortment of gemstones. 'Gggnngh…'

'A pretty speech, Grimcrag, but motivated by gold-lust rather than concern for my storage facilities I fear, eh?' The old man laughed at the dwarf's obvious discomfort.

'Well, I just thought–'

The wizard swept his arm dismissively around the chamber. 'The Finger sits in such company as makes this little lot worthless, and you, my friends, may have it all. All I want is the Finger.'

'Lots of treasure then?' Grimcrag had that pensive look that usually preceded a new adventure. Johan crossed his fingers behind his back. It looked as if Grimcrag was on board at least. The wizard nodded.

'Plenty of orcs and other hellspawn to test the mettle of my Ulthuan-crafted blade?' Jiriki leant out of the window, looking straight downwards, his words a careless whisper. The wizard nodded. Johan exhaled with relief; he'd thought that the elf would be the hardest to convince. Jiriki looked over his shoulder, staring the wizard straight in the eye. The old man nodded again. After a moment, the elf shrugged and looked out of the window once more. This time he shouted: 'Hey, Keanu, can you hear me down there?'

'Ja! Vot's happenink?' The unmistakable voice drifted faintly upwards 'Is jung Anstein turning into a Toad yet?'

'No, my friend. We just wondered if you fancied liberating a fortune in jewels and gold from some of the greenskins you hate so much?'

There was a brief pause.

'Ja! Of course! Vot schtupid Qvestion!'

THE MINOTAUR bellowed and roared as it charged down the narrow underground passageway. Johan backed away fast, holding his sword in front of him. During his years of schooling to be an Imperial Envoy, he'd obviously missed the 'Minotaurs: Etiquette and Handling Thereof' lessons. His sword looked ridiculously puny, even to himself. Still, if he was going to die, he might as well go down in a way worthy of one of Grunsonn's Marauders.

'Come on then, come on then!' he shouted, inwardly preparing for a painful demise.

The minotaur grunted and slowed to a stop. Its head swung slowly to and fro as it sniffed the air warily. Its teeth were still bared, but it obviously wasn't quite so keen to face Johan as a few seconds previously.

Anstein blinked, and regarded his sword with new respect. Perhaps Grimcrag had given him a magic one by mistake. He waved it at the minotaur again for good effect. 'You want some? YOU WANT SOME?'

The minotaur growled loudly and backed off towards the darkness from where it had emerged scant seconds earlier. To the young adventurer, it already seemed as if hours had passed since he'd first seen the beast. Time moved like glue.

'Um… you craven coward, come taste my blade!' Johan took a step forward, much emboldened.

This was obviously too much for the massive beast, as it turned tail and fled into the darkness. Johan heard its cloven hoofs beating a rapid tattoo on the rough stone floor. He was just sheathing his sword, in pride and relief, when Grimcrag, Jiriki and Keanu came hurtling around the corridor.

'Hey, did you see that, I just…' Johan's voice tailed off in terror.

The Marauders were looking at him with open horror and revulsion, and Johan could see what was coming – these were trained warriors who reacted first and regretted their actions later. Well, sometimes.

'No, it's all right. It's me – Johan!' he shrieked, wondering if somehow he had been enchanted to look like a fearsome creature. This was crazy. It was also much too late. As if in slow motion, Johan saw two arrows flash from Jiriki's bow, even as Keanu hurled a wickedly barbed spear, and Grimcrag's massive axe hurtled through the air. Even under the circumstances, Johan had to admire their reactions.

Still in slow motion, he backed away, dropping his sword in abject terror. The missiles crossed the short space between them. Johan mouthed silent curses. The axe glinted in the air.

Johan's improvised escape stopped abruptly as he backed into something big and hard. Something that growled. Something whose foetid breath touched him for a split second. Something whose beady red eyes regarded him balefully in the instant before it was simultaneously decapitated by a large axe, pinioned by a spear and spitted by two arrows to its black heart.

With a growling gurgle and a fountain of viscous black blood, the immense troll collapsed and died, one viciously clawed hand dragging Johan down with it. His desperately flailing arms caught a knobbly projection of rock, which came away in his hand. Hitting his head hard on the granite floor, the last thing Johan heard was a dull grating, rumbling sound. Even as he passed out it occurred to him that they may well all be about to die.

A BOOTED FOOT prodded Johan Anstein in the ribs. Callused fingers tugged roughly at his jerkin. Foul, caustic liquid was forced down his throat. A harsh voice shouted at him in a barely understandable tongue, as powerful and (from the smell) none-too-recently washed arms wrenched him moaning to his feet. Even in his groggy haze, and with his head smarting badly, Johan knew that something awful was about to happen. Maybe everyone else was dead. Maybe he was the last of the Marauders.

He blinked and tried to stand unaided, swaying dizzily but determined not to give his captors the satisfaction of seeing his weakness.

'Vot you think, Grimcrak, not holt his Liquor?'

'He'll be alright, had a nasty knock on the head. Go easy on the lad,' Jiriki said.

'Knock some sense into him perhaps.'

'Now now, Grimcrag, the lad's done fine by us so far, give him credit,' the elf chided. 'We'd not have found the concealed door otherwise.'

Waving away another slug of the noxious brew Grimcrag was toting, Anstein looked slowly about him. He quickly ran his hands over his bruised body, checking that nothing was missing. Apparently not. A thought trickled sluggishly through his battered brain. It eventually came to rest.

'What concealed door?'

As one, the Marauders stepped aside to reveal a large portal, where before there had been only a rock wall. Evidently the piece of stone Johan had grabbed as he fell had been some kind of hidden trigger mechanism.

'Are you sure it's the right one?' Anstein asked nervously. 'I've seen what happens when you lot go poking around for treasure behind secret doors.'

'You've got the map, young 'un,' Grimcrag grunted, still affronted that Johan didn't want any of his beer, 'and all the other stuff from the wizard too.'

'Let's just open da verdamten Door, ja?' Keanu enthused, drawing his sword.

Grimcrag began to smile, and a split-second later he had his savage axe firmly gripped in both hands. 'OK! Let's maraud!'

'Hold it, hold it!' The elven voice cut the air. 'Johan's right for once.' Jiriki was squinting at the inscriptions on the doorway. 'These are very old and powerful runes, and we don't want to break them without good reason.' He traced their shapes with a slender finger. 'Very good reason indeed.'

Grimcrag peered at the symbols, muttering under his breath. 'Good workmanship this. Old. Powerful.' The dwarf turned to Johan. 'OK, young 'un, get the stuff out, let's be 'aving you. Who knows what'll be along in a minute?'

'Ja, Monsters, Dragonz even!' the Reaver chipped in enthusiastically, looking at the dark recesses in the narrow passage, perhaps to spot any lurking behemoths they had missed earlier.

Johan reached into his backpack and pulled out a selection of objects given them by the wizard. One was an old map, which Johan rolled out on the stone floor and weighted down with some bits of troll. The warriors hunched over the map, illuminated by the flickering light of their torch.

JOHAN CAREFULLY packed the objects away again one at a time. He had a bag to hold the Finger of Life when they found it. There was also a simulacrum of the artefact, to be placed exactly in the spot where the Finger rested. Apparently it contained enough power to paralyse the guardians whilst the Marauders made their getaway. This bit had worried Johan a great deal, nervous as he was about powerful artefacts and cursed guardians, but he feared to say anything as the other warriors had taken the announcement in their stride.

Johan had also been given a magical talisman, which would re-seal the runes on the doorway – if the accompanying instructions were closely followed. That bit had worried him too, but the others had pointed out that if push came to shove even Grimcrag could run pretty fast. Finally, there was the agreement signed by the wizard that any other treasure they liberated was theirs to keep: all he wanted was the Finger.

'OK, this is definitely the place, I've got the gear. Let's do it.'

'Vot's da plan then?'

Grimcrag scratched his bearded chin thoughtfully. 'Well, in my experience, places with secret doors – ones which are magically locked by old and powerful runes, mind – spell two things.' He paused a moment and counted on his stubby fingers. 'The main one is treasure. Gold.' At the thought, his eyes closed wistfully for a few moments.

'And the second?' Johan prompted.

'Ah, the second...' Grimcrag scowled and looked fierce. 'That'll be all the hideous monsters defending the gold, all destined to die by my blade!'

'Und mine also!'

Jiriki looked heavenwards, arms folded. He tapped his foot impatiently. 'And the plan is?'

Grimcrag beamed. Jiriki began to grin. The Reaver's barking laugh cut the dank air.

'We all know the plan, don't we? It's the same one we've always used,' Grimcrag said politely, before lowering his voice to a rumbling, menacing rasp. 'We goes in, we kills 'em all, we takes the loot, we legs it. Gottit?'

'Clear as a bell, my friend.'

'Ja, Kunnink!'

Johan blanched in terror. 'Is that it? Shouldn't we at least–'

But it was too late. Grimcrag and Keanu rolled back the great stone doors, ready to rush the inevitable horde of monsters. Jiriki had an arrow nocked, the string on his fine elf bow pulled taut.

A moment later and they were all reeling back in shocked surprise. Rather than the expected flood of zombies, Chaos creatures, orcs or worse, they were completely blinded by a burst of pure white light. The brightness threw the tunnel into stark whiteness, and the Marauders fell to their knees, their hands covering their eyes. The torches they carried were dropped, to gutter and die on the floor, but no one noticed, such was the intensity of the light streaming from the long-sealed cavern.

Johan hurled himself to one side of the stone doorway, where he lay panting in terror. After a moment he found that he was, surprisingly, still alive.

Johan blinked. 'It's just light!' he called out, standing up warily and dusting himself down. Shielding his eyes and peering around the doorway, he saw the others walking into the light, black silhouettes against the brightness.

'Get in here, manling, sharpish!'

Johan staggered forwards, tentatively entering a chamber where the air was crisp and sweet, and the sound of soft breathing resonated peacefully. As his eyes grew accustomed to the glare, Johan gasped in astonishment. They were in a low roofed, circular chamber at least thirty feet in diameter. The walls were bright white, and radiated the light which had assailed them.

This was not what had caused Johan to gasp. In a circle around the walls of the cavern there was a ring of stone slabs, perhaps twenty in all. On each, bedecked in the finery of princes, was an elf warrior of such beauty and nobility that it was almost painful to look upon them. They slept, and theirs was the soft breathing which filled the air. Each was in full war gear, each held an elaborately styled sword to his chest. Each looked to be a king.

'Ancient elf lords, livery of Tiranoc, the sunken kingdom,' Jiriki spoke softly, his voice tinged with awe.

But even this was not what had caused Johan to gasp. At the centre of the chamber, surrounded by the sleeping elf lords, was a plain yet elegant plinth. elf and dwarf runes were inscribed in its surfaces, the spidery grandeur of the elven sigils contrasting with the powerful majesty of the dwarf work.

Atop the plinth sat a finger. A black, wizened finger. A wrinkled, mostly decayed, scabrous thing of great antiquity. Despite its obvious age, Johan was under no illusions that this was what these princely lords were here to protect.

Grimcrag looked over at Johan and laughed. 'Don't be taken in, boy, one false move and these charming lads will be revealed in their true shape. Vampires, I wouldn't wonder. Daemons even. Don't touch 'em.'

Johan paused, doubt assailed him. Then, with trembling steps, he made for the central dais. Jiriki was already there. The elf stood by the plinth, reading the inscriptions as best he could. 'These are beyond me, but they are probably powerful runes of protection akin to those on the doorway.'

'Vot Treasure?' Ever down to earth, the barbarian was scouting the chamber, looking for secret compartments where the great treasure trove might be found. 'Nothink here. Not vun think.'

The dwarf looked around and sniffed the air, shaking his head in evident disgust. 'Good point, meathead. We've been done!'

'Never mind that now,' whispered Johan. 'Let's get the Finger and get out of here – we can sort out payment later, when we get back.' Once more, he was sure that something awful was about to happen. Sweat beaded on his forehead.

They converged on the central dais. The Reaver's sword weaved, testing the air, and his eyes darted nervously about the chamber. Grimcrag stood close by, legs apart for balance, his axe held firmly in both hands. Jiriki reached out for the finger – as he touched it, the breathing of the sleepers faltered in its regular rhythm.

'Leave it, Jiriki!' Johan screeched. 'Remember the instructions: the simulacrum!'

The elf recoiled from the finger as if struck. He nodded to Johan, eyes wide. Grimcrag guffawed, a nervous cough of a laugh.

Johan carefully unwrapped the simulacrum from his pack. It looked little like the blackened stump on the plinth, but the wizard had assured them that it held magic properties enough to contain the guardians for a while at least. Johan reached carefully with his left hand for the aged finger, his right simultaneously manoeuvring the simulacrum into place. As he grasped the finger, a shudder went through the sleepers. Quick though Johan was to remove the artefact, one of the lords abruptly awoke, sitting upright and reaching for his sword.

'WHO DARES–' he began, but his voice was cut short as Grimcrag's axe removed his noble head from his elegant body. Jiriki winced. Johan placed the simulacrum on the dais. The sleepers resumed their slumber, although now their breathing was disturbed, and they fidgeted restlessly in their sleep, as if in the throes of nightmares.

'Goddit, ja?' Keanu asked.

Johan nodded.

'Let's go,' growled Grimcrag.

They made for the door, half expecting a hideous trap to be sprung as they left. Jiriki paused by the defiled slab, his forehead furrowed by lines of uncertainty.

'Come on, Jiriki, it was him or us,' Grimcrag said softly from the doorway. 'If I'm wrong, at least it's not you 'as been kin-slaying, and I'll owe someone due reparation.'

Hesitantly Jiriki joined them outside the chamber. 'We're all in this together, my friend. Let's hope we're right.'

In the passageway, Keanu had a torch re-lit, and the warriors carefully closed the stone door behind them, shutting out the white light and plunging themselves into gloom once again. Johan handed the magical talisman to Jiriki, who passed it around the doorway, realigning the broken runes once more.

'There you are, see!' Grimcrag exclaimed. 'That wizard knows what he's up to all right – all bar the treasure, that is…' His gruff voice trailed off, and he spat on the floor.

'Somvun get da Treasure first?' Keanu suggested, striding off along the corridor with lantern held high.

'Mebbe so,' grunted the dwarf. 'And wait for us!' Johan and the grizzled dwarf followed the barbarian.

Jiriki joined them a moment later, a puzzled frown still on his face. 'The problem is, if we think for a moment, that the chamber had lain undisturbed for ages. We found it as it was sealed, runes unbroken. No one has been there before us.'

'And that means–' Johan added after the required moment's thought.

'No treasure!' Grimcrag scowled even more ferociously than usual. 'As I thought, that wizard has some explaining to do once he's got 'is precious Finger back!'

Dispirited, the adventurers made their way to the surface and the long trek back to civilisation. It seemed that the quest was, at least from their own point of view, a failure.

'At least ve're gettink da Finga,' Keanu commented, attempting a glimmer of cheer as they trudged out of the broken down cave entrance 'Und ve can see da Daylicht vunce more.'

Grimcrag looked around the desolate hillside. It was starting to snow again. 'What good's that to us, eh? Daylight won't keep us warm, nor pay our expenses neither.'

Jiriki laughed. The situation had tickled his elvish humour. 'And all for a mummified bit of man-flesh that is worth

nothing to anyone except our misguided patron. We can't even
sell it to anyone else.'

Grimcrag snorted and stomped off into the snow, followed
by the barbarian, now wrapped tightly in his bearskin. The
dwarf's gruff voice floated back towards the elf, who was stow-
ing his bow to avoid the string being ruined by the damp air.
'Not funny. Not funny at all!'

Bursting into a bright and spirit-raising melody, the elf ran
lightly after his companions, leaving Johan shivering in the
entrance. A plan was growing in Anstein's mind, a plan so devi-
ous that it might just work.

'Hold on you lot! Hold on!' he shouted, rushing off down
the hillside after the vanishing figures. In a few minutes he
caught them, waiting for him in the lee of a large boulder
which offered a little shelter from the elements.

'Make it quick, lad,' Grimcrag said through gritted teeth.

'Yes, yes, but listen to this idea,' Johan began, hopping from
foot to foot.

'Ideas, pah!' spat Keanu, his breath steaming in the cold. He
stabbed Johan in the chest with an iron hard finger. 'Dis hole
grosses Dizazta ist 'coz of your verdamten Planen.' Johan had
noticed before that the barbarian's accent thickened to near-
incomprehensibility when he got angry.

Even Jiriki shook his head wearily. 'I think you've got us in
enough of a mess already with your pipe-dreams, lad. Leave it
alone, eh?'

As the three Marauders turned to go, Johan jumped in front
of them, eyes gleaming.

'Listen, you miserable beggars. We've got the Finger, right?'

'Ja, so vot?'

'The Vizard, sorry, the wizard wants it, right?'

'Yesss, go on…' Grimcrag was interested. He could see the
glimmerings of a plan happening, a plan which might involve
some gold.

Johan seized his chance and blurted out the whole scheme.
'We get old Gerry the butcher to make us a finger just like the
real one. After all, the wizard has never seen it.' Johan counted
the points off on his fingers. 'Then we take the real finger and
bury it somewhere secret nearby.' Jiriki was nodding in
approval. Johan held up another finger. 'We take the fake finger
to the wizard and try and get an explanation from him. He

won't let us in the tower if we don't have something to wave at him.'

'Klevva lad. Be Kontinuing.'

'Well, as I see it, once we're in the tower, he'll either spin us a yarn, or offer us some gold by way of apology. If we get some treasure, we go back and get the real finger for him. Otherwise, we tell him he's got a fake and sell him the real one. Simple! We can't lose!' Pleased with himself, Johan swelled up with pride.

The others, standing by the boulder on the desolate hillside, assessed the plan.

'Butcher, ja?'

'A simulacrum of a simulacrum, I like that.'

'Treasure and gold after all!'

'Well?' enquired Johan after a minute or so. 'What do you think?'

Grimcrag grabbed him by the shoulders, staring sternly into Johan's eyes. The dwarf's black eyes gleamed ferociously. Johan thought perhaps now something awful was going to happen after all. The others crowded round, looking over Grimcrag's shoulders to see what was going on. Johan felt his back meet the cold stone of the boulder. He gulped.

'Manling,' Grimcrag began, speaking slowly and with deliberation. 'Of all your harebrained schemes…' He stopped, and Johan cringed inwardly at what was to follow. 'This… is the best so far!' With a whoop of joy, Grimcrag threw his helmet into the air, caught it again and set off down the hillside at the nearest he was ever going to get to a sprightly jog.

Jiriki grinned. 'This is going to work, lad – he's even singing his favourite song!' Punching Johan cheerfully in the chest, the elf set off after the dwarf.

'What song?' Johan shouted, wincing from the blow.

'Komst, lad, let's go.' The Barbarian sprang catlike down the hillside.

Still smirking with satisfaction, Johan began picking his way down the treacherous slope. Even though he was concentrating hard on not falling over, his ears caught the unmistakable sound of the Marauders in full song as they descended the hill. After a moment's hesitation, Johan threw caution to the wind. Well, no one from the Empire was around to hear him.

'Gold gold gold gold!
Gold gold gold gold!
Wonderful gold!
Delectable gold…'
It was all going to be all right after all. Probably.

THE WIZARD WAS pleased to see them, skipping excitedly as he undid the myriad locks and bolts to his tower.

'You have it, you have it?' he fussed, leading them by torch light up the steps 'Of course you have, I saw it from the window.' The wizard turned around on the steps and reached out a bony hand. Johan thought he saw a rather greedy glint in the eyes which peered out from the shadows of the heavy cowl. 'I'll carry it from here on now, shall I?'

His eyes were mesmerising, and Johan felt his hand reaching unintentionally into his back pack. 'You can carry it now,' he intoned dully. Johan was barged aside by a sturdy armoured figure, who broke the spell with a characteristically gruff outburst.

'Not till the tower, that was the deal. We deliver it to the top of the tower. Always does things to the letter, we does. We've got honour!' Grimcrag's voice was laden with sarcasm, but if the wizard noticed he did a good job of not showing it, running off cheerfully up the steps.

'Very well, my friends. Hurry along, hurry along, I have a kettle on for a nice hot drink.'

'Hrrumph!' Grimcrag added, but they followed the excited sorcerer up to his den nonetheless. Five minutes later and they were sitting around his table, glasses of a hot, mead-like drink steaming before them. None of them touched a drop.

'Come along now,' the wizard chided, rubbing his hands together gleefully 'Drink up, we have much to celebrate!'

Johan smiled glassily and made to take up his glass, but the Reaver stopped him with an iron hard forearm. 'Njet drinking!'

'We always keep clear heads when concluding business. Nothing personal, you understand.' Jiriki's silky steel voice decided the issue.

'Of course. You are… professionals.'

Shaking his head to clear what felt like a thick fog, Johan thought he caught the edge of a snarl in the wizard's voice. The Marauders made no move. There was a heavy silence.

'Well?' the wizard exclaimed after a moment, and there was no mistaking the impatience in his tone now. 'Where is it?'

Grimcrag turned to Johan and winked. He was enjoying this immensely, although the canny dwarf had noticed that there were no treasure chests lying around this time. 'Where's all the treasure then?' he enquired of the wizard, as politely as a hard bitten dwarf who has been dragged to the perilous ends of the world for absolutely nothing could manage. 'Where's the gold?'

The wizard waved a hand dismissively and smiled. 'I took your advice and moved it. It was a lot of worthless clutter. All locked away safely downstairs, never fear.' He patted the large ring of keys under his cloak. They jangled comfortingly. 'Now, if I might insist, the Finger of Life, power of goodness, please, as agreed. I have waited long enough, and we do have a deal!'

'Ahem!' The dwarf cleared his throat after a moment's thought. 'Johan, the Finger if you please!'

All eyes were on the table as Johan Anstein, ex-Imperial envoy and latest accidental addition to Grunsonn's Marauders, unwrapped the prize for which they had fought so hard.

The wizard gasped. Johan thought that they'd been tumbled. But no, the wizard was enraptured by the burned and charred chicken leg that sat before him. 'May I take it?' he whispered, reaching out a scrawny hand. 'Oh, it's a beauty!'

Privately doubting his aesthetic judgement, the Marauders nevertheless nodded in concert. The wizard was almost in their trap. So far so good.

Then, with a speedy move which they would not have dreamed of witnessing from one so apparently old, the ancient wizard swept aloft the 'Finger' and simultaneously gave a loud and triumphantly sinister laugh.

'Mine, it is mine at last!' he roared, holding the chicken leg above his head. As the Marauders looked on in shocked disbelief, the old sorcerer leapt onto the table, scattering maps, charts and wizardly tomes onto the floor of the tower. Discarding his grey robe with a dramatic flourish, the wizard was revealed in a jet black gown, covered in unmistakably necromantic symbols.

'Vot?' Keanu began, backing away. It had taken enough beer to get the Barbarian into the wizard's tower in the first place, and seeing their patron revealed as a foul necromancer did nothing for his nerves.

Fully aware that the evil wizard was wielding anything but a potent magical item, Grimcrag and Jiriki remained seated, grinning to themselves. Johan, a little unnerved, tried to follow their example, and managed an idiotic teeth-clamping grimace.

With a face like thunder, the dark wizard looked down at them. He regarded them balefully. 'Idiots!' he hissed. 'Now you see the truth!' Glancing at the Finger, the sorcerer grinned wickedly. Snake-like eyes glittered in his long, bony face.

'This,' he continued, 'this is one of the long-lost fingers of the Dread King, foul lieutenant of Nagash himself.' He capered in delight on the tabletop. Johan recognised insanity when he saw it, and by anyone's book this was a whole chapter to itself.

'You doubt me?' shrieked the sorcerer, regarding their placid expressions. 'Why should I lie? I have searched for this for ages. I am old beyond my mortal span, and now, with this, I gain ultimate power and immortality!' Spittle flew from his foam-flecked lips as he ranted.

'Why didn't you retrieve it yourself, old man?' Jiriki asked quietly. 'You've obviously known about it for years.'

The sorcerer threw back his head and cackled maniacally. 'That's the joke, you see, that's the joke.' Doubled up in laughter, tears rolled down his hollow cheeks. Suddenly his squawking laughter stopped, and he stood straight, regarding the warriors with a baleful glare. Pointing at Jiriki, he laughed derisively. 'Your kin, ages past, locked the claw away beyond my reach. Sealed it so that none like me could enter the chamber. Guarded it with twelve mighty elf lords for all eternity.' He spat on the floor to mark his disgust. 'But I waited. Oh yes, I was patient. I tracked the resting place of the Finger and I plotted and planned. Many tried and failed whilst I brooded long in my tower. Then you arrived and all was clear. I needed you as pawns to do my bidding, just as my great undead armies will do!'

He studied the warriors as if they were mindless vermin, all but unworthy of his gaze. 'I needed you to go, unwitting, where I could not. You would unknowingly breach the defences set up by your own kind, and retrieve that which was rightfully mine.' The sorcerer laughed. 'Your lot ever was to be lured by greed and avarice.'

'And now?' Grimcrag asked, nodding for the others to stand up. 'What happens now?'

The sorcerer paused for a moment, head cocked to one side. 'Ah yes, what happens now...' He coughed to clear his throat, and solemnly adjusted his robe about his scrawny body.

'Now I must kill you all. You have been a great help, and it is a great shame of course, but really you have to die!' The wizard chuckled ruefully, and brought the claw down to point at the Marauders. 'Doubtless you will later join my hordes of undeath which will march across the world, but now YOU – MUST – DIE!'

As he finished his speech, he closed his eyes, and portentously threw out his arms, waving the claw at Grimcrag and the Marauders.

Despite knowing the impotence of the device, Johan found himself flinching. He need not have worried.

The sorcerer opened his eyes and frowned, puzzled. The Marauders watched him, transfixed by his performance. The wizard drew in a deep breath and tried the ending again: 'MUST... DIEEEEE!'

When this didn't work, and he noticed the grins on the warriors' faces, he began to suspect that all was not well. Tapping the claw on the palm of his other hand, he jumped off the table and quickly found himself backed up against the turret wall. 'Die...?' he whimpered feebly.

'We weren't born yesterday, mate!' Grimcrag grunted. 'Eh, Johan?'

The Marauders closed in on the pathetic, misguided and evil old man.

THE WHITE RADIANCE faded and vanished as the great stone door slid into place once more. This time around, the Marauders had taken the precaution of bringing two other long-standing sorcerous acquaintances to supervise the resealing of the runes protecting the vault, and to work out how the secret door could be brought back into place. Then, and only then, could they really forget about the whole affair.

There wasn't much Johan could do except stand by with a torch and a sword. Keanu was doing the same: torch to illuminate the others' work, sword to deter any would be intruders. Johan was mightily relieved that no monsters of any description had turned up yet. In contrast, the barbarian was staring intently down the rough hewn passageway, and Johan was sure that the Reaver did not share his sentiments.

The two wizards – one bald and portly with fiery red gown and ruddy cheeks, the other tall and gaunt with flowing and sombre purple robes – stood back from the doors to admire their handiwork. After a few minor runic readjustments, they proclaimed their task completed.

Jiriki had already declared that the elf sigils were largely unbroken, and should stand the test of another few thousand years without any strain.

Grimcrag had enquired, checking over the dwarf runes on the portal, if that was really the best that could be expected from shoddy elf work? 'Aha!' he declared, stubby fingers probing the recesses around the stone-wrought door frame. 'I've found the catch to young Anstein's secret portal.' As far as his stout build would allow, Grimcrag pressed himself flat to the surface of the door, and reached his hand into a dark crack at one side. His eyes were closed to mere slits and his tongue protruded from between his compressed lips in concentration.

'Votch for Skorpion, Grimcrak!' Keanu whispered, all too familiar with the sorts of creatures to be found simply by probing one's fingers into the myriad small nooks and crannies to be found in any hostile dungeon.

'Thanks, musclehead, that's just what I don't need to hear!' grunted Grimcrag. 'This thing was built by dwarfs, so it must be set up to… ahhh, that'll do it!'

With a muted grating sound, a sheet of roughly surfaced rock began to slide slowly down over the rune-encrusted doorway. In a few minutes the secret chamber would be invisible to all but the keenest search. As they stood and watched the monumental slab descend, they all heard the unmistakable sound of scrabbling coming from within.

'Ee's Voken up then,' the barbarian stated impassionately.

'Looks that way,' Grimcrag added.

A barely discernible voice reached them through the stone door, which was already at least halfway covered by the descending slab. Grimcrag strode forward and listened to catch the words.

'Don't leave me here… The light it pains me so… My powers are nothing in here… Please, I implore you!'

Grimcrag rapped on the stone door. 'Hush now, you'll wake 'em up – and I'll wager you don't want that!'

The scrabbling redoubled, but was soon blocked out as the massive slab slotted into its final resting place with a solid booming thud and a cloud of dust.

When the air cleared, they were standing in a nondescript and gloomy passage once more.

Grimcrag rubbed his hands together. 'There now, a job well done.'

'Many thanks to you, Marius, Hollochi,' Jiriki added gracefully, bowing to the two wizards.

'Least we could do after that nasty business with the Crown of Implacable Woe,' replied the Bright wizard cheerily, whilst the Amethyst mage simply gave a single, sombre inclination of his head.

'Ja, tanks a lot!' the Reaver added. 'Now ve're getting to da Alehaus.'

Without further ado, the party of adventurers set off towards daylight and a well-earned tankard or two.

Grimcrag hung behind and walked alongside Johan, filling the latest addition to the Marauders with pride. 'Well, lad, it could've turned out worse,' the dwarf stated. 'At least we've done a good service to folk hereabouts.'

'Oh yes, Grimcrag, all-told a jolly successful quest, eh?' Johan agreed happily.

'Well, I wouldn't go that far. We're not dead, and he–' Grimcrag cocked a grubby thumb over his shoulder. 'He's locked up for good'n'all, but...' The dwarf sighed sadly. 'Not even a snifter of any gold.' His shoulders sagged as far as his battered armour would allow.

Johan grinned and reached into his pack, retrieving a large bundle of keys. They jangled comfortably.

'Oh I don't know about that, Grimcrag. Whilst you lot were busy bundling him up, I took the liberty of borrowing these.'

Recognising the keys, the dwarf's jaw dropped in surprise. 'I'll be blowed!' he exclaimed. Further up the passageway, heads turned to see what the commotion was about.

Johan lifted up the keys and jangled them merrily above his head. 'It's a big tower, I know, but somewhere there's a heck of a lot of gold going begging – and the way I see it, he still owes us for the job!'

Relieved and uproarious laughter filled the dingy tunnel. In a moment the buoyant adventurers burst into song, Grimcrag leading and the others taking up the refrain:

'Gold gold gold gold!
Gold gold gold gold!
Wonderful gold!
Delectable gold…'

As they marched along, Grimcrag patted Johan paternally on the shoulder. 'Yer one of us now, lad,' he said between verses. 'Ain't it grand when a brilliant plan of mine comes together!'

THE DOORWAY BETWEEN

Rjurik Davidson

'I WANT THEM DEAD and my property returned to me.' Baron von Kleist leaned forward as he spoke, the light throwing shadows across his thin face. He was a tall, gaunt man fast approaching middle age, clean shaven, his black hair slicked back like a raven's wing. And although he wore a simple cloak, secured over his shoulder with a plain clasp, he had the air of nobility about him. Perhaps this was due to the very simplicity of his attire, for true nobles have no need to dress flamboyantly, to show off with frills and lace. Only the new nobility needed to prove their credentials with gaudiness and show.

Or at least, that's what Frantz Heidel thought as he sized up the man opposite him. The witch hunter leaned back against his chair and glanced around the inn. Logs crackled in an open fireplace, yellow flames lazily throwing out heat. A few old-timers leaned up against the bar, heads drooping forwards as if they were gaining weight by the minute. In the opposite corner, a group of young men sat and laughed, their faces ruddy from cheap wine. The innkeeper's daughter served them, making her way from behind the bar, through a wave of suggestive comments, to the young men's table. Bechafen, Heidel thought to himself, could be any town in the Empire.

Heidel dressed plainly himself, his clothes a series of simply-cut browns and greens, perfect for the wilderness. His face mirrored his attire, brown straggling hair falling around his ears, lines etched into his skin, thin lips. The only remarkable feature were his eyes, deep and dark. It was as if behind them whole vistas of passion and zealotry were concealed. Only the pupils allowed a glimpse, as if through a keyhole into a blazing room. He turned back to regard the nobleman.

'The destruction of evil, that is the task I've set myself. It is my vow to seek out this cancer that grows daily in the world. And when I find it…' Heidel let his voice trail off.

'A noble cause, undoubtedly.' The baron smiled slightly. 'I understand you burned a man just three days ago. Tell me, have you ever destroyed an innocent by mistake?'

'Never.'

'And how can you be sure?' The baron's eyes were alive with the challenge.

'Witchcraft, sorcery and other forms of corruption are revealed by the stench that wafts before them. Evil betrays itself at every turn. Those who are sensitive feel its presence – I know I am in darkness when I cannot see,' Heidel said rather distractedly. He leaned forward, his voice gaining conviction. 'The innocent have nothing to fear, for they walk in the light. But the guilty will reveal themselves, and they should tremble because only the gods and light and truth can cleanse the world of the foul existence of corruption.'

The baron seemed satisfied with Heidel's reply and leaned back, sipping his dark red wine. A moment later he placed the glass back onto the table. 'So this job is suited to you? You can track down this evil band and – how do you put it? – cleanse them. The Dark Warrior has the heirloom, no doubt. When you have cleansed this foul brood and retrieved it, you will return it to me. Seven hundred crowns for its safe return. You can find me here when you return.'

'Tell me, baron, when this band attacked your wagon, how did they know to take the heirloom?' Heidel poured himself another small measure of wine from the ceramic carafe.

'I brought all my valuables with me when I chose to settle here, in Bechafen. They took us by surprise on the road and my men fled, the cowardly fools, leaving the follower of Darkness and his band to take what they wanted. Naturally I am somewhat embarrassed, so I trust that your task will be kept private.' The baron covered one thin hand with the other, as if to show what he meant.

'And what does this heirloom look like?'

'It is a pendant, silver, set with a blue gem. It is beautiful like a clear sky above the ice-stilled Reik in winter. When caught in the light it throws a thousand tiny sparks of silver into the air, and the blue becomes as deep and rich as the oncoming night.'

'A beautiful object.' Heidel smiled, picturing the gem in his head with its changing blues and its flashing silver reflections.

'My most precious,' the baron said earnestly.

'You must be quite concerned.'

'I am sick with worry that I might never see this precious thing again.' Then the baron shook his head from side to side, as if in disbelief that the pendant could ever have been stolen.

'Well fear not, your lordship. I shall return your heirloom to you, and in doing so, give these foul obscenities their just desserts: an eternal sleep in a long, cold grave.' Heidel's voice was firm, solid, emphatic. 'I will need to find a guide of course, someone who knows the land—'

'Ah, I have already thought of that,' the baron interrupted with a wave of his hand. 'I know just the man. He's a tracker, familiar with these parts. Karl Sassen. I shall send him word to meet you here at the inn.'

'Well, if this Sassen is able to do the job, then we should be able to leave tomorrow.' The witch hunter raised his glass high. 'To success in our mission,' he said.

'To success,' von Kleist echoed, smiling broadly.

THE TRACKER, SASSEN, arrived mid-morning. Heidel was reading *The Confessions of Andreus Sinder*, a book full of the most personal and incisive perceptions into the nature of evil and darkness when there was a sharp rat-tat-tat on the door. He placed the heavy volume aside almost reluctantly and admitted him.

Sassen was a little man, sprightly like a small animal. His body seemed perpetually tense, as if he might need to spring from danger at any moment. Heidel couldn't help but think he looked like a weasel, a view accentuated by his long nose and soft, thin, facial hair.

'Come in,' Heidel invited and Sassen followed him into the room. Heidel sat down but he was disconcerted when the tracker, instead of doing likewise, began to walk around, stopping only to inspect Heidel's possessions.

'A nice long-coat,' Sassen said in a soft high voice, more gentle and articulate than one would expect from a tracker. He rubbed the fur of the lapel between thumb and forefinger.

Heidel agreed uncertainly, unsure of what to make of the little man.

Sassen touched the hilt of the dagger on the small table by the side of the bed, but Heidel, getting increasingly annoyed, noticed that the tracker had cocked his head and that his eyes were on *The Confessions of Andreus Sinder*.

'When do we start?' The tracker turned and, for the first time since entering the room, looked Heidel straight in the eye.

Heidel, by this time, was struggling to contain his anger. The tracker had no manners. How dare he wander into Heidel's room and begin to peruse at his leisure! Heidel bit his tongue and struggled for a moment before responding. 'You realise the danger of the task?'

The little man scrunched his face up. 'I'm not a warrior.'

'It is our joint task to recover the baron's heirloom, so together we must do whatever is necessary. If that means you fight, then so be it. I will not complain about having to help with the tracking.'

Sassen looked confused for a moment, as if there was something faulty in Heidel's logic, then nodded in agreement. 'Very well,' he said before sitting down on the bed and picking up the heavy tome which lay there. 'This book,' the tracker said. 'I have heard of Andreus Sinder.'

'You are an educated man?' Heidel was both impressed and curious.

'Oh, not really,' Sassen said with a self-deprecating smile. 'I've learned to read a little: just a word here and there.'

For the first time Heidel warmed to the man with the rodent's face. Humbleness had always been a virtue to Heidel

Sassen continued: 'I heard that Sinder was something of a sinner in his youth. Corrupted, they say, before he understood the true nature of evil.'

'But he renounced the darkness,' Heidel countered instantly, 'and believed that his knowledge could be used the better to combat it.'

Sassen smiled momentarily, revealing sharp white teeth. 'Could that be true? That a man could turn his back on darkness, when once he revelled in it?'

'It appears to be the case,' Heidel admitted.

'Then you have entertained the thought, Herr Heidel, that you might benefit from delving into forbidden acts and unhealthy practices?' Sassen smiled and his leathery face was cunning and mischievous.

Heidel's eyes flashed dangerously. 'There are some,' he noted, 'who say that they would never consider such a possibility. They argue that one can never be sure of one's resilience, that only the strongest can return to the light after tasting such sweet and poisoned fruit.'

Sassen stood and began to pace, intensely interested in the discussion. 'And you agree with this position?'

'No,' Heidel stated resolutely.

'There is surely no alternative.' The tracker seemed pleased. Evidently he believed he had cornered Heidel. 'Only such a position can be held if you wish to avoid experimenting with the Darkness yourself, and yet see some value in the *Confessions*. Otherwise what would your approach to Sinder be?'

'I would have killed him.' Heidel's voice was steady, adamant.

'Even–'

Heidel finished Sassen's question: 'Even after he had confessed the error of his ways.'

Sassen stared fixedly, as if in disbelief, his small mouth open, revealing the small, sharp teeth. Heidel himself sat quite still, feeling almost guilty to have crushed what little intellectual argument the tracker had mustered – but knowing without question that he would have done just what he had declared.

Later, after the pair had worked out a basic plan for the task ahead, Sassen left to organise the supplies: saddle-bags, his sword, blankets, food, and so on. Heidel, too, readied himself. He put on his old brown leather coat, hiding the chainmail he had donned for the battle that was surely to come. On his head he placed a black, broad-brimmed hat, weather-beaten and

stained with sweat. He attached his sword to his waist and
checked the long bow and quiver that he would carry on the
saddle of his grey mare.

Was it true, Heidel wondered, that he would have killed
Andreus Sinder, the author of one of the most erudite tracts on
the nature of evil, a text filled with piecing insights into the
darkness in all its manifestations? Almost without realising it,
he picked up the *Confessions* from where it lay on the table. He
turned the cover over in his hands, feeling its weight. He
rubbed his fingers across its cover. The leather was soft and sup-
ple. Instinctively he opened to the first page where the
manuscript began. He read the first lines:

Only by my participation in these unnatural events did I under-
stand the true gravity of these horrors. Only then did I know the
need to burn twisted evil with the bright flame of the sword.

Heidel placed the book down, lost in thought.

HEIDEL MET SASSEN by the gates of Bechafen in the early afternoon as the sun was just beginning to break through the
lumbering clouds overhead.

From Bechafen they rode out on the road that ultimately
led to Talabec, passing through a series of small hamlets surrounded by green rolling fields. Their path ran south,
though later it would turn gradually west. Cattle and sheep
stood lazily about, munching on the grass and occasionally
turning their soft dull eyes towards the two men and their
horses as they rode by. Beyond the cows stood fields of
wheat and barley, turning gold in the late summer. A farmer
steering a cart carrying grain passed in the opposite direction; when he saw Heidel he bowed his head and would not
look at him. Then a merchant train carrying barrels and furs
clanked by, its heavily armed outriders giving them hard,
silent stares.

Finally a couple of young nobles on dashing black horses
galloped across the fields and crossed the road in front of them
without greeting, disappearing into the distance in pursuit of
some unseen prey. After that they were alone on the worn path
which meandered through the tree-dotted scrubland. Slowly,
inexorably, the road turned westwards.

As they rode Heidel felt distinctly happy. At last, he told
himself, on the trail of evil again.

'Lord Sigmar,' he prayed under his breath, 'protect me on this journey. Let me return safely, the scalps of my enemies in my hand.' He never knew if the gods heard his prayers, but praying always seemed a wise idea. For if they did hear, perhaps they would deign to look over him.

As if trying to fill the silence, Sassen began to tell Heidel about his life, though the witch hunter would have been quite happy not to hear it. The little man had lived in the country hereabouts for many years and had spent time hunting and clearing the land. Once, though, he had sailed the seas with a group of Norsemen, raiding unprotected towns, pillaging fat merchant ships. But since then, he assured Heidel, he had decided to work permanently around Bechafen. Heidel was not sure whether to believe the tracker. Sailing with Norsemen? Sigmar keep him, he thought; let the little man have his fantasies.

'The baron told me that the attack on his goods occurred some ten miles from Bechafen,' Sassen continued. 'He says the band of brigands headed east into the forest, towards the mountains.'

'How did he discover that?'

'After the attack he and his men returned to the carts, only to find them plundered. A fresh trail led off into the woods.'

Heidel nodded silently and disappeared back into his own thoughts as they rode on.

The scattered vegetation around the road slowly transformed into forest: first a copse of trees here; then a slightly larger copse there, then they came quicker and faster until there was only a wall of thick greenery. Heidel was most comfortable in the wilderness. There was something about its simplicity. Danger was swift and direct: wild beasts searching for food; the descent of the winter snows; the surge of the stormy sea. Heidel's worries were equally simple: finding a camp-site out of the weather; keeping warm and dry; saving enough provisions for the journey. Evil was stark, clear, easy to locate; creatures of darkness wandering the woods, raiding small villages, or hiding in the mountains. Heidel's task was simple: to find them, and to eliminate them.

Cities were another story. Affluence made Heidel uneasy. The machinations and intrigues of the courts, great glittering balls with ladies hiding their pockmarks under white paint and rouge, lords and princes wallowing in a sordid world of whores and white powders. Nothing was simple, everything was veiled and obscured. People spoke and acted according to complex codes and signs that had to be interpreted. A friendly greeting could conceal a serious insult. Your best friend could be your worst enemy. Simplicity and directness were seen as colloquial and quaint. Danger came in all sorts of guises, all manner of forms. He could never move in that society. They brought malevolence upon themselves. He could not, he would not, protect them. Better to leave that to witch hunters like Immanuel Mendelsohn.

Heidel leaned over and spat on the ground at the thought of the man.

Mendelsohn, a self-proclaimed witch hunter, was a nobleman by birth. He had grown up amongst the lords and the ladies – and the whores. He could move with ease in high society: with his frilled silk shirts, his brown curly locks, his floppy hats and pointed leather boots. And, for all this, Mendelsohn was not above suspicion. After all, it is a short step from silk shirts to other pleasures of the flesh. First came the finery, then the women and the illicit substances. Then came corruption, sure as night followed day. No, Heidel did not like him or his kind. Heidel did not like the aristocrat's search for fame, his love of publicity, his attempt to turn everything into a drama. Mendelsohn gave witch hunters a bad name and it would not surprise Heidel if one day he would have to go after the noble himself. That stray thought brought an ironic smile to his lips.

Heidel shook his head and banished Mendelsohn from his thoughts. He recognised that such thoughts had a habit of turning him distinctly surly. He looked around at the forest. The trees seemed to be getting thicker, more twisted, the underbrush more prickly and uninviting. Sassen rode beside him in silence, tracker's eyes now intent on finding the trail of the quarry.

Maybe four hours after they left Bechafen, Sassen suddenly called a halt. He reined in his horse and leaped down to the road. He crept, head down along the edge of the forest. It appeared to Heidel as if the little man was actually sniffing for the trail. Then the tracker looked up suddenly and stated: 'Here it is.'

Heidel dismounted too and walked over to him. On the ground were a series of scuffled tracks leading into the forest. Without Sassen he would have ridden straight past it.

The way into the forest was marked by several broken branches and the tracks, still distinct after two days without rain, leading into the darkness. Once into the trees it would be hard going. Branches hung low like outstretched arms barring the way; roots twisted like tentacles from the ground, threatening to trip them.

'Do you know this area well?' Heidel asked the tracker.

'Fairly well. It's all pretty much like this, I'm afraid. But that means it will hamper the band as much as us. We'll have to walk, anyway.' Sassen wrinkled his eyes, an annoying habit that Heidel had noticed; the little man always squinted when he spoke.

'It doesn't look like we'll be able to travel at night,' Heidel said. He looked to the sky, as if night was about to fall then and there. But it was still deep and blue with clumpy white clouds rolling slowly overhead.

'Unlikely,' Sassen agreed. 'We'll just have to make the best of the day.'

'Fine. Then we had better begin.'

FOR FOUR DAYS they pushed through the forest, the gnarled branches of the trees blocking them and their horses, thorns and bushes scratching against their legs, drawing blood wherever the skin was exposed. In no time Heidel's hands were covered in a delicate latticework of dried blood. The days were dark as the sun was shut out by the canopy overhead. But if the days were dark, the nights were blacker still. Even the shadowy forms of the trees disappeared into the night.

Every day passed the same. They awoke at first light and departed as quickly as possible. During the day they pushed on as hard as they could for, according to the baron, the bandits would have two days' start on them. If Heidel and Sassen pressed on with this pace they could catch them within a week at most, less if the band had made more permanent camp somewhere. When they caught them, surprise would be the key. Heidel would stand no chance against a united group; he would have to pick them off one by one.

On the morning of the fourth day since entering the forest, Sassen stopped and inspected the tracks, an action that had become increasingly regular. 'They are less than a day away from us.' He peered up at Heidel and squinted.

Ahead of them they could see twenty feet at the most. At any moment they might stumble upon the prey. That could mean death or worse. In these close confines, the hunters would become the hunted, and the black warrior's horde would surely crush them. Often Heidel heard rustling close to them in the forest or fluttering amongst the branches above, but whatever it was remained unsighted. He assumed they were just the movements of birds and animals, but they made him jittery anyway.

Perhaps to ease his tension Sassen kept trying to strike up a conversation, trying to get Heidel to tell of his exploits as a witch hunter.

'How many have you put to death?' he asked one time.

Heidel glared at him.

'You are grim, Herr Heidel.'

'Better to say nothing at all, than to say nothing using many words.' The witch hunter spoke plainly.

Undeterred, Sassen continued: 'I hear you burnt a man only last month. What for?'

'He was in league with corruption.' Heidel practically spat the sentence out, the words so filled with revulsion and disdain.

'What did he do?' Sassen inquired timidly.

'When I arrived in this particular village many were falling ill. It was like a plague.' Heidel's voice rose in intensity as he spoke, passion beginning to creep into his account. 'At first I could not discern the cause of this illness. I studied the victims and found that they had great red swellings beneath the skin. Under the armpits, on the neck, between the legs. As a test I punctured one of the victim's swellings, and from the wound squirmed a writhing mass of worm-like creatures, all purple and yellow and bulbous. Alas, the victim died. Later I tried to cleanse a victim by applying fire to his swellings. But the strain was too much on his body.'

Heidel glanced at Sassen, who looked on with a mix of disgust and excitement.

'Continue, continue,' the tracker said, pulling his thin beard with his fingers and licking his lips.

'I realised that the only victims were men, and so turned to the origins of the illness: if I could determine the cause then perhaps I could save these poor people. It took me but a day to find the truth. I interviewed the men and found that those who fell ill first had something in common. All were suitors of a woman, a particular woman. Searching her house I found nothing. But I was undeterred. I pressed the woman for the names of all who courted her. Under duress she produced a list, and all on that list were ill… all save one, the keeper of the inn. I found in that man's cellar a cauldron full of writhing, squirming larvae. These he would feed to the men when they were drunk, placing them in their ale. Somehow they would eat their way through the flesh and the insides. And so he was burnt at the stake that very night.'

'But why, why did he do it?'

'He called it an act of love. He loved her, but she did not return her feelings. As a result he hated her other lovers and decided to kill them. But as he acted out his drama he lost his mind. His hatred for these particular men turned into a hatred of all men. Soon it would have become a hatred of all the world and everything within it. That way is the path to darkness.'

After he finished there was silence for a moment, and then Sassen burst into a high fit of uncontrollable laughter.

'You think it funny?' Heidel's eyes flashed and his hand moved unconsciously to his sword.

'No, no, of course not.' Sassen suddenly looked worried and did not ask any more questions of Heidel.

AROUND NOON on the fourth day, the trail they had been following suddenly met a path, wide enough for two carts, leading away to left and right. Once it must have been well used, but now was overgrown, with the trees threatening to close in once more. Sassen handed his horse's reins to Heidel and bent down to examine the tracks.

'They passed to the left,' he said, 'but there are other tracks here, that come from the right. Someone on a horse. It looks like he dismounted, for there are new footprints. Here, see?' Sassen pointed to the new tracks. 'Perhaps he met the group here and has joined them.'

Heidel peered down. There was a small group of hoof-prints, one over the other, as if the horse was made to wait for some time. Next to them were the fresh prints of a boot.

'They are soft-soled,' Sassen noted. 'See how faint the tracks are.'

'Well, with only one horse they can't have gone far. If we mount here we may catch them today. How old are these tracks?' Heidel peered down at the tracks himself.

'Perhaps half a day.' Sassen squinted in the direction that the tracks led, as if he might yet see the band travelling away from them.

'Then we shall ride slowly – and tonight we shall come upon them in a hail of fire and light.' Heidel's eyes flashed at Sassen. The tracker smiled grimly and looked away.

They rode throughout the rest of that day and, as it became dark, Heidel turned to Sassen: 'You must set up camp here. We do not know how far away the band is, but we must take no chances. I shall walk ahead and begin the work, using my bow. I'll be back before morning. Do not light a fire, for I want you here when I return. Otherwise…' Heidel had nothing more to say, so he nodded, dismounted, took his bow and quiver, and began the walk.

Sassen left the path behind him for a clearing, the two horses in tow. 'Good luck,' he called out to the witch hunter, who did not acknowledge him.

THE NEW PATH was wide and above him he could see the stars. It was a relief to feel the open air again and to feel the fresh wind. 'Sigmar,' he prayed under his breath, may the forest be kind to me tonight. 'And Ulric, god of battle, to you I pray also: together may we come down upon these abominations and cleanse them with blood and steel.'

And his heart began to sing, as it always did before he went into battle. For something stirred in him before he killed. It was as if his soul was suddenly in harmony with the world, as if there was some secret melody, some logic, which things and events travelled along. Truth, that was what it was. When a foe squirmed upon his sword – that was truth. When the light in a mutant's eyes dimmed slowly, and then faded to black.

The road opened out into a large clearing. He found them there, camping around a small fire. Already they were drunk or intoxicated, and he smiled silently. Baron von Kleist had been right: these were evil things that needed cleansing. Darkness undermines itself, he thought

There were seven of them. Six things: neither men nor beasts but something in between, twisted and vile. And the warrior, dull in his black and heavy armour, his face hidden by a great helmet. Some nameless black meat was charring on a spit above the fire. Bottles of liquid lay strewn amongst the creatures, who rolled around on the ground amongst the dirt and their own filth. Only the warrior sat calmly on an overturned log, contemplative and evil.

When three of the corrupted men-things began to make their way from the clearing down a slope away to the right of him, Heidel seized his chance and followed them. He crept as quietly as possible, a shadow in the darkness, yet cursing under his breath as he heard the twigs breaking beneath his feet. But the creatures didn't hear him, for they were crashing down the slope carelessly. After a minute they came to a small stream flowing gently, the sound of water over rocks floating through the air. All three dipped waterskins into the water, splashing their filth into the clear stream, and turned to carry them up the hill.

It was then that Heidel struck. His first arrow hit the leading beastman in the neck, piercing its soft fur and sending blood gushing through its bear-mouth.

Pandemonium broke loose. In a whirr of motion a second arrow whisked through the air, another close behind. Two hits and a thing with tentacles fell groaning. A last beastman hissed like a gigantic snake; something heavy crashed into it from behind, screaming and lashing out. Then Heidel retreated back into the darkness. An excellent initial foray; three creatures dead.

Praise be to Sigmar. Blessings upon the name of Ulric.

WHEN HE ARRIVED back at the clearing where he had left the tracker, he found Sassen sitting silently between the horses. It was still dark and the chill bit at his face. Sassen was shivering despite being wrapped in a blanket.

'A fine night, Sassen. In the darkness I struck against malevolence, and Sigmar was on our side.' Heidel spoke fast, breathlessly recounting the night's events. 'We must ride before dawn. The sun will soon rise and we must catch them again before they have a chance to move or find us unawares. The darkness will give us cover.'

The crisp air was motionless as they rode. Before long the eastern sky began to lighten. Finally, as they came close to the quarry's camp, the sky had turned gold and red and pink, but the sun was still hiding behind the tree-line.

Heidel glanced at Sassen and wondered if the tracker would be of any use in the fight. The little man had a short sword at his side, but until now it had only been used to hack at bushes and branches. It had not yet tasted blood, unless the stories of sailing with Norsemen were true. Perhaps this would be the morning of its baptism.

When Heidel judged that they were close to the camp, he hissed for them to halt, and they tied their horses to a tree.

'Let's hope that they have not heard us,' he whispered to Sassen. 'Are you ready for this?'

The tracker looked at the ground, then to the sky, and finally nodded briefly, pursing his lips. The fear emanated from him like a scent.

Heidel's mood had changed since his joyous return from his initial foray. Perhaps he could feel Sassen's fear, and somehow he had taken it as his own: an uncomfortable, dissolute, emotion. He felt a terrible sense of foreboding. And though he prayed to Sigmar and Ulric once more, his heart refused to lighten. Instead it was weighed down, leaden. For a moment Heidel felt the inevitability of defeat. How could he face that dark warrior, that faceless, soulless thing – all darkness and metal, terrible and sublime? The warrior had seemed just another man in the night. But as the sky became light, its image in his head to grow in stature; it was as if the very light was eaten by evil, which turned the warrior into something else entirely. Now he was ten feet tall, his armour hardened, impenetrable.

Heidel shook himself. 'Fool,' he muttered under his breath. But despite his reassurances he still felt the sands of uncertainty shift beneath his feet.

They crept along the side of the track and before long came to the camp. Heidel was almost surprised that the creatures were still there. Three corrupted mutants sat in a circle facing outwards, in their hands jagged and vicious blades. There was a chicken-man. Behind him crouched something with what Heidel first took to be a shield on his back, before he realised that it was a shell that has grown from the man's flesh. And finally there was another, a truly foul, corrupt thing which made Heidel rage with fury and sick with revulsion when he a saw it. Where its head should have been there was merely a gaping mouth dripping ooze and slime, pink and putrescent.

The warrior was nowhere to be seen.

'Sassen,' he said, 'the time has come to mete out justice.'

They began.

HOW BEAUTIFUL, Heidel thought, as his arrows arched their way across the clearing in the still, crisp dawn air: rising ever so slightly in their flight, and then dropping subtlety, before plunging into flesh and blood. For a moment he forgot the combat, and was content simply to watch the arrows sail, their beauty as they fulfilled their purpose, to fly and to strike.

Then the serenity of the arrows was broken and everything became violence and death. The chicken-man suddenly began hopping uncontrollably, thrusting himself into the air, surprisingly high. The manic leaping was disturbing to watch, the body pulling tight, thrusting repeatedly against the ground. The corrupt body, thrusting and twisting, twisting and thrusting, blood spraying under incredible pressure; the last actions of a doomed creature in agony. So much blood.

Heidel's next arrow struck the second monstrosity, piercing its shell, forcing it to thrash and grasp aimlessly at the shaft protruding from its back.

The witch hunter charged, his sword in hand, Sassen scurrying alongside him, howling at the top of his voice. Heidel quickly lost sight of the tracker as the third creature came at him. He realised with disgust that its body was covered with gaping, slavering, teeth-filled orifices. Its arms were tough and wiry, and the witch hunter knew that if it clutched him those mouths would suck his life. There would be no escape from its clutches.

'You are doomed, spawn!' he cried as he thrust his sword forward, driving it into the creature's belly. It slid along his blade, up to the hilt, yet there was life in it still. It grasped at him, and held him in its wiry arms, pulling him closer, ever closer still. The strength of its arms was immense, and he felt the mouths as they bit into his flesh.

'Sigmar!' he screamed, and tried to push himself away. But it held him fast.

Desperately he twisted his sword and dragged it upwards, and he felt warm blood and entrails on his hands. There was a terrible bird-screech wail. The fiend's grasp weakened. It slid to the ground.

Heidel staggered back, sword hanging loosely in his hand, sweat and blood dripping over his eyes. He was vaguely aware of Sassen fighting something on the other side of the clearing. Weakly he spun around – and something huge and black loomed before him.

The warrior was seven feet tall, a great battle-axe in its mailed fist. Heidel felt dwarfed by it, as if he stood before something from another age, something eternal. For a moment he was motionless, paralysed by awe. He realised that this would be the moment of his death. From behind his opponent the sun had risen all red and gold. Its rays gleamed off the black armour and blinded him. The only thing he could see was the silver pendant, set with a brilliant blue gem, hanging tantalisingly around the warrior's neck.

Then a mailed fist struck him in the face, throwing him backwards. Heidel scrambled desperately to the side as the great battle-axe plunged into the earth. He felt the rush of air as it flew past him. Heidel swung his sword sideways and felt it clatter off armour. A deep laughter followed, a laughter so unnatural and mocking that it filled Heidel with rage. The rage became strength and he leaped to his feet and jumped backwards. The axe whirled close to his belly, threatening to gut him.

'Laugh now! But you will die screaming!' Heidel screamed.

But only laughter was returned.

Side-stepping to the right, Heidel lashed out, aiming at the elbow where only the black plates separated revealing only chainmail. He connected, and felt the sword bite, before stumbling sideways and backwards away from the lethal axe whirling towards him. As he stumbled his foot clipped something – a stone, a root – and his balance shifted, his leg remained stationary, yet his body lurched forward. Desperately he tried to pull his foot forward. Finally he succeeded, in time for his knee to brace his fall.

The warrior was now behind him, unsighted. The terribly notion seized him that something huge and sharp would plunge into his back or cleave his skull. He threw himself to the side and heard a great roar, felt the rush of air on his cheek as if it was a spring breeze.

With great effort he leaped back onto his feet, twisted his body, arcing his sword in one great circular motion. There was a clang as the blow struck his opponent's chest, denting his breastplate and forcing the monstrosity back a step. Glancing around, Heidel noticed the slim figure of Sassen duelling lithely with a beastman, sword flashing time and time again.

Heidel raised his hand to wipe the sweat from his forehead eyes. Soon it would blind him. He lashed out at the colossus as it advanced once more, and again found himself dodging the deadly axe. The witch hunter struck and struck again, and each time the same pattern repeated itself. He thrusting and slashing, his sword glancing off the black armour. The warrior heaving his great axe and plunging it into the thin air: air in which only an instant before Heidel had stood.

Heidel had struck well, denting the armour, drawing blood from between the plates where only chainmail protected the fiend. Yet he knew he stood no chance. One blow from the axe would fell him. Then it would be over. His blows were too small, too weak. Perhaps they drew some strength from the warrior, but Heidel was tiring faster.

Then the inevitable happened: Heidel fell backwards over a corpse. Sweat dripped down into his eyes so everything became a blur. Above him the huge black-armoured warrior stood. Behind the monster, the sun shone with a surreal beauty and the immense, ancient axe glinted cruelly. Heidel knew he was dead. There would be no escape.

A sudden explosion, and it was like time slowed to a crawl. A massive dent appearing in the side of the warrior's helmet. Another explosion: the dent pushed further in, and a thousand tiny holes appeared, as if someone had thrust needles repeatedly through the metal. The warrior backed away, suddenly staggering, blood and streams of yellow filth dribbling from beneath the vast helmet. The huge body fell like the edge of a cliff into the sea; foul steam and dust was thrown into the air with a gigantic crash. The dust seemed to hover in the air for a second and then was whisked away from the enormous body by a sudden gust of wind.

Heidel sat and stared, his ears ringing, sweat dribbling into his eyes. Through the ringing came a startling voice.

'Just in time, hey? You know, Heidel, old man, you really should pick better odds.'

Heidel turned his head. There stood a fop: dressed in a frilled silk shirt, a floppy soft hat on top of hair curled into ringlets, a tiny perfectly trimmed moustache, and wearing soft, pointed leather boots. The man held two smoking pistols in his hands.

'Mendelsohn,' Heidel said flatly.

SASSEN HAD taken care of the shell-creature and was now busy piling the bodies together. Heidel was relieved that the tracker had not been killed in the fight. He had lost track of the little man for most of it, but apparently Sassen could handle his sword after all, and though a trickle of drying blood ran down his left arm, he was not badly injured.

'Only a scratch,' the little man had said quietly when Heidel asked about it. The tracker seemed distracted, as if something was on his mind. Heidel assumed it was the result of the combat. He had seen many men shaken after a battle; some were so distraught they were speechless, wept like children, or moaned worse than the wounded.

They were determined to burn the foul bodies. Mendelsohn and Heidel began collecting wood and building the fire up into a pyre.

'You must have passed me in the night,' Mendelsohn grinned. 'I must say, I'm a bit upset that you only left the warrior for me.'

'Have no fear, Mendelsohn. The Empire is crawling with corruption. You should know that, from the circles you move in,' Heidel snapped.

Mendelsohn smiled for a reply and picked up a fallen log, swathed with damp and rotting bark. 'Damn this, it'll ruin my shirt.' He held the log away from his body but bits still fell onto the silk cuffs.

'I'll go and fetch the horses,' Sassen called out from the clearing. He had finished piling the bodies together as best he could and seemed anxious to be away from this place of death and corruption. Heidel nodded in agreement and the tracker disappeared off down the path.

When they had built the fire high enough, Heidel began to throw on the corpses, cringing as he touched their diseased bodies. He was in turmoil. Mendelsohn, the aristocratic dandy, had saved his life. Had the flamboyant fop not arrived, he would now most certainly be dead. But Heidel felt humiliated, bested, and could not bring himself to show gratitude. He had known Mendelsohn some years, long enough to realise that the paths they walked were different ones. He did not entirely approve of that which the noble had taken. Begrudgingly he turned to the other man.

'You arrived at an important time. Thank you, Mendelsohn.'

Mendelsohn raised his head and gave him a brilliant, handsome smile. 'You make it sound like we had a merchant's meeting. "You arrived at an important time..." – otherwise I would never have sold the silver spoons!' A moment passed. 'Oh, call me Immanuel; "Mendelsohn" sounds so formal.'

Heidel struggled for a moment with his manners, then said: 'And you, you can call me Frantz... I suppose.' A moment later, 'So the baron, he hired you too?'

'The baron?'

'Baron von Kleist? He set me upon this task.'

'I know of no Baron von Kleist.'

Heidel stopped for a moment, thinking. 'The baron hired me to recover an heirloom, a most precious thing, that these foul beasts stole. They attacked the caravan which he was taking to Bechafen.'

Mendelsohn looked concerned for a moment and pulled on his small moustache with his fingers. 'This band attacked no caravan. I followed them from Bechafen myself, all the way. Never let them stray far from my sight the whole journey. Where is this von Kleist from?'

'From Altdorf or somesuch. He was moving here to escape the pressures of the capital.'

Mendelsohn pulled harder on his moustache. 'I know most of the nobles in Altdorf, but I have never heard of a Baron von Kleist. What was this heirloom of which he spoke?'

Heidel walked to the massive armoured corpse of the dark warrior. The thick metal plates which covered the body were impressive. Great strength would be needed to carry such weight. Even now the enormity of the body and the armour were frightening, as if the Warrior might suddenly leap once more into life.

Heidel was also struck by the stench that emanated from the corpse, flies buzzed and disappeared into the cracks between the plates. He shuddered, imagining what was beneath the armour. The flies preferred what was hidden

beneath the plates to the bloody mass that had been the warrior's head.

'A pendant, spectacular. It was around the neck of this–'
Heidel began, then stopped. There was nothing: the pendant
was not there. He looked up at the noble.

'Gone?' Mendelsohn raised his eyebrows inquiringly.

Heidel nodded and turned slowly.

'Sassen.'

IT TOOK THEM half a day to find trace of Sassen's flight. They rode
two in line, Heidel sat behind Mendelsohn, clinging as lightly
to the man's back as he could. At twilight they came across
Sassen's roan, dead by the side of the path.

'He took my grey mare,' Heidel said impassively.

'Aye, and this poor beast looks a little grey itself.'
Mendelsohn smiled brilliantly.

Heidel could not understand this incessant cheerfulness.
'Immanuel, how in this world of darkness, do you remain so–'

'Happy?'

'Yes.'

'It's not happiness, it's…' One of his slender hands described
a little circle as he thought of the right word. 'It's a sense of
humour.'

Heidel thought about that for a moment.

'A sense of humour is one of the ways to fight the darkness,
Frantz. If the world is a duality, caught between light and dark,
day and night, good and evil, then we understand humour as
the opposite of… Damn, I can't think what it's an opposite of
right now but…' Mendelsohn threw his arms in the air. 'It's a
good opposite anyway.' He laughed to himself.

'Immanuel?' Heidel said seriously.

'Yes.'

'You're a very strange man.'

They rested for a while as the sun went down, ate some dried
fruit, salted pork and bread, and let the horse graze. They had
reached the point at which Heidel and Sassen had broken
through the forest and reached the wider path. To the north lay
the thin track along which they had followed the evil band. To
the east the wider path continued, the way Mendelsohn had
ridden. Both led to the Talabec-Bechafen road.

'Did you follow me all the way?' Mendelsohn asked.

'No, we cut through the forest from the north. It looks like Sassen is returning that way. Perhaps he thinks it will be quicker.'

'Well, if we follow the wretch directly he will stay much the same distance ahead of us. If we return to Bechafen on the trail that I took, we will cover more distance but will be able to ride. It's a risk, but it means we have a chance of cutting him off. If however, he reaches Bechafen before us, I fear we will have lost him.'

For three days they rode and it was like a nightmare broken only when they stopped to eat or sleep at night. But sleep was hard to find. To his great irritation, Heidel would doze off only momentarily before being jolted awake. As he lay half-asleep he felt the constant motion of the horse beneath him, as if he was still riding. At other times he felt the roots and rocks digging into his back, every knot and twist. So he spent most of his time in a strange twilight world of insufferable insomnia.

When sleep finally took him, he dreamed strange dreams: of riding the same horse as a cloaked figure. He was too afraid to talk to the man, for he knew that something was not quite right. Once, in the dream, he touched the figure on the shoulder, and the man turned. The face was for a moment caught in the shadows. But as the wan moonlight touched the face Heidel screamed: for it was a corpse, cadaverous and rotten, and curling down from its shrivelled scalp was a cascade of perfect brown ringlets. It had touched its cheeks with rouge, in a gesture monstrous and sickening, and on its face was a grin of yellow, decaying teeth.

'Humour,' it said to him, 'humour is the opposite of...' And those words echoed in frightful ways. But no matter how he tried, Heidel could not get off the horse.

ON THE FOURTH DAY they reached the road, and there they bought fresh horses from a passing merchant for a thousand crowns. More, thought Heidel, than he had been offered for this task. They enquired and found that a small, weaselly man, riding a grey mare, had passed within the hour.

They caught their first distant glimpse of Sassen as he entered Bechafen – the tracker riding slowly towards the town's great wooden gates.

'My poor mare,' Heidel muttered, noticing the beast's head drooping with fatigue.

The sun was going down behind them, the chill in the air starting to bite. They followed Sassen's route through the gates, past the two guardsmen who looked indifferently on all those who entered the town. They trailed Sassen as inconspicuously as they could, trying to keep groups of people between them. They were fortunate that there were many on the streets: labourers heading for their favourite tavern, street vendors packing up their goods for the day, farmers driving their carts towards the gates and the hamlets surrounding Bechafen. In any case, Sassen did not check behind him; he did not seem mindful of pursuit, as far as they could tell.

As the two witch hunters made their way through the busy streets, they kept as far behind as they could, and at times feared that they had lost the tracker. But just as they were losing heart, peering desperately into the distance, one of them would notice Sassen heading away down a side street, or just turning a corner in the distance. On and on he went, leading them across the centre of the town, and finally they entered the wealthier quarters, trotting past great rows of town houses, hidden from the road by high walls.

Sassen entered the grounds of a decrepit and decaying building, its eaves cracked and splintered, tiles missing from its roof, a garden overgrown with weeds and grasses. The tracker tied the exhausted horse to a dying tree and disappeared around the side of the house.

'Do we enter now, or rest and return later, refreshed?' Mendelsohn asked.

Heidel noticed that Mendelsohn's handsome face was weary and lined; his eyelids looked leaden, weighed down.

'We could rest now and return later,' Heidel replied. 'If we do we will be able to deal more easily with whatever evil we find. However I fear to tarry, for evil left alone can prosper and grow.' He paused wearily and squinted. 'I say we enter now, and administer the cure for whatever corruption we may find.'

Mendelsohn nodded his head emphatically. 'Let us finish this business. Later we may rest.'

They tied their horses to the front gate and walked into the front garden of the house. Mendelsohn loaded his pistols while Heidel looked around, sword drawn.

'There must be a back way in,' Heidel whispered.

They crept around the building, daring a peek through the side windows. The place seemed empty; no furniture cluttered the rooms, no fire warmed the air.

The back door, peeling paint clinging to its wooden panes, swung loosely on its hinges. Beyond they could see an empty corridor leading into a shadowy room. As they entered, it occurred to Heidel that the place seemed even more decaying from the inside. The floors were covered with grime and dust, and thick, matted cobwebs hung low from the ceiling. For a moment he felt that he had entered something dead, as if he stood in the dry entrails of something that had once moved and lived. Colour had once adorned these walls; people had once laughed in these rooms and hallways.

They searched the ground floor, and found nothing. Upwards they ventured, but all the rooms were empty.

'It seems we must enter the cellar,' Mendelsohn ventured. 'Though the prospect displeases me.'

The stairs led down into the deepest darkness. Into the very bowels of this dead creature, thought Heidel. He pushed the idea from his mind, for it unnerved him. He was not usually quite so morbid.

Eventually they reached the floor of a dry and empty room. A burning torch hung on the wall facing them, holding back the darkness. Heidel strode across and took it. To his left a narrow tunnel, chiselled through the rock, descended into yet deeper darkness.

'I do not like this, Immanuel,' Heidel whispered.

'Me neither. Yet I fear the solution to which we seek lies deeper down this tunnel. We are left with but one option. Light the way for me.' Mendelsohn walked through the tunnel opening.

Heidel followed, holding torch in one hand, blade in the other. To himself he began to pray: 'Ulric, watch over me. Sigmar, guide me.'

The tunnel descended slowly for a hundred paces or so, then levelled out. The floors were smooth as if worn by years of use, but the narrow walls and the roof overhead were craggy. Many times Heidel or Mendelsohn clipped outcrops of rock with their shoulders, arms or knees. The air down here was fetid and foul. Moisture, cold and clammy, clung to the walls and dripped down from the roof, while small puddles splashed underfoot. The two witch hunters could not see very far ahead of or behind them, and the unseen weight of the earth overhead enclosed them. Heidel was in gloomy spirits and Mendelsohn said nothing. Though remaining level, the tunnel wound now left, now right, and before long Heidel had lost all sense of the direction in which they moved. With every step the sense of utter foreboding grew in him.

The stale odour of the still air seemed to increase with each step. With nowhere to go, no fresh air cleansing the tunnel, the smell accumulated into a gagging, noxious, stench that began to sicken Heidel. It brought to mind worms wriggling in dead meat – warming slowly in the sun. Nausea washed over the witch hunter in waves until finally he could bear it no longer and exploded into a fit of coughing.

The noise echoed weirdly down the tunnel. Mendelsohn jumped at the sudden break in the silence and turned. For a confused moment, Heidel's fears leapt from his unconscious: as Mendelsohn had turned, he had imagined his face to be emaciated and cadaverous, a rotting skull, just like the face in his dreams. He gasped and his heart leapt in his chest. But as soon as he had started, he realised that it was no so. Mendelsohn was just himself.

'What will the ladies of the court think of me now?' Mendelsohn smiled his handsome smile, trying to brush the smell from him with fluttering shakes of his hands. 'I shall have to buy myself some expensive Bretonnian perfume to rid myself of this foetid odour.'

Heidel could not help himself and broke into a shy smile. He did not mention his nightmarish vision, however, and Mendelsohn's words did little to allay Heidel's fears. The pair began walking again and after twenty paces or so the dread had returned. All was the same as before: the stench, the darkness, the water, the loss of a sense of direction. Then just when Heidel felt like suggesting they turn back, a dim light beckoned before them.

HEIDEL AND MENDELSOHN crept forwards until they could peak into the chamber beyond. It was a cavern, smooth walled and dry, perhaps two hundred feet long and just as wide. The towering roof disappeared into the darkness above. It must have been a mausoleum of some sort, or perhaps a part of the

Bechafen catacombs. Desiccated corpses lay on great stone slabs; bones littered the floor, jutting up at odd angles, in a veritable sea of human remains. Hundreds of narrow holes were cut into the walls, from which more bones protruded. From everything rose the stench of death and decay.

In the middle of the room stood a stone contraption, somewhat like an arch, maybe ten feet high, beneath which stood Sassen. The little man looked up towards the top of the archway, stepped back, turned on his heels and walked out of Heidel's sight. To the witch hunter, the tracker had never seemed so like a weasel, with his pointy, pinched little face, his furry little beard, his beady eyes squinting.

From somewhere out of sight, a familiar voice rose to break the deathly stillness, and echoed down the tunnel. 'Come in, Heidel, I've been expecting you. And bring your friend.' It finished with a burst of uncontrollable laughter.

All hope of surprise was gone, if they ever had it, and Heidel felt bitter defeat. Wearily he and Mendelsohn stumbled through into the shadowy mausoleum, arms limply hanging by their sides.

'You've come to witness my triumph, of course. Welcome, Herr Heidel, to the Bechafen catacombs.' Baron von Kleist stepped into the flickering torchlight towards the arch. A few paces behind him, Sassen loitered more shyly. Swathed in a black robe, the baron appeared tall and thin to Heidel, much like a cadaver himself. The torches that lit the mausoleum threw great shadows over his body. His skin seemed to be pulled too tightly over his head, and his eyes and mouth seemed to disappear into gaping blackness. His face seemed transformed into a skull. The baron laughed again.

'Witness my work: from here Bechafen shall fall! Here I shall open the doorway between life and death. I will conquer death, vanquish nature, and these pitiful bones will rise once more!' The baron turned slowly around in a circle and raised his arms up in triumph. He was looking at all the bones and corpses as if they were all the riches of the world; as if, instead of lifeless, rotting bodies, they were gems inlaid with silver and gold.

Heidel's face twisted in fury. 'This is blasphemy, infernal sorcerer! And for that you will pay! Sigmar damn you!'

'Why such harsh words, witch hunter? In condemning me you are only damning yourself. It was you, after all, who was

responsible for the return of the key to that doorway between.'
The baron dangled the pendant before him, taunting the witch
hunter. 'My so-called "guards" ran away with it. So I turned to
an employee of an entirely different kind. I thank you for its
safe return.'

Von Kleist gave a mocking half-bow. Behind the baron,
Sassen gave a strange little high pitched laugh. Heidel
gripped the hilt of his sword in anger. He yearned to swoop
upon the little man and repay him for his betrayal. Heidel
could feel Mendelsohn tense and tremble in fury beside
him.

'You have been corrupted, necromancer, and for that you will
be sent screaming to the abyss,' Mendelsohn stated simply, as if
he was passing sentence. For a moment the baron was taken
aback by the confidence in the witch hunter's voice.

But then von Kleist smiled. 'And what of this?' he asked as he
reached up and implanted the brilliant blue gem of the pendant into the top of the stone archway. A harsh light arced from
the gem, sulphur-bright, searing away the shadows of the cavern. A rank smell, as if of burning metal, filled the stale air.
Slowly the entire floor seemed to move; the sea of bones
swelled into waves. A jaundiced murmuring rose discordantly
on the air – and the bones began to move!

Heidel felt unhinged, delirious at the sight, as ages-dead
bones ordered themselves: as thighs re-attached themselves to
hips, as jaws began chatter, as mottled arms and withered
skulls rejoined their bodies. The cavern echoed with the
hideous scraping of bones as they slid, as if sentient, in search
of the right joint, the correct aperture, with which to connect.
The horrendous reek of death choked the air as the entire collection of corpses and body parts shifted and roiled around
each other. To Heidel it seemed a hallucination, yet he knew its
awful reality. This was no time for dreaming; they must act, or
they would die here.

The witch hunters moved with lightning speed. They leaped
high and scrambled over moving skeletons, slashing out with
their rapiers at claws which tried to grasp them. Heidel kicked
at cadaverous hands, pushed himself further forward using
skulls as hand-holds, ribs as footholds. He struggled to balance
himself on the shifting sea of bones beneath his feet, which
seemed to lurch ten feet one way, then ten feet another. He felt

nails begin scratch at him, jaws bite. More than once he felt sharp pain and his blood flow.

Heidel heard two explosions in swift succession, and watched Sassen fall howling, his face ghastly white, two holes blasted in his chest. He glanced around wildly, but could not see Mendelsohn. The witch hunter had only moments before he would be drowned in a sea of gnashing corpses. Desperately he tried to reach the baron, slashing frantically as he tried to carve a path through the shifting bones.

Baron von Kleist was prepared. Beneath his breath he muttered something arcane and guttural. From his suddenly outstretched hand a ball of livid red flame shot towards Heidel, who ducked uselessly as searing fire wrapped itself around his body. Someone screamed agonisingly, a wail which rose and rose until Heidel wished that whoever it was would stop. Then, as it finally died out, the witch hunter realised that he, Heidel, had been the one screaming. He raised his head to see another fireball speeding from the baron's hand. The fire embraced him again; his agonised wail broke unbidden from him once more. As the pain died he saw, from the corner of his eye, Mendelsohn, who had scrambled rapidly over the rising bones and reached the arch. The other witch hunter stood behind the baron, arm raised with a stone in hand.

No, Heidel screamed inside, mouth barely able to form the words. Mendelsohn! You're facing the wrong way...

Mendelsohn faced not towards the baron, but towards the arch. The stone came down, with all the force that Mendelsohn could muster in his body – directly onto the blue gem of the pendant set into the arch. A third vast fireball exploded around the hellish cavern, but this time the fire did not touch Heidel. This fire was white and searing, and it flowed from the gem in the archway like a river of flame. Flame that engulfed Mendelsohn and tossed the baron aside with its force.

Around Heidel the bones shuddered, as if in memory of agonising pain. Then they collapsed like puppets with their strings severed.

With renewed vigour, Heidel leaped forward and landed before the baron, who was struggling onto his hands and knees amidst the scorched cadavers. Heidel kicked out and von Kleist was flung backwards. The baron scrabbled, belly exposed, hands desperately searching for purchase on the carpet of bones. The witch hunter thrust downwards, feeling the sword pierce vital organs, slip between bones.

A look of shock crossed the baron's face. 'No!' he howled. 'This cannot be!'

'Know this, necromancer!' Heidel cried. 'I am a witch hunter. I will seek out evil wherever it raises its misshapen head, and I will wipe its pestilence from this world. You are leprous and corrupt. Return to the abyss from whence you came.'

When his words finished, the baron was dead.

Heidel rushed over to Mendelsohn's side, but was too late. In destroying the pendant, the flamboyant witch hunter had destroyed himself.

HEIDEL DID NOT stay long. He muttered a few words under his breath, a prayer of sorts:

'What is it to be a witch hunter?
To toil endlessly against the dark.
What then will be our reward?
We ask for none and none is received.
When can ever we stop?
When the cold grave eternal calls us to rest.'

Heidel stood and turned to leave. But he stopped himself, bent down and picked up a metal object from the floor. It was an ornately carved pistol, the silver a little blackened with soot. He turned it over in his hand. It was heavy, yet fit well in his palm.

Well weighted, he said to himself. I think I will learn to use this, he said. Yes, I think I will. Then he placed it beneath his belt.

I might not buy a silk shirt though.

In his head he heard Mendelsohn's voice. *Humour is one of the ways to fight the darkness*, it said.

Heidel smiled briefly and began the long walk back to the surface of the town.

MORMACAR'S LAMENT

Chris Pramas

MORMACAR WAS drowning in a sea of agony. Although he longed to surrender to the undertow and let the pain consume him, he continued to struggle towards consciousness. Far off he could hear voices but he couldn't understand what they were saying. He strove to listen, to somehow bring the voices nearer. After a torturous struggle, the sea calmed, the voices became clear and Mormacar opened his eyes.

'He's awake,' a gruff voice said, 'bring him some water.'

Suddenly a cup was at his lips and water coursed down his throat. Although it was warm and stale, the water tasted sweet beyond words. He looked up into the scarred face of an old elf with tangled hair and only one ear, and asked in a cracked voice, 'Where am I?'

The old warrior looked down on him, pity on his face, and whispered, 'I'm sorry, son, but you're in Hag Graef.'

Mormacar groaned and grabbed his throbbing head. He had thought it couldn't get any worse. How wrong he was. Hag Graef was the most notorious of the dark elf slave cities, a city of doom and death where untold prisoners were worked to death and from which no one had ever escaped. He began to wish he had simply been slain in battle, along with the rest of his Shadow Warrior band. The Forsworn, however, missed no opportunity for cruelty, especially against their hated foes from Ulthuan.

Sitting up, Mormacar looked about him. He was in a dark cell of crude stone, its floor covered with rank straw. He shared the cramped room with a dozen other prisoners, many elves like himself, but also some humans and dwarfs. All of his fellow prisoners looked dirty and weary and many bore bruises and welts, plainly gifts from their dark elf tormentors. A stout door closed them in and one sputtering torch added the smell of smoke to the stink of the windowless cell.

'Rest now,' the old elf said. 'You won't get another chance.'

'Thank you, brother,' the Shadow Warrior replied. 'May the Everqueen bless you. I am Mormacar of the Night Stalkers. May I ask your name?'

'Galaher,' the man said tersely.

'Galaher?' Mormacar cried. 'Surely not Galaher Swiftblade?'

'Some used to call me that,' the scowling elf hissed. 'Now I am just Galaher, a slave like you. Leave me be.'

Mormacar was momentarily stunned and could not speak. Galaher Swiftblade alive! The Shadow Warriors had produced few greater heroes and he was long thought dead. Mastering himself, Mormacar reached out and grabbed Galaher's arm. 'Please forgive me if I offended you, Galaher, but everyone on Ulthuan thought you perished on Eltharion's raid on Naggarond. With you alive, our escape is assured.'

Galaher knocked Mormacar's hand from his arm. 'There is no escape from Hag Graef save death,' the old fighter replied, his voice hollow, 'and only fools seek death.'

Mormacar could hardly believe this was the same Galaher from the stories. His shock must have been plain, for Galaher's face softened a little.

'Be strong. Endure,' the elf continued. 'And hope that Tyrion brings an army here and razes this place to the ground.' Galaher looked away, as if he searched his own soul for the dying embers of a long-held dream. 'Any other course is pure foolishness.'

Mormacar stared incredulously at the old elf. 'I can't believe you, of all people, are telling me to submit to the lackeys of the Witch King. Never! I will try to escape from Hag Graef, with or without your help!'

'Then you'll die,' Galaher said simply. Without a further word, the scarred warrior turned his back on Mormacar and crossed the cell.

The young Shadow Warrior lay back, a storm of emotions coursing through him. It pained him to see one of the great heroes of his people dead of spirit, but he could not take Galaher's advice. It was the duty of every elf to escape if captured by their ancient foes. Why couldn't Galaher see that?

Mormacar was so wrapped in thought that he didn't notice another presence until a deep voice jarred him back to his senses. 'The old elf's fire died out long ago. Don't waste your breath on him, elfling.'

Mormacar slowly got to his feet, grimacing in pain as he drew himself up to his full height. 'Who dares to insult Lord Galaher Swiftblade?' he said icily.

Facing him was heavily-muscled human, who stood a head above the defiant elf and whose dirty face was framed by thick braids. 'I am Einar Volundson of Jaederland,' the giant boomed, his Norse accent thick, 'and I insult every member of your gutless race!'

Before Mormacar could reply, one of the other prisoners near the door hissed, 'Be silent, they are coming!'

Everyone in the cell quieted. The Shadow Warrior and the Norseman stared at each other, their antagonism wordless yet potent. Outside, the thump of heavy boots echoed in the hallway. When the pounding advance stopped, the air was rent with the screech of grinding metal as a distant door opened. Then the screaming started.

The Shadow Warrior looked at his cellmates, seeing the terror etched on their faces. He would die, he resolved, before he would live in fear of the dark elves. The heavy footsteps continued, at last stopping in front of their door of the cell. The prisoners looked at each other as keys clattered outside, but if they sought solace than they found none.

The fear in the cramped room was palpable as the heavy portal swung open slowly to reveal three cruel-eyed dark elves. Their leader, a tall woman clad head to toe in black leather, feigned demureness as one of her henchman mopped fresh blood from the front of her leather vest. She could have been beautiful, but her raven hair and striking features were ruined by the twisted sneer on her pale face. Her gloved hands lovingly cradled a long whip, which seemed to writhe with a life of its own under her expert caress.

Her henchmen, two lithe, heavily mailed guardsmen armed with ornate maces and wicked blades, barked in unison, 'On your knees for the Lady Bela, scum!'

The witch elf watched with pleasure as the prisoners fell to their knees. Mormacar hesitated for a moment, but complied when he saw even the cursed Norseman obey.

Lady Bela walked slowly around the small cell, her boots clicking on the rough stone. She stopped in front of Mormacar, who met her stare with one of his own. 'What have we here?' she purred as she stroked Mormacar's face with a slender hand. 'This one is still defiant.'

'One of the new batch, mistress,' offered one of the guards. 'We'll break him soon enough.'

Lady Bela stared at Mormacar, drinking up the hatred in his eyes. His skin crawled as her hand continued to caress his cheek. 'Oh yes, I like this one. He's got spirit.' Entwining her whip around his head, she tugged him closer. 'Tell me, slave, what is your name?'

'You'll get nothing from me, you murdering bitch!' Mormacar shouted and spat in her face.

The dark elf guards rushed forward, maces raised, but Lady Bela waved them away. Still holding the high elf with her whip, she pulled a long pin out of her hair and jabbed Mormacar lightly in the side of his neck. The Shadow Warrior jerked as his body was swept by a burning sensation. Then all feeling went dead and he could not move a muscle. Lady Bela smiled lasciviously and pulled a small blade from her belt. Seeing the blade, Mormacar strove to move, to knock it from her hand, but his body let him down and he remained as still as a statue.

'That's much better, isn't it?' she asked, wiping the saliva off her face. 'I must say I do have a weakness for the lively ones.' Her blade flashed out and slashed Mormacar's chest. 'They provide much better sport than these others, don't you think, Rorga?' Again the blade swept down, this time cutting Mormacar's ear. Her grin widened as she tightened the whip around his neck and pulled him closer still.

'Yes, my lady, great sport indeed,' said one of the dark elf guards, staring meaningfully at the other prisoners. 'Will he be the one then?'

'A fair question, Rorga,' Lady Bela replied, pausing as if in contemplation before turning once again to her motionless prey. 'What do you think, slave?' she asked Mormacar, with a cruel smile. The Shadow Warrior tried to speak, tried to scream out his defiance, but the witch elf's poison was too potent and he could only gurgle in response. Lady Bela laughed. 'Oh yes, slave, I agree completely.'

The cruel witch elf knelt to inspect her handiwork. As the blood welled in the wound on Mormacar's chest, she closed her mouth over it and drank greedily. Then she stood, smacking her lips contentedly. 'It is always refreshing to drink blood that isn't tainted by fear. A rare treat, Rorga, especially here at Hag Graef. I think I'll keep this one awhile.' Lady Bela regarded Mormacar afresh and her eyes lit up with excitement. 'In fact, dear Rorga, I think this noble elf is perfect for my plans. Victory must be assured, after all, and I fear I can't count on Galaher any more.'

'As you wish, mistress. Who's it to be then?'

Lady Bela turned her attention away from the paralysed Shadow Warrior and looked over the rest of the prisoners, tapping her chin with a finger. She stared long at old Galaher. 'You'd like to die now, wouldn't you, sweet Galaher?' The old elf stared vacantly, and remained silent. 'But no. While it is a tempting thought, one cannot be too careful where the gods are concerned.' She turned around. Elf, man, and dwarf shrank under her gaze, all trying to avoid catching her attention. Finally, her eyes settled on a swarthy human whose numerous tattoos bespoke years of piracy. 'That one will do. Take him to Khaine's altar.'

The guards moved forward and seized the frightened prisoner. He began to scream and struggle but a few blows from the dark elves quietened him and he was dragged unconscious from the cell. Lady Bela once again regarded Mormacar, at last unlashing her whip from his unmoving form. Stroking his face as if he were a beloved pet, she purred, 'I'll be seeing you again.' Then she turned and strode from the cell.

The other prisoners stared at Mormacar as if he were already dead.

MORMACAR WORKED in the mines, as he had every day for the past two weeks. As a pair of overseers looked on, the wretched slaves toiled in the near-dark, scrabbling out ore in the humid tunnels for the anvils of Hag Graef. Those prisoners who dropped from exhaustion and refused to rise had their throats slit by the dark elves. The lesson was not lost on the other prisoners. Nor could they help but notice that the prisoners' ranks grew thinner each day, as more and more of their number were dragged off by the Lady Bela's minions. Death hung like a pall over the squalid prisoners of Hag Graef, and most had become resigned to their fate.

Mormacar refused to give in. His muscles quivered with hatred as he swung his pick into the hard rock, imagining that the unyielding stone was the soft flesh of the Lady Bela. Every day another prisoner was taken to Khaine's altar. At night he saw their faces and heard their screams, but even in his dreams he was powerless to help them.

But now his grim endurance was to prove its worth. While the Lady Bela had been engaged in her deadly work, Mormacar had slowly cut away at one of the support beams at his end of the long tunnel. This passage had been dug in haste, and the supports groaned under the weight of the rock overhead. Now one good blow would smash the weakened support beam and hopefully cause a cave-in.

Mormacar swung his pick into the rock again, but scarcely paid attention to what he was doing. His attention was fixed on the hated overseers, who even now were striding down the tunnel to inspect the work. Out of the corner of his eye he saw the cursed Norseman working across the way and resolved to watch him closely. Humans were never to be trusted. Galaher, despite what he had said back in the cell, Mormacar knew he could trust. The old elf would come through in the end. He could feel it.

When the overseers were scant feet away, Mormacar hefted his pick and smashed it into the weakened support beam. The beam shuddered from the blow and dust fell from the ceiling. Mormacar's heart leapt, but his elation was short lived. The beam held.

The overseers whipped their swords free of their scabbards. One of them spat, 'That was your last mistake, slave,' and strode forward, blade at the ready. Mormacar hefted his pick, determined at least to die a warrior's death.

The other overseer followed his compatriot, but hissed, 'Remember the Lady Bela's orders!'

'Damn that witch!' snapped the first dark elf, his voice hot with bloodlust. 'This wretch is mine!'

The tunnel was eerily quiet. All of the other prisoners had stopped their work, watching the unfolding drama with dumb fascination. Mormacar looked down the tunnel, hoping to see Galaher coming to stand at his side. But the old elf just stood and stared, his pick dangling from his weathered hands. Suddenly the silence was pierced by a echoing crack. Glancing to his right, Mormacar saw that the Norseman had smashed the weakened support beam on the other side of the tunnel. The beam shuddered and fell, loosing a rain of falling rocks.

Mormacar instinctively leapt out of the way, but the dark elves, surprised by the falling debris, were knocked to the ground. Before they could rise, the Norseman and the Shadow Warrior were upon them. Mormacar smashed in the head of one of the dark elves, while Einar swung at the other, pinning him to the floor. The Norseman hurriedly stripped the dying elf of his sword and dagger.

Above them the ceiling groaned menacingly. As uncounted tons of rock shifted and slid, dust and debris fell in streams. Mormacar turned to the stunned prisoners, most of whom still stood at their work stations. 'Get out of here!' he yelled furiously.

That was enough for most of them, who dropped their tools and ran up the tunnel. Mormacar and Einar followed them, grabbing torches from their wall brackets along the way. They ran desperately, hearts pounding, until at last they came to an intersection, where the ramshackle band halted to rest. A dull roar echoed up the tunnel, as more of the ceiling caved in behind them.

The two warriors exchanged looks of grim satisfaction, pleased with their handiwork. Looking around at the other fugitives, the Norseman asked, 'What now, elfling? Is this as far as your plan goes?'

The Shadow Warrior answered without hesitation, 'Now we follow the tunnels down and look for a way out.'

'What do you mean "down"?' Galaher spoke up. 'There's naught down there but cold ones and endless tunnels. The best you can hope for is to starve to death. We must go up and try to find an escape route there.'

'I know it sounds crazy,' Mormacar said, looking around at the desperate throng, 'but I've thought this through. You yourself said there was no way out, Galaher. Now we've all seen dark elf war parties in the tunnels, haven't we? Well where do they go? I think the Forsworn have an underground way through the mountains and I mean to find it. ' His compatriots looked dubious, and shifted uncomfortably in the gloom. 'Above are countless soldiers, thick walls and stout gates,' Mormacar continued, speaking quickly, as if he could feel the crowd slipping from him. 'If you go up, you'll surely die. My way we have a chance.'

Chaos erupted as all of the fugitives began to talk at once. Mormacar tried to break in, tried to calm their fears and make them see sense, but had little chance as the panic-stricken fugitives babbled about what to do.

Eventually, the Norseman lost his temper. 'Shut up, all of you!' he bellowed, his angry words bringing immediate silence. 'You're acting like children. There are only two choices, up or down.' Einar pointed to Mormacar. 'The elf and I go down. Who will join us?'

Mormacar looked at the others, sure that they would see sense. If the oafish Norseman was convinced, surely his elven brethren would join him. He was shocked when not one voice rose up in support.

'I'm sorry, lad,' said Galaher gravely, 'we know what we must do.' The others nodded in agreement and clustered around the old elf.

The Shadow Warrior could scarcely believe his ears. It seemed the former slaves were prisoners still, if only in their minds. He started to speak but Einar cut him off.

'Don't waste your breath, Mormacar,' spat the Norseman in disgust. 'Let's go.' Spinning on his heels, the furious giant stomped down the tunnel.

Mormacar hesitated, hoping even now that someone would join them. None stepped forward. With sadness in his heart, he approached Galaher and pressed a sword into his hand. 'You'll need this, brother,' the Shadow Warrior said quietly. Then he turned away and followed Einar down the passage.

MANY HOURS LATER, the two warriors stood in a large cavern which was dimly illuminated by glowing fungi. Peering intently down the three passages that descended further into darkness, Einar, for once sounding hesitant, asked, 'Well, which way now?'

Mormacar considered each of the tunnels carefully before answering. 'I think we must follow the right-hand path.' He indicated barely discernible marks. 'See all the bootprints there? It is clearly frequently used.'

'Which makes it that much more likely we'll run into some of the dark elf scum,' Einar said, grinning as he ran his fingers up and down his blade.

'True, but remember that we are trying to escape, not to settle the score,' Mormacar said levelly, 'That can wait for another day. Agreed?'

'Cease your prattle, elfling,' Einar scoffed. 'The blood of berserkers runs in my veins. I do what I must.'

'Fine,' the elf said curtly, suppressing an urge to comment on the apparent foolishness of all Norsemen. 'Let's go.'

By Mormacar's estimate, the two warriors were already several leagues underground. After leaving the other prisoners behind, they had hurried down a cavernous tunnel that shot through the bowels of the earth, turning neither right or left. The sounds of the other fugitives had soon been lost as the two warriors continued their descent. Wary of both pursuers and whatever unknown dangers might lie ahead, they had nonetheless set a quick pace. Eventually they had come to this large cavern. Now, as they made their way down the right-hand passage, they were quickly confronted with more choices, as passages split, caverns multiplied, and tracks became ever harder to identify.

Shadow Warrior and Norseman pressed on urgently, stopping only to drink from the few streams and stagnant pools they happened across in their wanderings. Eventually, after what must have been many hours, sheer exhaustion dictated that they stop and rest, and the two collapsed next to a evil smelling pool. They sat in silence, breathing heavily and occasionally drinking the scum-covered water at their side. The weeks of overwork and under-nourishment at the hands of the dark elves were taking their toll. And now that they were deep under the earth, the icy chill made a mockery of their ragged clothing.

'Perhaps the others were right after all,' Mormacar ventured, shivering as he choked back some of the vile water. Suppressing the urge to retch, he sprawled on the ground, his muscles aching with every movement.

The Norseman snorted. 'The others are surely dead already,' he replied. 'At least we are still alive.'

Mormacar accepted this assessment without comment; he knew Einar was right. Sighing, he added, 'I never expected to end my days like this, wandering under the Land of Chill. Curse the day those hellspawn captured me!'

'The day I was caught was a dark one as well,' Einar said softly, his face betraying shame and despair. His voice trailed off. Abruptly, he shook his head as if to clear it, and stared at Mormacar. 'Tell me, how did you come to be in hellish mines of Hag Graef?'

A black look crossed over Mormacar's face as he remembered his last day of true freedom. By his own estimate, it was probably no more than two months since his capture, but it seemed so long ago. 'I was travelling with a band of my brethren, the Night Stalkers of the Shadow Warriors. We've been fighting the thrice-damned dark elves for centuries on Ulthuan and it's a war that never ends.' As Mormacar talked, he held his head high and his exhausted slump became a proud pose. 'While other of my kin live in shining cities and try to forget the Witch King's bloody hordes, my folk scour the Shadowlands for invaders and bring red death to the Forsworn defilers.'

Thoughts of what the dark elves had done to his homeland filled his mind, and Mormacar strove to push down the hatred that welled-up in his heart. Consumed by his own emotions, he failed to notice the grin of approval break out on the Norseman's face. 'In any case,' he continued, 'my brethren and I set an ambush for a raiding party. We thought to trap them, but fell into a trap ourselves.' His voice grew quieter 'While we rained death on the Forsworn below, another group of them surprised us from behind. Before I could even unsheathe my sword, one of the cowards struck me from behind.' He spat in disgust. 'The next thing I knew, I awoke in Hag Graef.'

Einar nodded, having heard many similar tales in the slave pits. 'Those evil scum do not fight with honour,' he noted. 'Poison, foul magic and tricks are not the weapons of true warriors.'

Mormacar could not but agree. Strangely curious about this barbaric human, the Shadow Warrior asked, 'What of you? How did you come to be so far from frozen Norsca?'

'That is a tale worthy of the skalds, elfling,' the Norseman replied, 'although I doubt any lived to take the story back to Norsca.' He shook his head as he continued, 'Ah, a black day it was indeed. I was sailing with Grimnir Ogre-kin, as fierce a reaver as ever prowled the Sea of Claws.' Einar settled back, as if the two of them were drinking mead in front of the hearth. 'We'd just raided an Empire merchant fleet and our holds were heavy with booty. Then a great storm blew out of the east, like the breath of the gods themselves.' Mormacar cracked a smile. Storytelling came easily to the Norseman. 'My ship was separated from Grimnir's and we tossed on the seas for three days. When the storm finally blew its last, we were adrift and mastless.' Einar shook his head and dropped his gaze to the ground. 'It was then that the dark elves found us. It was a fearsome sight, a castle that floats on the sea, filled with sea serpents and worse. Truly an abomination sent by Mistress of the Damned herself.' The Norseman crossed his arms in front of him, making an ancient ward against evil. 'Seeing its towering walls and countless warriors, I knew that we would soon be dead.'

'It was a black ark that you beheld,' Mormacar said. 'None can stand against them.'

Einar nodded but he was talking quickly now, his blood racing as he was caught up in remembrance. 'I swore a vow to the Father of Battle to die before surrendering. Soon the murderers boarded my ship and we fought like berserkers that day.' Suddenly, Einar was on his feet, braids flying wildly as he shook his head back and forth. 'I wish the skalds could sing of the deeds of Halfdan Wolfclaw, Skragg the Grim and Canute Shield-breaker, for few have equalled their skill at arms. One by one, though, all were slain, pierced by bolts, hacked down by swords or felled by black magic.' He stood there, shaking his fist at unseen foes while Mormacar looked on, wondering if the Norseman had lost his mind. 'My heart cried out for vengeance as more and more of the dragon-cloaked corsairs boarded my ship. At last, only I was left alive.'

Mormacar could see that guilt stained the Norseman, guilt at not dying with his shipmates like a good captain should.

'I lay about me with my axe, slicing and cleaving, but I could not kill them all. When the bodies were piled up high around me, one of their foul wizards ensorcelled me.' Einar slammed his fist into cavern wall and howled in frustration.

'Instead of letting me die with my crew, the captain of that evil vessel took me to Hag Graef in chains. When we escape, I will hunt him down and feed him his own heart. Only then will my comrades be avenged.' Story finished, Einar slumped to the floor in despair. His hand, now bloody and torn, was still clenched tight as he continued to relive that fateful day.

Mormacar stared at the Norseman, impressed despite himself. 'I think you may have missed your calling, Einar. You should have been a storyteller yourself.'

Einar chuckled a little at this and Mormacar joined him. For a short while, they forgot the mistrust between elf and man and enjoyed the laughter together. But the moment ended quickly, as the harsh reality of their situation intruded upon them once more. An uncomfortable silence descended on the two fugitives and Mormacar feared that Volundson would sink back into his guilty despair. But then Einar forced another laugh to break the silence. 'If you liked that tale,' the Norseman said, 'let me tell you of the battle at Brienne. Grimnir's wrath was something to behold that day–'

'Einar, shut up,' whispered Mormacar, squinting in obvious concentration. The Norseman bristled, but Mormacar's insistent gesture silenced him. 'Do you hear that?' asked the elf.

'Hear what?'

'Listen closely, I heard something.' The Shadow Warrior stood up silently and crept over to one of the passages.

Volundson followed, listening intently.

After a minute, the Norseman said, 'I don't hear anything, elfling. Have your wits left you?'

'Follow me, you oaf,' Mormacar hissed, yanking his dagger free from his belt. 'And be quiet.'

THE ELF PADDED silently through the dank and gloomy passages, followed clumsily by the big Norseman. At each intersection, the Shadow Warrior would stop, listen, and then pick a new direction. After a few minutes, even Einar could hear the clash of metal and the shouts of combat.

'What now?' Einar asked. 'Who knows what lurks this far under the earth?'

'Whoever it is,' the elf whispered, 'let's hope they know a way out of here. This way, and try harder to be quiet.'

A gruff belch was all he got by way of a reply. The two fugitives set off again, easily able to follow the echoing cacophony. The minutes passed slowly, as each warrior wondered what lay ahead. They were concentrating so much on the noises that they all but tripped over the body of a dark elf lying in the passage. His head had been ripped from his shoulders and was nowhere in sight. Mormacar stuck his dagger in his belt and took the dead elf's sword. Slowly, silently, the two warriors inched ahead.

Finally, they came to a large cavern, whose circular shape and smooth walls made it seem man-made. Peering inside, they beheld a furious conflict. Battle cries, howls of pain and triumph, and the sound of clashing steel filled the air. Around a dozen dark elves were locked in combat with savage lizard creatures. These green and black scaled monsters walked on two legs and wielded crude spears and clubs with considerable skill, although Mormacar and Einar did not fail to notice that they used their razor-sharp teeth at every opportunity. The cavern was already littered with corpses, both elf and lizardman, and the fight had clearly become a grim battle of attrition. Most of the smaller lizard creatures were dead already, but their larger cousins were putting up quite a fight.

Two in particular towered above the battle, their huge spears smashing in elf skulls with unmatched strength. As the fugitives watched, one of these gargantuan lizardmen was felled by a savage attack from a frenzied witch elf. Her twin blades danced over the slow-moving reptile, slicing scales and driving deep into the monster's vitals. With a bellowing death scream, the creature fell backward, crushing a dark elf warrior beneath its ponderous bulk. Jumping onto the monster's carcass, the witch elf beheaded the monster with one blow and a rapturous howl of 'Blood for Khaine!'

Mormacar, utterly transfixed by this titanic clash, suddenly realised that he looked into the twisted face of Lady Bela. The Shadow Warrior's blood turned cold, and he was so full of loathing at the sight of her that he almost didn't notice that the battle was coming to him. One of the Forsworn had broken and was running right towards the hidden fugitives. A small, crested lizardman and the other hulking giant chased the fleeing warrior. Einar and Mormacar fell back down the passage and waited in a small alcove. Mormacar could feel the cold, hard, rock against his back but the sword felt good in his hands. Presently the terrified dark elf ran around the corner. Before he even realised that he faced a new foe, the Forsworn found Mormacar's cold steel in his belly. Face to face with his enemy, Mormacar watched the life drain from his victim's eyes. Stepping back, he let the body slide off his sword and fall to the ground.

Overcome by all-consuming hatred, he hadn't even noticed that Einar had split the crested lizardman nearly in two. There was no time to celebrate, however, as the crash of clawed feet and an ominous bellowing reminded both of them of the other imminent threat.

The huge lizardman, a mighty spear grasped in its clawed hands, stalked around the corner, roaring fiercely. Einar and Mormacar looked at each other, then jumped forward to attack. Although slow to react, the beast had scales as tough as hardened steel and the two warriors found that their blows were all but ineffectual. The raging beast hissed angrily and smashed Einar to the ground with the butt of his spear. In the same movement, its heavy tail snaked out and slammed down on the Norseman's chest, knocking the wind of him.

While the beast was momentarily fixated on Einar, Mormacar seized his chance. Balancing lightly on the balls of his feet, he took his dagger in his right hand, steadied himself, and then threw the wicked blade at the scaly monstrosity. The beast reared back in agony as Mormacar's dagger flew straight and true into its eye. The Shadow Warrior grasped his sword in both hands and drove it into the creature's exposed throat. Black blood gushed from the wound, showering the elf and causing him to lose his grip on the blade. The lizard creature, two blades buried in its flesh, stood there stupefied for a few moments, then fell forward with a ground-jarring crash.

Einar sat up, looked at the Shadow Warrior, and marvelled, 'Truly a feat for the sagas. The Father of Battle has blessed you today.'

Mormacar motioned him to be silent. The elf quietly recovered his weapons and did his best to clean the blood off their hilts. No new foes ventured down their passage and eventually the sounds of battle began to fade. Soon all was quiet.

* * *

As THE TWO warriors crouched in the passage, wondering who had won the brutal battle, animalistic howls of 'Khaine' grimly answered their question. Then they heard the Lady Bela, her usually icy voice hot with the joy of bloodletting. 'We leave in ten minutes,' she said simply. 'Be ready.'

'But lady,' one of her warriors objected, 'what of the wounded and the missing?'

Even from where they sat, the two fugitives could hear the ferocious slap Lady Bela delivered to her soldier. 'You insubordinate wretch, if you ever question me again your entire family will go to the altar of Khaine! Anyone too wounded to travel is to be killed, as are all these lizardmen who yet offend me with their breathing. Now, move! It's a long way to Arnhaim and we wouldn't want to disappoint our high elf brothers.'

The remaining dark elves did their work quickly and soon the whole band marched off in the darkness.

'Faster,' the Lady Bela urged, her voice now distant, 'we've got a prediction of victory to deliver.'

When their footsteps could no longer be heard, Einar boomed, 'That was refreshing. It's been too long since my last battle. I would have preferred dark elves to lizardmen, but a fight's a fight.'

'You are familiar with those things?' Mormacar asked, gazing down at the corpses at his feet.

'Only by reputation,' the Norseman replied. 'I've heard stories of these creatures but I never believed they truly existed.' They walked carefully into the cavern but found nothing but the slain. 'Leaving aside the question of what these lizardmen were doing under Naggaroth, what are we going to do now?'

The Shadow Warrior considered the question and decided quickly. 'I think we should try to follow the dark elves.'

'I see,' the Norseman sneered, 'you miss your girlfriend already.'

Mormacar glared back at him. 'No, you brainless oaf, but if anyone knows the ways out of these caverns, it's the Lady Bela. Did you not hear her say they were heading to Arnhaim?'

'Aye, I did,' Volundson said, 'but I've never heard of it.'

'It's a high elf bastion south of Naggaroth – but it must be a thousand miles away. I don't know what Lady Bela's plans are, but she must be stopped.'

'Speculate later, elfling. If we're going to follow them, we should do so quickly.' Looking about the cavern, Einar's eyes lit up. 'But not before availing ourselves of the opportunity for booty.'

'How can think of treasure at a time like this,' Mormacar asked incredulously.

Einar, already sifting through the backpack of a dead elf, pulled out a parcel. 'If you're not interested in treasure, I suppose I'll have to eat all this food by myself.'

Mormacar nodded approvingly. 'Perhaps you are not such a fool after all, Einar Volundson.'

After gathering up all the food, clothing and weapons they could carry, the two warriors set out after Lady Bela. If they looked ridiculous in the ill-fitting clothing of their former tormentors, they did not care. They were warm, they had food in their bellies for the first time in days, and they were still free. And they intended to stay that way.

THE FOLLOWING WEEK was a hellish one for the two fugitives as they trailed their former tormentors through the labyrinth of caves far beneath Hag Graef. They had to stay near enough to Lady Bela's band to follow their tracks but far enough away to avoid detection. They ensured that one of them was always awake, keeping watch and waking the other if their foes moved. They could not even light a fire, lest they draw unwanted attention to themselves, so they continued to navigate by the eerie light of the fungi.

The Lady Bela travelled at a terrific pace and rarely sent out scouts. Indeed all her attention seemed fixated on some distant goal, although neither of the two fugitives could say what that might be. Despite their fatigue and the darkness, man and elf would not be left behind. The followed the Forsworn with a manic single-mindedness, so desperate were they to see the light of day again. As the days passed, uncharted by sun or moon, Mormacar and Einar dropped into a monotonous, numbing routine. Conversation had died out after only a few days. It was all they could do to keep going.

When the dark elves finally did stop, the two fugitives, tired and dazed, nearly stumbled into the large cavern occupied by their foes. But the Norseman saw the glint of steel in the gloom and pulled his companion back down the tunnel in silence until they found a small cavern full of dripping stalactites. Despite the slimy floor, Mormacar flung himself down and immediately fell asleep.

The elf awoke to the sound of drums, and at first thought he was back in fair Ulthuan. But a quick look at Einar, who looked nearly dead as he sat on watch, brought his dreaming mind crashing back to reality. 'Einar,' he whispered, 'what's going on?'

The Norseman slid back a few paces, but kept his eye on the passage ahead. 'It sounds like a foul ritual of some sort,' replied Einar, his voice full of loathing. 'You slept through the chanting, but it's been going for at least an hour by my reckoning.'

Mormacar nodded, and rubbed the sleep from his eyes. Gathering up his few possessions, he asked, 'Shall we pay a visit to the Lady Bela?'

The Norseman grinned. 'I was hoping you'd say that, elfling. If I sit here any longer, I may well turn to stone.'

The two warriors crept forward. Mormacar still cringed at what the Norseman considered to be 'moving quietly', but the drumming and chanting drowned out even his blundering. After a few minutes they approached an enormous cavern lit up brilliantly with dozens of flaming torches. The bright illumination was almost too much to bear, so used were they to the dim light of the caves. A few minutes of blinking and quiet cursing and their eyes had adjusted enough to see into the chamber beyond. They crept closer still, and it was then that Mormacar spotted a jagged column of black rock that thrust up from the floor. Signalling Einar with his eyes, Mormacar dashed the few yards to the column, followed quickly, if not gracefully, by Einar. Safely obscured, they crouched behind the rock and peered inside.

At the far end of the cavern was a tall altar of glassy black stone carved with evil runes and darkly stained. A hooded figure lay chained to this hideous slab, his frantic straining useless against the strong steel of the manacles. Surrounding the altar were four mighty stalagmites, and upon each of these was chained another hooded form. Below the altar, dark elf warriors beat wildly on a dozen drums while half-clad witch elves danced around the cavern singing the praises of Khaine, god of murder. Presiding over this scene, her face glowing with ecstasy in the torch light, was the Lady Bela.

'This is truly a place of evil,' whispered Einar, his gaze transfixed on the spectacle before him.

Mormacar nodded in response. This is what Ulthuan would be like without the constant vigilance of the Shadow Warriors, he thought grimly. But even his brethren were but a breaker against the dark tide of Naggaroth.

The wailing of the witch Elves reached a fevered pitch, and Lady Bela began to dance around the altar, lashing about with her whip in a fit of rapture. As she passed each of the stalagmites, she tore the mask from the face of the bound victim. Mormacar's heart caught in his throat as he recognised all four as prisoners from his cell who had gone upward with Galaher to try to escape. Seeing the terror on their faces, there was no comfort in knowing that he had chosen the right path.

Now all the assembled dark elves began to chant, 'Khaine! Khaine! Khaine!'

Lady Bela pulled a jagged blade from her belt, threw her head back, and howled like an animal. 'Lord Khaine,' she intoned, her voice hot with passion, 'accept this sacrifice!' With that, her blade swept down and plunged into the chest of a screaming victim. Mormacar could watch no more and he turned away, his heart heavy. He could hear the laughter of Lady Bela, and the scuffling of her minions as they fought over the crimson prize he knew she had thrown them.

But realising this was no ordinary ritual, Mormacar steeled himself and turned his head back to watch. And as the last heart was torn from the last victim, a dark mist began to rise around the altar. It seemed that Lord Khaine was listening.

Einar dropped down behind the rock they were hiding behind, and pulled Mormacar down with him. 'Haven't you seen enough?' he said, his voice full of disgust. 'Or are you waiting for Khaine himself to appear?'

Mormacar knocked the Norseman's hand away. 'This ritual is important, Einar, and we must find out why. If it's too much for you cover your eyes!'

The Norseman bristled, and anger flashed in his eyes. Standing slowly, he spat, 'I've seen more blood than any gutless elf. Pray you never know how much!' Then he turned his gaze away from the Shadow Warrior, and once again looked down on the Lady Bela.

Mormacar, cursing fate for throwing him together with this lout of a Norseman, did the same.

During their heated exchange, the black mist had surrounded the altar and now Lady Bela seemed to be adrift in clouds of inky darkness. She swayed back and forth above the altar, running the flat of her blade over the still-hooded form bound there. 'Lord Khaine,' she shouted, 'I ask for your favour in exchange for one final gift!' She grasped the hood and tore it free. 'See!' she growled. 'Galaher Swiftblade!'

Mormacar froze in horror as the hood came free. There was poor Galaher, beneath the knife of the murderous Lady Bela. Instinctively, he pulled his blade free and made to leap over the rock, but strong hands restrained him.

'Don't do it, elfling!' Einar hissed urgently. 'You'll get us both killed!'

'Let me go, Volundson! It's Galaher down there!' Mormacar strained against Einar's arms but couldn't break free.

'Remember your own words,' the Norseman whispered in his ear, as he struggled to hold back to writhing elf. 'We will have our vengeance later. Now, we must escape.'

Mormacar struggled half-heartedly but his body slowly relaxed. As much as he hated it, he knew the Norseman was right. But Galaher! What of Galaher?

As if in answer to his unspoken question, Lady Bela's voice echoed through the chamber. 'Lord Khaine, even now our armies are on the march. Accept the blood of this elf Lord as a sacrifice fitting your dark majesty!'

Once again the chants rose high, and the Lady Bela's knife plunged down. If she had hoped for a howl of fear, she was disappointed. Galaher had long ago become resigned to his fate, and the sharp blade brought him the eternal rest he craved.

Mormacar wept silently as Lady Bela sacrificed Galaher Swiftblade to her dark god. Einar held him but there was no need; Mormacar knew what he had to do.

Lady Bela dropped her knife, so she could hold the elf's heart in both hands. 'Lord Khaine, this heart is yours!' she intoned. 'In return, I ask only one question. Will it burn with the fire of victory, or shrivel with the decay of defeat? Hear your humble servant and know that victory will bring hundreds more to your bloody altars!' Gripping the heart tightly, she tore it free from Galaher's body. Holding it high, she shouted, 'For you, Lord Khaine, and victory!'

'For Khaine and victory!' howled the assembled witch Elves. Every eye in the cavern was fixed on the pulsing heart. No one moved, no one breathed – and then the heart exploded in black flame that licked up and down Lady Bela's arms. She embraced the flame like a sister, and shouted one word with indescribable joy: 'Victory!'

The dark elves screamed with delight. Lady Bela lowered the heart and looked with pride on her savage minions. Smiling her cruel smile, she tossed the flaming heart into the boiling mist below the altar. The black flame ignited the unnatural mist, and the heart exploded to form a vortex of swirling energy.

Lady Bela mounted the altar and with a shout of, 'To Arnhaim and victory!' she dove into the vortex and disappeared. One by one, her minions followed her lead.

Soon, Mormacar and Einar were alone in the great chamber with the bodies of the slain. As the two dumbfounded warriors looked on, the vortex began to shimmer and shrink. Mormacar quickly regained his senses and shouted, 'Quickly, Einar, we must follow them!'

The Norseman, eyes wild, said, 'Are you insane?'

'If you want to live, follow me!' Mormacar yelled. With that, he vaulted the rock and ran towards the shrinking vortex. Einar hesitated for a moment and then barrelled after him. Without a word, Mormacar dove into the endless blackness that hung over the floor.

Einar shouted, 'The gods love a fool!' and flung himself after the elf as the vortex winked out of existence.

MORMACAR LANDED hard on cold stone. A few seconds later, Einar appeared from nowhere and nearly fell on top of him. From the expression on the Norseman's face, he seemed entirely surprised to be alive. Warding himself against evil, the superstitious Norseman asked, 'In the name of all the gods, what was that?'

Mormacar stood up and listened intently. Mindful of the chanting and howling of the dark elves, which could still be heard from a nearby tunnel, he whispered, 'That was the darkest of magics.' Mormacar could feel the taint on him, and he brushed furiously on his ragged clothing in a vain attempt to wipe himself clean. 'It must have been some kind of gate. We could be anywhere now.'

'Then we have little choice,' Einar replied, at last rising from the cold floor. 'We must follow Lady Bela before her trail is lost.' Mormacar nodded in agreement. Their path was clear.

So the two warriors wearily resumed their previous routine. They followed Lady Bela and her minions, keeping their distance as best they could. Her pace had once again accelerated, and they pushed themselves hard to keep up. Two days later, the tunnels took a definite upward turn. This small victory gave the two fugitives a renewed burst of energy.

Early the following day, Mormacar stopped without warning, and Einar crashed into him, sending them both to the ground. 'Mind yourself, elfling,' the angry Norseman whispered. 'I've killed men for less.'

'Forget bloodletting for a single moment and smell,' Mormacar said insistently.

'Smell? I think you've eaten too many strange mushrooms these past few days.'

Mormacar grabbed the Norseman and shook him. 'Use your senses! Can't you smell the fresh air?'

Einar drew his hand back to strike the agitated elf, but paused and then broke into a toothy grin. 'Aye, I can smell it. Fresh air, elfling! It can't be far now.'

The two pressed on through the day, noting excitedly the widening of the tunnel. Then, without warning, they simply emerged above ground. It was night, so they had not seen light ahead, but there was no mistaking the stars above. The two warriors looked at each other and could not speak. What words could describe their feelings after such an ordeal? They simply clasped hands and laughed. They laughed at their fate, laughed at their luck, and laughed at the stars. And the laughter was real because it was theirs and they were free.

Looking about, they saw that they had emerged in the shadows of a imposing chain of mountains. Jagged spires reached for the heavens, towering above the exhausted fugitives. Below them stretched a valley, perhaps once fertile but now full of withered trees and blasted earth. Still, Einar and Mormacar could not help but find the sight full of beauty. Compared to the mines of Hag Graef and the terror of the underworld, this place was paradise.

Warily now, lest a wrong step end their journey in tragedy, elf and man crept down into the valley spread out below them. They searched amongst the withered trees for a sign of their foes, but found none. When they were sure it was safe, the fugitives made camp and then slept.

They awoke the next day refreshed, but their eyes burned in the dawning sunlight. It suddenly seemed so bright, so used had they become to the darkness below. Walking under the barren trees of the forest, Mormacar and Einar slowly regained their eyesight.

That night, Mormacar consulted the stars and tried to figure out where they were. 'I don't know how the Lady Bela did it, Einar, but we are only about two hundred miles from Arnhaim. We could make it there in nine days if we push ourselves, twelve if we don't.'

The Norseman chuckled, scratching at his ragged beard. 'Something tells me, elfling, that you want us to push on ahead.'

'You are no fool,' Mormacar said. 'I don't know what Lady Bela has planned, but we must stop her.'

'So be it. We can rest behind the walls of your bastion.'

Without further discussion, the two warriors continued their great trek through the wilderness, leaving the vast Black Spine Mountains behind. Of Lady Bela and her dark elves, they saw no sign. It was as if the witch elf and her minions had been swallowed alive by the ancient forest.

Einar and Mormacar spent the days travelling and the evenings swapping tales. They were pleased to find that the further east they travelled, the greener the land became. They soon left the blasted forest behind and entered a region of wild grass broken up with copses of trees. The crossbows they had looted from the dark elves allowed them to hunt some game. The Norseman turned out to be a fine trapper, which more than made up for his lack of aim. And thanks to Mormacar's ability to build a nearly smokeless fire, they were able to enjoy their first hot meals in memory. By the week's end they had shaken the worst effects of their imprisonment in Hag Graef.

At the end of the seventh day's march, Mormacar spotted a wispy plume of smoke to the east, where a series of low hills rose above a forest of pine. Cautiously, the two warriors headed towards it, hoping to find a friendly settlement of some kind.

Coming to a gentle hill, Einar and Mormacar quickly climbed it. Dropping to the ground, they crawled the last few feet to the top and then peered below. Bile came to Mormacar's throat as he realised what they had stumbled upon.

Beneath them lay an entire dark elf army. Mormacar looked in horror at the spectacle before him. The plains below were covered with the tents of the Forsworn, and the once-green grassland had been turned brown and lifeless beneath thousands of boots. It seemed all of Naggaroth was going to war, and the elaborate tents flew the shrieking banners of the dread cities of the dark elves.

Hundreds upon hundreds of warriors swarmed across the camp, united in their hatred of their high elf kin. The executioners of Har Ganeth, fearsome in the billowing black cloaks, strode amongst the crowd, their brutal axes sharpened and ready. Savage witch elves danced lewdly around a great cauldron of blood. Black armoured knights whipped their reptilian steeds into readiness for the battle ahead and engineers worked feverishly to build more of their dreaded repeating bolt-throwers. It was as if the Witch King himself had vomited forth a black stain onto the green lands below.

'Einar,' Mormacar whispered, 'they mean to attack Arnhaim!' His heart sank when he thought of his kin in the unsuspecting city.

'Aye, elfling, the words of Lady Bela now ring true.' Einar looked into his companion's eyes and, seeing the fire that burned there, knew their ordeal wasn't yet finished.

'We must reach Arnhaim first and warn my people,' the Shadow Warrior said, his voice strained. 'The Forsworn must be stopped.'

'You know I have no love for your folk, Mormacar,' the Norseman replied, 'but to thwart the dark elf scum I will gladly help you and your kin.'

Mormacar gripped Einar's hand. They had fought and bled together, their fates bound inextricably together. The Shadow Warrior stood, then turned to make his way down the hill. His keen eyes quickly picked out the skulking forms of two dark elf scouts who were silently making their way up towards them.

'Einar!' he yelled, unloading a bolt at the nearest scout.

The Norseman turned about as a speeding dark elf bolt pierced his left leg. Mormacar's missile also found its mark,

burying itself in the scout's chest. Norseman and dark elf both
fell to the ground, as the two remaining combatants closed.
Mormacar drew his sword but kept the repeating crossbow
hanging loosely in his left hand. The scout smiled wickedly,
unsheathed his own blade, and charged up the hill. Mormacar
parried a brutal overhead blow, brought up his crossbow, and
fired it point blank into his enemy's stomach. The scout fell
back with a grunt and rolled down the hill. The Shadow
Warrior ran to finish off his foe, but could not plunged his
sword home before the wounded scout had screamed long and
loudly.

'Einar, let's get out of here!' the elf shouted, his eyes picking
out the shadows of more enemy scouts.

'I'm not going anywhere on this leg,' the Norseman said
gravely. 'Leave me and go warn your people.'

Only now did Mormacar see the Norseman's wound. Einar
had tugged the bolt free and tied off the bleeding, but he could
hardly walk. 'Einar, I can't just leave you here! Not after what
we've been though.'

'Yes, you can, because you must. Together, we'll never make
it, but alone you just might.' The Norseman smiled grimly.
'Perhaps now I can make an end for myself worthy of a saga. I'll
hold them here as long as I can. Now, go!'

Mormacar embraced the big Norseman. 'Einar Volundson, I
swear this oath before all the gods: the skalds will sing of your
bravery this day.'

WITH A LEADEN HEART, Mormacar turned and ran down the hill.
He wanted to turn back, to stay until the bitter end, but he
knew that he couldn't desert the people of Arnhaim. Even now,
he could see dark elf soldiers rushing towards Einar. The
Shadow Warrior doubled his speed, determined to make his
friend's sacrifice meaningful. Einar stood alone on the hill, a
sword in either hand and death in his eyes. His life would not
be sold cheaply.

The Shadow Warrior made it to the forest, and already he was
breathing heavily. Diving behind a fallen tree trunk, he stopped
to scan for pursuers. There were none yet. The dark elves' attention was fixed on Einar, who lay about him with mighty strokes
and sent his foes reeling down the hill. Mormacar tore his eyes
from Einar and, moving quickly, plunged into the forest and

headed east. He needed to skirt the enemy camp if he was going to make it to the plains beyond. As he ran, he could hear the bloodthirsty howls of the frenzied Norseman. The Father of Battles was surely proud that day.

Mormacar had been reared in the wild expanses of the Shadowlands, and spent his life waging a merciless war on the Forsworn. Now he used every iota of his instinct and his training to slip through the woods unnoticed. He could hear the pounding of hooves and the shouts of the search parties, but he was a ghost in the shadows. Striving to keep his pace steady, Mormacar darted from tree to tree, his passing silent and leaving no sign. It took him nearly two hours to circle the dark elf army and he could now see the plains beyond. He was close, and the hated enemy was almost behind him.

Suddenly, the quiet was shattered by the thunderous approach of a Forsworn war party. Heart pounding, Mormacar threw himself flat and crawled into a tangled bush. The sharp branches cut his face and hands but he uttered no sound. Sitting perfectly still, he waited as the dark elves approached. The horses had slowed their pace as they entered the forest, and now Mormacar could only hear the gentle clip-clop of hooves and the jangling of harnesses. The sounds got louder as the Witch King's minions approached, and Mormacar gripped his crossbow tightly with his sweaty palms.

The dark elves broke out of cover, and the Shadow Warrior could see the wiry forms of three dark riders atop their midnight steeds. They circled the area slowly, scanning the ground for some sign of their quarry. When the riders found nothing, they regrouped and began to ride deeper into the forest.

But a chance glance from the last of the retreating horsemen aroused his suspicion. This rider broke off from his companions and cantered toward the concealed elf. Mormacar noticed too late that a piece of his cloak had torn off and was now clearly visible, hanging in the branches of the bush. Cursing himself for his carelessness, Mormacar readied himself as the dark elf approached.

The remaining horsemen now turned their steeds and galloped towards the hidden high elf, skilfully guiding their horses around the intervening trees. The foremost rider, spear extended, moved ever closer.

Mormacar launched himself out of the bushes with a yell. The evil steed reared in surprise, its rider dropping his spear while seeking desperately to calm his snorting mount. Mormacar stepped to the side of the stomping beast, and levelled his crossbow at the other two dark riders. With cold precision, he fired the crossbow twice in quick succession at the approaching horsemen, the infernal mechanism of the Forsworn weapon now turned against its masters. Both bolts found their mark, and the stunned dark elves fell from their saddles, wounded or slain. The last of the dark elves had regained enough control of his mount to leap from the saddle and tackle the weary Shadow Warrior. Both elves fell to the ground and the Forsworn smiled cruelly as he felt Mormacar's bones crunch beneath his weight.

Mormacar felt the breath knocked out of his body, and could only struggle as the dark elf rained blows down on him. The dark rider pulled a gleaming dagger from his belt, his other hand at Mormacar's throat. The Shadow Warrior thrashed desperately, trying with all his might to wrench the blade free. As the two mortal foes struggled, Mormacar's empty hand closed around a rock. Smiling grimly, the Shadow Warrior shifted his weight, and smashed the jagged rock into the skull of his foe, caving it in with one great blow.

The dark elf crumpled to the ground and Mormacar struggled to his feet. He grabbed the reins of the dark elf's mount and swung himself into the saddle. Nothing would stop him from reaching Arnhaim. Nothing!

Leaving the dead and dying behind, Mormacar raced out onto the plains and kept on riding. He could almost feel the hot breath of Lady Bela on his neck, and whipped the horse furiously to coax every ounce of speed out of the swift beast. Even though he rode at a full gallop, he would turn to look for dark riders every few minutes, but the crucial first hours saw no pursuit. All too aware of the power of dark magic, however, the Shadow Warrior rode on as if Khaine himself was in pursuit.

For the better part of a day, Mormacar stayed in the saddle and drove the horse on. Finally, the dark steed could take no more: it threw the Shadow Warrior from the saddle and collapsed. The huge steed rolled in the tall grass, whinnying in pain.

Mormacar lay in the grass, agony shooting through his shoulder. For minutes, or maybe it was hours, he drifted in and out of consciousness. He could tell that his arm was broken and his body seemed to be one big bruise. Gods, but he was wrecked. Perhaps he should surrender to the screaming pleas of his body and rest? But what of Arnhaim?

He could still hear the horse screaming in pain. It thrashed in the grass, surely dying. And its howls took him back to the altar of the Khaine. Once again he was in dark temple at Hag Graef, prisoner of the Lady Bela, forced to watch his kinsmen fall under her knife. And he could not decide if the screams of the dying horse reminded him more of the victims of Lady Bela, or of her bestial witch elf minions. But he did know that he would gladly give his life to spare his brethren in Arnhaim such a fate. There was no more time to waste. He had to push on.

So steeling himself, Mormacar rose, every joint and bone straining with the pressure. But he staggered forward... east, always east towards Arnhaim. As he crossed icy streams and tore his way through obstructing brambles, he lost track of time completely. It was all he could do to put one foot in front of the other, to ignore the pain in his shoulder and cover those final miles. When his body threatened to fail him, he thought of those who had already fallen in the struggle. The faces of his dead friends seemed to hang before him, urging him on. He saw his Shadow Warrior brethren, slain in foul ambush. He saw the prisoners of Hag Graef and Galaher Swiftblade, ruthlessly sacrificed by the Lady Bela. And he saw Einar Volundson, now surely dead. For all of them, and his kin yet living in Arnhaim, he forced himself on.

So Mormacar passed the night, stumbling in the dark in a desperate bid to bring salvation to the last high elf bastion outside of Ulthuan. As the morning haze evaporated under the burning sun, he saw it. In the distance, rising above the well-ordered fields of the outlying farms, a shining tower of pure white, surrounded by stout battlements and sharp elven steel. Arnhaim! Arnhaim at last!

He stopped, overcome with emotion, all his pain forgotten for that one instant. He had done it. He had escaped from Hag Graef and come in time to warn his kin of the impending attack. He looked forward to watching Lady Bela wither under a crushing defeat, and hoped he could face in her the battle to come. Only when his blade clove her in twain would justice be served.

Eyes closed, Mormacar smiled then, thinking of his sweet revenge, and failed to notice the tell-tale hiss of a speeding missile. His head jerked up as it struck his throat and pain shot through him like fire. He fell to his knees, blood oozing from the terrible wound. He reached out to the horizon, reached for the tower of Arnhaim but his hand grasped at nothing. His life ebbing away, Mormacar tried to cry out, to warn his brethren in Arnhaim that doom approached. But no sound emerged from his ruined throat, and he fell forward in a heap.

'Forgive me,' Mormacar thought, his head full of visions of Einar, Galaher, and his kin, 'I have failed you all.' Then he surrendered to the pain, and it consumed him utterly.

'HE'S DOWN!' an icy voice shouted. 'Let's take a look.' Three figures rose from the tall grass and walked over to the body of the fallen elf. They looked him over silently, poking the body to make sure the arrow had done its work. Seeing his haggard form, bloody and dressed in a ragged dark elf uniform, their faces filled with disdain.

'Look at this Forsworn scum, he's filthier than a pig,' a disgusted voice said.

'What was a lone dark elf doing so close to Arnhaim?' said a second.

'You can tell by the state of him,' the icy voice said, 'he's clearly a fugitive. We get these strays now and again. Throw him in that ditch and let's continue our patrol.'

'But sir, shouldn't we alert the garrison, just in case.'

'There's no need to rush, brother. We'll report in at the end of the day, as usual. What could happen by sunset anyway?'

THE BLESSED ONES
Rani Kellock

SIGMAR, STOP *your hammering!* Jurgen Kuhnslieb thought, as the throbbing pain in his head intensified. He winced and shielded his face as the inn door creaked open, admitting a bright lance of sunlight which seemed to pierce his very eyeballs. Grimacing, Jurgen gestured to the barkeep, who turned and studied him with a dour expression.

'My usual,' Jurgen said; it was more of a groan than a sentence. The barkeep looked unimpressed. The customer slumped before him – with his shabby slept-in clothes, his cropped black hair and dark, blood-shot eyes set into a keen, blowsy face – already owed money and did not look to be paying up any time soon.

'You've not paid your tab from last night,' the barkeep rumbled.

'Come on,' Jurgen moaned, struggling vainly through his hangover to muster some charm, 'just one. For your favourite customer.' The barkeep looked away. 'Look, I'll have the money in a few days. There's this man coming in from Altdorf...'

Jurgen trailed off as the barkeep turned away in disinterest.

Sigmar! Jurgen thought; another place in Nuln he couldn't get served. If this kept up, he'd soon end up barred from every establishment in the city. If only that last job hadn't gone so terribly wrong – Heinrick and Eberhardt betrayed and slaughtered, and Rolf good only for begging since he was caught by Pharsos's men – they would all have been rich, at least for a little while. And Jurgen wouldn't be slinking around in dives like this trying to avoid Hultz the Red-Eyed, the small time crime-baron who seemed to think the whole mess had somehow been his fault; probably for no better reason that he was the only one who had survived the bungled job with all his appendages intact. Then there was the other matter: a few gambling debts which had, well, got out of hand.

No wonder Jurgen was rapidly becoming very unpopular in this city.

Jurgen became aware that a particular kind of silence had descended on the inn, of a sort usually reserved for the presence of the city watch, or strangers who were obviously out of place. Jurgen resisted the impulse to turn around, not wishing to attract attention.

A young man, the apparent cause of the hush, sauntered up to the bar next to Jurgen and gestured imperiously to the barkeep. He was dressed in fine clothes, and clearly in the wrong part of town.

'Tell me, do you know a man name of Jurgen?' the newcomer addressed the barkeep. His manner was languid, but his dark eyes held an intensity that to Jurgen did not bode well. The barkeep risked a glance at Jurgen, who shook his head almost imperceptibly, but the young man caught the exchange and he span like a cat to face Jurgen.

'No need for alarm, sir,' the man smirked, his eyes coming to rest on Jurgen's left hand as it inched towards the knife concealed beneath his jacket. Jurgen paused, waiting for the stranger's next move. 'I've sought you out in order to offer you employment.'

'What are you talking about?' Jurgen said, taking the opportunity to size up the stranger. His dark eyes were set into a handsome, though somewhat pallid face; one which – by both appearance and demeanour – indicated a kinship to one of Nuln's noble families. His head was crowned by neat fair hair which fell loose over his shoulders, which Jurgen noted were somewhat stooped.

'I have come here on behalf of my master, who wishes you to... acquire a certain item for him.' The man studied Jurgen, his voice low. 'A very special item.'

Jurgen leaned forward and hissed: 'Not here, you idiot!' The thief flicked his eyes toward the barkeep, who was standing too close, steadily ignoring the impatient cries of thirsty patrons and cleaning an already spotless glass. The noble's smile tightened, but he nodded to the private booths at the rear of the inn and strode towards them purposefully. Jurgen followed cautiously, quickly checking that the knives secreted throughout his person were accessible.

Both men seated themselves in the enclosed booth and once again appraised each other. There was a moment of charged silence, broken first by Jurgen: 'So who are you? Who's your "master"?'

'My master wishes to remain anonymous, and who I am is not important.' The habitual smirk returned to the face of the young man. 'You may call me Randolph.'

Jurgen suddenly realised where he had seen the stoop-shouldered look that this Randolph possessed: it was common among the students of Nuln's famous university. Being wealthy and unused to manual work, they quickly became hunched when forced to lug about huge tomes of lore. Perhaps this Randolph was also a student at the university; this would explain his pale complexion – the more diligent students barely saw the light of day, spending their time endlessly studying books in the huge university library.

'Alright, "Randolph". What's the job?'

'My master has long wished to acquire a certain object, which recently came to his attention as being in the possession of a local merchant specialising in exotic artefacts,' Randolph paused, and fished a small pipe from his pocket. 'However, the dealer was not willing to part with the piece, much to my master's sorrow. Now we must resort to more discreet methods of obtaining the painting.'

'A painting?' Jurgen asked, incredulous. 'You want me to steal a painting?'

'It's not an overly large piece; you should be able to carry it alone. Once you have the painting out of the place it's stored in, you'll only need to move it a short distance to where we can take it off your hands,' Randolph filled the pipe with a pinch of herbs, and pulled a flint from his pocket.

'What are you offering,' Jurgen grimaced as the lit pipe began to emit sickly sweet fumes, 'assuming I accept this job?'

'Oh, you'll accept. One hundred gold crowns now, and nine hundred more once we have the painting.' Randolph paused for a languid draw from the pipe. 'The amount is non-negotiable.'

Jurgen felt his jaw go slack. This fee was totally out of his league; the old gang would have been happy to pull two hundred crowns for a job. Sigmar! Jurgen thought. Just who does he think I am? Jurgen recovered himself and found Randolph studying him, a quizzical expression on his face.

'S-sounds fair... Hmm.' Jurgen did his utmost to appear casual.

'You accept the commission?' Randolph arched his eyebrows.

'Uh... Of course,' Jurgen smiled weakly.

'Very well. Here's your advance,' Randolph said, rising from his seat and nonchalantly tossing a bag bulging with coins onto the table. 'The merchant is Otto Grubach, of Tin Street, in the Merchant's Quarter. The painting lies within a safe inside his office.'

'What's the painting?'

'The piece is titled *The Blessed Ones*, by the artist Hals,' Randolph said. He carefully extinguished his pipe and replaced it in a pouch by his side. 'I shall meet you in two days, here, to discuss delivery. That'll give you time to examine the premises.'

'Fine.' Jurgen grasped the bag and weighed it in his hands. 'Uh, look: what made you choose me for this?'

'You came highly recommended by a previous employer – a man known as Hultz.' Randolph flashed a knowing grin and strode purposefully from the booth.

Oh Sigmar, Jurgen thought, as his insides lurched with dread.

GETTING INSIDE Nuln University was no problem for Jurgen, who had a carefully nurtured friendship with the regular gate guard. It had been some time since he'd last had cause to visit the academy, but the feeling of discomfort he experienced with each visit returned on cue. It was more than just the intellectual and social snobbery of the university's inhabitants which set

Jurgen on edge: there were the stories, whispered in the dark corners of taverns throughout Nuln, concerning terrible and secretive goings-on within the academy walls. Of course, Jurgen was too much of a sceptic to believe even part of most of the tales he heard, but he was also cautious enough not to dismiss them out of hand. As the old saying went, Where there's smoke there may well be dragons…

Jurgen was here this time, within the musty dormitory complex, visiting an old friend, Klaus von Rikkenburg II. Klaus was the third-in-line to the Rikkenburg family fortune, built over centuries from the local wine trade. Klaus rejected the traditional third son profession of priest and elected instead to study at Nuln's famous university, a decision his family welcomed.

They were less impressed when he proceeded to almost completely ignore his official studies in order to pursue regular extensive studies into the quality of his family' vineyard produce, and its market competitors, alongside much research into the anatomy of local womenfolk. His family concluded Klaus had 'fallen in with bad sorts', which – as Klaus proudly pointed out – his association with Jurgen was testimony to. Jurgen considered Klaus a good friend, one that had not hesitated in the past to use his influence and intelligence to help him out of not a few tight spots.

'It's good to see you again, old man.' Klaus, having fixed his guest a drink, swept the clutter from an ancient-looking chair and seated himself. 'Where in Ulric's name have you been these last few months?'

'Uh, you know, saving the Empire and all that.' Jurgen glanced around the small dormitory room and shifted awkwardly; he'd made a seat of a low, over-stuffed cushion and was beginning to regret it. 'Well, I suppose I've been in a bit of trouble actually.'

'Really? Jurgen, I am shocked,' Klaus grinned, raising a mocking eyebrow.

'That's not important. I wanted to ask you about someone.'

'Yes?'

'I got approached by this young aristocratic-looking man who wanted me to do this job, right? Only he wouldn't tell me his real name, or who he was working for.' Jurgen paused for a quick sip of the spicy-sweet wine Klaus poured for him. 'Thing is, I reckon he looked a bit like he could be a student of the university, so I thought you might know him.'

'There are a lot of students at this university, Jurgen,' Klaus paused to gulp down a half-glass of wine. 'Well I suppose it's worth a try. What's he look like?'

'About my height, pale, dark eyes, blond hair down to his shoulders–'

'You just described half of the student population,' Klaus smirked.

'Smoked some horrible sickly-sweet weed, smirked a lot, bit of a fool. Come to think of it, he reminded me of you.'

'This tobacco, it smelt a bit like rancid perfume? I don't believe it!' Klaus seemed genuinely surprised. 'That sounds… Tell me, did he walk around like this?' Klaus stood and did an impeccable burlesque of Randolph's haughty demeanour.

Jurgen laughed loudly, almost spilling wine all over himself. 'Yeah, that's the one. Then again, all you aristocrats look that way to us common folk.'

Klaus grinned. 'It sounds like Eretz Habemauer; he was in my art history class. He's been smoking that disgusting Araby weed ever since he took up with Count Romanov last year.'

'Who's he?' Jurgen leaned forward, carefully setting his wine on the floor.

'Lives on the Hill. There are some odd stories about him. There used to be a lot of big parties in his manor, but they stopped because many of the noble families didn't approve of the things happening at them.'

'What do you mean? What was going on?'

'Well, I don't know for sure. But some say that they were taking riffraff – if you'll pardon the expression – off the street and, well, using them for entertainment.' Klaus paused while he carefully refilled his glass. 'Eventually all the bodies began turning up and people started asking questions, so his little soirees stopped. Or perhaps the count has been more discreet since.'

'By the gods…' Jurgen leaned back, exhaling slowly. 'So what's Habemauer to Count Romanov?'

'Romanov seems to have taken him as his protege, and now it seems Eretz shares the count's mania for exotic intoxicants and obscure relics. He really is a clown.' Klaus snorted with derision. 'Did he really ask you to do a job?'

'Yeah. He offered a heap of money, on behalf of his "master", for me to steal a painting. By someone, Halls or something–'

'Hals?' Klaus demanded sharply.

'Um, I think–'

'Not *The Blessed Ones*?' Klaus stared at Jurgen intently.

'Yes. What do you know about this?'

'I studied the finer arts once, mainly to annoy my parents, and gave a dissertation on mythological art: ancient pieces which are legendary, despite the fact that nobody can be sure they even exist. *The Blessed Ones*, by Hals, was one such piece: rumours of its whereabouts keep turning up but the painting's never been found,' Klaus pondered his wine glass for a moment, swirling the contents gently. 'The thing is, well, this old painting was supposed to grant the possessor, erm, eternal life. So, well, naturally, many people are interested in finding it.'

'Then this could be big...' Jurgen was standing abruptly to leave. 'Klaus, I'd better go. Do you think you could find out any more about this painting, or Romanov?'

'I can try.' Klaus sat forward but did not rise. 'So this painting is in Nuln?'

Jurgen offered a guarded shrug of his shoulders by way of a reply. 'Thanks for all your help, Klaus,' he said, before briskly turning to leave.

'Not at all, friend,' Klaus called as Jurgen hurried out of the door, slamming it shut behind him. The impact stirred up motes of dust coating the ancient door frame. 'Not at all.'

JURGEN DODGED his way across the city, hurrying through dingy lanes and twisting back alleys. Few knew Nuln as Jurgen did, which was the only reason he had managed to evade Pharsos's men when the last operation had blown up in their faces. Jurgen would be sad to leave this place, but he suspected his departure from this corner of the Old World was long overdue.

As he raced through Nuln's filth-strewn streets, already choked with the first leaves of autumn, Jurgen's mind sped. He knew Hultz was out for his blood, so being hired at his advice could only mean this job was, in one way or another, a death sentence. His every instinct told him to stay away from this strange employer and his obscure artwork. And yet... if this priceless painting really lay within the merchant Grubach's shop, then a solution to Jurgen's cash-flow problems could be at hand.

Jurgen slowed as he reached the end of an unkempt alley, stepping over an unconscious drunkard, to find himself facing the small merchant's house lying at the end of Tin Street. Ducking back into the alley, he squatted down against a broken crate. Fishing a small hand-mirror of beaten brass and a tiny wooden box from the pockets of his jacket, Jurgen proceeded to apply the contents of the box – a pair of dark eyebrows and a styled goatee – to his face. He carefully moulded these new features until he was satisfied they appeared authentic. Jurgen contemplated his rather shabby clothing for a moment, reflecting that it was a pity he could not afford the time to purchase a more appropriate outfit. Or the money, of course.

Taking a deep breath, Jurgen assumed the bearing of a servant on an important errand and strode purposefully from the alley. He stopped smartly before the narrow, two-storey building, adorned with worn, leering gargoyles. The building was flush with its neighbour on one side, with an alley on the other. Approaching the double front doors, he heard faint sounds from within. He rapped briskly on a solid door.

The noises inside ceased for a moment, then cautious heavy footsteps approached. The clunk of a beam lifting was heard from within, and the door opened slightly to reveal a thick-set man. His face – a jigsaw of scars – held an expression of extreme annoyance, which only deepened at the sight of Jurgen.

'We're closed,' the man growled. Jurgen quickly shoved his foot into the small space. He had to suppress a howl of pain as the man slammed the door on to his leather boot.

'Take your foot out of the door, now, or you'll be carrying it home in a sack.' The scarred man's voice dripped with malice.

'My master would be most disappointed if I returned without having spoken to the merchant Grubach,' Jurgen contorted his voice into the whining-yet-superior speech common to the servants of nobility.

'You ain't hearing too good,' the man snarled, and pushed his face closer to Jurgen's. 'We're closed. Begone, you worm!'

Jurgen struggled to maintain his composure as he felt the man's hot breath on his face, and was about to back off when he heard the faint shuffle of a second figure behind scar-face.

Jurgen stretched to peer around the thug's head at the interior of the store, and was rewarded with a glimpse of a rather pudgy figure peering at him from round the corner of an ornate dresser. The figure immediately ducked back behind the antique.

Jurgen raised his voice: 'A pity! Lord DeNunzio will be most upset. I had come to lay a considerable bid for–'

'Lord DeNunzio sent you?' The pudgy figure said, emerging cautiously into the light. Jurgen resisted the impulse to smile; the invocation of the name of one of the wealthiest and most powerful families in the city rarely failed to gain the attention of those of a mercantile persuasion.

'Yes, Herr Grubach. His Lordship was most interested in a piece you have acquired.' Jurgen did his best to speak confidently; not easily done with the thug snarling into his face.

'Well, of course!' The merchant's manner changed, a congenial tone entering his voice, although he still appeared extremely nervous. 'Come in, do! Please allow the poor man in, Hans.'

Hans scowled, but stood back from the door and gestured impatiently for Jurgen to enter. Jurgen stepped smartly into the store, then proceeded to make a show of smoothing down his clothes and examining his boot for scuff marks. Hans's scowl deepened. Jurgen took this opportunity to quickly scan the cluttered store.

'DeNunzio's page boys are lookin' pretty shabby these days,' Hans rumbled sarcastically.

Jurgen ignored him imperiously, as did Grubach. 'Which piece was your master interested in?' The merchant wrung his hands, and glanced about distractedly. Jurgen got the feeling that Grubach wished to get rid of him as quickly, though as politely, as possible.

'A certain vase. Milord provided me with a detailed description… Ah! I believe that is the very piece there.' Jurgen indicated a large vase, which stood at the head of some stairs to the rear of the shop.

'Ah… I'm terribly afraid that piece has been, hmm, sold.' The refusal came haltingly from Grubach, and Jurgen could see he was cursing himself for selling for what must have been a far inferior price to that which would be offered by one of the wealthiest men in Nuln. 'Still, I should think Lord

DeNunzio would have nothing to do with such... such an inferior piece. Perhaps he would be more interested in something like this?'

Jurgen was led through the cluttered store to examine various vases, urns and other assorted containers. Grubach became increasingly agitated, casting nervous glances about each time he ushered Jurgen to the next piece. Hans, by contrast, was like a rock, unflinchingly inspecting Jurgen's every move.

A section of the second storey had been cleared of artefacts, and a large tub half-full of water had been placed beneath a leaking section of ceiling. 'Must be quite a hazard in this business,' Jurgen commented pleasantly. Grubach assented, grumbling that the roof repairer was due but had not yet shown.

It took less than twenty minutes for Grubach to show Jurgen every piece of glassware and pottery in the place. Only one section of the shop remained unseen: a door to the rear of the building, which judging by the layout of the building led to a fairly small room.

'Any more pieces through here?' Jurgen asked casually, knowing he was pushing things.

'No! Em, no, just my office.' A look of panic crossed Grubach's eyes for a moment, before he brought himself back under control.

Hans placed a heavy hand on Jurgen's shoulder, gripping it tightly: 'You've seen all the pieces that are for sale,' he said, talking slowly and deliberately, 'and I think it's time you left to consult with your master. Don't you?'

It was Grubach, strangely, who answered the somewhat rhetorical question. 'Er, yes,' the merchant appeared rather distressed, caught between the need for politeness to the servant of a powerful man, and his need to be rid of the same, 'I do have some pressing tasks to attend to, so if that's all...'

'More than sufficient, thank you,' Jurgen began moving towards the front doors, though in truth he had little choice since he was being bodily propelled towards them by Hans's vice-like grip on his shoulder, 'Lord DeNunzio will be most grateful for your time.'

Jurgen was shoved onto the street, tripping and falling into the dust at the final push from Hans. The door slammed shut, and the heavy bolt slid loudly back into place. Jurgen rose and dusted himself off, thinking hard. He was sure from the way Grubach had behaved that the painting was present, and the theft actually seemed relatively simple. There were obviously complicating factors: he would be working alone, for one thing. Grubach's nervous manner did not bode well either. Romanov had probably alarmed him with suspiciously large bids on the painting. Jurgen suspected that if the burglary was not performed immediately – which meant tonight – the piece would most likely be transported to a safer location. That did not leave long to arrange matters...

Jurgen strode off briskly down the street, remembering to retain his servant's poise until he was some streets away.

From the alley opposite the house, a dark figure emerged, looking decidedly sober now. The figure paused to make sure it was not seen, then skulked off after Jurgen.

WOODEN SHINGLES shifted under Jurgen's feet as he stepped cautiously across the rooftop. He checked his movement for a moment, and then crept on more carefully, testing gingerly for loose tiles in the darkness with the point of his boot. His planning would all be for naught if he lost his footing now and plunged to become a bloody mess on the cobbled street below. The faint light emitted by a thin blade of moon, poised overhead like an assassin's knife, picked out the edge of the building in front of Jurgen. He crouched down, crawling slowly to the lip of the two-story precipice. Jurgen looked down into the street briefly and then wished he hadn't: he had never been much good with heights, which was a considerable liability in his chosen profession.

Jurgen steadied himself, slowly unhooking a small device from his belt. It was essentially a compact, three-pronged grappling hook, to which was tied a length of slim and sturdy cord. It had taken almost an hour of cajoling, wheedling, and finally a sizeable deposit of gold before Konrad, a nervous, small-time fencer, had agreed to lend it.

Taking a deep breath, Jurgen regained his feet and concentrated on the stone gargoyle on the roof of Grubach's house opposite. He swung the hook around his head, letting it gather momentum before releasing it to glide across the intervening space. The grapple-iron looped about the statue and caught, one of the prongs finding purchase in the nostril of the hideous effigy. After testing the line, Jurgen secured his end of the rope to a disused flagpole.

Jurgen tried to quell his quickening breaths as he pushed himself gingerly off the roof, dropping a few feet as the line adjusted to his weight. Sigmar save me, he thought, fighting to remain calm as he dangled two stories above the cobbled ground of the alley below. After a few deep breaths, Jurgen settled into a desperate rhythm of hand-over-hand for what seemed like hours, then suddenly found himself dangling against the opposite roof. Jurgen carefully lowered himself to the relative comfort of the tiles below him.

He rested briefly before ascending the slate roof cautiously, to the point at which the roof-leak inside the house had been. Sure enough, some of the tiles had slipped, leaving a small cavity leading into the darkness of the building's attic. Working carefully, Jurgen eased the surrounding tiles out of place, carefully piling them next to him until he had made a sizeable hole.

Jurgen lowered himself though the hole into the cluttered darkness of the attic. After some careful blundering, he managed to find his way to the trapdoor leading down into the building proper. Easing the trapdoor up gently, he surveyed the room below. Lamplight emanated upwards from the ground floor, but Jurgen heard no sign of any occupants. He slithered through, pulled a knife from his jacket, and began a stealthy descent of the staircase, checking cautiously over the banisters for possible assailants; Hans, in particular, he was not keen to face. The room appeared empty, however, the only sign of any occupancy a single lamp burning on a table.

Jurgen crept to the door Grubach had told him led to his office, listening carefully for sounds of occupancy. Once again, there was nothing.

What in Sigmar's name is going on here? Jurgen thought, as the unlocked door opened readily to his touch.

Beyond lay a small office, containing a small desk holding neat piles of documents, and a large wooden cabinet. The cabinet had evidently been moved from its regular place, where it had concealed a sizeable wall safe which now stood open and empty but for a few papers. Jurgen was almost ready to weep with frustration – when he noticed a painting, about the size of a large child, which lay propped against a low table in a shadowy corner of the room.

Jurgen carefully approached the painting. A strip of moon-light through a window provided no more than a glimpse of the subject contained within the gilt-edged frame: the green of forest trees, the pale pink of bare flesh, and then an angular face of raw crimson, staring insane and demented from the canvas. Jurgen shuddered and turned away, feeling nauseous. Steeling himself, he turned back to check the small signature in the bottom-right corner of the canvas, and made out the name 'Sena Hals' penned in strange script.

A sheet of black cloth on a table nearby made an adequate cloak for the grotesque painting. Jurgen shouldered his prize and proceeded towards the back door that led from the office to the street.

As Jurgen moved to open the robust oak door, he noticed that it was already ajar, and swinging slightly in the autumn night breeze.

JURGEN EMERGED from the building into a narrow lane, its cob-blestones slick and gleaming in the moonlight. A light rain had started, and Jurgen had trouble keeping his balance on the slippery surface as he wrestled with his bulky load. As Jurgen stumbled along, he became suddenly aware, by the innate and indefinable sixth sense which had allowed him to survive thus far in his profession, that he was being followed. He took a quick glance over his shoulder, making out a vague blacker-on-black silhouette of a figure as it crept towards him.

Jurgen slowed and peered ahead in the gloom of the lane's end, although he already knew there would be at least one more in front; footpads rarely worked alone. The few Jurgen had ever associated with had been callous, spiteful, stupid cow-ards. Men who lived by preying on the weak, who all feared – despite their desperate bravado – ending up like their victims: trapped, friendless, alone, bleeding to death anonymously in some dark alley.

There, a second, inching his way through the darkness. Jurgen stopped. He knew he couldn't possibly escape carrying the painting. Yet he could not leave it. The painting was his new-found hope, a way to repay the borrowed time he had been living on. Jurgen backed up against the wall, awaiting a move from the strangers.

The stalkers knew they were spotted and emerged from the shadows. There were only two, which at least Jurgen could be thankful for, and they appeared to be typical street thugs, though well-equipped. Their swords, drawn as they approached, were of a fine make, not the usual rough-hewn barracks-quality usually wielded by street ruffians.

'Good job, Herr Jurgen,' the shorter man said, a menacing undertone belying the compliment. 'We'll handle it from here.'

Jurgen had no doubt the man's tone would not have altered one bit, were he to be uttering the phrase Give us what we want and you won't get hurt.

'What about my payment?' Jurgen spoke casually, desperately trying to formulate some kind of plan. 'I'm not delivering the goods until I get what… what Romanov promised me.'

'Very well. If you come with us to the count's estate, you'll get your payment there. You don't expect us to carry that kind of money around, do you?' The short man smiled, or attempted to; a strange grimace strained his face. The taller thug, who seemed a little slow, guffawed at his companion's wit.

So Romanov is behind this after all, thought Jurgen; at any other time he would have felt pleased with his cleverness. But in the small thug's facial contortions and hard, dark eyes, Jurgen knew that the only payment that would be made at Romanov's manor would be with his own life. He had to get out of there fast. He did the only thing he could think of.

'Here you go!' Jurgen hurled the painting towards the small man, and immediately sprang towards the tall hoodlum, smashing the surprised thug in the face with a quick jab. There was a crunch of cartilage. The man screamed as he reeled backwards, one hand flying to his shattered nose. Jurgen pressed home his advantage, drawing his knife and slashing in one quick motion. The man screamed again and collapsed to the ground, clutching desperately at his side.

Out of the corner of his eye, Jurgen saw the smaller hoodlum, who had dropped his weapon to catch the precious canvas, scrambling forward on his knees to retrieve his sword. Jurgen span and stamped down on the base of the blade, just as the man grasped the hilt. The thug looked up, fear and defiance in his eyes. Jurgen gritted his teeth and brought the pommel of his dagger down on the man's head.

* * *

JURGEN SHOOK uncontrollably as he raced through the streets with his heavy burden, all caution gone. The immediacy of death never failed to make an impression on him. The two bloodied men he had left back there would most likely survive; Jurgen was not in the habit of killing unnecessarily, and he did not intend to start now. He had two new enemies in Nuln, however, for men like that did not easily forget such moments of vulnerability.

If he had been calmer, the thief would have been rather embarrassed to admit that he had not planned as far as where to go once he actually had the painting. So he stopped, gasping for breath in a shadowy doorway, and considered his options. He could not go to the inn he had been lodging at, nor any others, since the bulky package would start rumours flying immediately. All his regular underworld bolt-holes were off-limits, since there was no one he could trust not to hand him straight to Hultz, or even Romanov.

Jurgen was stumped for a moment, the panic welling up inside like dark spring-water, and then he had it: the one place he could go, where no one would think twice about a man carrying a strange artefact. Jurgen grinned in the darkness.

THE UNIVERSITY gatekeeper greeted Jurgen with a nod and detained him a moment with his latest joke, something vile about dwarf and halfling procreation. Jurgen hardly listened, just chuckled politely and strode into the academy, the man still chortling behind him.

He made his way to the dormitory houses without difficulty, though several times he was amicably jostled by inebriated students returning from a long evening at the local tavern. Arriving at Klaus's small dormitory house, Jurgen set down the painting and knocked heartily on the door.

Movement sounded from within, but there was no further reaction. Sigmar, thought Jurgen, he's probably completely smashed.

'Come on, Klaus, it's me! Open up!' Jurgen hammered again.

It had been a long night; he was exhausted, frozen and scared. All of which might help to explain why not until the last, even after the door was flung open, after he was seized by rough hands and dragged into that nightmare room of blood and torment, did he suspect that anything was in the least amiss. By then, of course, it was too late.

Two huge thugs gripped Jurgen's arms, and he hung between them like a sack of grain. The small room was a shambles, although the violence done to the furnishings was minimal. There was some glass on the floor from a broken decanter, and some papers had also been trodden into the rug. It was the blood, which seemed to saturate every surface and piece of furniture in the room, which coated the floor and rug in a sticky mess, that created an impression of such brutal vandalism. The gore was from one source: Klaus von Rikkenburg II, who sat slumped in a bloodied mess, tied into a previously opulent chair by lengths of thin cord. Behind him stood Eretz Habemauer, the one Jurgen had known as 'Randolph', a gore-spattered pair of pliers in his hand and a pouting smile on his lips.

'How fortunate! Who would have thought you would have friends in such circles, Jurgen? And you have brought a little present also, hmm?' Eretz gestured to a third thug, who lifted the cover on the painting for the noble to inspect. 'Ah, how beautiful. Best put it away. Wouldn't want to contaminate the precious thing now, would we?'

The thing in the chair convulsed suddenly, then began moaning piteously. Jurgen's heart turned over; poor Klaus was still alive! Eretz appeared to derive amusement from the display, for his pout became a wry smirk.

'Your friend does have surprising endurance. Had you arrived earlier you could have enjoyed the show; I fear Herr Rikkenburg will not be with us much longer.' Eretz paused with mock regret. Jurgen's tensed with rage. 'Well, we had best be off. I think it's time for you to meet the count.'

'Can I...' Jurgen choked on his words, though with anger or sorrow he could not tell, 'can I have...'

'Hmm? Oh yes, of course. It must be very sad for you,' Eretz said, with the indifference of handing a coin to a beggar.

Jurgen approached the mangled form of Klaus, who was suddenly beset with violent coughing. Jurgen bent to speak to his friend, though the right words escaped him.

'Klaus... I'm... Sigmar!' Jurgen mumbled, his stomach turning. 'I'm so sorry, Klaus.'

The figure jerked his head up at the sound of Jurgen's voice, its ruined face staring straight through him. 'Jurg–' An explosion of coughing. '…Is that you?'

'Yes, friend. I'm–'

'Jurgen… the pain… it's evil. Watch… blood, don't let your blo…' Klaus's body was wracked with an especially violent fit of coughing. When the attack ceased, the figure was still.

The two thugs stepped forward and seized Jurgen, and he was led away. Away from the ruined room, and from his dead, ruined friend.

JURGEN SAW LITTLE of the Romanov estate, crammed inside a darkened carriage. The manor, however, he had ample time to survey as he was pulled forcibly from the coach and shoved up the wide entrance stairs. The exterior gave an impression of ageing splendour: a once-great edifice falling into disrepair, the combination of neglect and the passage of time taking their toll.

The interior, in contrast, contained opulence the like of which Jurgen had never before set eyes on. Its crumbling passages were graced with a plush red pile carpet, and vivid tapestries and silks hung from the walls. The huge, antiquated rooms were decorated with chairs and couches with velvet upholstery, and strange sculptures and statuettes of exotic origin.

Jurgen was led into a large study, with shelves of books lining all four walls and a fire crackling in a sizeable hearth. Reclining on an opulent chair with a large tome on his lap was a middle-aged man, tall, with dark hair greying at the temples. He turned towards the new arrivals with irritation.

'Eretz, what is this?' the count – for Jurgen had no doubt this was he – spoke with annoyance, 'What are you doing here?'

'This is Jurgen Kuhnslieb, your lordship, the thief I hired.' Eretz spoke proudly, like a cat triumphantly depositing the corpse of a bird onto his master's bedroom carpet. 'He obtained the painting, and was attempting to keep it from us, as I predicted, when we intercepted him.'

'You have the painting?' Romanov sat up, his eyes burning with sudden intensity.

'I viewed it myself. We were… interrogating someone, a student, to find out what Jurgen was planning. I knew–'

'Where is it, man?' The count stood impatiently.

'Fyodor and Willem are preparing it as we speak.'

Romanov nodded briskly and stalked past Eretz, who hurried after his master. Jurgen was shoved after them by his large minder.

'So,' Eretz was gabbling, racing to keep up with Romanov's long strides, 'my spies followed the thief to a student's house. I knew this scholar, one of the Rikkenburgs, from my studies. He had even given a dissertation on *The Blessed Ones*. I knew that as soon as this petty burglar found out about the true powers of the painting, he would try to take it for himself. I had to find out what he was planning.'

The group reached a long set of stairs, and began the descent into the bowels of the manor. Eretz continued his report. 'We were fortunate that the thief, having somehow evaded the men I set to tailing him, came straight to the student's room with the painting just as we were finishing up! Of course, I had considered the possibility that he might return...'

The count stopped and turned, directing a piercing look at his excited protégé. 'You took a considerable risk, against my explicit wishes, doing this. You were extremely lucky that things have worked out as they did.' Romanov spoke briskly, with controlled malice. Jurgen seemed forgotten. 'There are more important things to consider now. Be silent!'

The party descended the remainder of the staircase in a hush, only the sound of their footsteps on the ancient stone filling the charged silence. At the base of the stairs, lit by guttering torches, stood a large wine-cellar, containing rows of dusty bottles on racks. Romanov gestured to Eretz, who walked sullenly to the opposite wall and lifted a small flagstone to reveal a short, steel lever. Eretz struggled briefly, then with a grating of stone on stone, a section of the cellar wall swung ponderously outwards.

Beyond lay an unusual sight, a chamber of beauty and horror. One half of the room was adorned with the sweeping silks, extravagant furniture, and fine candelabras common to the rest of the manor.

The other half, set on a cold stone floor, was filled with aesthetically-placed instruments of torture. Jurgen could discern a few of the usual suspects: the rack, vices designed to fit various appendages, and an iron maiden, its exterior decorated with a naked woman carved in alarming detail. Many of the remaining devices were far more bizarre and exotic, and Jurgen could only guess at their uses – though he suspected that guesses would soon be unnecessary.

At the opposite end of the chamber, two men were carefully arranging the covered painting on a large easel, which stood before an altar of stone draped with a silk cloth.

A small jade statuette of a beautiful androgynous figure, a cruel smile upon its lips, stood on the altar, its feet immersed in a low stone dish containing a dark liquid. Jurgen felt the hairs on the back of his neck rise as a feeling of deepest dread filled him.

Jurgen was manhandled over and deftly tied to a large cross-beam planted into the bare stone. At a gesture from Romanov, Jurgen's minder exited the chamber, the stone door rumbling shut behind him. The count turned to Jurgen.

'Listen carefully, vermin. You are about to witness something so wondrous I doubt your petty little mind can even comprehend it. Enjoy the privilege, for your death will soon follow, even as my everlasting life is assured.'

Romanov turned away, and walked purposefully to the painting, the two servants respectfully standing aside. Meanwhile, Eretz had taken a short flaxen whip from a rack of tools on the wall, and was walking slowly towards Jurgen, a coy smile playing across his face.

The first blow caught Jurgen unprepared. A casual flick of Eretz's wrist sent the point of the whip stinging across the thief's right cheek. Jurgen gasped and stifled a cry. A second flick lashed above his left eye, sending blood trickling down his face. This time Jurgen did cry out, equally from despair as from pain. Romanov, who had been stooped in an examination of the painting, turned in annoyance.

'Stop that, Eretz! You can entertain yourself with your trivial games, or you can observe history in the making.'

The count stepped back from the painting, studying it with the eye of an aesthete while Eretz looked on respectfully. Jurgen, blinking away blood, was also drawn to the picture within the frame, his eyes widening in horror at what he saw there. The image was of a forest glade with a shallow pool, in which figures bathed and lounged around in various states of undress. All of the figures were attended by oddly-proportioned red-skinned daemons, who appeared to cater to all the whims and desires of their human masters. The image was disturbing enough to Jurgen, but what induced such terror in him was a figure he recognised within the painting. Even from this distance, Jurgen could clearly make out the merchant, Grubach, lounging by the pool. His face was plastered with a strained grin, but his eyes stared wildly from the canvas in horror and desperation.

Neither Eretz nor Romanov seemed to notice anything amiss. Romanov produced a ceremonial knife from the folds of his robe, and held forth his left arm. He carefully made a light cut, catching the flow of blood on his finger. He studied the crimson drops for a moment before stepping towards the painting. Unnoticed, Jurgen struggled with his bonds, testing for a weakness.

'Immortality is mine!' Romanov cried theatrically, and smeared his blood onto the canvas.

For a moment nothing happened, and Romanov glanced about uncertainly. A light mist then began to seep from the painting, and the frame seemed to glow slightly in the candlelight. The bloody smear began to sizzle, seeping slowly into the canvas. The count stepped back in wonder and a low hum filled the air. The canvas appeared to pulse, the image distending, and abruptly two figures flowed out of the painting, forming before the awed count. They resembled the daemons in the picture: tall, spindly red-skinned creatures, with wide grins painted onto their distorted faces. Jurgen redoubled his efforts, and was rewarded with a loosening of his left wrist's bonds.

The two creatures spoke as one, their horrible sensual voices echoing through the room: 'Lord Slaanesh is grateful for your sacrifice – the eternal service of your immortal soul!'

Romanov stood in stunned horror as the two creatures seized him by the shoulders. One of the guards, prompted into desperate action by the plight of his master, leapt at a daemon with a desperate sword swing. The creature reached out, easily seized the guard's arm with one long clawed hand and twisted it into an unnatural angle. A languid swipe of razor-sharp claws separated the man's head from his body, and he collapsed to the ground.

Eretz and the remaining servant looked on in shocked disbelief as their master was dragged, screaming, pleading, into the

accursed painting, flesh flowing like vapour, until all three figures were gone. The room was filled with a palpable silence,
though a lingering aftershock remained, like the ringing in the
ears after a blow to the head.

Jurgen took his chance. Twisting his freed left arm, he
plunged his hand into his clothing, snatching his last remaining knife, hidden on his inner right thigh. Jurgen quickly cut
himself free from his constraints, as Eretz and the guard stood
staring at the painting in disbelief.

Jurgen lunged forwards and despatched the guard expertly.
Eretz span to face the thief, white fury suffusing his face, and
lifted his whip. Jurgen raised his arm to defend against the
coming strike, only to find his extremity suddenly entrapped in
the whip's coil. Eretz yanked the whip, sending Jurgen sprawling on the cold stone floor.

'It's all over now, Eretz,' Jurgen implored from his place on
the floor, 'It was Romanov's mistake. There's no need for us to
kill each other.'

'You cannot possibly understand!' Eretz screamed with rage.
'You are nothing! Nothing!'

Jurgen received a painful kick to the ribs. He gasped, then
jerked the whip from Eretz's hand, rolling quickly away across
the floor. He scrambled to his feet as Eretz charged. Jurgen's
desperate stab pierced Eretz's shoulder, but did little to stop the
maddened acolyte, who seized him by the shoulders and
slammed him backwards into the stone wall. Jurgen's head
bounced off the chiselled rock, and he slumped to the ground,
stunned. A savage kick to his jaw flattened him, blood and pain
exploding in his mouth.

Jurgen pushed himself upright, shaking his blurred vision
clear, to see that Eretz had picked up a heavy, shoulder-high
candelabra, and was advancing intently. Jurgen blinked,
attempting to clear the blood from his eyes. He raised his hand
up protectively in front of him, the bloodied dagger still
clasped in it.

Eretz laughed maniacally at his feeble resistance. 'Good
night,' he said, hefting the candelabra.

Jurgen looked up, sighing painfully. His blurred eyes strayed
as he awaited the final blow, and came to rest on the malevolent painting sitting just a few feet away. Jurgen continued to
stare, as a curious thought struck him. Eretz, puzzled by

Jurgen's behaviour, followed his gaze, then quickly turned back, eyes wide as he reached the same thought a moment too late.

Jurgen tensed his arm and flung the bloodied dagger – a wild, inaccurate throw, but it found its mark. The knife clattered against the painting, blood spattering across the canvas, before falling to the floor. Figures began to move within the painting.

Eretz emitted a scream of rage and despair. Jurgen closed him eyes tightly, though he could not stop his ears to the terrible sounds that filled the room.

WHEN HE OPENED his eyes some time later, Jurgen found the room silent, except for the low crackling of a small fire on the plush carpet, started by the fallen candelabra. Jurgen got to his feet slowly, steadying himself against the wall. He stumbled forward towards the painting, then stopped himself. He carefully cleaned his bloodied hands on his clothes, and then gingerly picked the painting up, setting it down on the growing flames.

The search for a mechanism to open the door sent him into a brief panic, but at last the lever was found. Just as he was stepping through the open door, a terrible wail sounded behind him, and he turned back briefly.

From the burning canvas then emanated all manner of horrific screams, some monstrously alien, some undeniably human. He ran, blundering though the wine cellar and scrambling up the stone steps. As he fled, he was certain he heard the anguished cries of Eretz howling in agony once more.

And then, at last, Jurgen stumbled through the still manor house and out into the chill night. The first wisps of flame were already rising into the dark sky behind him.

DARK HEART

Jonathan Green

THE WOLVES ARE running again. I can hear them panting in the darkness. I race through the forest and the night, trying to out-pace them. The trees seem to throw themselves in front of me to slow my progress. Leafless branches reach for me as I crash on.

Behind the wolves I sense another presence, something evil. It follows my flight with menacing eyes. I feel a cold chill take hold of my heart. With every heartbeat the wolves are getting closer. There is nothing I can do to escape.

And then, in time with my pounding pulse, I hear the beating of wings. Strong, slow gusts of frigid air caress my body. With every beat I feel their power increasing. Great black wings close around me, their leathery warmth shrouding me from the numbing darkness. The sickly sweet smell of blood fills my nostrils. I cannot help but breathe in great lungfuls of the rank air. The wings enclose me totally, suffocating me. Even through the darkness I can see the red veins pulsing.

Blood flows in the endless night. It surrounds me, rising ever higher. Or is it I who is sinking deeper?

Then I am drowning. I gasp for air but instead the hot life-fluid pours into my parched throat. Its viscous sweetness cloys in my mouth. I cannot help but swallow. As I do so my senses are flooded with feelings of darkest ecstasy.

I am in the place of blood again.

'AND I SAY we stick to the plan, just for once, and keep on to Ostermark!' The slim man's sharp eyes glared at the rest of the band from under a fringe of unkempt black hair.

Torben Badenov scratched his neatly-trimmed black beard. The tallest of the mercenaries, his hefty frame making him an imposing figure, could see that the disgruntled Yuri was in one of his stubborn moods.

Oran Scarfen looked up from polishing a dagger. 'Oh you do, do you?' he retorted.

The mercenary band was gathered before a signpost at a t-junction in the road over the moors. Shivering, they pulled their furs tighter around them against the chill of approaching night. They were all dressed in a similar fashion with tough, leather boots and they still wore their thick winter cloaks. With their assortment of swords and axes they were the very picture of hard-bitten fighting men.

'It's almost dusk,' Alexi, the leather-armoured old soldier from Nuln pointed out as he finished rearranging his backpack. 'We ought to start looking for somewhere to stay for the night.'

Yuri pointed an accusing finger at a smartly dressed, black-robed Kislevite. The man's left eye was covered by a patch that made him look both distinguished and mysterious. 'Well if Krakov here hadn't've got falling-down drunk–'

'As usual!' snorted the weaselly Oran.

'– and let the damn horses wander off, we wouldn't be in this mess.'

'That's right. We would've been in Ostermark by now,' agreed Stanislav, a heavily-built mercenary, his ham-sized hands resting firmly on his hips.

Torben paused in cleaning his blade and turned his gaze on the cringing Kislevite. Krakov's face was scarlet, and he was staring at the ground with embarrassment as he shifted guiltily from one foot to the other.

'We could've been enjoying the hospitality of the Slaughtered Troll by now,' Stanislav, the great bear of a man continued, a dreamy look in his eyes. 'I would've drunk old Alexi under the table–'

'As usual,' Oran muttered.

'– and Serena would be sitting on my lap right now, saying how much she loves me.'

'Like she does any fool who's more generous than he is sober,' Torben laughed.

Stanislav scowled at the band's raven-haired leader, but not for long. His broad face broke into a grin. 'That's my Serena, and it does a man's heart good to hear it.'

'But we're not in Ostermark!' Yuri sulked.

'We should head for this place, Ostenwald,' Alexi suggested. 'It's only five miles away.'

'I agree,' Oran stated firmly.

Torben looked up at the signpost again. It was the only man-made object in sight on the blasted heath. The main body of the sign was a sturdy stake hammered firmly into the ground with an arrowed board pointing towards the east, carved with the name 'Ostermark'. The letters had then been picked out in red to make them stand out further. Pointing in the opposite direction was a much smaller, age-weathered sign, no doubt a remnant of a previous signpost. The faded lettering, once painted with an unsteady hand, read 'Ostenwald, 5 miles'.

'I thought we were looking for work, especially since Krakov lost our horses,' Yuri complained. 'We should head for Ostermark!'

'Yuri's right,' Torben declared, sheathing his sword. 'The village may be closer but look at the sign: it's tiny. I've seen bigger signs on privy doors. I bet this Ostenwald isn't much more than a few hovels and a hen house. There probably isn't even a tavern!' He was in full flow now, gesticulating expansively. 'No, there won't be any work for us there. Ostermark it is. We'll press on for a couple of hours, camp by the roadside for the night, and be there in the morning.'

Dusk was drawing on, the last lingering rays of the sun giving way to twilight, as the party set off along the eastern road.

THEY HAD BARELY been on the road for ten minutes when the thunder of hooves approached on the road behind him. Torben turned, along with the rest of the band, and at once saw the carriage speeding through the grey twilight towards them. As one, the mercenaries threw themselves out of the way, landing in the dirt at the side of the road.

Torben looked over his shoulder as the vehicle bumped past them. Plush red velvet drapes flapped from the windows of the black carriage. A family crest picked out in gold on its side also attested to the fact that its owner was someone of noble background and with, no doubt, the riches to match.

The silhouettes of two figures could be seen in the driver's seat at the front of the careering vehicle. The coachman lay slumped at the reins: Torben assumed he was dead. Next to the body, a young woman was struggling to control the racing horses but without success. The carriage was out of control.

In seconds Torben was up and running after the carriage. As he drew level with the vehicle, Torben grabbed hold, leaped and swung himself up into the driver's seat next to the young woman. Gasping with her exertions, she shot him a wild-eyed look.

'If you'll allow me, my lady,' the mercenary said, flashing the terrified woman a smile, and gently took the reins from her. Coaxing words to the horses from the mercenary captain were accompanied by a firm hand on the reins.

By now Stanislav and Yuri were running alongside the horses, the creatures' bridles in their hands. In only a few moments the frightened animals had slowed to a trot, and then came to a halt. The carriage came to rest behind them.

Torben turned again towards the young woman. His eyes widened as his gaze progressed upwards from her delicate ankles and the gold-braided hem of her blue velvet dress. Her features were delicately set within the slender frame of her face. A stray tress of auburn hair caressed a pale cheek. Anxious emerald green eyes peered back at him from beneath the hood of her travelling cloak.

Her dress was of the latest cut and made from the finest materials. A silver brooch, inlaid with gemstones, held her cloak in place. All these things, along with the opulence of the carriage and the quality of the horses, no farmyard nags, spoke to Torben with money's voice.

'They killed my driver!' she blurted out, having recovered her breath.

'Who did?' asked Torben, startled by her outburst.

'The villagers. Oh, please help me!' she gasped.

'You are safe now,' Stanislav said, trying to reassure the girl.

'I– I wish it were that simple,' she said with unashamed despair.

'What is it? What's the matter?' Torben pressed.

'I must get to Ostermark! I must petition Lord Gunther for his help!' Her voice carried a vehemence Torben would not have expected from this waif-like girl. 'A terrible evil has arisen in my village.'

'Ostenwald, you mean?' Krakov asked.

'The same,' she nodded. 'I know you will probably find this hard to believe... but the dead have risen from their graves!'

'Oh, I don't know. We've seen a few strange things ourselves,' Torben said by way of encouragement.

'Those who have not already fled are now under a foul curse! I flee for my life, for they chase me even now!' The young woman peered anxiously back over her shoulder, before continuing. 'I must get help! I just hope that the fortune my late father left will be enough to persuade Lord Gunther to put an end to this evil. As commander of the militia he will be able to send armed men to stop them. He will surely help after all the years he served with my father in the Elector Count's cavalry!'

The girl looked exhausted through fear and anxiety. Torben took her cold, trembling hands in his. 'Do not worry,' he said, reassuringly. 'We will help you on your way.' The mercenary jumped down from the carriage, pushing the coachman's body before him, and placed a firm hand on the black-robed Kislevite's shoulder. 'Krakov, make up for losing our mounts by driving... I'm sorry, I didn't catch your name,' he said, looking up at the woman with a smile.

She looked down shyly. 'I am the Lady Isolde.'

'By driving the Lady Isolde to the city.'

The one-eyed Krakov needed no more encouragement and clambered up into the driver's seat. Torben supposed that he was pleased to be getting a lift to Ostermark ahead of the rest of them; no doubt the thought of a rest from the endless ribbing had also entered his mind.

'Let's see if you can keep hold of these horses: after all, at least these are tied to the carriage. We'll see you in the Slaughtered Troll tomorrow, at noon.'

The mercenary captain was suddenly aware of shouts in the distance. Peering through the dusky gloom, Torben could make out a crowd of peasants charging towards them from the direction of Ostenwald. Their hair was lank and matted, while their clothes were caked with mud. The crazed mob was howling rabidly and the mercenary could just make out gruff shouts of, 'Stop her! She has to die!' They were waving an assortment of axes, clubs and farm implements above their heads; others carried blazing torches.

'It's them!' the Lady Isolde screamed, looking back in horror at the approaching crowd. 'You must kill them!'

Having caught sight of the mercenaries, the villagers appeared to become even more enraged, the front-runners putting on a burst of speed.

'Don't worry, we'll deal with them,' Torben said coolly. 'Go – now!'

With a loud cry, Krakov whipped the horses into a gallop and without another word the carriage sped away towards Ostermark.

'I don't think they're going to be open to the idea of civilised discussion,' Alexi said, unslinging his bow from his shoulder as he eyed the dishevelled villagers.

'Well there's five of us,' Yuri said, notching an arrow to his own bow, 'and–'

'Lots of them,' Stanislav finished.

'So let's even up the odds,' Torben smiled, taking aim along a flighted shaft. 'When you're ready, lads!'

Five black shafts shot across the dimming sky. Four of the mob's leaders stumbled and fell, and remained still.

'Never mind, Oran,' Torben chuckled as the fifth arrow embedded itself in the road. 'Better luck next time, eh?'

The rat-faced man cursed under his breath. 'Never did like long-ranged weapons,' he muttered. 'A dagger, up close. That's more my style.'

The deaths of their fellows did nothing to halt the rampaging crowd but merely seemed to spur the men on, if men they were. From their bedraggled appearance Torben could almost believe that they were nothing more than the dead risen from their graves!

'And again!' Torben called over the furious shouts of the lynch-mob. A second volley of arrows soared through the air and found their mark in the seething crowd.

Then the villagers were upon them. The mercenary band just had time to drop their bows and unsheathe their weapons. The battle lasted only a few minutes. In a series of well-practised strokes, the trained soldiers despatched the crazed thugs. Placing a foot against a man's chest, Torben pulled his sword free of his last opponent's body. The man fell spread-eagled onto the road, the sharpened fence-post he was using as a club rolling from his hand. The mercenary looked around for another opponent but there was none.

'Well, that was kind of easy,' Stanislav stated.

'Nothing to it for fighting men like us,' Torben boasted.

'So maybe there was something to her ladyship's story after all,' Yuri pondered.

'Maybe there was,' Torben agreed. And yet at the back of his mind he couldn't help thinking that the villagers hadn't really behaved as if driven by dark sorcery. They had still cried out in pain like the living.

'She said she needed help,' Yuri reminded his companions.

'And she mentioned a family fortune!' Stanislav added.

Torben stroked his beard with a large, rough hand for a moment. 'Tell you what,' he said, finally, 'why don't we go and sort out whatever's going on in Ostenwald. Then Lady Isolde will reward us, instead of this lord that she's gone to petition.'

All but one of the others smiled and nodded in agreement. Torben looked at them, grinning broadly at his own cunning suggestion.

'I told you we should've headed for the village,' Oran muttered under his breath.

I AM RUNNING AGAIN. Branches whip across my face. Sharp twigs, like a crone's fingernails, tear my skin. I can no longer hear the wolves behind me.

I burst free of the tangled wood and stop. A menacing shadow looms up tall out of the darkness. I am standing at the foot of a grey, stone tower. Against the pall of night, small black shapes flit around its ruined turrets.

And then I am flying with the bats. My wings beat against the night as I circle the tower in a jerky spiral. Beneath me the crumbling walls taper as they stretch towards the ground. The moon hangs waning in the sky, seemingly only wing-beats away. Its chill light illuminates an arched window near the top of the tower, and from within the opening a figure watches me. Cruel eyes stare out of a face as cold and white as the moon. Their gaze pierces my soul. I recognise the face. It is a face that has haunted my dreams for an eternity. It is my own.

* * *

THE WHETSTONE scraped along the edge of the blade, and off the end with a deep ringing sound. The flickering firelight picked out the noble, yet haggard, features that gave the young man an appearance beyond his years. He paused in his preparations and looked up at the moon. 'It is almost time, Walter,' he stated with finality.

'Aye,' the ageing manservant replied. 'Tonight the beast will finally die.'

Pieter's eyes glazed over as he remembered for the hundredth time the events of the last seven days.

A week ago he had been a different man, care-free and full of youthful optimism, firm in the knowledge that he loved another with a passion and was loved in return in equal measure. Now he was a shell of his former self, dedicated to one purpose only and his actions fuelled by his desire for vengeance. How he longed for those carefree days of youth that now seemed years ago.

But it had been only seven nights since Pieter Valburg, only son of the mayor of Schwertdorf, had returned from the wars to find his beloved Rosamund on her death-bed. They had known each other since childhood, Rosamund's father being the lord of Grunwald, only ten miles from Pieter's own home. It was no secret that their families had always planned that they should marry but over the years a youthful friendship had grown into deeply-felt love. The union of the houses of Valburg and Reichter would go ahead to the delight of all, founded on true love and with no sham of affection.

But then the Elector of Ostermark had called on the services of brave young men throughout the province to defend against the incursions of orcs and goblins from within the Great Forest. Pieter himself was called up and he rode away to war with equal measures of anticipation, for what was to come, and sorrow, at having to leave his dear Rosamund. But he knew that he would eventually return bringing glory and honour to his family.

Indeed, in time, the Battle of Riesenbad was won. Pieter returned home at a gallop and made straight for Grunwald. The first signs of spring were visible in the land and the sun was shining. However, upon his triumphant arrival at Lord Reichter's house, Pieter was greeted with the most tragic news. While he had been away fighting, his betrothed had been taken seriously ill by what the family physician described as a 'disease of the blood'. Rushing to her chamber he had found Rosamund a pale, wasted shell of the woman he had left only a few months before. That night he kept vigil by her bedside, but overcome by tiredness after his long journey he finally, if unwillingly, gave in to sleep.

He had been woken as the clocks chimed midnight to see a shadow slip from the room through the open window. He looked immediately to his betrothed only to find her already dead.

The black veil of mourning was drawn over the household and at the physician's urging Rosamund was buried the very next day. But during the very next night her grave had been disturbed, by wolves the gravedigger had said, and her body taken. For most that was the end of it, but Pieter knew better. On his return to his family home, Walter, his family's oldest and most loyal retainer had taken him aside and told him the legend of Count Morderischen.

It was said that during his evil lifetime there were no depths of depravity to which the lord of Ostenwald Tower would not sink. He was even accused of stealing and eating babies from the local villages. A hundred years ago the bloodthirsty count had been put to death by the enraged peasants and imprisoned inside the Morderischen family tomb. The village of Ostenwald lay only a league away and to Walter it was clear what had happened. Somehow the monster had returned from the dead and taken Rosamund.

Other people told Pieter not to listen, dismissing Walter as a superstitious old fool. But in his grief Pieter was prepared to accept any story, no matter how outlandish. He had always thought himself a rational man but his anguish needed an outlet. If there was any chance that what Walter told him was true he had to follow it up – he had to go to Ostenwald.

'All is ready,' Walter said, carefully placing another sharpened whitethorn stake on the ground next to the fire.

'Tonight my love will be avenged,' Pieter said. It was not a point to be debated. Placing the whetstone against the gleaming edge of his grandfather's sword he resumed sharpening.

TORBEN STOPPED at the cross-roads around which Ostenwald huddled and looked around. Before him was a patch of dying

grass that he assumed was the village green. The eaves of the
low buildings were picked out by the silvery light of the rising
moon. A number of miserable-looking women and children
returned his gaze before doors and shutters daubed with sacred
symbols were slammed shut and locked.

'Friendly lot round here, aren't they?' Oran said sullenly.

'We should pity these people, not mock them,' Alexi said and
Stanislav grunted his own disapproval.

Torben had seen places like this on many occasions. They
were in a run-down village inhabited by a fearful populace,
who dared not venture out after dark.

'There's something wrong here,' Yuri said quietly.

'Oh, you noticed,' Oran sneered.

Ignoring the bickering of the others Torben continued his
survey of the village. Overlooking it, atop a wooded hill, the
pinnacle of a ruined and overgrown tower pointed into the
night's sky like a twisted finger. Torben looked from one mercenary to the next.

'Come on, let's not waste any time where we're not welcome,'
he said gruffly. 'Her ladyship said the dead have risen. To the
cemetery!'

THE MOON'S COLD, unwelcoming light cast eerie shadows among
the tombs and gravestones as the mercenary band advanced
through the cemetery. 'I don't mind telling you, I do not like
this,' Oran carped to anyone who might be listening.

Yuri froze. 'What was that?' he hissed.

'What was what?' Stanislav asked.

'I heard something. A skittering sound, like the shifting of
loose soil.' His words slowed as he realised what he was
saying.

Torben turned. 'Hush, you fools!' he hissed. 'There's nothing
th–'

The mercenary captain heard the snap of a twig behind him
and spun round, half expecting to come face-to-face with the
living dead. But looking back at him were the steely eyes of a
stern-faced, smartly-dressed young man, almost a head shorter
than Torben and still very much alive. He had a finely-honed
sword gripped in one hand, pointing at Torben chest. Behind
him stood a hunched and balding old man, stiff in his formal
servant's attire.

'Who are you and what are you doing here?' the young man hissed.

Torben smiled broadly, keeping a close eye on the gleaming blade. 'My name is Torben Badenov and these are my companions. Our business is our affair. I could ask the same of you.'

'I am Pieter Valburg. My reason for being here is an honourable one.' Torben raised an eyebrow. 'I have come to avenge the death of my beloved.'

'In a graveyard?' Oran burst out incredulously. 'Who killed your sweetheart?'

'The vampire who is buried here,' the old man stated coldly.

'A vampire? What makes you so sure?' Torben said.

Pieter began to explain: 'Walter, my retainer, says–'

'This old man? What does he know?' Torben declaimed, gently lowering Pieter's blade with his hand. 'We too have come to sort out what's going on here but I'm sure it has nothing to do with the living dead! We should talk.'

'THIS IS IT: the Morderischen family tomb,' Walter said sombrely, nodding at the grim edifice before which the seven of them now stood. Grotesque gargoyles leered down from the edge of the circle of light cast by the old manservant's lantern. Beyond the rusted railings and chained iron gates, stone steps led downwards into darkness.

'So this is where your vampire is supposed to reside.' Torben took in the carved skulls that reminded the observer of the ever-present certainty of death.

'Homely, isn't it.' A hint of uncertainty tinged Oran's usual sarcastic tone.

'The legend goes that one hundred years ago a priest of Sigmar, assisted by a band of noble adventurers, defeated the evil creature who dwelt in that tower over there on the hill,' Walter explained.

Torben again looked towards the grim structure, now overgrown with thorns. Its silhouette stood black against the deep blue of night.

'The victorious priest imprisoned the count in the tomb of his forefathers here,' the old man continued. 'The villagers, in revenge for the murders the monster had perpetrated, wrecked the tower.'

'So why all the trouble now?' Alexi asked.

'It would appear that, after a century, the power of the ward-ings used to seal the tomb have faded and the horror inside has reawakened.'

'Look at this place!' Yuri exclaimed. 'The gates are locked and rusted up. No one's been in or out of here for years. You're wrong, old man.'

'No, it is here,' the retainer insisted. 'Its kind are not stopped by locks!'

The moon was high in the night's sky and Torben was aware of a disconcerting howling coming from the direction of the wood.

'We cannot delay,' Pieter pressed, anxiously. 'We must enter the tomb.'

Torben tested the chain securing the gates. 'Come on, lads,' he managed to say with forced levity. 'We might as well take a look now we're here. Stanislav, if you would be so kind…'

The bear-like ex-soldier stepped up to the gates, lifting the double-headed axe from his belt. With one effortless swipe the chain was shattered, the sound of the broken links rattling onto cracked flagstones echoing around the silent cemetery. Taking hold of the rusted iron bars Torben tugged on the gates. Metal grated on stone as corroded hinges screeched in protest at being forced to open once more.

The party paused, listening to the echo fade between the gravestones.

'Remember, it shall be I who lands the killing blow,' Pieter insisted. 'I owe it to my Rosamund.'

Torben nodded. Taking a step forward, he peered into the darkness of the crypt.

An angry hiss from behind them made the whole party turn round sharply. By the moon's cold light they could see a figure crouched, cat-like, on the bough of a tree, the wind whistling mournfully through the branches. The man's lank hair waved behind him in the breeze and he appeared to be wearing the ragged clothes of a nobleman. More figures moved among the shadows of the cemetery, emerging from behind gravestones and tombs. Their various forms of dress revealed them to be men and women from all parts of society.

'What do you want?' Pieter challenged the advancing figures, unable to hide his nervousness.

'We want you,' the nobleman in the tree hissed.

'Our lord must feed,' a young peasant woman hissed. 'He will feast on your life energies.' The girl smiled and Torben saw the first glistening points of fangs breaking through bleeding gums.

'By Sigmar!' Alexi gasped.

At that moment the vampires attacked. The creatures sprang at the mortals, fingernails raking the air as they tried to tear at the adventurers' throats. Swords were yanked from scabbards and battle was joined.

'Take them while they are still weak!' Walter commanded.

'Weak?' Oran gasped, deflecting a taloned fist with his sword. 'I'd hate to see them when they're feeling stronger!'

Torben counted half a dozen or so among the brood. All had obviously still been young when they died, just as they were young in undeath. Despite that, the vampires fought with agility and strength increased by a supernatural vitality.

Torben swung his sword at the inhuman noble. The stroke opened a great gash across the vampire's chest through his shirt. The man stumbled backwards at the blow and collapsed over a gravestone.

'One down,' the mercenary said to himself with a grin, and span to face the other creatures.

Torben suddenly found himself hurled bodily to the ground with the hissing nobleman furiously tearing at the mail armour over his jerkin with its talons. Twisting to one side, the warrior used his bulk to throw the clawing vampire from him. Quickly getting to his feet, he watched open mouthed as the wound he had dealt the man closed bloodlessly before his very eyes.

'By Queen Katarin's sword!' he exclaimed. 'What does it take to stop these things?'

It was all the mercenaries could do to fend off the vampires' slashing claws. Torben was horrified at how the creatures caught their blades with bare hands, showing no discomfort whatsoever. And all the while their assailants cursed them.

'The coming of our master is at hand!' a vampire proclaimed. 'Can you not feel it?'

Torben could almost believe that the wind rose as the words were spoken.

'You will all fall before him,' the peasant girl snarled, 'and he will drain your very lives from you!'

Out of the corner of his eye Torben saw Oran duck as another undead youth launched himself insect-like from a gravestone. Oran sent the vampire sprawling onto the ground with an up thrust punch from a bony fist. But as soon as the rat-faced mercenary was crouched, with his dagger drawn, the vampire was also on its feet again, ready to attack.

Stanislav was backed up against the tomb, struggling to fend off a vehement attack from a fanged maiden. Yuri looked up panting, his fringe flopping in front of his eyes. He had blood on his face, although it was not clear whether it was his own or his attacker's.

The peasant girl leapt at Torben. Without hesitation, he parried her outstretched claws with his sword but even this did not stop her. The girl continued to advance, even as her left hand flopped uselessly at her side.

'They won't die!' Yuri yelled as a farm-hand, his body a mass of open wounds, picked himself up once more and continued his assault.

'The beast must be killed!' Walter shouted over the clamour of battle. 'It is the unholy energies which he draws to this place that keeps them alive! If he dies, so will they! Hurry!'

The old manservant darted off, his lantern a bobbing sphere of light vanishing down the steps into the tomb.

'Where does the old fool think he's going?' Torben exclaimed in disbelief.

'We cannot let him go alone!' Pieter shouted back. Evading a blow from his attacker, Pieter followed.

'You go. We'll deal with these,' Oran said, sinking his blade deep into a vampire's side.

Torben looked towards the tomb. If this was the sort of opposition they could expect to find out here, then down those stone steps was the last place he wanted to go.

LEAPING DOWN the steps two at a time, Pieter stumbled to a halt at the bottom, just ahead of the puffing Walter. Pieter took in every detail in the crypt as he realised abruptly that he had at last reached his goal.

They were standing at the edge of a long rectangular chamber which continued beyond stone archways to both left and right. Burnt-out torches rested in sconces around the walls. The reassuring orange glow cast by the lantern illuminated the vaulted ceiling of the crypt, but picking out glowering gargoyles much like those that adorned its exterior. A number of stone coffins lay within the tomb. Several had been smashed open, their lids now so much broken masonry scattering the cracked flag-stoned floor. In the centre of the chamber stood two tombs, grander than the rest. Only one still remained intact. Standing before it was a young woman, beautiful in death as she had been in life, still wearing the white shift in which she had been buried.

'Hello, Pieter.' Her voice was richly seductive.

Pieter stared back at her, open-mouthed. 'Rosamund!'

'I don't believe it, young master,' Walter gasped.

Rosamund's long black hair cascaded down over her shoulders, as luxurious as Pieter had ever seen it. Her ivory skin glowed with an inner vitality and her captivating blue eyes looked back at him longingly. To see his Rosamund alive again, when he had held her cold, frail body against his after her heart had stopped beating, was beyond rational comprehension.

'I've missed you, Pieter. Have you missed me?' Her voice was soft as velvet.

'But... you're dead,' was all he could manage.

'I was dead, Pieter, but now I am truly alive,' she said.

'This can't be real,' he spluttered, raising his sword.

'But it is, Pieter. Join me and nothing will ever separate us again.'

'She's no longer your sweetheart, master!' Walter insisted but Pieter only half-heard him. He was gripped by terrified indecision. He could still hardly believe what he was witnessing. The only rational explanation for Rosamund being here now was that she had become like those creatures he had just encountered and yet that in itself was irrational!

'It only takes a kiss,' Rosamund said. 'One kiss and we can be together, forever.'

He began to lower his sword. To be together, that was all he had ever wanted. Pieter stepped slowly forward, gazing into Rosamund's sparkling blue eyes as tears ran from his own. At the edge of his consciousness, he could hear Walter's desperate voice. But with every step the voice became quieter and quieter until he did not notice it at all. All he heard was the soothing voice of his beloved and all he saw was her radiant smile, welcoming him back into her embrace.

And then his mind was awash with a series of confusing images. Walter was between them, a sharpened stake in his hand. And Rosamund no longer had her arms outstretched to embrace him. Instead taloned hands were raised, ready to tear out his throat, while ugly fangs protruded over her sweet cherry lips.

There was a flash of lantern-light and Walter's arm bent down at the elbow at an awkward angle. The old man cried out in pain but his screams became a horrible gurgling as Rosamund's head darted snake-like towards his neck. Walter's body went limp and was flung aside like a rag-doll, landing heavily on top of the unopened coffin. Hissing and spitting the vampire that had once been his sweet Rosamund moved towards Pieter. Horrified, he looked on, stunned into inaction.

'Wh– what have you done?' he spluttered, aghast. 'Rosamund would never have harmed another creature!'

'That was the old Rosamund,' the creature hissed.

'And you are not her!' Pieter roared, raising his sword.

Rosamund's eyes were suddenly wide open in shock. The vampire let out a blood-chilling scream as a rusted spear tip burst through her chest, sullying the white shift with black, half-congealed blood. The broken shaft of the railing had pierced her dead heart. When she stopped twitching, her talons dropped to her side and her eyes closed for the last time. The girl's body slumped to the floor and lay motionless. Torben let go of the broken railing and span about, panting for breath. Pieter was standing completely still, staring fixedly at the corpse of his beloved.

'She was no longer human,' Torben said, his voice full of regret, 'she was a thing. She is at rest now.'

The young man said nothing.

Looking back to the girl's body, Torben saw that she had indeed found the true peace of death at last.

The body of the old retainer lay slumped face-down over the lid of the unopened sarcophagus. A trickle of blood from the dead man's torn throat glinted darkly in the flickering lantern-light. Only half aware of what was happening, Torben watched as the precious, life-giving fluid collected in a small fissure in the coffin lid, then trickled through a crack into the sarcophagus

* * *

SOMETHING STIRS ME, like a voice calling me back to somewhere I once knew. In the all-encompassing darkness I feel myself floating upwards. It is as if I am rising from the dark scarlet depths of an ocean. Above me lapping crimson light beckons.

I can see things beyond the surface. It is as cold as the grave but I can feel the warmth of living bodies close by. I can hear the beating of their warm hearts. I can smell the sweet blood in their veins, hear it pumping through their arteries, taste it in my mouth.

And I know what it is to hunger again.

PIETER WAS SUDDENLY aware of a cold wind blowing through the crypt. Leaves from outside were lifted in spiralling eddies that danced among the tombs. 'We have to finish it,' the young man stated with grim resolution, taking a whitethorn stake from his pack. Torben Badenov nodded.

Bracing themselves against the lid of the coffin, they pushed with all that remained of their strength. With a hollow grating noise, the stone lid slid slowly across the top of the granite sarcophagus. Pieter winced and turned away gasping as stale air, heavy with the stench of decay, escaped from the coffin along with a wisp of red mist. Opening his eyes, he peered cautiously into the sarcophagus.

Inside the stone coffin lay a skeleton, the skull thrown back as if the occupant had died in tortured agony. To all intents and purposes the skeleton appeared to be human, apart from the extended fangs that forced the jaws open in a rictus grin. Finger bones ended in long talons while a portion of the ribcage was shattered.

The wind was rising rapidly and Pieter could feel the hairs on the back of his neck rising. A miasma of dark energy crackled around the edge of the coffin. Pieter could feel its it tingle in his fingertips. His pulse quickened.

Walter's blood had collected in a small pool beneath the remains, where it had begun to bubble and hiss strangely, evaporating to become a cloud of red steam. Pieter was unable to tear his gaze from the skeleton, as through the mist he witnessed a terrible transformation. Flesh was coalescing out of the red cloud and attaching itself to the bones. Cords of sinew stretched over the skeleton, pulling the joints into position and binding them together. At the same time tendrils of muscle

lashed around the calcified remains, swelling and twitching
with new life. Despite his panic, Pieter found himself thinking
that the effect was not unlike watching a wax candle melting in
a fire, only rapidly in reverse.

As the musculature crawled over the vampire's chest, the broken ribs were pulled back into place and knitted together.
Pieter could see a leathery black organ swelling inside the
ribcage with every bellows-like convulsion. Uncurling ears
peeled away from the skull and stretched into bat-like points.
Balls of yellow fat condensed in the eye sockets as the corpse
continued to re-flesh under Pieter's own horrified gaze. New,
red-raw eyelids flicked open and the men looked into the
night-black pupils of an evil creature who had been born of
darkness centuries before.

With a roar, the dead torches around the walls burst into
flame. The wind had risen to a gale. Glancing at Torben, Pieter
could see that the mercenary's hair was standing on end – as,
he could feel, was his own.

'Quickly! Do it now!' Torben yelled over the howling gale.

Pieter raised the stake over the vampire's regenerating body.
With a shout born of fury, frustration and despair he plunged
the whitethorn down towards the creature's black, pumping
heart.

His hand was suddenly halted as, with lightning speed, the
vampire's own skeletal hand seized his wrist in a grip of iron.
Pieter watched helplessly as the skinless horror sat up in the
coffin, meat still solidifying on its bones. An unnerving hiss
escaped from between the vampire's fattening lips and a
pointed tongue darted from between its bestial fangs.

Then the mercenary was between them, the rusted railing in
his hands once more. With one vicious thrust, the spear-like tip
passed easily through the creature's ribs and punctured the
black bag of muscle that was the vampire's heart. The half-
formed, undead creature opened its mouth to scream, jaw
ligaments tearing, but its useless lungs had already begun to
collapse. All that issued from the dying vampire's throat was a
rasping breath that stank of death and decay.

The crypt was suddenly a hive of activity. Somehow free of
the vampire brood, the rest of the party burst into the tomb.
The hulking Stanislav ran forward, a sexton's spade gripped in
his hands. With one swing, the blunt edge of the spade

separated the vampire's head from its shoulders and sent it sailing across the crypt. Its corpse began to decompose at once. New-formed flesh shrivelled and turned to dust, swirling around the coffin in tiny eddies. In seconds all that remained of the vampire were a few crumbling bones. Stanislav strode over to the corner of the crypt where the creature's head had landed. With one stamp of his boot, the deformed skull was shattered against the flag-stoned floor.

The mercenary leader looked down at the contents of the coffin and ran a hand through his thick black hair. 'I told you we should have gone to Ostermark,' he said.

THE GREAT BONFIRE hissed and crackled as the bodies of the vampires were burnt to ash. The funeral pyre bathed the graveyard and particularly the Morderischen family tomb in flickering orange light. Yet despite the eerily-moving shadows the carved gargoyles did not seem quite so menacing anymore. Pieter sat staring disconsolately into the flames, looking at something in another time and place. His eyes were dry. He would shed no more tears.

He had been wracked all night with conflicting feelings of grief, unfairness and anger. Rosamund was gone. Walter was dead. In one night he had seen what cruelties the world had to offer. Pieter looked down at the slab of stone covering Walter's grave, on which he sat. The wolves would not have him.

It was less than an hour from dawn and the moon was beginning to set. Although none of them had slept, Torben and his companions were preparing to leave.

'How's your arm?' Torben asked Yuri.

'Better now it's bandaged,' Yuri said.

'Thank Sigmar the creatures out here dropped dead when you killed that monster in the crypt,' Stanislav said.

'We'd all have been dead men otherwise,' Alexi agreed, hitching up his sling.

'We'd better be off.' The mercenary captain was in good humour after the night's events. 'We've got to meet up with Krakov and the lovely Lady Isolde,' he said with a grin. 'Come one, lads. We'll be in Ostermark by noon.' He turned to Pieter. 'What will you do now?'

The young man shrugged.

'You could come with us,' Torben suggested almost casually. 'Besides, we need you as a witness to what happened here last night.'

'That's right. The Lady Isolde will believe a man of your breeding,' Yuri said.

'Why not?' Pieter said with a shrug.

'Oh fine,' Oran muttered quietly. 'Another pocket to split the gold with. Just what we need.'

'That's settled then,' Torben said with a smile. Adjusting his pack, he turned towards the lightening sky to the east. 'I hope Krakov's got the first round in.'

FROM THE BASE of the tower on the hill overlooking Ostenwald, the Lady Isolde watched the funeral pyre burn with piercing green eyes. She inhaled deeply, savouring the smell of the roasting corpses carried on the breeze. The mercenary band had been a good choice and the girl's distraught sweetheart an unexpected bonus.

She turned her gaze from the cemetery and patted the head of her newest servant almost affectionately. The shrivelled one-eyed thing dressed in black, ill-fitting clothes at her side grunted in response as a cat might purr at being stroked. 'Good boy, Krakov,' she breathed. She had never had a Kislevite in her thrall before.

Those fool priests a century ago had underestimated her. They had thought that her brother was the stronger of the siblings and so had spent longer binding him inside his coffin. That had been the advantage she needed as over time the charms sealing her own tomb had lost their potency.

Now her cruel brother would never control her again. She would become the mistress of Ostenwald Tower and the surrounding countryside. The peasantry would be as cattle to her, there merely as a source of sustenance or assistance as she saw fit.

'Sleep well, brother,' the Lady Isolde purred and a smile parted her full red lips. As she smiled, the last rays of moonlight caught the glistening point of an elongated incisor.

THE CHAOS BENEATH

Mark Brendan

IN THE DANK, subterranean depths of the Marienburg Grand Sewer network, more than effluent was being carried along the crumbling, cavernous conduits. The stark glare of the flaming torches held aloft by four sinister, robed figures projected dancing shadows upon the tortured frame of a man dragged along the waste channel between them.

The captive was clad in fine, black leather britches and riding boots. Above the waist he had been stripped, revealing a gaudy patchwork of lurid bruises and angry red weals where a lash had bitten him, and most disturbing of all a mass of blisters and scabs which traced an unearthly, sinuous pattern where he had recently been branded on his breast. The cluster of sores formed a circular hub, from which a broad point projected from the bottom left quadrant, and a lithe tail twisted away from the top right to form a design as strangely fluid as the flames which had imprinted it onto the victim's flesh. A sack of purple velvet covered the man's head and was securely knotted around his throat, so that he was forced to stumble along, being shoved, kicked and whipped in the correct direction.

Passing beyond the grand arches of the main channel, they entered a little-used part of the system, where the walls once more narrowed about them like the jaws of a great serpent. It was here that they came upon a bizarre little iron bound door and the journey came to its end as the cultist bearing the lash unlocked the portal and the group passed into the dim glow beyond.

The room within was of a comfortable size to accommodate perhaps twenty or more people and had a high, vaulted ceiling. Low swirls of thick, choking incense from braziers situated around the walls carpeted the tiled floor. The central area of this floor was dominated by a huge mosaic, with a pattern delineated in slivers of coloured glass, marble and shell which bore a strong resemblance to the brand seared on to the prisoner's torso. At the centre of the design, four shackles anchored to the floor by thick steel chains awaited a victim.

On the opposite side of the chamber from the door was a slightly raised platform, upon which stood a large throne of twisted black wood and purple velvet. A tall, feminine silhouette rose from this throne and came down from the platform to stand before the circle. Like the other cultists she wore a long, deep purple robe, but rather than being belted by a simple cord, hers was a thick leather belt with a large, wrought-iron skull for a clasp. Also, there were long vents up to her hips in the sides of the robes, beneath which she wore fine purple velvet trousers and soft, doeskin boots. The tall figure wore her hood down, in contrast to the other disciples, and her face was concealed by an ornate black ballroom mask shaped like a raven. Delicate mother-of-pearl inlay chased around the eye slits of the mask, behind which blazed violet irises, and edged the elegant beak too, whilst a spectacular spray of midnight black feathers held soft golden hair back from her temples.

'Let the offering be brought forward to the circle,' she announced in a clear, cultured voice. At her behest, the four cultists thrust their prisoner forward into the circle and more robed figures hurried forth from the shadows to spread-eagle him in the centre of the mosaic. Only once he was securely shackled to the floor was the bag removed from the prisoner's head. His face bore none of the marks of the torment his body had suffered in the cultists' care, and for the briefest of instants his clear grey eyes locked upon the dreamy violet orbits of the figure looming over him, before he closed his eyelids in despair and submission. His jaw was clean shaven, and his features lean and predatory, with a suggestion of strong lineage in both his high forehead, with its sweeping collar-length black hair, and in the long, straight line of his nasal bridge.

'Well, well, well,' the woman mocked. 'Obediah Cain, second lieutenant of the Church of Sigmar's Holy Inquisition in Marienburg. You are welcome as our very special guest of honour. Indeed, you might even say that we need you.'

'Do what you will with me, witch!' groaned the man on the floor. 'Remember that when judgement comes, it is final!'

'It is good that you have given up all notion of redemption, and you are now looking to history for vindication,' the masked woman spat. 'For when M'Loch T'Chort, Weaver of the Ways, High Daemonic Prince of Twisted Destiny and Misguided Fate, comes to seize possession of your miserable skin, the last thing he needs is some lost soul contesting his right to it.'

With that, she delivered a stinging kick to his ribs, causing him to whimper as the scabs on his brand cracked with the force.

'It's such a shame that we have to inflict punishment on your earthly clay before our lord can take up residence within it, but as you witch hunters are always so fond of demonstrating, the prisoner's co-operation isn't adequate grounds to carry on to the next stage of the procedure. You, more than anyone, should appreciate what is required to ensure the veracity of any actions or claims made by a prisoner, because, after all, their co-operation might be a falsehood to avoid torture. Isn't that the option presented to your victims, witch hunter?' she asked, bending down so that her face was close to his own pained visage. 'Isn't it, you pious worm?' she howled when he did not answer, and dug the points of her gauntleted fingers into the weeping wound on his chest.

'Yes! Yes it is, damn you!' sobbed the broken man squirming on the floor.

'Very good,' she said evenly, and stood up once more. 'Then let us begin the rite.'

The dozen or so cultists in the room took up positions around the circle and began to sway rhythmically, chanting in alien, melodious tongues an otherworldly mantra of damnation which rose up from the strange vaulted room and out into the still night beyond, inviting a thing which should not be into the realm of living men.

Led on by the strange, powerful sorceress, the cultists' performance became more frenetic, their exhortations more desperate, and a singular change began to take place within the eerily lit room. The heavy clouds of incense drifting languidly at waist height coalesced in the centre of the chamber, above the recumbent witch hunter, and then spiralled upwards into a point like some grotesque, ectoplasmic worm rearing its swollen bulk out of the foetid soil. The tip of the apparition dipped towards the unconscious man's face and infiltrated his mouth and nostrils, feeding itself, coil after coil into his twitching, choking body.

The ritual's leader suddenly ceased her rapturous chanting to command, 'It is time. Let the sacrifice be brought forth for the Sanguinary Binding!'

From a curtained alcove in the shadowy chamber, a nightspawned abomination of uncommon vileness shambled into the circle. It was a man in stature but, through constant exposure to the warping malignancy of the Chaos lord, Tzeentch, his head had puckered and inflated like an over-ripe fruit, the skin thick, wrinkled and lurid pink in hue, his mouth a broad, grinning slash filled with row after row of sharp, blackened fangs and his scalp studded with starfish's suckers in place of hair. His left arm, too, had become severely mutated and was grossly elongated and jointed in four places, covered in tough pink skin like his face, while the hand on the end of the offensive limb had grown to absurd proportions and its eight thick fingers were hollow tubes. In the daemonic limb he held a struggling lamb, while in his other, human hand he carried a large sacrificial knife. Taking up position over the witch hunter, the mutant prepared to complete the ceremony with a blood sacrifice.

Despite everything that Obediah Cain had been through, some spark of his original consciousness yet remained untainted by the invading entity, and the unacceptable presence of a Chaos mutant hovering over him stirred that faint ember into scintillating action. Cain did the only thing he could under the circumstances – he brought his knee up sharply, as far as the chains would permit, into the creature's shin. It was enough to cause the mutant's leg to buckle and deposit him in a heap on top of the witch hunter. The sacrificial lamb scurried free and gambolled around the room, adding to the confusion.

When the mutant picked himself up from the witch hunter's body, ready to give the prisoner one final taste of pain before the ritual erased his soul forever, pain and shock registered upon his grotesquely leering visage. Others, too, had noticed the unthinkable thing which had befallen their great plan and began gasping and crying out in fear and dismay.

'You fool! What have you done?' shrieked the sorceress.

The mutant backed away, shaking his bloated head, his eyes never leaving the terrible sight in the centre of the circle. The sacrificial knife jutted from beneath the chin of their prisoner – but worse than that an ephemeral glow was intensifying within Cain's open mouth and his cheeks were beginning to bulge with warp-born energies. Then the coruscating wash of power seemed to contract in upon itself.

The cultists eyed one another with deep trepidation. The mutant continued to back off, still shaking his head in pained denial.

Suddenly a brilliant, prismatic cascade of light erupted from the corpse's hideously stretched mouth, an otherworldly illumination which seemed to siphon the flesh from the cultists' bodies where it touched them, drawing out their substance in little lumps which evaporated within the searing beams. In the space of a minute, the screaming and pleading was done. A dozen charred skeletons clattered to the stone floor.

Obediah Cain's body writhed and jerked with unholy vigour, then sat bolt upright tearing the steel bonds from their fittings as though they were a child's paper chains. With an impatient gesture he yanked the knife from his throat and cast it aside. After a deep, gurgling cough, he clamped a hand over the hole in his voice box and uttered in a horrible, reedy, burbling timbre, 'Nec-ro-mancer! I must find a necromancer!'

'I'M SORRY, de la Lune, but after careful consideration the Guild's senior tutors have concluded that you are simply not possessed of the finer skills of meditation and concentration required to make the grade as a qualified Wizard in this academy.'

Michael de la Lune perched on the edge of a comfortable leather chair in the opulent office of Paracelsus van der Groot, the Marienburg College of Magic's master of apprentices. Across the magnificent teak table, strewn with arcane trinkets and scrolls, van der Groot was telling him the awful, unbearable news that he had failed his apprenticeship. De la Lune was a slight man, who had witnessed the passing of no more than twenty summers, and his boyish, Bretonnian face wore an expression of crestfallen astonishment. A lock of dark, wavy hair fell across his forehead as he hung his head in defeat.

'But don't take on so, lad,' continued the corpulent van der Groot, toying with one of his enormous rings in embarrassment, 'There are plenty of careers wanting for resourceful, educated fellows like yourself. Have you considered perhaps something in one of the mercantile professions – they're always looking for accountants and administrators. Or if you still want to work with magic, how about the Alchemists' Guild? I know a few people there and everything they do is academic. Not quite so esoteric as our stuff, eh?

'I could get in touch with–'

Against all the protocols, the young man dared to interrupt one of the masters and spoke for the first time since entering the office. 'Please sir? By your leave, I think I'd just like to collect my belongings and be gone.'

'Yes, yes. I understand lad,' van der Groot said breezily. 'I know it's a sore blow to you young ones to be told that you've failed, but only a few ever succeed. There's no shame in it, so you stay in touch and–'

There was the sound of the door shutting.

Michael strode down the tangled web of corridors which burrowed through the great edifice that was the Marienburg College of Magic. He kept his head down on the way to his private quarters, ignoring the greetings of other wizards of his acquaintance along the route. His head was a whirl of confusion and resentment. What had he done to fail the test? He had thought this establishment to be an enlightened one. After all, hadn't they offered him a second chance after he had failed the entrance exam to the exalted Altdorf college. Though he had long suspected that entrance to Altdorf's college had more to do with money than ability, and he reasoned that his Bretonnian lineage being of freeman stock, rather than the aristocracy who more usually gained admittance there, was the real reason that he failed the exam. However, he couldn't understand why the establishment which had eventually permitted him entry to the field of his beloved magical research would now turn their backs on him. Their reasoning seemed to be beyond him.

Michael reached his spartan quarters and began packing such meagre possessions as he owned into the sling bag which had accompanied him from his home city of Lyonesse four years earlier. What would become of him now? It was a bitter irony that he had travelled so far, learning two new languages in his pursuit of magical expertise and the Classical script employed in conjuration, just to seemingly have to return to Bretonnia with nothing to show for it but a couple of apprentices' parlour tricks. Oh, he might stay in Marienburg as van der Groot had suggested, but that would be taking an almighty risk with his dwindling funds. If he couldn't find some way to sustain himself here then he might end up a beggar or worse, and he was in no mood for taking chances at present. It would be much more sensible, he reasoned, to use what money he had left to buy passage back to his homeland whereupon he could take up employment in his father's textile trade, much though the idea pained him. On the face of things, however, he didn't see any other reasonable options open to him.

'Damn it! Everything is a mess. Damn magic and damn merchants too!' he muttered, swinging the heavy satchel over his shoulder. With that, he left the little room he had inhabited for the past four years for the final time and headed out of the building.

BLINKING OWLISHLY in the light of day, Michael passed beyond the portals and out into Guilderstraase, pausing briefly to hand his room keys over to the gatekeeper. Eyes which burned with intent unknown marked him as he proceeded down the broad thoroughfare, then a dark figure hurried from the alley whence it had observed him so that it might intercept the youth before he passed from sight.

Michael was still in a condition of shock, his thoughts lost in fanciful notions of how he would spend the rest of his life, when a hand clapped down heavily upon his shoulder. Michael almost leapt clean out of his skin at the sudden contact and whirled to face whoever it was that presumed to be so familiar.

It was a tall man, garbed in the traditional attire of the religious puritans who made the vanquishing of heretics their lives' work: wide-brimmed hat, leather britches and high riding boots, a half cloak worn over a blouson shirt, and a burnished steel gorget to protect his neck from Vampires. At his belt he wore a long, heavy bladed sabre and a fine duelling pistol, along with pouches for powder and shot.

'Forgive me,' wheezed the stranger in a voice curiously thin and consumptive for one so impressive of stature. 'It was not my intention to startle you.'

A witch hunter! Michael's heart dropped into the pit of his stomach. Just when he thought things could get no worse, along came the practitioner of wizardry's worst nightmare. These religious zealots were notoriously indiscriminate in their inquisitions, and many an innocent whose only crime was an interest in sorcery had suffered torture and death under their regime. It would be a bitter irony indeed if he were to get into trouble for practising magic now of all times, and he briefly wondered if the gods were having sport with him.

'What can I do for you?' asked the young man guardedly.

'Please. You have nothing to fear from me,' continued the witch hunter in his unhealthy tone of voice, 'My name is Obediah Cain. Would I be correct in assuming that you have come from the College of Magic?'

'Well, yes, but I won't be going back there. My apprenticeship came to an end today, and I shan't be going on to indoctrination in the higher mysteries.'

'Ah. I am sorry to hear that,' answered the man, his eyebrow and the corner of his mouth raising a little in unison. 'Despite that, I should still very much like to talk with you concerning your days at the college. If you can spare me the time over a drink that is?'

'Alas, it seems that I have all the time in the world now, and a drink would be most welcome at this juncture.'

THE TULIP was a ribald establishment in a side street off Guilderstraase, patronised mainly by labourers and menial workers. Cain had suggested it so that they were not likely to encounter any of Michael's erstwhile colleagues, and any reservations the youth had about entering such a bawdy house in his academian attire were dispelled when he saw how the presence of the witch hunter discouraged the clientele from even a cursory glance in their direction.

Cain himself refused to drink with Michael, proclaiming that his religious asceticism would not permit him to partake of alcohol, but he generously provided the youth with a jug of foaming table beer from which he could refill his tankard.

'So what's this all about then?' enquired Michael once he had properly introduced himself to the sinister witch hunter. He was eager, he realised, to get this encounter over with, since he instinctively mistrusted this strange man. But at the same time a resentment for the world of magic and wizards which had so cruelly rejected him was beginning to fester in the undertow of his shattered emotions – a resentment which was stirring up faint notions of respect for the work of such men as Cain, even as he spoke.

'As you can imagine, where I am involved it is about heresy, blasphemy and cult activity!' Obediah Cain smiled.

'You surely can't think that I–' Michael blurted, but he was silenced by an impatient wave from the witch hunter.

'No, no, no, lad! Of course I don't think a failed apprentice is involved. But answer me this: why do you think capable young men like yourself fail at that academy all the time?'

'Well, I mean, the course is very rigorous, isn't it? It takes a high degree of spiritual fortitude as well as academic prowess. They told me that only rare individuals are cut out for such a challenge,' Michael answered carefully, not yet prepared to damn his erstwhile colleagues, but somewhere deep inside he was starting to entertain the notion that damnation was perhaps their lot.

'Ha!' Cain spat. 'And do you suppose that all those bloated old men up at the college are possessed of such purity? Don't you believe it, lad! Why, you can reckon the sins of the flesh on their fat carcasses like the bites on that serving wench's neck. They haven't the moral fibre to do what they ask of you young apprentices who fail, but they'll happily take your money. No, the easy route to arcane power is the path trodden by their well-shod soles, and that means bargains with daemonic powers. Dark magic and necromancy, pacts with Chaos daemons is their mystical currency, you mark my words.

'Now listen well, young Michael de la Lune. I have it, from an unimpeachable source, that there are ancient books of necromancy, and the unguents used in the mummification rituals of distant Araby, in the college libraries.'

'No, it's surely impossible,' Michael gasped, shaking his head to clear the ale fumes, aghast at the enormity of what he was hearing. 'I spent four years in that place. I would have known.'

'Do you think that such a well-established secret society would reveal itself to a mere apprentice? Even one under their own roof? Now I'm not saying that everyone at the college who isn't an apprentice is in on this. That would be madness.' Cain smiled enigmatically. 'But certainly the top echelon of the guild are guilty of the vilest crimes against the Church. I'm appealing to you now to perform a deed that could save countless souls. You're the only one who can do it Michael. I can't go in there, so I want you to go and steal the books and the oils and give us solid evidence to bring these blackguards to trial.'

It all seemed to make sense to Michael in some awful, surreal sort of way. He prayed earnestly that the witch hunter with the strange voice was labouring under a gross misapprehension, but now that those things had been said, he knew he had to find out whether it was true for his own peace of mind. He had spent such a large part of his life within those walls, under the tutelage of those implicated, that he must discover the truth. And if the truth should prove as the witch hunter would have it? Then damn all practitioners of magic! He would name every last one of them to clear the taint of their sorcery from his soul. He must keep reminding himself that he was no longer a wizard, and the only thing of any consequence now was the pursuit of truth. He had been lied to for long enough; although Michael knew not what was to become of him in the years to come, he determined that honesty would characterise it.

'How will I know?' Michael asked quietly, 'You said yourself that such a society, if it exists, has kept its secrets well hidden.'

Cain smirked triumphantly and reached down inside his boot.

'I have a map.'

MICHAEL EMERGED from his hiding place in one of the smaller, and lesser-used libraries of the Marienburg College of Magic. It was a strange twist of circumstance indeed which had caused him to return to this building the very next day after he had been evicted from it.

Obediah Cain had remained with Michael during the previous day, and had provided for the youth's comfort generously, paying from his own purse for both their lodgings. The next morning Cain had instructed him on using the map and drilled him thoroughly on the need for secrecy in the mission he was about to perform for the good of the Old World. Cain had also provided him with a curious little serpentine charm of blackest obsidian, hung upon a pendant of brass. The witch hunter assured him that the talisman would negate the power of any wards he might encounter in liberating the evidence he sought, but also warned him that whilst wearing it he should be quite unable to use any of his own magical powers, such as they were.

As to what pretences Michael would employ to gain access to the college, Cain left him to his own devices. So Michael had simply used Paracelsus van der Groot's invitation to keep in touch in order to convince the gatekeeper to permit him access.

Following the spidery lines traced upon the parchment map, the young man crept stealthily through the familiar halls. Although it was late at night, he knew there would still be many powerful Wizards awake within these ancient walls.

After a fraught journey, he eventually arrived at the location of his quest. The Library of Forbidden Mysteries was on a floor which had always been deemed off-limits to apprentices and it was a part of the building he had never before visited, since he was an obedient student. Although the room was unlocked, various magical alarms and warding devices existed to discourage the excessively curious. Those who had tried in the past to gain unwarranted access to this place had paid the price of their folly by expulsion from the academy, or worse in some cases.

The atmosphere within was one of timeless serenity, and thus far the power of the witch hunter's talisman seemed to be holding out. Most of the dusty volumes on the creaking shelves seemed to be historical texts warning of the dark side of magic, texts which chronicled and cautioned the unwary against the machinations of Chaos and evil rather than actually instructed one in the Dark Ways. Nevertheless, even the knowledge that such practices existed at all was deemed too unsafe to reveal to impressionable apprentices.

According to the parchment given to him by Cain, the things he sought were in a safe behind the large portrait of the rather stern-looking founder of the college, Zun Mandragore, that hung upon the back wall. Perspiration pricked Michael's forehead as he tremulously reached his hand out to the heavy frame of the picture. Gently sliding the portrait to one side the map proved true, for sure enough a bulky steel safe was embedded in the wall.

But before he could react, a previously invisible rune on the metal safe door blazed with arcane power. There was no time to react: a brilliant bolt of cerulean lightning arced from the rune at his hand... only to fizzle into harmless ozone an instant before he betrayed himself with a scream. Gingerly Michael shook his head as the coppery tang of blood wet his tongue where he had bitten his lip in alarm, and then resumed his task with vigour, desiring only to be free of this oppressive place. The world of Magic had turned upon him so quickly and profoundly now that he no longer experienced wonder and awe in its presence, just fear and revulsion.

Feverishly Michael dialled the combination provided with the parchment, vague questions about how such a map had come into existence subsumed by his excitement. The door swung open without a sound. Before him lay an enormous volume, bound in what seemed to be very soft, thin leather, entitled *Liber Nagash vol. III*, together with six stoppered vials of brackish liquid. He quickly stuffed the contents of the safe into his satchel and fled the room.

'BOUND IN THE skin flayed from the backs of living men,' Obediah Cain breathed almost reverentially. A small table set before him in their small upstairs room in the Tulip inn was dominated by the hulking tome. It was a Classical translation, the witch hunter had been explaining, of one of the original nine treatises on necromancy penned by the Supreme Lord of the Living Dead, Nagash of Nagashizzar himself. 'And here too, the sacred preserving fluids of the ancient Tomb Kings,' continued Cain in a sort of distant rapture. 'Natron, imbued with the dust of cadavers, to bind a spirit to empty, dead flesh, and protect the carnal vessel from the ravages of time.

'However, I grow weary now, young Michael, and I must rest. Know that there is yet one more thing I would ask of you on the morrow before you shall be properly compensated for your service. A dangerous thing in which we both must share but,

before all that, I would urge you to read… here for example…'
A slender finger tapped the dry parchment page. 'The binding
ritual used to create mummified undead creatures such as the
Tomb Kings themselves. Read this and drink deeply of the cor-
ruption and easy power with which your former tutors dabble.
Fore-warned is, after all, fore-armed.'

With that, Cain swung his legs up onto his bunk and passed
immediately into such a deep stupor that it almost seemed to
Michael that he was not breathing at all.

It seemed odd to Michael, who in his own estimation might
be a touch naive but certainly wasn't gullible, that this champion of holiness, this supposed paladin of temperance, should
encourage him, a young disgruntled practitioner of magic
denied the way to naturally progress his art, to read forbidden
texts. As far as Michael knew, one could be burned at the stake
for simply having seen such a work as *Liber Nagash*, never mind
actually having read it. The young man suddenly grew very suspicious and deeply afraid of his strange new mentor.

However, he determined to read the extract, as Cain had
decreed, in order to perhaps gain a clue as to what was going
on, but no more. He would have to play along for the time
being, until he found out what Cain's game was and then act
in whatever small way he could. He was scared, but a sudden
determination not to mess this up, as he had done the rest of
his life, steeled him and prevented him from bolting from the
room that instant and catching the first stagecoach to Bretonnia. Eyes darting sideways, as if he dared not the read the words
he was even now taking in, Michael began to read.

IF ANYTHING, despite his long rest, the witch hunter seemed even
wearier the next day. Michael himself didn't exactly feel in the
peak of condition himself, and noted the deep black rings
under his own eyes whilst shaving his downy chin in the tiny
silver mirror he carried. It was afternoon, Michael having spent
most of the night poring over the crumbling pages of *Liber
Nagash*'s mummification ritual. Abhorrent lore permeated his
mind, but unlike weaker men, Michael had no desire to exploit
this easy power, which he knew would only lead to self-serving
evil. Nevertheless, a part of his innocence had gone forever
with the knowledge that vast earthly gain could be bought for
the meagre price of one's soul. His optimistic idealism, already

damaged by rejection from the college, was further under-
mined with the realisation that in these dark times there would
be no shortage of desperate people prepared to pay such a
price. Somewhere deep within his soul, a vow to set this bitter
world of greed and opportunism to rights was starting to take
shape.

For his daemonic part, M'Loch T'Chort could feel the hold he
had over Cain's body growing weaker by the hour. He knew
that he did not have much time left to salvage his diabolic plot.
He was pleased to note the taint of horror on the boy, and
could sense a nascent treachery flowering in him. Although the
daemon prince could not read the minds of men, he was possessed of certain intuitions for the darkness in their hearts, and
he felt assured that Michael's corruption was now advanced
enough to offer the young man a daemonic bargain. Until that
time came, he must conserve his energy.

Michael found the witch hunter to be uncommunicative for
the remainder of the day, and noted how he had never once
seen the man eat or drink anything. When Michael suggested
they dine, Cain grunted non-commitally and tossed a few cop-
pers in the youngster's direction, but did not stir from his bunk
when Michael left the room and descended the stairs to the bar
alone.

WHEN THE evening finally drew around, the witch hunter was
suddenly galvanised into action. The cadaverous figure rushed
around, collecting up his belongings and instructing Michael
to bring the oils and the book. Michael hurried to comply, fear
of Cain and curiosity about his intent blending in equal measure to bring about his obedience. The witch hunter was
obviously in a hurry to be away from the Tulip, and Michael
almost had to run in order to keep pace as Cain strode out of
the premises.

'Where are we going now?' Michael enquired guardedly as
they left the inn.

Cain smiled in a paternal way. 'To the sewers, lad. There is to
be a ritual this very night and I need you with me.'

'Why don't you just inform the authorities and let them deal
with it? It sounds terribly dangerous.'

'Ah,' said Cain with a snort, 'we prefer to work independently
of such institutions, and I want you to positively identify the

participants. We'll observe quietly and bring them to trial later, so I can guarantee your safety.'

This explanation rang false to Michael but, with no one else to turn to, he knew he had to rely on his own resources to get to the bottom of this mystery. So it came to pass that he found himself scurrying along behind the bobbing lantern of the witch hunter on the slippery walkways of Marienburg's sewer network. They had entered through a disguised door in the cellar of a silent, shuttered town house. Before descending, Cain had slipped away for a moment before returning bearing long robes of purple velvet. They were a disguise, Cain explained, that would allow them to get close to the ritual.

After slogging through the foul, dank underground for what seemed like hours, eventually they came to the threshold over which, only scant days before, the cultists had dragged the tortured body of the second lieutenant of the Church of Sigmar's Holy Inquisition. M'Loch T'Chort, struggling to maintain a grip on the dead body of Cain, went about the room, igniting flambeaux held in sconces to illuminate the scene for a plainly shocked Michael.

Grey traces of ash delineated the skeletons of those whom the daemon prince had consumed in panic, in order to fuel the strength he had needed to hold on to the rapidly expiring body of the witch hunter. In one corner of the chamber, a lamb stood tethered, contentedly munching on a bale of hay. M'Loch T'Chort had clearly made some preparations for his salvation before ascending to the surface of Marienburg.

'What– what is going on?' Michael asked slowly.

'You are,' the witch hunter hissed. 'To better things!' He leapt up to the throne and snatched up a parchment.

'You see this?' he continued in a wild voice. 'This is a contract I have prepared for the one who would solve my dilemma. This contract holds the keys to the greatest magical mysteries of the age! Its clauses have been set down in the name of the unchallenged master of magic, Lord Tzeentch himself! Aid me now and sorceries beyond your wildest imaginations shall be yours to command, if you but dedicate yourself to the service of the Changer of the Ways!'

Michael stood open mouthed in astonishment. He had expected some sort of elaborate con trick, but nothing of this magnitude. 'So you're not a real witch hunter then?' was the best he could manage in that frozen moment.

Ignoring the young man, Cain's face become deadly serious and his hand grasped the hilt of his sabre. 'I am the High Daemonic Prince of Twisted Fate and Misguided Destiny, from the nethermost planes of the Void!' he hissed. 'Do you accept these terms?'

Michael's mind raced. He was terrified, but also strangely thrilled. Temptation was before him, or death. What would he do?

'I– I accept,' he announced, struggling to keep a level tone of voice. 'What is your dilemma?'

'Excellent!' Cain wheezed. 'I will talk plainly. I am a spirit from beyond this world, and the body I have acquired is dead. It cannot be brought back to life, and I do not have the energy to sustain it much longer. However, the necromantic process of mummification will preserve the corpse and allow a spirit to control it. I believe you are now familiar with that ritual.

'I want you to carry out such a ritual and then spill the lamb's blood over me, a requirement I have as a daemon to indefinitely exist upon this realm, for reasons too complex to explain to you just yet. I will now prepare.'

Cain hastily stripped off his clothes and lay in the circle on the floor. Michael saw now the hideous wound that was the source of the witch hunter's speech impediment, and no doubt the demise of the real Obediah Cain. He wondered briefly how the great man had come to such a tragic end, then falteringly began the rite. He poured the natron potion over the body before him in the prescribed fashion, enunciating the words from the pages of *Liber Nagash*, using the vocal techniques he learned at the college to craft the phrases into vibrations of mystical power.

Within moments, dark energy gathered in the room, its easy, exhilarating flow threatening to consume the boy with more and greater secrets yet. There was the scent of lightning in the air, and death.

When he completed the mummification process, Michael untethered the lamb and fetched it across to the ritual circle. Then, taking a deep breath, he reached down for the sacrificial knife. Now would come the part of the ritual which completed the binding.

However, instead of picking up the dagger, at the very last moment Michael swept up the witch hunter's sabre instead. Its wicked steel blade incised the still, dark air with a hissing silver arc as it plunged towards the form on the floor. For the second time in its short existence, the lamb had a narrow escape and skipped away unharmed as Obediah Cain's blood poured out onto the mosaic. There was no redemption for the daemon prince this time. The ex-apprentice had totally severed Cain's head. The glassy eyes blinked once in astonishment before expiring forever.

'Never underestimate humans, daemon filth!' Michael gasped, still clutching the sword in both hands, his whole body heaving in uncontrollable spasms.

M'Loch T'Chort's grasp upon the Earthly Plane had not totally loosened yet, however. Tendrils of vapour began to emanate from the corpse's neck, rapidly ballooning into a twisted, ropy tentacle. Behind the tentacle a burgeoning cloud of foul gases pumped out of the awful, headless body. As it formed, howling, enraged mouths manifested across its horrendous surface. It was a dank, nebulous obscenity which writhed and billowed before Michael's panic-stricken eyes with an oozing, hypnotic plasticity.

It reared up before the young man as a towering column of smoking, stinking Chaos, its absolute horror profoundly changing his outlook on the world forever, and turning his luxuriant black locks snow white in the passing of but an instant in its unholy presence.

'Innn-ssect!' sputtered the ephemeral nightmare. 'I sshaall crussshh you!'

And then the most intolerable of all the violations of nature, beyond anything Michael ever dreamt possible, unfolded before him. For the headless body of Cain rose jerkily to its feet. It groped towards him, the dank cloud of daemonic essence dancing above it, whispering its vengeance in grossly distorted tongues. It was all too much and Michael turned and fled for the door, sick with the knowledge that humanity could never stand against abomination of this magnitude.

Before he could make good his escape, though, M'Loch T'Chort reached out purposefully with Cain's hand, making a curious sign with the fingers, and the door slammed shut with such force that the brickwork of its frame cracked from the impact.

'Now, boy!' wheezed the daemon. 'I will flay the meat from your bones and eat your very soul!'

In panic, Michael shrunk against the wall, trying to steel himself for the inevitable end and turned his eyes away. White hot light burst all around him. Michael was shocked rigid and, blinking his eyes seconds later, he wondered if he was in the Halls of Morr.

But no, he was still in the chamber and had somehow survived the daemon's magical assault. Not three paces from him, he saw to his horror, the last wisps of M'Loch T'Chort slithered free from Cain's ruined neck and the witch hunter's corpse slumped, almost gratefully it seemed, to the ground.

The daemon was yet abroad, though, hovering like a wrathful thunderhead of pure magical essence in the centre of the room, swelling rapidly as hatred and rage fuelled its murderous purpose. Knowing that it had to be the end for him this time, Michael's mind, which had been feverishly calculating ways to survive this ordeal quite simply overloaded, and pure instinct took over. Rolling himself into a tight ball on the floor, he unconsciously clutched the amulet at his neck and prayed over and over to Sigmar as the hellbegotten daemon cloud washed over him. There was an awful, agonised wailing like the lament of a legion of tortured spirits... then nothing.

After a moment, Michael risked opening his eyes again, just in time to watch the last flickering trails of M'Loch T'Chort's magical form disappearing between his fingers, into the curious little obsidian talisman he wore at his throat – the very talisman that the fiend had given him.

'So THAT WAS a daemon,' Michael said to himself.

He looked thoughtfully at the remains of Cain, who had given his life in the battle against these plagues and vexations of decent folk, and reached for the sword with which the witch hunter had set out to right such wrongs. Hefting the sabre and picking up the pistol from the floor, he gauged the weight of them both. They felt good. He had carried on Cain's good work, ensuring that the heretic-slayer's death had not been in vain.

It had been the first thing he had done right in his entire life, he reflected

'Truth? Inquisition? Balance?' he muttered, donning the wide-brimmed hat that Obediah Cain would definitely be needing no longer, and scooping up the other belongings of the late witch hunter.

'Work to be done,' Michael de la Lune, one-time apprentice sorcerer, said in a stronger, more determined voice as he left behind the carnage of the small cultist's chamber. As he strode through the sewers, a strange gleam shone in his eye and he clutched the witch hunter's sabre in his white-knuckled fist.

PARADISE LOST

Andy Jones

'WELL, JOHAN, y'see, it's like this…' The gruff dwarf voice hung for long moments in the hot tropical air. 'Sometimes yer has to take the big chance…' The voice trailed off. 'Ain't half hot, though.'

'Snowkapt Mountinz, I see Snowkapt Mountinz.' Indecipherable babble escaped from Keanu the Reaver like steam from a leaky kettle. 'Ja, und schtreams, und kold, kold fountinz…' Even the barbarian's delirium was thickly accented.

Johan Anstein, ex-Imperial envoy, groaned inwardly and manoeuvred a fragment of sailcloth to shade himself from the merciless ravages of the sun. The young, would-be warrior peered with squinting eyes at the dwarf sitting stoically at the rowlocks.

'But Grimcrag, what are we going to do?' Anstein's voice was little more than a croak, his tongue thick and furred in his mouth. He could feel the sun hammering down on his head, even through the thick tarpaulin he had draped across his blistered shoulders.

The young man pointed what was (to his mind at least) quickly becoming a skeletally thin arm at the recumbent elf lying in the bilges. Jiriki rolled softly with the swell of the sea.

'He hasn't moved all day, and Keanu thinks he's back home in Norsca.'

Johan studied the barbarian lolling in the steersman's seat. Wearing nothing but a loin cloth and horned helmet, the Reaver glistened menacingly.

'Take mich Home, Momma!' the barbarian gargled, his teeth chattering uncontrollably.

'Don't you be worryin' about yon elf, lad,' Grimcrag interjected. 'He's always doin' that suspendered animalation trick of his when things get tricky.' The dwarf deftly prodded the comatose Jiriki with a boat hook. 'See, nothing!'

Grimcrag scratched at his beard and spat overboard. 'It's old musclehead I'm worried about. I don't think he can take many more days without anything to drink. He's getting beerhydrated, and it'll be the end of him, mark my words.'

'No sign of land?' Johan asked hopelessly.

The dwarf performed what under normal circumstances would have been an almost comical double take. 'Oh yes, didn't I mention it? We're about thirty yards away from a lovely landing berth. I can see the tavern from here… OF COURSE THERE'S NO BLOODY LAND!' Grimcrag snorted in derision, and continued scratching despondently at his beard.

Johan slumped back under the tarpaulin. 'That's it then, we're done for.'

Minutes later, he had drifted off into a restless, sun-driven daydream.

'GOLD, LAD, GOLD! More than you can imagine!' The dwarf voice resonated with barely controlled excitement.

'Yes, but it's not Lustrian, or from the Lost Kingdoms at all: it's in a storm-wrecked Bretonnian galleon.'

'Never mind that, it's ours for keeps now.'

'It's sinking fast!'

'We've got time, lad, and this boat can hold plenty.'

'Wouldn't we be better scavenging water and food?'

'VOT? S'YOU MAD?'

A madly canted deck, so far down in the water that it was not much of a climb at all even in their weakened state. Crazy angles, creaking hawsers, the desolate flapping of ripped and tattered sailcloth. Not so different from their own recent fate.

Keanu barging the others aside impatiently, muscles straining as he pulled at the iron ring on the deck hatch. Nothing… then the screech of swollen wood on rusted metal.

A black square leading down into nothingness. The stench of stagnant death and decay. The slap of lazy waters in the dark bilges below.

Heat-bloated bodies gently bumping against him in the darkness. Foetid water climbing quickly over their waists. Fish swimming blindly about their legs. The discomforting feel of being ghoulish carrion, unwelcome visitors intruding upon the rest of the dead. Heavy crates. A race against time and the horror of joining the bodies in the hold for ever.

A portion saved. Exhaustion. The sad sight of a once-noble vessel slipping ignominiously below the waves, leaving at its last nothing more than bubbling froth and a few shards of timber.

The endless sun by day and the chill blackness of night. Day after day after day in a boat piled high with nothing but gold. Death's shadow never seemed far away. Who would succumb first?

'Sail ahoy!'

Hope!

'You sure, elfy?'

'Yes, it's some kind of corsair.'

'Wave everything! We're saved!'

'Hide the gold, lad!'

'Where, for heaven's sake?'

'Halloo! Halloo!'

A brine- and barnacle-encrusted tramp. A patchwork of old repairs over older repairs. A grimy grey sail. Tar and smoke-blackened timbers. A ruined figurehead jutting like a broken tooth. The most beautiful ship Johan had ever seen.

A grizzled, suspicious face. A toothless grin, a hooked hand. A swarthy bunch of no-hopers. Angels in disguise, no doubt.

'Well 'pon my soul, if it ain't the great mister lardy-dardy I-wouldn't-hire-your-ship-if-I-was-in-the-middle-of-the-Great-Ocean-on-a-tea-chest Grunsonn himself…'

'Vot?'

'Grimcrag, you didn't?'

'Not exactly, lad… I think he missed out the bit about the tea chest leaking…'

A diplomatic elvish voice: 'Look here, Black Hook Pugh Beard or whatever your name is, are you going to help us or not?'

'Depends, eh, lads? Shall we help the hoity-toities?'

A chorus of despicable cheers and catcalls.

'Dependink on vot, 'zactly?'

'Got'ny gold in those boxes?'

'Ja!'

'No!'

'For heaven's sake, Grimcrag. Yes, yes, yes, just get us off this blasted boat!'

'You'll be wantin' water then?'

'Ja.'

'Yes.'

'Mmph!'

'Definitely.'

Ropes and grapples snaking down. Chests brim full of Bretonnian gold hauled up on board. A fishermen's net lowered. Salvation in sight. Four sun-bleached souls about to end their week-long torment. Heaven is nigh.

JOHAN STIRRED in his heat-drenched half-sleep. He already knew the ending of this particular dream. He'd seen it for real, and dreamed it a hundred times a day since. His eyes opened a crack, as he wondered yet again if maybe, somehow, this was all a dream, a very bad one. Perhaps he was really lying on silk sheets at home in Castle Baltenkopf? Pitiful hope seized his heart.

But no, here was the boat, and there sat the disconsolate form of the renowned Grimcrag Grunsonn, unceremoniously stripped down to filthy grey vest and long johns. The lugubrious dwarf still wore his iron-shod boots and his helmet, but his armour and precious axe were tucked under his bench for safekeeping. Johan blearily noticed that today the dwarf had rolled his sleeves up. Perhaps the sun was finally getting to even him.

Johan turned over and quickly drifted off into fitful sleep again, the endless monotony of the slap-slapping of the sea against the boat's flimsy side a familiar lullaby. After a few hours of blissful oblivion, the dream came on again.

THEY ARE SCRAMBLING up the net, grinning madly to one another. Even Grimcrag has forgotten the thought of his gold in the joy of rescue. Fresh water? A bath? Food? What it is to have friends!

Halfway up and disaster strikes – the net falls away, plunging them down into the sea. Uproarious laughter from above

When they surface, the ship is already drifting away. Their small, sorry boat is dragged alongside by the current for a moment, as if forlornly hoping for a tow.

The corsairs laugh cruelly, jeering at the Marauders from the safety of the gunwale.

'Come back!' Johan gurgles.

'MY GOLD!' shrieks Grimcrag.

Jiriki and Keanu swim with strong, accomplished strokes towards the boat.

The pirates throw down some water skins and a few barrels of salted fish.

The Marauders clamber, exhausted, into their floating prison cell once more. Ironically enough, there is more room without all the gold. At least Johan can stretch his long legs.

Grimcrag is inconsolable, shouting curses southwards long after the pirates' sail has dipped below the distant horizon. The sharks circle. In the boat they all know they are doomed.

JOHAN WOKE with a start, a sharp stabbing pain in his heart warning him that finally his time was nigh. He had hoped that he would not be the last to die. He didn't think he could stand that. At least they hadn't eaten each other. They still had their honour.

It was so hot he could barely breathe. Eyes closed, he groaned softly. What a way to go. The stabbing pain intensified, followed by a repetitive dull thumping ache in his head. After a moment, Anstein opened his eyes.

Grimcrag stood over him, staring open-mouthed at the horizon. Waking up to the view of a dwarf's badly-sewn long johns crotch revealed secrets to the young adventurer that lesser men had died for merely talking about in casual conversation. The dwarf was absent-mindedly stabbing him in the chest with a marlin spike, whilst simultaneously stomping nervously up and down on the ex-envoy's head with a heavily booted foot.

'Pack it in, Grimcrag,' Johan croaked through sun-dried lips. 'Just lie down and die quietly like the rest of us.'

The dwarf mumbled something through his salt-encrusted beard.

Johan thought he had misheard. He painfully raised his head, and pawed feebly at the dwarf's long johns. His breath came in rasping sobs. 'What did you say?' He was surprised to see that the dwarf was weeping. Must be a delayed reaction to the loss of so much gold.

Salty tears ran down the grizzled dwarf's cheeks, mingling with that already tangling his beard. Johan strained to hear his cracked whisper. 'Land, lad. Marvellous, green, grassy, diggable bloody LAND!'

KEANU WAS mostly awake and rowing hard by the time they approached the beach, rounding the rugged headland into the sheltered cove beyond. So far, the island had seemed an impenetrable fortress, with cliffs on every side, but the sight of this sheltered cove took Johan's breath away. A strip of white, white sand stretched for perhaps a quarter of a mile, with projecting horns of rock sheltering the cove from the open ocean. Coral reefs made bizarre living citadels in the clear water, and also created a natural barrier against any heavier swells.

Negotiating towards a gap in the reef, Keanu muttered something about catching a chill, and Johan could see whisps of steam escaping from beneath the barbarian's helm. Clearly the man needed rest soon.

'See all that green, lad?' Grimcrag shouted, pulling on an oar. 'That shows there must be water on the island somewhere.' The dwarf was wearing a relieved grin along with his boots and underclothes, and had obviously heroically put the matter of his gold to the back of his mind for a while.

Despite Johan's best efforts, and the crazed shouting and whooping of them all, they had failed to rouse Jiriki from his deep slumber. Grimcrag had explained that it sometimes happened like that – and the Reaver had grunted something about 'Vontink a lie in, praps' – but Johan could see that the dwarf was concerned.

Johan trailed a finger in the clear waters, watching the myriad schools of fish flash in the sunlight beneath him. He had taken an hour at the oars, rowing around what looked to be a huge lump of jungle-covered rock, and now he was taking a well earned rest. So many fish.

Then Grimcrag shouted for him to grab a boat hook and be ready to fend off. 'We're going through the gap in the reef, lad, and we don't want to hole her.'

As they navigated safely through, the elf slept on, snoring softly, his feet at the tiller and his head just behind Grimcrag's seat.

A few moments later and they were into the lagoon, five hundred feet or so from the white sands of the beach. Johan had once read a book from Araby about exotic fruits. Surely what he was seeing now were indeed the fabled, erm, barnarnowls or something; the exact name eluded him.

'Looks like we're in for a sojourn in paradise, eh, Grimcrag?' he shouted excitedly, pointing shorewards. 'See, corker nuts.'

The dwarf grinned deliriously, 'Yes, and jimjam trees too!'

Johan sighed contentedly, sat back at the tiller and peered at the fish again.

A moment later, Anstein, Grimcrag and Keanu made simultaneous exclamations.

'Grimcrag, there's no fish at all in the lagoon! Why d'you think that might be?'

'Hell, lad, what's that coming from the jungle?'

'Achtung! Valkink Lizarts!'

Johan's question was forgotten as all eyes swung forwards. All, that is, except for Jiriki, who was facing the wrong way and asleep anyway. A strange procession was making its way through the jungle and onto the beach. What indeed looked to be four- to five-foot tall, walking lizards were emerging in small groups, carrying bows, blow pipes and crude swords. Others were throwing quantities of fruit and flowers into the lagoon, while slightly larger lizards began blowing on trumpets fashioned from polished shells.

In all, Johan soon estimated there to be upwards of a hundred lizard men on the beach. So engrossed were the reptilians, that they didn't seem to have noticed the intruding boat. In fact, and Johan thought this most peculiar, they seemed to be studiously avoiding looking up or out to sea at all, as if terrified of what they might see.

'They won't be expecting us, make no mistake,' giggled Johan, his fish spotting momentarily forgotten.

'Vot is dey?' Keanu asked. 'Never seeink Nothink like dat before.'

'Dunno, Keanu, but best be on the safe side,' Grimcrag growled, reaching instinctively for Old Slaughterer, his trusty axe. Only once the mighty blade was wedged firmly between his stumpy legs did he recommence rowing. 'Johan, you're an envoy, this should be right up your street,' the dwarf grunted over his shoulder. 'Do something useful for a change.'

'Ja, Usevul.'

Johan looked at the throng of lizard men they were fast approaching, and racked his brain for the appropriate phrase or saying. Visiting ambassadors he was fine with, or representatives of the merchants' guild, but a hundred apparently semi-civilised lizards throwing fruit into a lagoon on a desert island was something different altogether.

'Well?'

'Ja, say Somzink.'

Feeling that his talents were obviously being called into question, Johan stood up and made his way to the front of the boat with what he hoped was an air of quiet confidence. From the way Grimcrag beamed toothily and nudged the steaming barbarian, he had succeeded so far.

Standing at the very prow, Johan cupped his hands to his mouth.

'HALLOO! HALLOO! DON'T KILL US – WE, ER, COME IN PEACE!'

Judging by the collective intake of breath from behind him, his speech had a dramatic effect on Grimcrag and Keanu. The lizards on the beach were immediately thrown into a state of high panic. Some buried their heads in the sand, others ran off into the jungle. Others feverishly threw more and more fruit into the lagoon. Johan saw one of them biting large chunks out his trumpet. A few braver souls, who unfortunately all seemed to carry bows, stood uncertainly on the shoreline, arrows knocked and ready.

'Now you've gorn and done it, lad,' Grimcrag muttered. 'At least try and smile, nice, like.'

Johan fixed his best diplomatic grin as Keanu and Grimcrag continued to row.

A moment later, something triggered the lizards into even more frenzied behaviour. Within a few seconds all save a dozen or so lonely warriors had vanished into the jungle. The creatures raised their bows uncertainly. Johan could see that they were still trying to avoid looking directly out to sea, which couldn't do much for their chances of hitting anything.

'Bound to be poison-tipped. I heard once that...' Grimcrag was rudely interrupted by an unmistakable elven shriek from the rear of the boat.

'AAAAAARGH! What in Tiranoc and the sunken realms is that!!!??'

'Oh good, Jiriki, you've woke–' began Johan as he turned, but the words died on his lips.

Perhaps fifty feet behind the boat, approaching them in a huge welter of spume and spray, was the biggest, most fearsome looking beast he had ever seen.

CONSCIOUSNESS slowly seeped back into Johan Anstein's wiry frame, like reluctant treacle leaching through the stygian depths of an old gravel bed. Something was tickling his face.

'Two sugars in mine, Grimcrag,' Johan groaned, keeping his eyes screwed firmly shut as he clutched his head to stop it falling off. Johan's skull felt as if the dwarf was enthusiastically excavating for gold somewhere behind his frontal lobe. 'Must have been some party,' he thought, groggy from what could only have been last night's excesses of ale. Cosy in his blanket, Johan desperately tried to let sleep reclaim him.

Something slimy and cold began wriggling up into Johan's nose. It was only then it occurred to a sluggish Anstein that he hadn't been to a party for weeks, not since three days before they set sail on that accursed boat. 'Boat...'

Johan frowned inadvertently in his slumber, as dislocated thoughts fell like dominoes through his drowsy brain: 'Boat... shipwreck... pirates... island... lizards... MONSTER!!!'

A swift moment later, Johan was very much awake and cautiously opening an eye, whilst keeping the other screwed firmly shut, just in case. He sneezed to clear his nose of what could only be an inquisitive worm, and blinked his one open eye. Total darkness. Either he was blind, or somewhere black and smelling of sandy earth. Somewhere black, sandy and with worms. Johan briefly wondered if maybe it was better to imagine he was blind.

Cautiously he edged onto his back, immediately encountering another problem. He seemed to be roughly wrapped in some sort of coarse material. It enveloped him in a manner

most unlike a blanket. The word 'shroud' drifted through the
backwaters of Anstein's stunned mind, on an unavoidable col-
lision course with his conscious thoughts. Struggling free of his
'blanket', Johan gingerly reached upwards with his right hand.
Almost immediately his nails scraped rough wooden planks in
the dark. Panic struck as quickly as the Dwarf Mineworker's
Guild when the pit-head bar ran out of Bugman's.

'Buried alive!' Johan gasped, thrashing out wildly about him
in the inky blackness. In every direction he hit wood almost
immediately. 'Oh No Oh No Oh No!' he shrieked, before lying
very still, like a desperate and cornered beast. 'Think, Anstein,
think!' he muttered, teeth chattering uncontrollably. A terrible
fear gnawed at his innards, threatening to return the blind
panic which had all but overwhelmed him a moment ago.

Johan recapped the situation aloud, in a vain attempt to
calm his pounding heart. 'The monster – that's why there were
no fish in the lagoon. That's what the strange lizardy men were
making offerings to.' Johan stopped for a moment as a violent
trembling fit seized his frame. It passed.

'We almost reached the beach, then it was upon us,' Johan
whispered slowly to himself, as the recollection of the dread
fanged monstrosity which had assaulted their tiny boat flooded
back into his memory.

He remembered it roaring in insensate fury. He remembered
its tiny, bestial eyes, staring fixedly at him from a cart-sized
head atop a mast-high neck. He remembered the water streaming in frothy torrents from its crustacean-encrusted back. Johan
remembered Jiriki loosing arrow after arrow at the beast. He
smiled as he remembered Grimcrag's axe, a whistling arc of
gold and red in the bright sunlight. He remembered the barbarian's war cry as the Reaver struck again and again with his
wicked longsword. He remembered the moment when the
beast began to know fear. He even recalled his own blade – a
cold sliver of silver pricking at the gargantuan monster's side.

Johan gulped in the darkness of his tomb as he recalled what
must have been seen as the moment of his own death. Tears
welled in his eyes, tears of sadness and frustration. At least he
would be remembered as a hero, killed fighting a great beast.
And they had slain it, of that he had no doubt at all.

Even buried alive, on a far distant isle, for that he surely was,
Johan allowed himself a grim smile as he remembered the sea

monster's death throes. Bleeding from a hundred or more wounds, it had threshed the water to a pinky red froth. Its cries had echoed around the cove over which it must have been undisputed lord for many years.

And Johan remembered its massive tail swinging round as if time had slowed, clearing the water like a fifty-foot yard arm. The others had instinctively ducked just in time, but Johan could clearly see in his mind's eye that he, alone, had not. He could remember a flash of pain and a great many stars, then nothing more, but now he nursed the bump on his head and silently wept salty tears of pain, fear and frustration. Buried alive! Johan desperately hoped he had been given a good send off at least...

Mad, blind panic swept over Johan again, carrying him like a broken twig before a mountain river in flood. He screamed, he yelled, he cried insanities at the darkness as he hammered and clawed weakly at his coffin lid for what seemed like hours.

Eventually he was exhausted, and lay panting in the darkness. It was no good. He was surely doomed to die, probably of asphyxiation when the air in the foetid hole ran out.

Johan slumped, beaten and dispirited in the cool blackness. He was ready, at last, to die. As one of Grunsonn's Marauders.

ON THE BEACH, the Marauders sat around a small fire and devoured chunks of half-cooked sea monster with gusto, as the eventful day drew to a close. On the distant horizon, the sun sank beneath the waves, its angry red orb extinguished for another day.

'Marooned in the middle of nowhere!' Jiriki muttered, picking delicately at a tender morsel.

Grimcrag stared wistfully out to sea, hot fat running down his bearded chin. 'Reckon that was as good a fight as any I've had for a while – thought it had us fer a moment or two.'

'Nah!' spat the barbarian through stringy haunch, black eyes gleaming in the firelight. 'Ve voss just Veak, dat's all, uddervise ve're killink it pretty damm Qvick, ja?!'

'S'pose so,' Grimcrag answered after a moment's chewing, before shaking his shaggy head as if to clear cobwebs away. 'Eeh, though, we're gettin' all maudlin and no mistake, aren't we?' The dwarf's eyebrows furrowed and he gestured with stubby fingers at the feast which lay before them. 'Look at this lot, 'nough to keep us going for weeks.' He turned to the others and smiled his broken-toothed, bearded grin. 'S'not all that bad, is it lads? Old Grimcrag saw you right in the end.'

Jiriki threw back his head and laughed sarcastically. The silvery note rang clear across the cove. He wagged a slender finger reproachfully. 'Oh yes, Grimcrag, everything's just fine!' The elf looked around them pointedly. 'Here we are, stuck in the middle of nowhere, with no boat, no hope of rescue, not even a map!' It wasn't often that the elf betrayed much emotion at all.

At this sudden outburst Keanu and Grimcrag sat open-mouthed, fat and saliva dribbling from their chins in equal measure. Jiriki sighed and kicked languidly at the sand before looking up and smiling sadly. 'Oh what's the use, we're stuck here!' Looking stern, the elf continued in an admonishing tone. 'Bear in mind though, Grimcrag, it's no use trying that "I'm your caring father" routine with us any more, you sneaky old miscreant, we've known you far too long for any of that nonsense to work – we're not young Anstein, you know.'

At the mention of Johan, the conversation ground to a halt. Keanu reached a ham-sized fist into the fire and lugged out a huge, crisped slab of meat, sizzling hot and dripping fatty juices onto the sand.

'Johan would like that bit, I'll wager,' Grimcrag grunted, nodding at the hunk of flesh. 'He always did like a nice bit of crackling.'

They paused in unison, the unspoken bond of untold shared adventures and brushes with death uniting the Marauders' thoughts.

A dull thumping and muffled shrieking intruded upon their reverie, and Keanu stood up, rack of monster in hand. He padded lithely across the beach to the spot where their battered rowing boat lay overturned on the sand. The thudding and shouting quite clearly came from beneath the upturned hull. Keanu reached down and carefully lifted up one side of the boat, peering underneath through the small firelit crack. A pair of wild and staring eyes greeted him, accompanied by animal-istic growls and mewlings.

JOHAN'S PANIC was rudely interrupted by one edge of his coffin being lifted away. Ruddy light seeped through the crack. A hulking shape awaited, accompanied by the unmistakable smell of charred and burning flesh.

'This is it then, Hell it is for me,' Johan burbled, terrified and miserable. At least he wouldn't be stuck in the dark for ever, which perhaps was some small consolation.

'Avake, jung 'un?' The unmistakable voice ripped through Johan's mind, and reality rapidly readjusted itself in his brain.

'Gghhh?' the ex-envoy burbled, wondering how Keanu came to be down in Hell too. Perhaps he had a visitor's day-pass.

'Head betta? Hungry?' Keanu's voice cajoled, but Anstein knew that devils and daemons could be very convincing if they wanted. He backed off to the far side of his coffin, trying to remember suitable holy signs or gestures. Something outside sighed patiently.

'Kom on out, you're Schleepink too long, ja? Nitemares also, by da look of it. All tangled unda da tarpaulin you are.'

The delicious tang of roasting meat reached Johan's nostrils and his grumbling stomach decided the matter in lieu of his concussed mind.

'Keanu?' he whimpered hopefully, 'Is it really you?'

Whatever stood beyond the coffin seemed to pause and ponder the question.

'Ja, 'f Korse, schtupid!' With one mighty heave, the barbarian lifted the boat away from Johan, who lay revealed, blinking in the firelight.

Johan shivered uncontrollably, wrapped in his tarpaulin-shroud, dazed and confused. An all-important question rose to the fore of his battered mind, back as he was, from the dead. Before he could stop them, his cracked and swollen lips had formed the fateful words.

'Can I smell... crackling?'

THE PATHWAY from the beach into the jungle was obviously well trodden, but the Marauders trod it with exceptional care. As they wound onwards through leafy glades, one moment they were drenched in tropical sunlight, the next they were plunged into the greeny darkness of the humid forest canopy.

Jiriki took the lead, gliding with silky footfall along the jungle track. The elf sniffed the air, listening intently at every turn. It was a source of some contention between Keanu the hulking barbarian and Jiriki the elf as to which had the most highly attuned senses. No one would argue that in the natural state, an elf's senses were keener than those of man or dwarf, but the Reaver had long proven himself to be something of an exception. His ability to pinpoint danger was second to none (except maybe Jiriki on a very good day), and he too moved catlike in the jungle, but staying perhaps ten feet from the path itself.

Grimcrag was still rumbling about 'All that sixth senses nonsense!' and snorting derisively to himself. He made no attempt at quietness, clattering along in his trusty armour, the clanks and bangings interspersed with frequent hearty belches. This disregard of any possible danger, to Johan's way of thinking, made something of a nonsense of the others' theatrical movements.

'Let me tell you, young Anstein,' bellowed the dwarf, receiving a recriminating stare from Jiriki and a muffled 'Qviet!' from a nearby bush. 'There's some senses what is 'stremely useful, and others,' the dwarf pointed at Jiriki's frozen form, 'what isn't.' Johan noticed that for all his brevity, the second part of Grimcrag's utterance was little more than a whisper. The dwarf belched, shrugging apologetically. 'Pardon me, lad, sea monster. Always repeats something awful, in my 'sperience.' The dwarf pushed his warhelm back and scratched vigorously at his grizzled scalp. 'Hot, innit?'

Johan nodded, peering cautiously into the gloomy canopy on either side. Everywhere, things were moving; unseen things that flapped, or scrabbled, or crawled, or just made atonal cooing noises in the distance. Sword drawn, the envoy felt decidedly uncomfortable as they made their way down the beaten track. He didn't want to go first, as that way lay almost certain first contact with them, and he didn't want to go last, as that way he was almost certain to be picked off without anyone else noticing. In actual fact, he didn't much like the idea of being on the track at all, as it was such an obvious place to set a trap (even the words trap and track were strangely similar), and the very thought of plunging off into the forest, as Keanu had, filled the young man with queasy unease.

'Anyhow,' Grimcrag carried on, waving his axe vaguely at the vegetation, 'what's the use of being able to creep about in the jungle?' Johan was about to enter a plea on behalf of forest lore, tracking, hunting and so on, but Grimcrag was in full flow. 'No, heightened and truly useful senses relate to real things, things you can touch...' The dwarf's voice tailed off, and Johan had a pretty good idea what he was contemplating, and it wasn't dusky maidens from Araby.

'Such as… gold?' He ventured, prodding Grimcrag from his reverie.

'Well, I s'pose that's as good an example as any,' Grimcrag whispered hoarsely. 'My senses can detect gold – and beer too, for that matter – from a distance of…' The dwarf stopped in his tracks and frowned.

Johan looked puzzled. Surely Grimcrag was not about to be overcome by a fit of honesty regarding his claims? Looking over his shoulder at the dwarf, Johan almost bumped into Jiriki. The elf had stopped dead still, managing to meld almost invisibly into the background. Only his bright red jerkin gave him away, and the best the elf could manage under the circumstances was to vanish to the extent that it looked as though someone had left their shirt out to dry on the bole of a tree. Of Keanu there was no sign.

Over his shoulder, Johan could see Grimcrag standing still as stone, eyes closed, nostrils dilated as he sniffed the leaden air. Sending darting glances all around in search of trouble, all Johan saw was further evidence of paradise. Yellow-white shards of sunlight flashed through the greenery, catching the heavy moisture in the laden air like glittering gemstones. Nearby, unseen, a stream trickled and gurgled seductively. A multi-coloured bird with huge wings sang sweetly as it glided between treetops far overhead. Water trickled off the mound of stark white skulls sitting by the bend in the pathway.

'Skulls?'
'A village!'
'Qviet, dammit!'
'BEER!'

THE SETTLEMENT appeared deserted – a collection of thatched mud huts, of curiously familiar design, situated in the middle of a sun-drenched clearing. Ringed by palm trees bearing coconuts as big as Johan's head, the village certainly looked idyllic. The tinkling burble of fresh, flowing water sounded from behind the furthest hut, and the only other sounds came from the jungle.

Stepping around the pile of skulls, which on close inspection seemed to belong to an assortment of creatures of all shapes and sizes, Johan peered at the dwellings laid out before him. Squinting in the harsh sunlight, the tatters of his sweat-soaked shirt sticking uncomfortably to his back, he stood stock still and watched for any sign of movement.

Having wisely discarded his scarlet blouse, Jiriki was a shadow amongst shadows. The last Johan had seen of him the elf had been somewhere to the left, behind a cluster of wooden, shed-like buildings. That had been at least ten minutes ago. Of Keanu there was no sign at all.

'Come on then, lad, no point in hanging about when there's beer to be drunk,' Grimcrag said cheerily. ''Sides, there's obviously no one at home.' With that, the dwarf strode into the village, his heavy boots kicking up little dust motes in the clearing. Somewhat more hesitantly, Johan followed in his footsteps.

In the centre of the cluster of huts, a small and overgrown pyramid thrust uncertainly towards the sky. Overhead, the palm trees which ringed the clearing sent branches scurrying as if to try and close off the immodest gap carved in the jungle canopy. Johan approached the structure for a closer look. He was troubled by the red-brown stains which marked the age-worn stone. Nonetheless, he tugged at the covering of lianas and vines, a twisted mat of root and leaf which conspired to convince the casual observer that this pyramid was, in fact, simply a strangely shaped bush or tree. Undeterred, the envoy pressed on, ripping and tugging at the tenacious growth. Johan had spotted something which he thought be of considerable interest, and wasn't to be put off easily.

So had Grimcrag, pulling aside a hastily thrown-together shield of palm fronds from alongside of one of the buildings. What he saw positioned in the cool dark of the side alley made the old dwarf gasp in surprise.

At that moment, a commotion on the far side of the clearing announced Jiriki's arrival, as the elf marched a captive lizard-creature into the clearing.

'Writing on stone!'

'Gentlemen, we have a captive.'

'Beer!'

The three adventurers all exclaimed at the same time. Jiriki's prisoner took advantage of the confusion by trying to scuttle off to the safety of a pond on the edge of the clearing. The elf hauled it back quickly with a tug on the rope which he had tied around its stomach. The creature sank down onto its haunches beside the elf, looking disconsolate. A long tongue shot out to grab a passing fly, but after a moment the bizarre reptile-man sat still, blinking its big eyes in the harsh sunlight.

'Not so fast, froggie. Stay where you are!' The elf tied the other end of the rope around a sturdy post which supported one of the huts, then turned to the others. 'Now, what did you say?'

'Writing!' Johan shouted, scraping furiously at the pyramid.

'Beer!' Grimcrag exclaimed, gesturing at the unmistakable shape of a large vat sitting in the cool shadows of the side alley. The dwarf had found a supply of hollowed coconut shells that obviously served as mugs, and held one beneath a cork bung on the side of the wooden vat. Removing the bung, the dwarf was showered in a dark brown liquid. A hoppy smell filled the warm and humid air. Filling the shell, he replaced the stopper, grinning happily.

'See, beer!' Grunsonn chuckled, downing the shell full in one capacious gulp. 'Good too, but maybe could have done with standing f'ra bit longer.'

'Never mind that, come and look at this lot!' Johan was beside himself. He had climbed almost to the very top of the pyramid, where a large clump of vines concealed some kind of ornate stonework.

The others walked over, Grimcrag slurping beer. The elf shook a warning finger at the lizard thing, which had crawled into the shade offered by the canopy of a nearby hut.

'Rik!' The creature gave a croaking burp, but made no attempt to untie itself, apparently resigned to its fate.

'Did that thing call you "Rick"?' Grimcrag asked, throwing the empty coconut shell away. The dwarf stood at the base of the pyramid, clenched fists on hips, staring belligerently up at the young man atop the construction. Bits of vine and moss floated down towards the dwarf. 'Wotcha doing, Anstein? This thing doesn't look too safe!'

'Rik! LsssRik!' said the lizard.

'And you can shut up n'all.'

Jiriki was peering intently at the base of the pyramid, where Johan had uncovered a patch of bare stone. Using a silk kerchief, the elf dusted some smaller fragments away from the surface, peered for a moment, then stood back in surprise. A clod of earth hit the elf on the head, but he made no indication of noticing.

'How?' Jiriki began, brows furrowing in surprise and consternation. 'What?'

'See, I told you, and that's just the start!' Johan's voice wavered with excitement.

'LsssRIK! LSSSRIKK!' In the shelter of the hut, the lizard thing was getting quite animated.

'Wot?' Grimcrag called, stomping over to where the elf stood mesmerised. The dwarf peered at the stonework. 'Wot is all the fuss ab– eh?' The dwarf stood as if frozen, a thick and stubby finger repeatedly tracing a carved line in the exposed stonework.

'RIKKRIKKRIKK!! LSSSRIKKK!'

'I... vill... Return...' whispered Grimcrag, reading the words inscribed on the base of the pyramid. A large clump of vines descended upon him, and he looked up, the spell broken. 'Unh?' grunted the dwarf, dropping his axe in surprise.

Jiriki was staring, mouth open, pointing at the top of the structure with a slender finger.

Johan Anstein, ex-Imperial envoy, was kneeling unmoving in front of the statue he had revealed at the very pinnacle of the pyramid.

'I'll be blowed!' declared the dwarf. 'Looks like a statue of one of them Norsey types.' He scratched his head, puzzled, leaving streaks of soil smeared across his brow. 'How'd that get 'ere then?'

Staring down at them from atop the small pyramid was the unmistakable form of a Norseman.

'Actually,' Johan began, 'don't you think it looks a little like–'

A spear thumped into the ground inches from Jiriki's boot, making the elf jump in shocked surprise.

'LSSSRIK! LSSSRIK! LSSSRIK!' This time, the croak was a chorus of many voices.

Very slowly, the Marauders turned round. They were completely surrounded by perhaps a hundred angry and agitated lizard creatures, all wielding spears, bows or blowpipes

'Poisoned, like as not,' Grimcrag exclaimed, reaching for Old Slaughterer. A cruelly barbed arrow shot into the sand, a mere hair's breadth away from the dwarf's reaching fingers. He hurriedly snatched his hand back, and a glassy grin crept over his face. For the first time in years, Grimcrag Grunsonn faced a multitude of foes without his trusty axe in his hand. In his heart of hearts, Grimcrag knew that this did nothing good for their odds of winning. It also made him horribly embarrassed. Caught short, he flushed bright red.

The lizards advanced, hissing noisily and brandishing their impressively sharp-looking weapons.

'Don't worry, Grimcrag, I won't tell anyone... even if this whole tragic mess is your fault!' Jiriki whispered, nodding at the dwarf's axe.

Their captive lizard nodded knowledgeably and burped almost to itself. 'S'Rikkitiz!'

INEXORABLY THE Marauders were being forced up to the top of the pyramid, where Johan stood swaying in the intense heat of the sun. Grimcrag could see his axe at the base of the pyramid, apparently of little interest to the lizard creatures which ringed the pyramid, gesturing with their spears and bows. Their hissed chanting was all but deafening. The Marauders glanced nervously about them, hoping to spy some way out of their hopeless predicament.

'A pretty pickle you've got us into, lad, and no mistake,' Grunsonn grumbled, sitting down on the top step. 'And us with no weapons 'n'all.'

Johan gasped in indignant surprise. 'What do you mean, Grimcrag? It was you who said the place was deserted. It was you that drank their beer.' The young man pointed at the axe the dwarf clutched. 'And what do you call that thing, a tooth-pick?'

Grimcrag was clutching his spare axe, Orcflayer, in one scarred paw, but his miserable countenance spoke volumes. 'It's not the same. Just don't feel right. It's all in the runes, y'see.' The dwarf gestured vaguely with the deadly looking axe at the throng of lizards before them. 'If them things kill me while I'm not using Ole Slaughterer, I'll, I'll...' His voice choked, and a tear crept into the old dwarf's eye. Grimcrag cast a shamefaced gaze at his boots. When he spoke again, it was with a small and tremulous voice. 'Well, I'll just never live it down.'

Jiriki slapped the dwarf on the back of his head, knocking his helm down over his eyes. 'Stop being so pathetic, Grunsonn;

we've been through worse that this, just.' The elf stood steely-eyed beside young Anstein, an arrow nocked in his fine elven bow.

At that moment, their attention was drawn to a commotion on the edge of the clearing. A huge lizardman, bigger than the others and bedecked in all manner of feathers, bones and other dubious finery, strode towards the pyramid. The creature had almost blue-black skin, and in one scaly clawed hand it wielded a long staff. As the Marauders watched, lightning-blue flames glittered balefully around its tip.

'Uh oh, they've got magic.' Johan manoeuvred himself behind the statue.

A crackling bolt of blue energy surged towards them, but even though it was lying at the base of the pyramid, the potent runes on Old Slaughterer drew and earthed the seething forces emanating from the shaman's staff. After a moment, the lizardman stopped trying to immolate the Marauders and stood nonplussed, its head cocked on one side like a bird. It studied them intently for a minute or so, then squawked something at its fawning retinue. They scuttled off and returned moments later, bearing some heavy-duty nets. The Shaman nodded up at the warriors, and licked its thin lips expectantly.

On top of the pyramid, Grimcrag stood up and set his lips in a stern pout. 'Ain't going in no net. Sharn't. Ain't no fish!' The dwarf looked at Johan and Jiriki, and grinned his familiar grin. 'Dunno what came over me, lads!.' Setting his helm to its correct angle, he whispered quietly to himself. 'Me old dad always said "It's not the axe as makes the dwarf", and 'appen he was right.'

'I hear you, my friend. Now is not the time for carping,' Jiriki agreed. 'Let's do it!'

'Oh heavens, there are hundreds of them, with magic and nets. We're bound to die now, aren't we?' muttered Johan, more in anger than fear. The deathly confidence exuded by Grimcrag and Jiriki was strangely infectious, and the two older Marauders were heartened by the sound of Johan's sword scraping clear from its scabbard.

At the base of the pyramid, twenty feet of very steep steps below them, the lizard things gathered. Looking up, they obviously weren't too keen to climb the steps, nets or no, not into the waiting blades of three belligerent warriors who had such an obvious height advantage over them. They rasped and burped amongst themselves, and a few launched arrows up to skitter and skip on the flagstones of the pyramid.

'Come on then, frog spawn!' Johan shouted. 'Come and get your legs chopped.' He turned to Grimcrag. 'Shame old Grail-mad Pierre isn't here, he loves frogs' legs.'

Grimcrag guffawed. Jiriki smirked.

'LSSSRIKK!' the lizards croaked as one, but they did not advance. The shaman reached the bottom of the pyramid with bounding steps, and squinted up at the warriors. 'Nrssssssss?' it hissed angrily at them, then rounded on its cowardly compatriots. After a few minutes of frantic hissing and croaking, the black lizard threw off its headdress in apparent disgust, and shook its mottled head resignedly. It shrugged its shoulders and pointed up beyond the pyramid top. The other lizards followed its gaze, and immediately went into a frenzy of excitement, hopping up and down and hissing enthusiastically.

Atop the pyramid, the Marauders watched, transfixed.

'Now what?' Grimcrag grunted.

'They seem excited about something,' Johan muttered, confused.

Jiriki turned to face the way the lizards were looking. 'Sun's going down. They'll wait for the dark.'

The others turned and looked. There was no denying the fact that the sun was sinking fast. Already its ruddy red globe fondly touched the top most branches of the trees, and soon it would drop out of sight completely.

'It sinks so fast in these climes,' began Johan.

'No wonder neither, it puts such an effort in all day. It's prob'ly 'zausted.'

'So what shall we do?' the elf asked.

'Do?' Grimcrag snorted. 'What d'ya think we're going to do?'

'Well,' began Johan, 'I, for one do not intend being butchered in the dark.'

'That's the spirit, young 'un. Let's go get 'em, eh?'

'Yes, well… oh hell, why not!'

Drawing themselves to their full respective heights, the Marauders prepared for battle.

At the base of the pyramid, the lizards realised that something was about to happen, and they began to form formal ranks of shield, spear and bow.

If still undecided in their hearts (and not one of them would ever admit that such was the case) the Marauders atop the pyramid had their minds made up by a familiar heavily-muscled figure who appeared in the dusk light around the path to the village. His voice reached them as a heavily accented bellow.

'Vot you vaitink for – Marauders or Mauses?' The barbarian was already at a run towards the lizards, the glitter of his sword a deadly sliver of malice in the dying rays of the sun.

'CHAAARGE!!!!' roared Grimcrag, leaping down towards the waiting lizard horde. He didn't even turn to see if the others were following. Battle cries to the fore and now to their rear threw the lizards into total panic. Despite the entreaties of their shaman, Anstein saw them turn to flee. Their path was blocked by a charging barbarian. A barbarian who wielded a two handed sword in his right hand and a heavily scarred iron shield on his left arm. A barbarian who howled like a wolf as he charged towards the assembled hordes of reptiledom with no apparent concern for his own safety.

Tumbling down the pyramid towards the lizards' backs, Anstein could see that this was going to get very bloody very fast. They obviously didn't take very well to surprises.

Then something very strange happened.

SEEING THE charging barbarian, the lizards flung their weapons aside, dropped to their knees and buried their heads in the sand.

Grimcrag, Jiriki and Johan came to a halt at the bottom of the pyramid. A carpet of lizard backs stretched away from them.

Grimcrag shrugged and raised his axe. 'Hardly seems fair! Still, never look a gift coin and all that.' he grunted, decapitating three lizards in one blow. Jiriki stopped the slaughter by adroitly tripping the dwarf over. Black blood was splattered everywhere, but the remaining lizards sat motionless.

'Oi!' exclaimed the dwarf, dragging himself to his feet. He made for the security of Old Slaughterer.

'Leave it, Grimcrag,' Johan hissed. 'Something's happening.'

Berserk, Keanu charged onwards, dimly wondering where the enemy had gone and why the floor was all lumpy. He slowed to a loping trot, then a walk, then finally stopped. He could see Jiriki, Grimcrag and Anstein all right, but he could have sworn that there was a whole horde of… Jiriki was gesturing at his boots.

'Vot?' he bellowed, still partly berserk, peering down. He was standing on the chest of a large lizard creature, a black-skinned one bedecked in feathers and bone. He raised his sword to strike.

The lizard's eyes bulged, but it managed to croak loudly. Keanu dropped his sword in surprise; the other Marauders did likewise. They all clearly heard the lizard shaman speak words – understandable words.

'Velkomsss God LosssErikkk. Long haff ve Vaited innit yessssss.'

The living carpet whispered at Keanu with the rustling, hissing squeak of a hundred lizard voices: 'LSSSRIKKK! LSSSSSRIKKK! LSSSSRIKKK!'

Grimcrag patted Johan on the shoulder. 'I'll be blowed! Maybe this isn't going to be so bad after all!'

SIX MONTHS IN paradise was probably enough for anyone. It was certainly enough for Johan Anstein. Much as he enjoyed lying on a beach being feted as a god by proxy – just knowing Keanu seemed to be enough to get you in the club – Johan knew that there was a whole world out there over the horizon, just waiting for the unique influence of Grunsonn's Marauders.

Still, he had had time to write up their adventures in his journal, the food was good, the natives friendly (except for the odd hostile glare from the extended families of those accidentally killed by Grimcrag and Keanu) and the weather beyond compare. As he curled his toes lazily in the warm sand, Johan pondered on his companions.

Grimcrag, certainly, was unusually happy, what with his beer and the cave full of gold which the dwarf was lovingly transferring to their patched-up and extended rowing boat in his secret cove. Johan sighed contentedly.

Only Jiriki was unhappy with the situation, his wanderlust frustrated by the confines of the small island. The elf had become quite solitary of late, taking to long sojourns along the cliff-tops on the lookout for ships. He had even built some warning beacons out of dead brushwood. He had meticulously timed the tides, how long it took to get a fire going, run to the boat and get out to sea. Johan really couldn't see the point, and hoped that Jiriki would perhaps relax a little when he realised that they truly were in the lap of the gods regarding rescue. They had not had so much as a sniff of a sail since their arrival six months ago.

Still, it was sunny and warm every day of the week... maybe they could stay awhile longer yet. Actually, it wasn't as if they had any real choice in the matter. Jiriki should jolly well wake up and–

His thoughts were interrupted by a familiar rasping voice.

'Anssssstein, 'vake?' The voice was that of Froggo, Johan's adopted lizard man. The young creature – apparently they called themselves 'skinkz' in their native tongue – followed Anstein everywhere, eager to learn as much as it could of the big, wide world beyond its island home.

'Yes, Froggo, me lad, I'm awake. Just musing.' Johan turned to look at the skink, which as usual sat a respectful distance away from its adopted mentor. On matters of gender, when pressed, the creatures had been ambiguous to say the least, and Johan was none too sure if Froggo was in fact a boy or a girl, or even whether they made such distinctions. Johan had pigeon-holed Froggo (he had quickly realised that he had no way in this world of being able to pronounce the creature's real name, which sounded like a cistern being flushed) as being a boy, for neatness' sake more than anything else.

'Musink?' the skink enquired, blinking its toad-like eyes and scratching a leathery patch of skin under its long chin. 'Vot meaninksss?'

'Another word for thinking, sort of... You know, your accent is terrible, Froggo; abominable, in fact!' Johan turned over and lazily threw a small stick at the reptile, which dodged nimbly out of the way. In return, it cheekily threw a small pebble which hit Johan square on the forehead.

'But better zan yoursss in my ssspeaks yessssss?' the lizard creature quipped, making the loud hissing noise in the back of its throat that Johan had learned passed for laughter in skink.

Johan jumped to his feet and chased the small scampering creature back to the village. It was nearly time for lunch.

Behind them, on the furthest visible reach of the ocean, the small black speck of a sail hove into view over the horizon. On a nearby cliff-top, a thin plume of black smoke clawed its way upwards into the heavy air.

IN HIS CAVE, Grimcrag worked tirelessly, piling yet more gold artefacts into the boat and tying them securely down. As he worked, he endlessly muttered to himself under his breath: 'Can't last, got to be a catch. Can't last, got to be a catch.'

The dwarf's arms and armour were stacked neatly to one side of the cave, glittering from the sparkling reflections cast by the clear water. The mouth of the cave was perhaps a hundred feet distant, a patch of white heat against the shadowy black of the cave. The slap-slap of water kept a constant rhythm by which the dwarf worked, stacking the gold items one at a time in a strange looking boat which was moored beside a natural stone jetty.

The boat was an odd mongrel contraption, new wood gleaming against older, more battered timbers. Its prow bore a proud dragon head, and there was provision for a small mast. Four old and rusted shields lined each side of the vessel, one to protect each of the oars which dipped into the cool waters of the cave. A bigger, steering oar was mounted at the higher stern, and the boat looked to be just what it was – a mix between the wreck of their rowing boat and a much older Norse longboat.

The soft pattering of booted feet disturbed the dwarf, and he instinctively reached for his trusty axe. A moment later and Jiriki's sun-tanned face peered into the cave. The elf had taken the most naturally to the tropical climate, and now looked healthier than the dwarf had ever seen him. 'Grimcrag?' he called, and from his tone, the dwarf knew that something was of grave concern. He stepped from the shadows.

'Here, Jiriki – what's up, old friend?'

The elf strode into the cave, grinning at the boat despite himself. He pointed at Grimcrag's construction and tapped a foot impatiently. 'Will that thing really float out of there?' The elf nodded towards the cave mouth. 'Weighed down by so much gold?'

Grimcrag spat on the floor, disgusted by the temerity of such a question. 'Course it will! What do you take me for?' The dwarf stomped up to the elf and prodded him with a stubby callused finger. 'While you lot've bin living it up with yer froggy friends,' Grimcrag's arm swept around the cave as evidence of his industry, 'some of us 'ave bin working blimming hard!'

The elf clapped Grimcrag on the shoulder and smiled. 'Splendid, my industrious friend, splendid. You know that, of all of us, I am least happy with our predicament, and now, we may have… an opportunity.' Jiriki headed back to the rear entrance to the cave, before turning once more to face the bemused dwarf. 'Come on, Grimcrag. We'll be using that boat of yours sooner than you'd imagine, I'll wager!'

'What do you mean?' Grimcrag began. 'I'm not using it for fishing, nor joyrides neither – look what happened last time…'

Jiriki winked conspiratorially as he stepped out into the daylight. His lilting voice drifted back into the cave. 'Come on, Grimcrag, grab your axe too – the tide's rising, the beacon's lit. By my estimation we have no more than an hour!'

'It's the sun, isn't it?' The dwarf frowned as he grabbed his axe. 'That, and all the time you've spent moping around those cliff-tops.'

But Jiriki was off and running. His last words, echoing around the cavern, persuaded the old dwarf that something important was happening: 'I've spied a sail. We have company!'

KEANU SAT ON his bamboo throne, two skinks fanning him with the feathers of some particularly large and gaudily-plumaged bird. Swathed in garlands of exotic flowers, the barbarian drank warm beer from his helmet; his feet rested in a bowl of cool water, which was replenished regularly by more scurrying minions. He faced out onto the village square, where the now spotlessly clean pyramid reared up into the sky.

On top of the pyramid, Keanu's likeness, or something approaching it, stared back at the barbarian. If he squinted hard, the entire village had a distinctly Norse look. Keanu sighed contentedly. If only it were nice and cold.

The Reaver burped loudly. 'Fang, da Legend vunce more, f'ya pleez.' Keanu gestured languidly at the black-skinned shaman, who stood in his ceremonial place beside the throne. He had named all the skinks in his 'hearth-guard' after his wolf hounds back home in Norsca.

Keanu fondly thought of the band of heavily-armed reptilian warriors as his very own Berserkers, although none of them had, as yet, betrayed any leanings towards going berserk at all. 'Not got the temperament fer it,' Grimcrag had explained at the last banquet, whilst Jiriki maintained that it was something to do with their blood being cold, or some such typical elf non-sense.

On a cue from Fang the shaman, a bigger lizard creature, stripped down to a loincloth, banged heartily on a brass gong strung up on sturdy wooden poles beside the throne.

Within minutes, the clearing was alive with skinks, all jostling for places from where they could hear the story again. Being a Norse barbarian himself, Keanu appreciated good tales. In his consideration, like a good wine, they improved with age. Not that any wine which came Keanu's way got the chance to enjoy its autumn years, but the principle was, he felt, a sound one.

After a while, the hubbub in the small square died down. Fang cleared his throat to speak the story on which the skink island civilisation was founded. With an imperious wave of his massive arms, Keanu bade Fang be silent. Standing, the barbarian addressed the assembled throng. Agog, they listened intently.

'Today,' Keanu began, his eyes sweeping the appreciative crowd, 'today I'm tellink da Saga, ja?'

'Ya, yesssss, ya!' the lizards chorused, rocking backwards and forward in delight. Fang smiled benignly and nodded his crested head.

'I'm keepink 'im short, koz nearly Dinna time,' the barbarian continued, striding to the front of the crowd. Already, a bunch of skinks stood ready to perform the odd ritualistic actions which always accompanied the story.

Keanu grinned: what a stupid bunch of lizards. He'd heard the story enough times that he knew it off by heart, almost felt it was of his doing. He'd give them a story to remember. He began, his voice echoing loud and strong across the clearing.

'Und so beginz da Saga of da Voyage of Erik da Lost, Great God Warrior of Norsca, und how he brought Kulture und Beer to Paradise.'

The miming lizards were ahead of Keanu already, making rowing actions as they envisaged the ship of Eric the Lost ploughing across the mighty oceans to this small island. Looking around, Keanu could see that the majority of the lizards had their eyes closed, broad grins of contentment splitting their leathery faces.

And so, at least for a few minutes, Keanu escaped from the real world of reaving and death, as he told the age-old story of Eric, great warrior king, and his voyage across the sea. He told of mighty storms and huge sea monsters (several mimers became carried away and bit each other at this point), of treacherous rocks and wicked pirates. He told of strange lands populated by strange creatures, of mighty heroes and deeds of wonder. And he told of how, after many years of travelling, Eric arrived at this fair land, which he took to be the fabled land of Lustria, and named it Ericland.

Keanu looked around the band of skinks and almost laughed aloud. He still couldn't really believe the next part of the story himself, although there was proof enough for anyone. The skinks doing the actions were confused by Keanu's expression: normally the story didn't stop here, and they were repeatedly miming planting a flag in the earth. Keanu hastily drew a breath and continued.

Eric and his wise heroes had stormed the island, killing all of the great lizard monsters who had once lived here. (Fang had showed Keanu the cave full of bones, and the barbarian had been truly impressed – Eric had certainly known how to fight judging by the size of some of the skeletons.) He liberated the skinks to true civilisation: true speech, freedom… and beer.

The next part of the story almost stuck in the barbarian's throat, such was the enormity of the lie. Now he told of how Eric and his noble followers had revealed the true horror of that evil and glittering substance known as 'Golt', and how those brave and selfless Norsemen had liberated the skinks from the horrid material of which they had so much, and hidden it in a far distant cave, never to trouble their idyllic lives again.

And finally, Keanu told of how the day dawned when Eric and his band of warriors had proven the true depths of their selfless love, by setting sail away from the island in their ship full of the hated gold, simply to get rid of it once and for all. Several of the skinks were weeping great salty tears at this part of the story, and not for the first time, Keanu marvelled at their gullible nature.

'Ja, but too much Golt was there for vun Schip, so as he vent avay, Eric was makink da Promise, ja?' Keanu shouted the words at the throng. They were all staring, a hundred pairs of unblinking eyes fixed on his face, hanging on every syllable. 'Und vot was dat Promise?' Keanu implored, secretly pleased with his performance.

As one voice, the skinks shrieked the words which ended the story every time it was told. Their voices echoed around the jungle, and several flocks of multi coloured birds took flight in terror. 'I VILL BE BACK FOR DA GOLD – SSSO DON'T TOUCH, JA?'

Exhausted, the assembly fell silent, and Keanu fell back onto his throne, gesturing for beer. The crowd abruptly erupted into applause, as they hooted and hissed and slapped their tails on the ground.

Fang smiled. His prophecies over the years had been borne out. He was the true priest of Erikkk. Everyone now knew that Eric had kept his promise, even if his warriors had changed a bit over the years. Especially the short, grubby, bearded one.

At that moment, the spell was broken as Johan, Froggo, Jiriki and Grimcrag rushed into the village square, panting and out of breath.

'Kean– Eric!' Johan shouted. 'We've got to go!'

'Vot? Going vere?'

'Forty-five minutes now!' Jiriki added.

The skinks were somewhat agitated, for they were not used to such an abrupt ending. Usually, when Fang was telling it, they got a good hour's sun bathing after such an energetic story, or at last half an hour in the cool water of the pond.

Jiriki ran over to the bemused barbarian, and whispered in his ear. The effect was electrifying. Like a scalded cat, Keanu was on his feet, weapons grabbed and running across the clearing in one fluid motion. The throng of skinks blinked and hissed uncertainly. Fang frowned, unsure as to what his lord was doing.

Jiriki ran after Keanu, shoving him in the back to keep him moving. Grimcrag and the others had already vanished down the path to the cave, the dwarf showing a surprising turn of speed.

Shaking himself free of the elf's grasp, Keanu glared at Jiriki and turned to face his villagers. 'Not Vurryink,' he hissed at Jiriki, before turning and bellowing at the hundred or so lizards. 'Now is da Time!' he began, raising his sword to the air. 'My Berserkers – Volf pack, Bear soldiers, Schnow Leopards, now is your Time to fight!'

The most inappropriately named groups of skinks scuttled off to collect weapons, growling and snapping at each other. A nimbus of blue fire already played around the tip of Fang's ceremonial staff.

'What are you doing?' Jiriki snapped, dancing agitatedly from foot to foot. 'We don't have time for this.' Keanu pushed the elf away and faced the skinks again.

'Now ve must be goink!' Keanu stabbed himself in the chest with his forefinger. 'Me, Erik, und my Varriors!' He grinned, showing sharp white teeth. The lizards were starting to look crestfallen. 'But not to be Vorryink! No! Ve take all da nasti Golt vith us to da land beyont da sea!'

At this, the skinks looked mightily relieved, and his 'Berserkers' started to look worried that there might be nothing to fight about after all. Keanu put them right, as he backed slowly away from them down the trail.

'A ship full of evil men is Komink, friends of, er, da big dead Lizart Monsters,' the barbarian improvised magnificently. 'Ya! S'right! Lizart friends komink to take you away! You stop them, ja? Stop them, my friend Fank! Lead skinkz to victor, ja?'

At this, Jiriki and Keanu turned tail and fled along the jungle path, heading to the boat and hopefully a slim chance at escape. Behind them, they heard growing chanting and shouting as the skinks prepared to fight for their island.

'You certainly got them going,' Jiriki gasped as they plunged down the muddy trail, vines whipping their faces as they ran.

'I'm makink da Divershun – they'll have to get everyvun ashore from da ship for da fight!' Keanu answered. 'Vot's da Hurri?'

'Diversion? Excellent plan!' Jiriki abruptly darted down a side trail. 'This way, Keanu. Tide's rising fast and we still have to get the boat out of the cave!'

A few minutes later and they burst onto the stony path which led to the cave. Hearts pounding, they had covered the distance to the mooring harbour in a scant five minutes. Ahead, Jiriki could see Johan dashing into the entry tunnel, and he knew it was a fair bet that Grimcrag was there already. Despite his bulk and shape, the dwarf could put on a ferocious burst of speed when need be. Particularly if time was of the essence, and the reward might be escape to freedom with a vast fortune in pure gold.

They plunged into the darkness of the cave, and headed for the heavily loaded boat. If Jiriki was right, and if they were very lucky, six months of not too arduous captivity were shortly about to end.

'AVAST THAT BILGE, mister mate. Bring the mains'l forr'ard and mainbrace the spinnaker!' Looking through the fine bronze telescope with his one good eye, Hook Black Pugh could see the plume of smoke rising from the island. As he studied the idyllic looking landscape, he shouted his orders over his braid-encrusted shoulder. As usual, old Yin-Tuan, first mate and veteran of a hundred such voyages, sighed resignedly and did nothing of the sort. Instead, the hulking first mate gave out a string of clipped, near-intelligible orders to the cut-throats who leaned eagerly over the port bulwark. As if already stung by the barbed whip hanging at Yin-Tuan's belt, the pirates brought the vessel around with a speed and efficiency which belied their ragged looks.

Pugh turned to his second officer, 'Teachy' Bligh, and sighed loudly. 'Aaargh, Bligh me lad, as fine an island fer a-plunderin as I ever did see!'

Bligh, hailing from Sartosa, was a nasty piece of work, all muscle and psychopathic intent. A grim smile split his normally emotionless face, and a familiar glitter came to his black eyes. 'Only island we've seen this past six month, sir. Lads need a bit of pillagin'.' He half-pulled his cutlass from its orcskin scabbard and looked around as if intending to pillage something right here, right now.

Pugh grabbed Bligh's hand and tutted. 'Now, now, Teachy boy, there baint none o'them Cathay slaves left to a-play with, you've bin and pillaged 'em all.' The pirate captain held his hook under Pugh's nose. The spike glittered menacingly in the sunlight. 'Yer don't want to go a-makin' me cross again, does yer?' Hook Black made a thrusting, twisting action with the hook. 'Or it might be spiky time fer you again!'

Bligh blanched visibly and clenched his legs tightly together. With a disconsolate grunt, he pushed his cutlass back into its scabbard. 'Okay boss, okay. I din't mean nowt. S'just...' Bligh's voice died away and a cunning animal gleam came into his black, dead eyes. 'The lads needs a good pillage, is all – they say it's bad luck as kept us away from land or plunder for the past six month, bad luck of that there Bretonnian gold we stole!'

Bligh stepped back, ready to make a run for it. After a moment's silence, however, his captain began rocking to and fro, giggling to himself merrily. The braid on his salt-stained jacket swayed with his rocking, and the faded medals on his once-red sash jangled in the sunshine. Throwing his black bearded head backwards, the pirate captain gave out a huge bellow of laugher.

'Curse o'the Grunsonns, is it?' he guffawed.

'Yer, that's right!' Bligh affirmed, looking around the rest of the crew for moral support. None was to be had: they all seemed to be busy swabbing decks or preparing cannons. A good few of them had climbed the rigging of the mainmast and were studiously making long needed repairs to the tattered expanse of a hundred bits of ancient stitched canvas that passed for the sail on the Dirty Dog.

Pugh's laughter abruptly stopped, and he stomped his iron tipped peg leg hard on the wooden planking of his bridge. When next he spoke, it was with the deathly calm he usually reserved for the last words his victim was destined to hear. He pointed his hook down at Bligh, who grinned nervously and held up his hands in something approaching an attitude of apology.

'Lissen, Mister Bligh, and lissen good!' Hook Black Pugh pulled his shabby tricorn down over his forehead, and glowered the length of the ship. 'And that goes double fer you lot of scurvy blaggards. Even you, Mr Yin-Tin-Tong or whatever y'name is!' He swept the fearful crew with his steely eye. 'You might be better sailors than I'll ever be…'

The pirates all exchanged confused looks at this frank admission, most unlike their hated captain.

'But!' Pugh turned back to face his crew, and there was fire in his voice. ''Tis my ship! My letter of marque from our Tilean Lords–' at this, all the pirates, including Pugh, made elaborate mock bows to one another, '–and my leadership what's got us an 'old full o'gold to take 'ome.'

Pugh paused to let the truth sink in. 'And now, me hearties, we have discovered a new island for our gracious lords.' (More mock bowing.) Pugh shook his right hand at the island, fast hoving into full view, his filthy lace cuffs dropping crumbs of bread and other detritus onto the floor.

'So break out the rum, me lads, and make it a double, fer today we makes our fortunes from our proud and noble patrons!' This time the pirates' bows were most sincere. Pugh held a finger to his lips as the cheers began to swell. 'ain't finished yet.'

He turned and pointed once more at the island. 'We'll call it Pughland, and it'll be a most profitable watering 'ole and stop off point for the fleets of Tilea, Bretonnia, Estalia, maybe even the Empire toffs.' He closed his eyes and a blissful smile split his raggedly bearded chin. 'Oh yes, me lads, and a bounty we will collect from each and every one. So no more bloody yellow talk of bad luck! That dwarf is dead and gone this six month back!'

The ship erupted into cheers and whoops as the avaricious gang envisioned the glories and riches to come. Bligh smiled menacingly and wondered how he could get rid of Pugh for good.

At that moment, the foppish voice of keen-eye Dando in the crow's nest rang out: 'War canoes, loads of 'em… and they're full o'bloomin' frogs!'

As one, the pirates rushed to the side of the ship and peered towards the island. Sure enough, a score or more slender canoes were heading straight for them. As Pugh focused on the lead vessel, he could make out a dozen or so fiercely betoothed lizards working hard at the paddles. Standing in the prow of the boat was a mean looking black-skinned lizard, wielding a large staff, about which a nimbus of light flickered ominously.

Hook Black Pugh snapped his telescope closed and turned to face his crew. He grinned maliciously. 'Tides a'risin' fast! Yin-Tin, turn her about. Grog-boy, open the gun ports. Teachy, get ready fer boardin'. Looks like we got us a fight!'

Like a well oiled machine, the pirates went straight to battle stations, the Dirty Dog heeling around so that her port guns faced the oncoming canoes. In short order, the barrels were run out of the gun ports, ten lethal iron-cast eyes staring grimly out at the frail craft of the lizardmen.

Pugh raised his scimitar, sunlight glinting off the oiled blade. On the foredeck, Yin-Tuan frowned and gestured with a brawny arm.

'Cap'n–'

'Not now, Yin-Tin!'

'But the elevation–'

'FIRE!' Pugh's blade swept down, and the world erupted in a roaring cloud of smoke and fire, as ten cannon balls hurtled towards the hapless lizardmen. Already several canoes were turning about to head back towards the relative safety of the cove.

They need not have worried. As the wily Yin-Tuan had realised, the small canoes were already inside the arc of fire of the great cannons, and their deadly cargo crashed over the heads of the desperately paddling skinks to turn the sea beyond into a welter of threshing foam.

'Fire lower, you idiots!' Pugh screamed, but the great cannons were already at their lowest elevation.

'Cap'n, no need to waste any more shot – the toads is runnin' away!' Yin-Tuan grinned toothlessly, his scrawny arm gesticulating excitedly over the side of the ship.

Pugh spun around, telescope raised to his eye. 'Aaargh, it be so!' The captain continued staring down the tube, scratching his beard with his hook. 'And they be putting a fair old distance between us and them 'n'all… are we a-driftin' with the tide, Mr Mate?'

With a timeworn sigh, Yin-Tuan gently prised his captain's fingers from the telescope and turned the brass tube around. Pugh visibly started, and his hat fell off, revealing a balding pate surrounded by a scraggy mop of stringy black hair.

'Aaargh! We can catch the scurvy frogs!' Pugh folded the telescope and secreted it in the voluminous folds of his jacket. Grabbing hold of a bell rope, he gestured with his hook over the port side of the galleon. As the action stations bell rang loud and clear over the still waters of the lagoon, Pugh squinted at the receding canoes. The manic glint which normally preceded grand slaughter was in the pirate's eye, and his thin lips were wet with spittle. 'Aaargh, me brave lads! Lower the boats, drop anchor, boarding all crew, women and children first, take no prisoners!' His cut-throat crew made for the boats, carrying marlin spikes, muskets and cutlasses.

Pugh shoved with a spur-booted foot to encourage any laggards to embark in the boats. 'Last one ashore is the lily-livered son of a toothless bar-crone from Marienburg!'

'So you'll be last aboard then, sir – shall I save you a seat?'

'Less of that, me lad or you'll feel the business end of me 'ook!'

'Err, are we all going?' Yin-Tuan frowned.

'Aaargh! That be so – not fair to deny some of me fine crew the pillagin' they deserve!' Pugh grinned, showing surprisingly white teeth.

'But all of–'

'Don't be so wet, Yin-Tong, it's not like the Bretonnian navy is about to show up, is it?' Pugh made a great show of scanning the horizon with his telescope. 'We ain't seen another sail for months!'

'But–'

'Get in that there boat NOW!'

Moments later and the long rowing boats splashed down into the warm, clear waters. Moments after that, some fifty cut-throats were rowing hard for the beach amidst much shouting and jeering. In the lead boat, Pugh could see that the lizard things had already disembarked, and the last few were disappearing into the jungle, leaving their canoes on the beach.

'Lily-livered sons of frogs!' he shouted 'We'll be eating thee afore sundown!' Turning to face his crew, he grinned maliciously at Belly Fat Dave, the ship's cook, his tongue licking his lips in eager anticipation. 'I hope you've got that there Tilean mustard you're so keen on, Mr Cook. I foretell a grand feast in a few hours' time!'

The fat and sweating cook was already sharpening several deadly-looking cleavers on a whetstone he always carried with him. 'Cap'n, theys going to taste bootiful!'

The pirates' boats surged towards the prey, like hunting dogs hot on the scent of a wounded beast. In Pugh's estimation, the isle was not so large, and once the lizards' canoes were burnt, the things would have nowhere to go, except into the pirates' waiting cooking pot.

'Faster, me lads, faster – I'll warrant there's gold an' jewels fer the pickin' too!' As one voice, Hook Black Pugh's scurvy crew cheered lustily and pulled harder on the oars. A few moments later, the prow of the lead boat ground against the soft sand of the beach, and a dozen hard-bitten pirates leapt eagerly ashore. They were confident that their great captain was going to deliver booty, treasure and grog in abundance to the dark holds of the Dirty Dog. He always did.

One way or another.

* * *

'ANSSSTEIN, SSSSSTOP!' A sibilant hissing filled the cave as the Marauders rushed into the welcoming darkness, Johan in front and just a little out of breath. He almost ran into a spear in the darkness, and they skidded to an abrupt halt, scant twenty paces from their boat.

'Go easy!' Grimcrag grunted, nearly tripping over his axe. 'Is that our friendly reptile?'

'Froggo?' Johan asked, confused by the flinty point which dug sharply at his chest. 'What's all this about?'

As his eyes grew accustomed the dark, Johan could make out perhaps a dozen shadowy figures, dappled reflections flickering on the wall in the dim light from the cave mouth. Lizardmen, hand-picked 'Berserkers' by the look of it – wielding spears and other dangerous-looking weapons. This felt an odd time for a goodbye committee, and the lizards' general demeanour suggested agitation.

'Maybe quarter of an hour left, Anstein. Look at the water level: the cave mouth will soon be impassable!' Jiriki's silky voice was edged with impatience, sounding like it was emerging despite clenched jaw and grated teeth. 'I – will – not – miss – this – chance!' The threat in the elf's voice was clear.

'Well, Froggo?' Johan demanded, trying to size up the situation. Glancing ahead, he could see that the rising tide had indeed already ensured that it would be a tight fit getting their outlandish boat out of the cave; in a few minutes the task would be impossible. He knew that they had very little time if they wanted their plan to work, otherwise they would be stuck on the island in the middle of a war between pirates and lizards, with no means of escape. The clock was ticking, and Johan knew that the last thing they could afford now was an unexpected run in with their lizard 'subjects' over some misinformed breach of tribal etiquette. Johan could see that the other Marauders had already made their decisions, and were imperceptibly moving into full combat readiness. More hissing and angry spear-gesturing, however, stopped them in their tracks.

From the shadows, Froggo stepped forward, with what passed for a sinister grin on his reptilian features. 'Anstein, you teach too well. I lissssten yessss, lissssten welll…' The creature bared sharp teeth and brought up its spear to point accusingly at the Marauders.

'What's it mean, Johan?' Grimcrag demanded gruffly. 'We haven't time for this...'

'SSSSHUTTUP!!' one of the Berserkers barked at the dwarf, whose stubby fingers were already twisting restlessly at the haft of his axe.

Froggo upended his spear and prodded Johan hard in the chest with the haft. 'Not godsssss no!' He prodded again for emphasis and Johan stepped back a pace. 'Not freindssss no! Not LossRikk no!'

A faint ripple of 'Losssrikklosssrikk' echoed around the cave. Froggo nodded and continued.

'Robbersss yes! Liarsss yes! Thieves yesssss!' the lizard man hissed, pointing at the boat. 'Gold! Richesssss in ressst of world!'

Johan rubbed his chest and sighed. 'Look Froggo, you really don't understand–'

'Yesssss, do undersssssstand!' the creature interrupted, tongue flicking rapidly in and out. 'Undersssstand too well!' Froggo took a step forwards and gestured towards the Marauders. His fellows shuffled forwards after their leader, not looking too sure of themselves but taking comfort in their superior numbers. Spears and dart guns were levelled at the Marauders, and a dozen pairs of reptilian eyes stared with unblinking ferocity.

The tide rose implacably in the watery cave. The atmosphere of urgency was almost tangible in the cool damp air.

Johan instinctively knew that this could get very nasty, very fast. Even under the situation, he briefly marvelled to himself that a few months ago he wouldn't have known anything instinctively at all, except perhaps how to serve wine to a visiting burgomeister or Tilean ambassador. Danger is a marvellous teacher, and Johan had recently been undergoing some very practical remedial tuition at one of the most infamous cramming schools around.

'Now, Froggo,' he began, backing leisurely in the direction of what looked to be a fairly safe alcove in the cave wall, arms raised in supplication. 'Don't do anything rash...'

'Noo, Ansssstein, this isss the time of Firssst Lord Froggo!' The lizard expanded its throat sac and croaked emphatically. If lizards are capable of a mad glint in their eyes, Johan rather fancied that he could see one right at this moment. 'King

Frogggo!' the skink croaked, raising its spear above its head as the others nodded and bobbed enthusiastically.

'Eh?' Grimcrag muttered, axe half-raised.

'Vot?' scowled Keanu, his sword somehow mysteriously out of its scabbard.

Jiriki seemed to have vanished completely, to the surprise of the lizards. Maybe the cold of the cave was getting to them, but compared to the lithe movements of the Marauders, they seemed to be distinctly slow. Then again, Grunsonn's Marauders in action did seem to have the ability to make time run like treacle. Whatever, there were a dozen of the enemy, so Johan decided to take no chances and quietly slid behind the rocks in his alcove.

'Yesss! You go! Now! Leave disss boat! Go and fight pii-iratessss!'

Froggo seemed to be getting quite agitated, and Grimcrag seemed to be getting the drift of what the skink was suggesting.

'You what?' the dwarf grunted, a dangerous edge creeping into his voice. Clearly Froggo wasn't listening too carefully.

'Leave now and live, meeessssssta Grimcrag,' he hissed, and his retinue prodded angry spears towards the dwarf's rock solid and disconcertingly squat frame. 'You go! We takessss da gold and ssship, and ssssail away yesss!'

The lizards hissed and burped appreciatively, clearly pleased at the prospect of sailing the high seas in their new found ship full of gold.

'What?' Grimcrag bellowed. 'Did I hear you right? Did you say "take the gold"?'

Blinded by his recently acquired confidence, Froggo nodded and licked his lips. 'Yesss!'

A moment's silence descended upon the cave, broken only by an urgent elf voice whispering, 'Do them, do them now!'

The skinks shuffled in the sand. Grimcrag looked like he might be about to explode. Johan peered at the scene through his fingers, almost daring not to look. Beyond the gaggle of lizardmen, the cave mouth looked awfully small. Water was lapping over the top of the jetty, and Johan doubted whether the bow or stern of the boat would clear the entrance already.

'We're going to be too late,' he mumbled to himself, aghast, 'and it's all my fault!'

In the event, Froggo decided the matter. The lizard hissed at Grimcrag and pointed to the tunnel at the back of the cave. 'You are not ssso tough! Take your beard and go!'

'Right, that's enough of that! That's enough of that! That's fighting talk and I'm your dwarf!'

The cave abruptly exploded into violent and bloody action, largely composed of a swinging axe, a lunging sword, a flurry of deadly arrows and a dozen screaming lizard men.

Johan closed his eyes tightly, and covered his ears too, just for good measure. This of course meant that he completely missed the arrival of another twenty or so hand-picked and heavily armed lizardmen via the back tunnel to the cave.

'GO EASY, LADS, they'll be around here somewhere.' The pirates edged through the jungle, following the path from the beach. So far they had quickly despatched the few lizard creatures who they had caught. They hadn't had it all their own way, though, three of their number falling to poisoned darts, and one being dragged into the jungle by something big which roared and hissed as it carried the screaming man away into the undergrowth. Four dead pirates for a half dozen dead lizards seemed poor trade to Pugh's boys, used as they were to attacking ships carrying nothing more hostile than a few easily-bribed guards and a hold full of shackled slaves. They were getting nervous. They knew the island wasn't very big, yet they had been marching for what seemed like hours. And they had left their ship completely deserted in their bravado and eagerness to kill.

Pugh recognised the restlessness amongst his men, and knew that he had to think of something fast. He knew that his lads weren't above following his own past example of slitting the captain's throat and making a quick getaway, no doubt led by a new leader rapidly self-promoted from the ranks. Pugh licked his lips and fidgeted with his hook, beady eyes scouring the jungle for signs of life. The path was well trodden, that was sure enough, but whether it actually went anywhere...

'Cap'n, here!' Yin-Tuan's excited voice broke the oppressive silence. Pugh spat on the sand and smiled, wiping a grimy cuff across his sweaty brow. He hurried up to where the first mate and 'Teachy' Bligh stood at a bend in the path with swords drawn and wolfish grins. A small stream could be heard running over rocks somewhere close by, and a pile of skulls indicated some kind of warning. The pirates ignored it, staring ahead around the bend.

'Aaargh!' exclaimed Pugh, beaming roundly and slapping his first mate on the back. Yin-Tuan coughed and swallowed a chunk of chewing tobacco, grimacing at the vile taste. 'Aaargh! Didn't I say as how we would catch em?'

Yin-Tuan and Bligh nodded, raising cruel swords as their captain gestured for the rest of the pirates to catch up. Soon a gaggle of cruel-eyed thieves and cut-throats peered around the corner, grinning and chuckling at the sight of the lizard man village laid out undefended before them. The pyramid in the centre of the village did not attract a second glance as the pirates spread out to begin the looting.

'Lets burn it to the ground, boys!' shouted Pugh. 'That'll bring the newts a-runnin', I'll warrant!'

Within a few minutes the first huts were burning, black smoke rising straight into the still dead air, no wind to disperse or blow it away. A few minutes later, the pirates discovered the beer vat, to evil cheers of great delight.

Amidst the carnage, Pugh stood on the bottom step of the pyramid with Yin-Tuan and Bligh. 'Very good, me lads, this'll do nicely! Reckon they'll be back any minute now, eh?'

Bligh just grinned wickedly and held up a razor-sharp cutlass until its silver blade glinted in the sunlight, reflecting the warm blue of the sea behind them through a break in the jungle canopy. Something caught his eye, and he suddenly looked away, across the clearing. 'What the–' he began, well-honed murderous instincts immediately to the fore, but his fears were quashed as a multi-coloured bird broke cover with a raucous atonal squawk which belied its beautiful red plumage. It fluttered and flapped clumsily to another tree, where it perched nervously on a topmost branch, obviously readying itself for more prolonged flight.

'Losing yer nerve, Mr Bligh?' Pugh enquired, and all the pirates in earshot laughed appreciatively. Pugh secretly thought that perhaps Mr Bligh was getting a little too big for his stolen gentry boots, and it wouldn't hurt if they were one less officer when they rejoined the ship. He grinned condescendingly at his second officer, who scowled back at him. Hook Black Pugh was happy. Things looked to be turning out just right after all.

* * *

JOHAN DUCKED DOWN, both so that his head would not scrape against the roof, and also to avoid the slashing blade of the sword wielded by a lizard who was frothing at the mouth with uncontrolled rage. Keanu had taught the skinks only too well 'Da Vay off da Berzerka'. The boat rocked alarmingly, and Johan grabbed at the bulwark to stop himself going overboard into the cold water.

The hissing groans of dead and dying lizards reverberated chillingly around the cave as the Marauders desperately tried to cast off. Blowdarts, spears and arrows hissed through the air all around them, and several struck the boat with dull thunks as they splintered the wood.

Grimcrag held the stern, his axe carving a glittering figure of eight in the damp air, an arc which no lizard man had so far stepped into and survived. Jiriki was at the dragon prow, shooting with deadly precision into the mass of reptiles which heaved around the small dock where the boat's stern was still tethered. Every so often, the elf turned and squinted at the diminishing arch of light which was the cave mouth.

'Cast off, for pity's sake, Keanu, cast off now!' Jiriki screamed, loosing another arrow into the throng. 'I have few arrows left, and we have no time at all!'

In the stern, ducking to avoid spears and darts, Keanu fumbled with the knot with which Grimcrag had secured the boat. 'Left unta Right und through… nyet, dammit! Right ova Left und bak… Nyet!'

Glancing down from his position at the stern, Grimcrag sighed as he saw the mess Keanu was making. 'For heavens sake, meathead, it's a simple bendshank!' The dwarf tried swinging his axe one-handed and leaning back to undo the rope, but his gnarled and stubby fingers could not quite reach. As the dwarf looked away, momentarily distracted, the skinks took their chances and swarmed towards the stern. Three were instantly decapitated, the glowing runes on Old Slaughterer hissing and flashing as the awful blade did its bloody work. The blade snagged on bone deep in the fourth lizardman's body, and Grimcrag almost toppled over as his momentum was abruptly stopped. Blood boiled from the lizardman's mouth as it collapsed on the killing blade.

'Bugger!'

'Kill them yessssss!' the lizards screamed as they swarmed up the side of the boat. There were so many of them now that they threatened to overturn the small craft, overloaded as it was with carefully boxed-up gold and jewels.

Grimcrag tried desperately to fend them off from his kneeling position in the bilges, as Keanu redoubled his efforts with the knots. The fight was now too close in for arrow work, and Jiriki's blade was a cold streak in the dappled light.

'By all the gods let's go!'

'Unnh! These floorboards ain't well made, them's all splinters. Not so quick, frogface!'

'Left unda Right unda back unda dammit dammit DAMMIT!'

Without really thinking what he was doing, Johan plunged into the fray, sword stabbing to left and right. Needle teeth snapped at him, scant inches from his face, and he seemed to be surrounded by a wall of steel and claws and sharpened stone axe-heads. The sharp smell of lizard washed over him, a mix of rubber and fish-heads, and scaly arms reached out to drag him from the boat.

Not to be stopped, Johan stabbed and thrust, peering into the gloom until he saw what he sought – the rope at the point where it passed over the rim of the boat side. His sword raised over his head before descending in a flashing arc. A burly lizardman blinked in comprehension and tried to stop the wicked blade, only to have his arm severed cleanly below the elbow. Black-blue blood fountained over Johan. The sword parted the rope and thwacked into the bulwark with such force that it was stuck fast. Even with a two-handed grip, Johan could not drag it free.

All around him, lizards hung onto the boat to prevent it drifting into the cave, and cold eyes stared at the ex-Imperial envoy. A forest of blades inclined towards him, and time slowed to a standstill. A face he recognised grinned evilly, twisted into a malevolent parody of the creature he had once counted as a friend. It wielded a spear in both hands, and as it thrust forward, Johan saw his death in the glittering black orbs of its eyes.

'Froggo, nooooo!'

'Ansssssstein oh yessssss!'

At the last moment, Johan felt himself thrown backwards by the scruff of the neck by what could only be described as heavily muscled fingers. A massive sword cleaved the air, barely slowing as it cleaved Froggo too. In the same gracefully deadly movement, and with barely a shift in his stance, Keanu reversed the blade and swept its razor edge along the side of the boat. A great hissing wail resounded, and a moment later the boat began to drift into the middle of the cave. Sitting up in the bilges, Johan was almost sick as he saw the row of perhaps a dozen clawed lizard paws still clutching the side of the boat like the broken sutures of a macabre wound.

'Get rowing!' Jiriki yelled, and Johan grabbed vaguely at an oar. Grimcrag was already pulling with a vengeance, and the heavily laden boat surged gamely towards the rapidly diminishing entrance. Even Johan could see that the water in the cave was almost at the high tide mark, and he doubted whether there was already any room for the miniature Norse longboat to clear the cave.

A rasping, scraping grinding sound assured him that he was right, when the proud dragon prow caught on the craggy rock of the cave roof. The boat ground to a halt immediately, throwing Keanu hard onto a heavy crate and ripping the oar from Jiriki's hands.

The elf lowered his head and closed his eyes. 'We've lost!' he whispered 'We're really stuck here now… and even we can't beat all the lizards on this forsaken island.'

Johan looked around wildly. Jiriki was right, there was no way that the boat was going any further. The cave roof sloped down towards the entrance, and their boat was firmly wedged in place by the ornate dragon headed prow. Glancing shoreward, he could see that the water was boiling as the lizardmen hurled themselves into the water and began swimming towards their frail craft. Johan knew in his heart what the skinks intended: they would turn the boat over and drown the Marauders by sheer weight of numbers and their superior aquatic fighting skills.

'It can't end like this!' Johan shouted, looking around for some way of escape. there was none. Despair clutched at his heart.

'Unngh!' grunted Keanu, clutching weakly at his sword, the wind knocked from his lungs by the impact with the heavy crate.

'Heads down, everyone!' Grimcrag shouted cheerfully, leaving barely a second for the Marauders to act on his sage advice, as once more Old Slaughterer was pulled back for a mighty swing. As he dove for the deck, Johan could see the sheer, grim, bloody minded expression which belied the dwarfs easy words. As the blade swung back, Johan could have sworn that he caught the words, 'Shan't – have – me – gold!' expelled through gritted dwarf teeth, and then the axe was hurtling towards its target. And Johan understood Grimcrag's intent the split second before the axe ripped through the proud dragon prow, sundering four feet of very solid and seasoned wood as though it was the pulpy flesh of an overripe fruit.

From his position on the crate, Keanu could only gulp appreciatively, heaving air into his lungs as he recovered his breath.

'That'll do nicely, eh?' Grimcrag gasped, gesturing over his shoulder with a callused thumb. 'Now we'd best get a move on, as we have company on the way!'

Johan and Jiriki needed no second bidding, and were already at their oars, pulling for all their might. Together, their efforts just matched those of Keanu, who heaved mightily on the opposite oar, corded muscles standing out on his neck and shoulders. Freed from the grip of the rocky roof, the boat leapt forwards almost eagerly, and Johan reckoned that with their lower profile, they might make it after all. Just. If they ducked.

'Pity; that figurehead was the best bit of the boat I reckon, good solid timber crafted by a skilled carpenter!' Grimcrag's voice drifted wistfully across the cave.

'Shut up and grab an oar!' came the chorus back.

'AAARGH! YES, me lads!' Hook Black Pugh beamed, surveying the burning village 'This'll do very nicely indeed!' Well satisfied with the pillaging so far, Pugh grinned broadly, scratching at his stubbled chin with the business end of his hook.

A few yards away, invisibly merged with the jungle, several hundred skinks looked on with murder in their cold eyes. Sharp daggers, spears, bows and poisoned darts awaited the signal, for they were determined that none would escape. 'When red bird flysssss away...' a feather-bedecked lizard man with blue-black skin hissed ominously.

If Bligh had not been so distracted by the flight of the brightly coloured bird, he might have noticed movement in the reflection in his highly polished blade. But even if he had seen it, he would probably have thought he was seeing things. For who could believe a smallish, makeshift mongrel boat, piled up with crates and so low in the water that it looked near to sinking... or the tiny reflection of the dwarf waving rudely at him from the tiller?

As it was, he saw nothing but an ugly red bird which caused his mates to laugh at him. And if there was one thing he hated, it was being made fun of. So he just stood at the base of the pyramid and fomented murderous plans for his captain. 'No one makes fun of Arbuthnot Bligh,' he muttered, and death was in his eyes.

With an ungainly flapping of scarlet wings, the strange bird took flight.

'YOU KNOW,' began Grimcrag, lounging on a hammock strung up on the poop deck of what was up until very recently an abandoned pirate ship, 'I don't think this could have worked out much better if I'd planned it.'

'You mean you didn't?' Jiriki chided in mock surprise, from his place in the shade of the mainmast.

Grimcrag ignored the elf and continued ticking off their successes on the callused fingers of his left hand. 'We've got a ship, lizard gold, our Bretonnian gold back, had a holiday...' The dwarf glanced around the poop deck. 'Have I forgotten anything?'

'Vot 'bout da Frogmeat stew?' Keanu shouted from the crow's nest. 'Dat vas gut!'

'I still can't believe you actually cooked him,' Johan muttered sulkily. 'Just 'cos he tried to force you to crew the ship with lizards.'

'You saw what he was going to do with that there spear, lad, let's not forget, eh?' He wagged a finger remonstratively at the ex-Imperial envoy. 'Him or us lad, him or us. And you do like a bit of crackling as much as the next man!'

Johan brightened up a little at the mention of crackling, and looked over the stern of the vessel. The sun glittered on the wake of the ship, and seagulls danced in the air, no doubt hoping for any detritus from the Marauders' last meal. 'You won't find any crackling!' Johan shouted through cupped hands, but his voice was lost in the wind in the sails.

The Dirty Dog sailed serenely away from the island into the setting sun, and a new chapter in the legend that is Grunsonn's Marauders drew to a close. Well, almost…

ON TOP of the small pyramid, grouped around the noble statue, Hook Black Pugh and the remaining pirates nervously eyed the throng of angry lizard kind gathered menacingly below them. To the pirates' consternation, the leading lizards were wearing what looked like Norse helmets. At least one of them was frothing at the mouth and rolling its eyes in its scaly head. A disconcerting bellowing and hooting reached the ears of the beleaguered pirates, as arrows clattered about the pirates' booted feet.

'Getting dark.'

'They're… berserks, ain'ts they?'

'Carn't be – can they?'

'Remember, their arrers is poisoned.'

'Looks like that one's got some kind of magic.'

'We're doomed and no mistake.'

'Aaargh! I'm sorry, me lads, looks like me luck's run its course this time.

'Hold on, what's this 'ere statue?' Pugh's deafening shout of pure frustration and despair echoed across the clearing.

'I don't believe it! It's that accursed barbarian! I knew THEY had to be at the bottom of this somewhere! Aaaaargh!'

WOLF IN THE FOLD

Ben Chessell

THE LIGHT IN the temple at night had been reduced to two iron braziers in deference to lean times. The stone pillars leapt into the resulting darkness, supporting a vaulted roof of pure midnight. An insistent drip of water had found its way through the tiles above and hissed into one of the braziers, as regular and relentless as a torturer's whip.

Magnus, named for 'The Pious', straightened from where he was squatting to cover his sandals with his robe, his sole meagre defence against the cold, and resumed scrubbing the altar. Chores were performed at night by the boys. Sigmar's altar must never be touched by an untrained hand and yet it must shine like a looking glass come morning. Magnus wondered if his namesake had ever considered this paradox, or indeed polished the altar. Certainly the Arch-Lector did not do so now, cocooned in his velvet sheets with a concubine like as not, his privacy enforced by gates and blades.

The knock on the huge doors caused Magnus to drop his bucket and spill water and sand on the piecemeal image of a rampant Heldenhammer which adorned the knave of the Nuln temple. The mosaic, picked out in tiles of blue, white and gold, made little sense to a viewer as close as Magnus. Six tiles comprised the hero's nose which only took on a convincing curvature with some distance and a fair amount of latitude on the behalf of the observer. Biting a curse sufficient to have him expelled from the seminary, Magnus circumnavigated his pond and made his way down the aisle, inhabiting for a moment the scoured footsteps of countless processions of now-dead priests. The knock was repeated: three sharp cracks made with a heavy object. Magnus conjured the image of the leaden pommel of a sword until he remembered the hammer, cast in bronze, that was fixed to the left-hand door.

The boy straightened his shoulders before he drew back the heavy bolt. A wet cloak knocked him to the cold floor. The body rolled off him and lay still as the storm beat its way into the temple. Magnus struggled to his feet and put all his weight against the door.

By the time he had forced the bolt into place, the man had dragged himself to one of the huge pillars and was leaning against its massive carved base. He was a tall man, with all detail of form muffled by the sodden cloak, perhaps more than one, which he wore like a shroud. His breathing was heavy and Magnus could see the man was not well. Both of his hands grasped his stomach as if he had eaten very poorly and in the second pond made on the floor of the temple that night Magnus saw curling fronds of blood.

The man spoke, with obvious difficulty, his voice fine wine in a rough wooden mug. 'Kaslain.' The name of the arch-lector.

'Arch-Lector Kaslain sleeps, as do all the priests. Might I find you a cot in which you could rest until they awaken?' Magnus was a good student and his lessons served him well on this occasion.

The man straightened himself a little and a flash of pain stained his features.

'I doubt,' a nobleman's voice, Magnus was sure now, 'I will see the dawn.' The boy could not deny that, from the size of the stream of blood, which was nosing its way to a drain beneath the altar, the man was unlikely to wake from sleep.

'Perhaps,' Magnus took a step forward so the man could hear him without straining, 'I might wake one of the other priests to give you audience?'

The expression might have been a smile 'My last words, the confession of the sins of my life, are fit only for the ears of the arch-lector.'

Magnus searched for the textbook reply but was interrupted.

'Perhaps it might help you, boy, if I told you who I was. You have heard, I presume, of Hadrian Samoracci?' The guarded but blank stare by way of reply convinced the man that he had not.

The man sighed and a licked a fleck of blood from the corner of his lip. The taste wasn't enough to carve an expression from the hard muscles of the man's face. He continued, the names coming out with the measured curiosity of a man more used to hearing them than speaking them: 'The Tilean Wasp? The Thousand Faces from Magritta? The Coffin Builder? There are other names.'

Ah, recognition.

'You are he?'

'I am.' A pause. 'And I wish, before I go kicking and screaming into Morr's blessed company, to purify my soul of the stains which are upon it. Can you be sure any lesser priest is so enamoured of your god that he can grant me that absolution? And, boy, are you the one to deny the arch-lector the greatest confession your cult has taken in his lifetime?'

There is a certain dignity, lent to a man, even a dying man, who asks questions which cannot be answered. Magnus walked quickly from the knave of the chapel and followed a route which he knew well but seldom traversed.

One must pause for thought, to find resolve for action, before waking the arch-lector of the Temple of Sigmar at Nuln. Magnus waited for several long moments with his small fist cocked before the door. The distance it had to cross was hardly the length of his forearm but any distance crossed for the first time is a journey in darkness. Magnus had to knock twice before a voice came from inside.

'Your holiness, a man is here.' The reply was predictably scathing and Magnus waited politely for it to play itself out. 'Your worship, it is a man of great import who asks for you by name. Even now his heartblood spills on the temple floor.' Over-poetic, perhaps, but Kaslain had a penchant for that kind of language in his sermons and Magnus took a gamble. The next response would decide the issue.

'Who is this man?'

Victory. Of a kind.

* * *

TWO LESSER PRIESTS came to carry the Tilean Wasp to Kaslain's chamber. The killer had drawn his hood over his face and Magnus's imagination couldn't help but conjure up the expression on the face which had looked on death so many times as he now went to face it.

As the almost funereal procession passed Magnus, the dark head lolled towards him and the faceless hole studied him. Magnus found something pressing to examine in the pattern of the marble. He had looked at this pattern many times, head bowed in prayer, and imagined grape vines, clouds, fish netting. Now he saw veins, like the pale cheeks of an elderly man.

Left to himself in the dying hours of the night, Magnus began to sponge the man's blood from the stones. Some had stained the mortar and Magnus scrubbed hard, removing most of it. His last act before retiring at dawn – he would be allowed to sleep until mid-morning devotions – was to open the temple doors to greet the rising sun. He stepped out onto the wide stone platform and fastened the doors to the walls by means of their hooks. Solid oaken doors.

Magnus was about to enter the temple and go to his few allowed hours of sleep when he was stopped by what he saw on the doors. The bronze hammers, usually fixed to each door had been removed, taken for polishing so Sigmar's temple would show no tarnish. He remembered the sound of the stranger's insistent banging on the door. He dropped the sponge and walked carefully back down the corridor to the Arch-Lector's private chambers.

KASLAIN PREPARED himself, but not as he would for any common final confession. The cult of Sigmar often received last testaments from dying men, promising them Sigmar's blessings on their journey to the land of Morr.

The ceremony was relatively simple but often the man receiving the blessing had travelled too far on that journey to understand much of what was said. Sometimes he had something he needed to say, a long-held secret which had ceased to be important to anybody but its bearer: an evil deed, perhaps, a disloyal act or a petty criminal doing. Whatever the exact nature of the event, each man amputated the memory and gave it into the keeping of the priest so the doing would not accompany him into the next life.

Kaslain had heard many sordid and foul acts recounted to him in this manner but they seldom made an impression on the ageing priest. He had too many such tales of his own to be impressed by the petty wrong-doings of some mud-spattered farmer or bloodstained soldier.

This man he prepared to see, however, was neither of those. What reckonings had he to make with Sigmar? Kaslain, dressed in his ceremonial garb and ready to receive his dying visitor, reviewed what he knew about the man.

The Tilean Wasp, so called because of a supposed mastery of the vile arts of brewing and administering poisons. The Wolf in the Fold, or the Thousand Faces of Magritta – he had these names apparently because of an ability to disguise himself with consummate skill and infiltrate his victim's camp.

For this he was perhaps most famous and there were numerous stories of his duping this guard or that official. The stories were often recounted as humorous rhymes, idle entertainment, and each ended with a corpulent public official having his throat cut or his belly stuck. One could make jokes out of the death of fattened bureaucrats as few cared for them, but Kaslain knew the truth was more grisly than such tales allowed.

Another name this man had acquired was the Coffin Builder, because of the sheer volume of murders attributed to him in a career which spanned almost twenty years. Everything known about this assassin was premised with 'perhaps' or 'supposedly' and almost nothing was held to be indisputable fact. No one knew his real name and nobody could recognise his face for what it was.

That, thought the priest, was about to change.

The boys carried the man into Kaslain's private suite and laid him on a divan. The couch had been covered with a canvas curtain to protect it from the blood which stained the boy's white robes and bare arms in generous brushstrokes.

Kaslain, not normally one for humorous comment, was unusually buoyant, commenting that the two boys were perhaps alone in having received wounds from the Tilean Wasp and lived to tell the tale. There was little laughter as the boys retreated and Kaslain pushed the heavy door closed.

The man spoke before the last echoes of iron and wood had been swallowed by the woollen mats and velvet curtains.

'Father, I have come to make my peace.' The voice had a sheathed edge about it.

Kaslain steadied his own voice. 'You can find here what you seek.'

'I know it to be true. It cannot be given by any man. You alone, father, can give me peace.' The man's words were chosen carefully.

'You are a man surrounded by much evil but perhaps we need not speak of it all. What would you have my ears hear and my heart absolve?' Kaslain repeated the ritualised phrases with no greater conviction than was usual, but his body was taut.

'Father, I wish to tell you of how I came to kill a priest.'

Kaslain's intake of breath was audible and abrasive, the extra air stabbing at his lungs. A priest! He would have to deal very carefully with the dying legend on the divan.

The legend coughed and opened his eyes. The blood staining his shaven chin underlined the eyes which stared at Kaslain. So devoid were they of any feeling that Kaslain thought the man was already dead. The priest froze in mid-gesture, as if his slightest movement might push the assassin over the edge before the all-important absolution.

The man called the Thousand Faces of Magritta struggled onto one elbow and looked straight at his audience. 'My name is Hadrian Samoracci.'

Kaslain raised an eyebrow. If the man was who he said he was, that made him the son and heir of one of the powerful merchant-noble families of northern Tilea.

'My name is Hadrian Samoracci and I have been twice bereft. The first time was long ago and does not concern the matter of which I crave absolution, except in so much as it made me what I am today. The second time, however, the second time occurred in the autumn which is only now dying. Dying as I am.'

AT FIRST I thought her to be a farmer's daughter. A simple farmer's daughter covered with earth, testament to her daily exertions in the field. She had hair the colour of the chaff she spread before the swine on the manor estate of the man who owned her. I saw her beside the road as I rode up to the manor for the first time and she fixed me with a stare which I did not understand – though I understand it now. Like knows like. Like knows like, and now she is dead. Such is the way of things and few think much about it. Just as the hawk preys on the hare and it is never the other way about, so the peasant works for the lord...

But I have not come here to waste my last breath on politics, and in truth, she was no hare. I have come here to use my last breath on the things that matter, at least to me. I have come here to spend my last breath talking of love and death.

I am a seller of death, almost a merchant you might say, or an artisan, or even a whore whose body is her only ware. I am all these things. My work takes me to strange places and I often have cause to touch the lives of the noble, wealthy and fortunate. Few men pay gold for the blood of a cobbler or silver to have a blacksmith's apprentice quietly drowned in the Reik.

The Count of Pfeildorf, a pole-cat of a man, maintained a manor house outside of the town of that name, for which he had nominal responsibility. A man had found me, found one of my men in Nuln and got a message to me: twelve ingots of Black Mountains gold for the death of the count. The gold safely in my vault, for I never extend the privilege of credit, I travelled to Pfeildorf, adopting the guise of a trapper of wolves – a subject I knew very little about, though I was to learn more.

Once in Pfeildorf, I took up residence in a boarding house of roaches and wenches and went to work. It was a simple enough matter to steal a horse and ride out to the estate each night. The count's personal security was extensive – a pole-cat but a paranoid one. His underlings were more accessible, however.

The count's chief man, castellan and gamekeeper, was a greasy pudding named Hugo. The count's flocks strayed on the hillside while Hugo plotted to increase his consumption of Bretonnian cakes, or pursued some similar activity.

For four nights I crept close to the flock, stealing a lamb. I would wrap the struggling creature in my cloak and carry it away so its noise wouldn't wake the dogs. Here my plan almost faltered for I could not bring myself to slaughter the animals with their fleece still yellow from their birthing. They were guilty of nothing. All my victims are guilty of something. Whatever you may say, you choose to be a killer's victim.

I left the lambs in my rank room where they consumed the straw mattress and soiled the floor, similar behaviour to most of the patrons of the establishment. Each morning I stood on

a crate in the market and plied my new trade. A wolf trapper I
was, on the trail of a rogue female, a killer from the north, a
huge brute of a creature which had taken halflings from out of
their houses. I made the creature into a fearsome scourge for
the whole district. Many farmer's woes were no doubt erro-
neously blamed on this fictitious blight and some even sought
to hire me to rid them of it. My fee was correspondingly high,
high enough that the poor shepherds could not afford my services. You may imagine that I found the work tiring but there
is an easy calm in playing out my strategies and I find great
delight in the invention of tantalising detail.

Eventually it happened. Hugo waddled into the square
escorted by one of the count's men. The duo approached me
and, after a brief haggle over the price, which I pointedly
refused to drop, engaged me to kill the wolf which had been
taking their lambs.

I was given lodging in the servant's quarters on the estate, a
pallet on an earthen floor. I have slept in worse places and I
have lain between silken sheets. My unique profession has
given me the opportunity to learn about the way others live
their lives, miserable and bleak, often before I take those very
lives. Take them and break them. But I am not without com-
passion, as you will see. As I have said, I saw the girl as I rode
in and her face stayed with me, though I did not know why.

My plan was simple: to range the estate making a show of
setting snares during the day and to scout by night, and decide
on the best way in which to gain entrance to the count's wing.
I was to be there three days, no more. Once I have devised a
plan I do not like to be distracted. Thus it was that I was
angered by Hugo's rousing me early on the second morning
and demanding that I explain the two missing lambs, taken the
night before. All of my snares lay empty and yet the animals
were gone. Hurrying because I feared my mock snares would
not stand close examination, I dressed and followed the track
up to the flock just as the count was being served fig and pheas-
ant breakfast in his feather bed.

I have some skill in reading prints in the ground and what I
saw surprised me. In the mud near the stream where the flock
drank I found signs of the abduction: here were drag marks to
indicate the demise of the lambs, here a little wool caught on a
thorn, here the prints of the shepherds arriving late on the

scene – and everywhere were the indentations of a large wolf. The wind, already cold along the stream bed developed a cutting chill. I followed the prints until they crossed and re-crossed the stream; a smart wolf, this killer I had supposedly created. A smart wolf manifested from thin air and imagination. I could do little but wait for the night which is usually my friend.

I am not a man who frightens easily, nor one who is used to fear. As the night settled over me, as it fell gently to earth and blanketed the greens in a cobweb shroud, a bead of sweat found the scar at the base of my neck and settled there. Most foolish of all, this man, this killer who is scared of nothing, was frightened of a beast of his own creation. After a brief discussion with the shepherds, who informed me they had had this wolf problem for some months, and who, gratifyingly, were more scared than I was, I positioned myself in the low branches of a large oak which spread itself over the flock like a priest blessing the multitudes.

There was no question of my falling asleep. Such vigils are common in my profession and besides, the perch was religiously uncomfortable. I watched as the moon traversed the sky, describing a pearly slice through the low western horizon. Morning was only a few hours hence and I had long ceased jumping at the shadows of the dogs, shaggy brown brutes from kennels in Averheim. It was one of these mutts who saw her first, however, or more likely smelt her. Even though she came from downwind, we could all smell her stench. It was a smell I have smelled before, many times. When a man is about to die, when he knows he stares death in the face, he has a certain smell. It is in his breath, or comes from his skin, I don't know, I am no physician. I smelt that smell that night on the wind. When I looked down from my perch she was there.

I have seen wolves before, but only in cages, rolling, barred wagons in the streets or in fairgrounds: 'Come bait the ferocious wolf, feed a mad killer with yer own hand!' She was a killer all right, but far from being mad. She moved with determination and poise. I slithered lower in the tree, silent as she, hunters both. Her approach put me downwind of her and I was almost overpowered by the stench of death which was her musk. As in an old Kislev folk tale, I had made a lariat from heavy twine and I balanced on the low bough, watching her.

She was fascinating, huge certainly, but agile and sure-footed. I imagined her yellow eyes as I watched the muscles shift beneath her flanks.

She moved quietly towards the flock. One of the dogs found the source of the smell and loped over. The well-trained mongrel bared its teeth and crouched on its forequarters, a language that the she-wolf would surely understand. As soon as she turned I was ready to spring my trap. She did not sway from her purpose, however, ignoring the dog's threat, and I detected something strange in her gait. She was hungry like a wolf, certainly, but she did not crouch low as a hunter would, walking rather at her full height past the snarling dog. This was too much for the mongrel which threw itself at her throat, a studded collar wrapped about his own. She turned, acknowledging the brutal assault. With a flick of her neck, which might equally have been contemptuous or desperate, she flipped the attacking dog and snapped its spine against the hard ground. Her unfortunate assailant yelped and rolled away trying to straighten a body which would never be right. I say 'contemptuous or desperate' because I could not read this strange creature, I had not the language. I should have sprung then and there but I waited, crouching in the darkness, in what could equally have been curiosity or fear.

The shepherds came then, with the other dogs. No doubt they wondered why I had done nothing, had not sprung my trap. Three young, strong men of Averland, armed with stout staves picked clean of bark during long, all-night vigils. Two more dogs, angry and frightened after the scream of their packmate. They would drive her off, perhaps before she took a lamb; anything else was unthinkable.

At the last minute I knew it would not be so, something in the way she moved, something in the unreadable curve of her ribs. I almost shouted a warning, but then I am no stranger to death, and these men were nothing to me. Besides, they outnumbered her. I have, I must confess, a sentimental attachment to the underdog, the lone wolf.

What followed was a lesson for a killer in killing. Again she waited until the last instant, turning as the two dogs came crashing in with their heavy skulls set in a charge. She rolled to the side and opened a gash on the flanks of the closest one with her bottom jaw, sending her victim in a scything skid down the stream bank. Before the other dog could recover she was on her feet and charging herself. She ducked under its guard and clamped her maw about its neck, spinning the animal in the air and crashing it sideways into a rock. The dog coughed once and lay still. The shepherds paused, fear and anger competing for their countenances. Anger won, as it so often does with younger men. They gripped their sticks tightly and strode in. The lariat hung loose in my hand.

She turned to look at the men and to my surprise she cowed. She looked away and lowered her tail, which flickered like a flame above her hind legs. The men rushed her and I read the signs an only instant before her ruse was revealed. The first shepherd was on his back with her paws on his chest before the second caught his brother's hand with a wild blow of his stick. The brother screamed and dropped his weapon. He brought his hand to his mouth as if the benediction of his lips might heal the shattered bones. The second shepherd turned in time to see their companion's throat rent by the wolf.

She was magnificent. I stood as I might in a theatre, watching the players enact a drama of such intensity that I dared not shift lest I disturb their concentration. The other two stood together, defensive now, not believing what they knew to be true. She circled them once, slowly, and then rushed in, felling them with an axe-like blow of her head. The three rolled on the ground and wrestled but there could be only one outcome. Eventually she shook herself free of the corpses and spun her coat like a hound who has come in from the rain. I watched, knowing somehow that there was more to see.

The wolf had hurt her hind left paw and she limped to the base of my tree. My breath was caged in my chest and I strained to keep it there. She sat against the roots and shook her coat again. The moon passed for a moment behind a cloud, or so it seemed, and suddenly I was looking at a woman, or perhaps a girl. A naked girl at the base of the tree, her shoulders slick with blood, her left foot stretched up to her face where she licked a cut on the soft skin beneath. I had stayed silent thus far but on this transformation I let the night air escape from my lungs in a rush and gasped for some to replace it. The girl's head snapped up and our eyes met, as they had met before. I understood her gaze then, as I had not before. A killer looked at a killer. Like knew like.

In an instant she rolled and before I could say anything, least
of all that I intended no violence to one so magnificent, she
was gone. She sped across the field, once again lupine, once
again perfect. I crept back to the manor slowly, avoiding the
blackest shadows, shaking my head as if to dislodge the images
of the night from my memory. When I awoke late the next
morning, however, they remained as clear as the day which
greeted me.

AFTER THAT my elegant plan had to be postponed and the
count's security was doubled. They found the bodies of the
three shepherds and the prints in the ground were clear enough
that even fat Hugo could read them.

'Werewolf,' he said, grimacing as if he had put his toe into a
bath too cold to sit in.

What angered me as I stood there, not far from the tree in
which I had perched the night before, was the man's
demeanour. An assumption of superiority over something he
could never hope to understand. From that moment I decided
I was on her side: wild, frightened, perfect killer over fat, tame
gamekeeper. After we held a solemn meeting about the best
way in which to trap the ferocious beast – my contributions
were fatuous and deliberately impractical – I went to seek her.

The farmers and workers on the count's estate lived in a village outside of the walled manor, a collection of huts and
thatched cottages huddled around the mill as if they wanted to
take up as small an amount of the count's fertile fields as was
possible. I felt eyes regard me from dark windows as I walked
up, stopping periodically to beat the sticking mud from my
boots with a switch of hedgerow. She was not hard to find. I
asked a few questions, not to be denied, this man from the
manor. The answers I got were not co-operative but the villagers said more than they meant.

I found her drawing water from the well. She saw me and
dropped her bucket, ducking behind the barn. I followed as
quickly as I could and this time managed to say that I meant
her no harm. She knew what I knew from the way I looked at
her; it is always in the eyes. She went inside the barn and I
stepped in after her, waiting for my eyes to adjust to the darkness, divided by slices of light between the planks. I smelt hay
and her.

The wolf's attack took me by surprise and I was lucky to have straw to fall on. She was on me and I remembered clearly enough the fate of an exposed neck to those jaws. But I am not a gormless shepherd boy. I brought my knee up into the creature's chest and gained my feet in time to meet another leaping assault. This time I pivoted on one foot and lashed out with the other. The manoeuvre cost me my balance and I once again tasted the hay but my boot connected with the wolf's ear and sent it sprawling. I leapt up, spitting dust and faced her again. She shook her muzzle, trying to dislodge the straw and a burr which had stuck there and I laughed.

'It seems we both have reason to regret this battle already.' I sounded more confident than I felt but such deceptions are my meat and drink. While we studied each other I was unclasping my cloak and searching the room for a weapon. 'Must we fight until one of us, most likely my good self, is cold meat?' There was a pitchfork holding up the thatch, wedged between two beams above my head. My pleading was having little effect and she lowered her head and crept forward into optimal pouncing range.

I watched her eyes; it is always in the eyes. Hers were yellow and savage, pools of amber malice, but there was a softness as well. I looked harder and almost fell into her trap. There was no softness, a sham designed to distract her sentimental opponent, accurately assessed by her predator's gaze. I recovered as she sprang. She was nearly quick enough, nearly, but I have been a killer longer than her.

I leapt upward, throwing my cloak in front of me and reaching for the pitchfork above my head. She flew head-first into the billowing wool and hit the ground awkwardly. As she skidded across the straw, I yanked down on the pitchfork and it came free. I crashed to the floor in a hail of straw and roof beams. The bundle of cloak and wolf thrashed about and I dealt it a heavy stabbing blow with the butt of the pitchfork. I stepped to the side as a section of the roof sagged dangerously and reversed the pitchfork, pointing the four tines accusingly at my cloak. The bundle therein was now a lot smaller and I released a breath which I did not know I had been holding in when I saw the girl's head emerge from one of the arm-holes. I made sure she remained covered in the cloak. My taste is usually restricted to women of more years and greater curves but I could not deny a certain attraction in this case. Nevertheless, I am nothing if not a gentleman killer. We crouched together in a shaft of sunlight in the corner of the barn, she rubbing a bruise on her shoulder and me working the straw from between my teeth.

Our conversation was short but enough to satisfy me that she was more afraid of her condition than any number of shepherds or farmers. I suggested she might wander farther afield on her night-inspired rampages, or perhaps wreak havoc among the deer of the forest. It seemed she had little control and I vowed to help her. We decided to make it possible for her to leave the village behind, and live somewhere a little more remote. Why? I left the village asking myself this question, suddenly unhappy, uneasy even, with the glib phrases I had made to myself about a killer knowing a killer. Certainly there was that. Perhaps I saw a little of my younger self in her savagery and I wished to help her over the hurdle from random savage into refined artist of death. Perhaps I loved her, though I doubt that. I am not so deeply sentimental.

Whatever the reason, I had determined to help her and would have proceeded along the simple course we had devised, returning then to my employer's task. Except that things did not happen that way, holy father. Another character enters on the scene of this little tale of mine, revered Kaslain, and writes a chapter whose authorship I will rue until my death.

That character and that author is *you*.

KASLAIN STOOD quickly, his heavy robe dropping from his knees to brush the flagstones. The killer on the divan looked at him.

'I have watched you as I told the tale and you knew from the beginning that it was your story, yet you listened. I had counted on your vanity, as sure a thing as any.' He smiled, mouth like a wolf's.

The arch-lector began a brisk walk towards the chamber door, the walk of a man who craves haste but dares not reveal his need. He stopped in response to a noise from behind him and whipped his head around. The man was no longer on the couch. In fact, the priest could not see him at all. A large stain of blood marked that he had lain there and a soft red pillow of flesh, a kidney!

Kaslain stared at it trying to understand. His mind groped in an unfriendly darkness. The kidney was too small to be a

man's – a goat's? How many times had he sacrificed a young
goat to Sigmar on this holy day or that? He remembered the
squeal of the squirming animal and the blood, always so
much blood...

The understanding of the ruse came upon Kaslain slowly but
powerfully, not to be denied. His face twisted in alarm and he
spun around. The assassin stood between him and the velvet
bell-pull which would summon his guards. He had divested
himself of his bloody cloak and stood, whole and hearty, his
face sporting a victor's smile. Kaslain lunged for the door and
the killer dropped low, lashing out with the toe of his boot and
catching the priest in the knee. The aged lector met the flagstones heavily and rolled beneath the gilt velvet curtains.

The Thousand Faces of Magritta stepped forward and gave
the curtains an authoritative yank. They fell, collecting in a
heap above the struggling priest. The assassin rolled the priest
with his boot, several times, until he was cocooned in velvet.
He gave the region containing Kaslain's head a solid kick and
the muffled cries ceased altogether. He then straddled the velvet grub and sat heavily. For a second, bizarrely, he adopted the
posture of a knight on horseback, hands on imaginary reigns
and rocked his hips to the imaginary rhythms of an absent
charger. This seemed to amuse him for a short moment but
then his face turned serious. He reached into his boot, removing a short stiletto. The Tilean Wasp leant forward with this
sting and began to cut a small window in the velvet wrapping.
Eventually he exposed the arch-lector's distressed face and
made a warning gesture with the blade, telling the priest that
he would end his life at the slightest cry for help.

'Your impatience is disappointing, Kaslain, and now you will
not hear the end of my story. A story which you wrote parts of
yourself, although I am writing this chapter, the last chapter in
which you appear. I told you that I must confess how I had
killed a priest. You are that priest, though I no longer have time
to tell you why you must die.'

MAGNUS CHANGED eyes at the keyhole but otherwise stayed
firmly in place, his back bent, his damp palms flat against the
wooden doors. He watched the man sit on the arch-lector and
angle his knife. He watched as the man slid it into the priest's
neck, muffling the victim's scream with a handful of curtain.

He watched the man turn and stretch his neck while he looked about for his escape route.

Magnus had seen and heard it all and had not been able to interfere. He hadn't been able to move, until now. But when he began to move he found himself moving the wrong way, his hands on the handle of the inner chamber rather than his feet fleeing down the marble hall. He watched, as if he were still an observer, his hand as it turned the handle. He drew breath when he saw the chamber within as if he had expected that the keyhole might have been showing a different reality to the one which now greeted him.

The assassin sprang to his feet. He moved towards Magnus, measuring his steps, all the time looking at the boy as if he were judging the distance between them so he might spring. After confirming Magnus was alone he gently closed the door and rested his back against it.

Magnus stared at the double line of blood on the curtain where the killer had cleaned his blade, until his concentration was absorbed by need to force air in and out of his lungs.

'The boy with the bucket?'

'Yes. Yes, but…'

'But you are more than that? Yes I am sure. We are each more than we seem.'

A pause. 'You are not injured.'

'So it seems.'

A breath. 'What will you do now?'

'I will finish my story. Isn't that why you came in here?'

EVENTS DID NOT follow my script. The players had their own motives and each proved to be his own author. Even my own script might have been written by another. How often had I been distracted from my work in such a way?

Hugo had a cousin who was a priest of Sigmar. He came, a young wisp of a man with straw for hair and a child's chin. He announced that he would watch the animals by night and he would catch this killer. He had all the eagerness of a soldier before his first battle but he had something else also, the bearing of an officer, though he had no troops. We were his troops and he strode among us imagining that we bowed and saluted.

The shepherds laughed at him, having had little to laugh at in the past weeks. Hugo made an announcement to the effect that his own authority was extended to his young cousin for as long as the priest chose to stay with us at the estate. The priest smiled a tight smile and gave a stiff nod.

He stationed himself in the field on the third night of his stay. He had brought a tome which he consulted before he took up his vigil, then he donned his white robe and strode into the night.

During this time I had not been idle. I had held two further conversations with the girl and each time she had agreed she would leave that night. Each morning I had discovered her, working in the field as if we had never spoken. I do not know for sure why she stayed, killing lambs all the while, but perhaps it was because she had found in me some kinship, some kindness which she would not willingly abandon.

We are complicated creatures and although I do not like interruptions to my plans I cannot say that I was not gratified to have her stay. I was unconcerned about the priest and here it was that I made my mistake – not that he was any danger to anybody, but it was his death which ultimately defeated my strategy.

They brought his body back, damp with dew and bent out of shape. No one had seen the boy die, the shepherds now being far too scared to share the night with the sheep, but the jaw marks left little doubt as to his killer. After that, events moved with an undeniable momentum. The count used his influence to contact Arch-Lector Kaslain in Nuln and appeal to the same sense of pomp and occasion which I was later to employ myself.

Kaslain came south with soldiers and witch hunters and they found her, as I knew they would. The soldiers went among the villagers with clubs and burning irons. Kaslain did not frighten me, though his performance had the desired effect on the peasants and staff at the manor. They bowed and scraped to his face and made furtive warding gestures to his back.

Though their methods were crude, they were effective enough and before Kaslain had spent two nights in the manor he had her. I would have killed him then, but I was more concerned in trying to save her. Helplessness is not a condition I am accustomed to or one which I accept lightly.

Our last conversation had been held in the same barn as our first. I was angry, fearful for her safety and frustrated by her stubbornness. She reacted badly to my anger and the meeting did not go well. I wish now it had been otherwise. I have never been skilled at recognising the actions of fate nor at accepting its whims. I tried to convince her in any way I could think of to leave but I knew it was for me that she stayed.

They came and found her and stuck her with their spears. She took three soldiers with her as I watched from among the crowd of villagers, head bowed and hooded. Her mother was there too, a woman with thin skin which showed the pattern of the blood as it flowed about her face. I never got to know her name. They lashed her to a stake and burned her at sun-set. My helpless fingers dug into my wrist and I made a quiet vow.

The tattered body took some hours to burn and produced an oily smoke, which caused the onlookers to cough and shield their eyes. Kaslain spoke a prayer to Sigmar, an obscene stave full of polite hatred and self-satisfied gall, standing with one foot on the ashen skull. I killed a soldier that night, I don't know his name; it is not a deed of which I am proud. I took him as he slept and mixed my tears with his blood.

In the morning I gathered her ashes in a sack from the ruined barn and commended them to the forest.

MAGNUS REALISED that the assassin had finished speaking and he lifted his head. The killer was wiping his cheek with a corner of the velvet curtain, cleaning away what might perhaps have been a tear. He stood and looked directly into Magnus's eyes. The stare was not comfortable.

'So that is my tale,' said the Tilean Wasp. 'Here lies perhaps my greatest kill and I feel little satisfaction. You are almost a priest: can you tell me why?'

Magnus chose his words carefully, grinding his sweating fingers against each other. 'I do not wish, sir, to be one of your kills, even one of the least. I have seen what happens to those who hear your confessions.' Dawn clawed at the crack beneath the door. 'Perhaps, however, I may venture, you have seen a lit-tle of what others see in death, or perhaps you know that you cannot but kill, even if you would rather love?'

A moment of contemplation, the time it might take for a tear to fall from an eye to the flagstones if there was such a tear, no more.

'Nonsense,' the assassin said plainly. 'I go now to pursue my lucrative trade, leaving you as the only one to have seen me as I am and live.'

'Why?'

'Because I may. You ask a lot of questions, boy.'

'I... I have another. What of the count? He still lives.'

'I go to visit him now. What shall my ruse be this time?'

'Sir, how am I to counsel you in these matters, one who can even disguise himself as himself?'

HUGO BEAT UPON the Count of Pfeildorf's door with fat knuckles. Two men were standing there in the late morning, the stone chamber which attended the count's inner door consumed by their combined bulk. Hugo's girth was natural but the other figure wore the hooded robes of a priest of Sigmar, and judging by their ornate finery an important one at that.

'Awaken, sir!' the wheedling voice pleaded, Hugo a man trapped between two superiors whose wishes were in conflict. 'I would not disturb you, sir, so early in the day, but I'm sure you would wish to receive so esteemed a visitor.'

The answer from within a bark of an inquiry.

'Who is it, sir? Why Kaslain, the Arch-Lector.'

FAITHFUL SERVANT

Gav Thorpe

THE SKY WAS filled with the beating of black wings and the screeches of ravens, crows and buzzards. The odour of decay was strong in the air as the flock circled in the warm thermals that rippled above the burning Kislevite town. Brought from many miles around by the rotting scent of food, the huge black birds circled lower, seeking the source.

Below them, Gorlensk was a scene of carnage and wanton destruction. Many of the buildings were little more than heaps of smoking ash, and all of those that still stood bore signs of the slaughter that had occurred. Bodies were piled haphazardly where clusters of men, women and children had been cut down where they cowered by their psychopathic attackers. However, the flickering flames and billowing smoke deterred the hungry scavengers, until the chill wind brought a much stronger scent of death. The flock moved onwards and downwards, seeking out the larger feast it promised.

The scene outside the town walls was no better than inside. The shadowy shapes of the scavengers skimmed low, using the trail of dismembered bodies to trace a gory path to the main battlefield, a mile or so north of Gorlensk.

The flock's excitement grew as the rotting stench of death grew stronger. Their cries becoming more raucous, the hungry birds scattered into smaller groups that flapped low over the battlefield, each picking out a tasty-looking target. Here the potential banquet would sate the hunger of even this massive flock. The armoured bodies of knights lay next to the gouged and hacked corpses of their steeds. The blocks of infantry had been run down as they fled, and the piles of their carcasses blocked the road and the scattered farmsteads they had tried to defend.

There were more than human bodies littering the field. The feasters of the dead cawed in alarm and avoided the unnatural corpses of Chaos warriors and half-animal beastmen which lay heaped by the dozen in some areas, their armour rent by massive blows. The ground was red with drying blood, a crimson testament to the ferocity of the battle. Rats scurried everywhere, their sleek bodies matted with dried gore, as they weaved through the carnage, disturbing lazy clouds of fat, blue flies. The heavy, bloated sun was perhaps an hour from dusk, giving the scene of death and decay an even bloodier cast.

Picking out the pile where the press of corpses was greatest, the birds plunged down amid raucous skrawks and the heavy beating of wings. The bulk of the flock had just settled down to picking at the body of a brilliant white horse and the tangle of bodies around it when something stirred next to them from the midst of the dead. One of the corpses, clad in what was once a white robe now stained with swathes of dried blood, shivered slightly and an arm shot upwards to grip thin air. A plaintive cry wailed across the field, sending the scavengers flapping into the air again.

Markus rose to consciousness with a shriek, awakening from a nightmare filled with hoarse battle cries and blood-chilling screams. His heart hammered on the anvil of his chest, and his breathing was laboured and heavy. His head reeled and a feeling of utter horror swept through him. Not daring to open his eyes for a moment, unsure of what might await him, Markus paused to take a deep breath and fumble the sweat from his brow with his aching arm. His sleeve was ragged and damp, and left a warm smear upon his forehead.

As his stomach settled and his nausea subsided, Markus opened his eyes slowly, terrified that the visions from which he had woken would be true. His attention was immediately drawn to the corpses scattered all around him and he knew that his nightmare was real. The crows had returned and he watched in disgusted fascination as they gnawed at bones and pecked at tender eyes and other soft delicacies. Markus felt his stomach heave at the sight, but as he retched nothing but bile rose up, burning his throat and leaving an acrid taste in his mouth.

Markus turned his head to take in the huge white shape lying alongside him and he groaned aloud. His beautiful war-horse had been a gift from a captain of the Tzarina's Winged Lancers, given to him in grateful thanks for the many blessings he had bestowed upon the captain's warriors. The white mare lay still, legs stiff and lifeless eyes open, a gaping, leaking wound in her side providing a feast for a swarm of vermin.

As he tried to rise, Markus whispered to his four-legged companion, though she would never hear his words. 'Farewell, faithful Alayma…'

As he sat, pain lanced through Markus's left leg, making him fall back, a startled cry ripped from his lips. The pain brought back a flash of memory.

THE HIDEOUS war cries of the beastmen surrounded Markus on all sides. A rust-edged halberd blade thrust out of the swirling melee engulfing him and caught a glancing blow on his armoured shoulder. There was a movement in the press, like a wave coming towards him. The swordsmen all around him were being pushed back as an enormous bestial figure, a brutal mace gripped in its clawed hands, strode forward, crazed eyes fixed solely on the priest. Markus raised his hammer in defiance, but his heart quivered as he looked into that monstrous, bull-like face.

Then Alayma took over, his mount more highly trained in war than Markus himself. Rearing high on her back legs, her steel-shod hooves flailed into the beastman's face, smashing it to a pulp. Twisting slightly as she landed again, the mare bucked, kicking out behind her with her powerful legs to send another mutant foe sprawling to the ground, its chest crushed. Without waiting for guidance the mare turned and leapt through the newly created gap, carrying Markus clear. As he dared a glance over his shoulder, he saw the last of the Imperial

swordsmen falling beneath the blades of the Chaos beastmen
and, as he had done so many times, silently thanked Alayma
for saving his life.

MORE GINGERLY this time, Markus managed to raise himself up
on his elbows and noticed for the first time the extent of his
predicament. In her death throes, Alayma had rolled onto his
leg, crushing it beneath her weight. The grim truth slowly
dawned on him and he whispered a prayer to Sigmar.

He was all alone on this blighted field of death, trapped
beneath the heavy body of the war-horse – and easy prey for
whatever creatures the fast-approaching night would bring. The
thought that Alayma, who had saved his life, would now be the
cause of his death, lay bitterly at the back of Markus's mind.
With a sigh of despair, the priest of Sigmar tried to recall what
twists of fate had brought him to such an unlikely end.

It had been a fine spring day when Markus had joined the
Emperor's glorious army. For weeks before there had been
increasing rumours of a large enemy force marauding through
the northern reaches of Kislev. Stories abounded of the
depraved Chaos horde, emphasising its merciless butchering
and unholy acts of destruction.

Word came through that the Tzarina herself had requested
aid of the Emperor, and shortly after came the messengers of
Elector Count von Raukov announcing the mustering of an
army. The recruiters came to Stefheim a week later, calling
upon all able-bodied men to join in this righteous fight.

Markus had not been drawn in by the well-crafted speeches,
drafted to stir men's hearts and make them feel honoured and
courageous beyond their normal bounds. However, as he had
watched the congregations of his sermons daily swell in size,
and noticed the fervent look in his followers' eyes, he felt his
own faith in Sigmar strengthening. The sacrifice of the normally peaceful townsfolk and farmers stirred Markus far more
than any amount of fiery rhetoric. The humble peasants had
looked to Sigmar for guidance and protection, and Markus had
felt beholden to help them.

Before the newly-recruited soldiers of the Empire marched
off to war in their ill-fitting new uniforms, Markus sent a
message to Altdorf notifying his superiors that a replacement
would be needed. When the tramp of marching feet

reverberated through the hills of Ostland, Markus's tread had sounded with it.

A SUDDEN MOVEMENT close by made Markus snap out of his reverie. A fat, black rat, well-gorged on flesh and slick with the fluids of corpses, had tugged at his robe and was now attempting to gnaw at his shattered leg. The priest looked around for some form of weapon, but could find nothing close at hand. Flinging his arms about him, Markus shouted hoarsely.

'Begone! Feast upon the dead. I'm still alive, you vermin!'

Startled, the rat scuttled under the broken neck of Alayma in search of a quieter feast. Seeing his mare's neck so strangely angled brought back another rush of memory to Markus.

WITH A ROUSING blare of horns sounding the attack, the Knights Panther and Tzarina's Winged Lancers charged the vile black-clad horde, spitting hundreds of deformed adversaries on their lances within a few minutes. As the impetus of the knights' charge was spent, the crazed enemy army surged back. A wave of deformed creatures bellowing in bizarre tongues smashed into the Empire and Kislev's finest cavalry and a sprawling melee erupted.

To Markus, things looked grim, as they were assailed from all sides by the demented followers of the Dark Gods. However, the armour of the knights was holding out and they smashed and thrust at the enemy with their swords or the butts of lances, holding the sudden onslaught.

Then something unimaginably ancient and terrible rose up amongst the ranks of Chaos warriors and beastmen. The hideous creation, born of the darkest nightmares, stood thrice the height of a man and bellowed orders in some arcane tongue that did not need to be understood to strike fear into the hearts of all who heard it.

'Blood of Sigmar...' whispered the leader of the halberdiers deployed to Markus's right.

The priest turned in his saddle and scowled at the hoary veteran. 'Watch your tongue, sir! This unholiness has nothing to do with Sigmar, but is the spawn of depraved and mindless enemies.'

The daemon's massive horns gouged armour apart while its claw-tipped hands wreaked a red swathe through all who tried to stand before it. The almost tangible aura of violence and malevolence that preceded it caused the Knights to retreat rather than face its unnatural vigour and savagery.

Faced with such unholy wrath, the men of the Empire began to give ground. As the monstrosity continued to carve a bloodied path of destruction through the ranks, the retreat turned into a rout and the brave soldiers turned to flee. Markus stood up in his stirrups and tried to rally the desperate men with prayers of courage and steadfastness. He had sworn to Sigmar that he would face these foes, and even if all around him was anarchy he would fight on, alone if he must.

'Hold fast!' he cried. 'As your lord and protector, Sigmar will see you through this carnage!'

It was to no avail and the panicked horde swept around him, embroiling him in a tumult of screams and pressing bodies. As the crying mass of men packed tighter and tighter, Alayma panicked and tried to force a way free, but there was no line of retreat.

Suddenly hands were grabbing at the reins and desperate faces lunged out of the throng, intent on stealing what they thought was the only route to safety – Markus's steed. Gnarled fingers closed around the priest's robes and tugged at him, and he felt himself falling. Markus kicked out at a bearded face and it disappeared into the crowd. He tried one last attempt to restore sanity.

'Hold! Sigmar is with us! These abominations cannot harm us if our faith is strong. Victory to the Empire! Attack!'

Markus's last words were drowned out by an unearthly bellowing and the screams of the dying came ever closer. Over the heads of the Empire soldiers he glimpsed the scaled form of the daemon prince. Its massive eyes were pits of darkness and a pile of battered bodies was heaped around it. It was so close now that Markus could smell the fear that crept before it.

A blade caught Alayma and she reared, whinnying. Knocked off balance by the press of fleeing soldiers, she toppled to the ground, crushing men beneath her weight. Markus heard a cracking sound, audible even over the hoarse cries of the panicked mass. He was scrabbling about in the blood-soaked mud when a boot struck his forehead. Darkness descended beneath unseen trampling feet.

* * *

WITH A START, Markus realised that the blow that had torn a rent in his horse's side must have come much later, when the victors spilled across the battlefield, hacking and ripping at everything they could find. Sigmar had been merciful and somehow he had avoided a killing blow while he lay oblivious to the world. At that moment, though, the baying of wolves reverberated across the surrounding hills and Markus corrected himself – he was not safe yet.

A shadow crossed him as something blotted out the setting sun. Turning his head in surprise, the priest saw a bulky figure silhouetted against the western sky, picking its way through the carnage. Markus's throat was too dry to call out but he managed a croak and lifted his arm to wave at the approaching figure, silhouetted against the deep red glare.

'Over here, friend!' he called. 'Thank Sigmar, I thought none alive but myself.'

The man turned abruptly and strode towards Markus. However, far from relaxing, the priest tensed as the figure came closer. He walked directly towards Markus with a determined stride that unnerved the priest. Markus thought that anyone wandering this blighted place would surely be wary of more Chaos followers lurking nearby.

As the shadowy figure came closer, the priest could pick out more details. The man was clad in thick armour and a horned helmet, and all about him were hung dire symbols of power, sigils of the Ruinous Powers proclaiming his status and allegiances. Otherworldly runes were engraved into the black enamelled chest-plate, inscriptions of protection and power that writhed with their own energy, written in a language no normal mortal could speak. It was plain the newcomer was no saviour.

Markus's heart fluttered and he struggled frantically to pull himself clear from Alayma's heavy corpse. Pain lanced through Markus's leg again and he collapsed on his back, whimpering despite himself.

Muttering entreaties to Sigmar, Markus tried to calm his ragged breathing and studied the approaching figure, who was just ten strides from him. He tried to speak, but his throat, dry with fear, just made a cracked, croaking noise. The dark warrior now stood perhaps three paces away, not moving at all. Dark eyes glittered inside the helm's strangely shaped visor, staring at the priest with unblinking intensity.

As his own eyes took in the immense scabbard hanging at the warrior's waist, Markus recoiled in fear, expecting a death-blow to come swinging down with every thunderous beat of his heart.

Markus flinched when the warrior reached up with a gaunt-let-covered hand, but the death blow did not fall. The stranger gripped the single horn protruding from the forehead of his helmet, then wrenched the helm free and let it drop to the ground.

Markus blinked in disbelief. The man in the bizarre armour was startlingly normal. His chin and nose possessed an aristo-cratic line, his dark eyes more amused than menacing without the confinement of the helmet's visor. The warrior looked straight into Markus's eyes and smiled. An icy shiver of fear ran through the priest. That seemingly benign expression terrified him more than the slaughter that had occurred earlier, or even the horrifying carnage wrought by the daemon prince.

The terror he felt was wholly unjustified and unnatural, and his spine tingled with agonising horror, though Markus could not fathom why the warrior was so frightening. This was no vile daemon from the *Liber Malificorum*, but a normal man. For some reason, this just increased Markus's panic and his whole body trembled with every shallow breath he managed to gasp.

When the Chaos warrior spoke, he found himself listening carefully and – despite the awful predicament he was in – try-ing to place the man's accent. He thought it might be from the Reikland, but the intonation and phrasing of the stranger's words seemed slightly mispronounced and somehow archaic.

'Are you afeared?' the sinister figure began. 'Does your blood coldly run with the sight of myself?'

Markus swallowed hard, and tried to look as defiant as pos-sible. 'You don't scare me, foul lapdog of evil! My master protects me from the ravages of your desperate gods.'

The dark warrior laughed, a deep, disturbing sound. 'But of course you must have divine protection.' He looked around himself extravagantly. 'Amongst this slaughter you alone lie alive and breathing, spared the fate ordained for your country-men. However, could it not be that someone other than your master has stayed the hands of your attackers?' The warrior lowered one knee into the crimson-stained earth and leaned forward to whisper in Markus's ear. 'Is your master so strong he could hide your presence from the gaze of the Lords of Chaos?'

This time it was Markus who laughed coldly, shaking his head in disbelief. 'Sigmar watches over his faithful followers; he loves them now as he loved them in life. Of course it is Sigmar who has spared me from death. My soul is pure. Your loathsome gods have no hold on me.'

The warrior laughed in mockery and stood up, wiping the filth from his armour with a rag torn from a corpse's jerkin. Markus ignored the disbelieving look directed at him.

'Sigmar provides my life and soul with every contentment they desire,' he spluttered bravely. 'There is nothing I want from your dark masters.'

The stranger moved across to Alayma's corpse, kicking at the rats that scurried underfoot. With a sweeping gesture, the Chaos warrior unhooked his dark blue cloak and laid it across the wide curve of the dead horse's body. After smoothing out a few creases, he sat down on the carcass, causing it to shift slightly and send more pain roaring along Markus's leg. The priest gasped. When his tear-misted eyes focused on the warrior once more, the strangely armoured man was still staring straight at Markus, with the same amused, almost playful look in his eyes, his mouth twisted in a slightly crooked smile.

'Did that hurt?' he said in a low voice. 'Or did mighty Sigmar prevent your mind exploding with agony for a moment? They say pain focuses one's mind. In my long experience, however, I have found pain to be a constant distraction, whether in the suffering or the infliction. You say your soul is pure – yet you have had doubts, no?'

Markus shifted uneasily, trying not to move his leg. As he looked away from the warrior's constant stare, the man laughed shortly, an unpleasant noise like the yap of a small dog.

'Was it pain or guilt that averted your gaze from mine?' the Chaos warrior continued smoothly. 'I once heard a philosopher say that life was a constant series of questions, with each answer merely leading to more questions, and only death provided the final answer to which there were no more questions.' The warrior paused and his brow briefly knitted in thought.

'Jacques Viereaux of Brionnes, I think.' He waved a dismissive hand. 'It doesn't matter. I have many such questions, and I expect you have even more. Shall we live a little, and exchange our questions for yet a little more of life? How come you here, Sir Priest? You are ageing. Nearing forty? Why would a slightly overweight, peaceful priest be found lying as a casualty on this forsaken field? What brought you forth from your shiny temple?'

Markus was confused; the stranger's words were baffling his pain-numbed mind. Gritting his teeth, he felt compelled to ask the questions burning in his mind. 'Just who are you, foul-spawned deviant? Why not kill me now? What do you want with me?'

The warrior's eyes almost glowed with triumph, the setting sun reflected in those dark orbs. 'Now you see! Questions and answers, answers and questions! This is life!' The warrior laughed again, slapping his hands on his knees. He calmed himself and his face took on a veneer of sincerity. 'I am called Estebar. My followers know me as the Master of Slaughter, and I have a Dark Name which you would not be able to pronounce, so "Estebar" will suffice.

'As for my being here? I have come for your soul!'

LORD SIGMAR, Father of the Empire, Shield of Mankind, protect me from evil…' That chilling horror Markus had felt when first seeing Estebar returned with even greater strength and he whispered a prayer to Sigmar, asking for guidance again and again.

As the desperate litany spilled from the priest's lips, the warrior bent closer, his voice a savage whisper.

'Your god will not hear you.' His arm swept back, taking in the expansion of death and destruction that spread for miles in every direction. 'Around this battlefield, my masters laugh and scream in triumph. The Dark Gods' power is strong here and your prayers will go unanswered. If you want salvation, you had best ask for it of other entities than your weak lord.'

Markus tried to spit in disgust, but the thin dribble of saliva merely dripped down his chin, making him feel foolish rather than defiant. 'I would rather be torn apart by wild creatures than to ask your insane gods for aid. If that is the best you have to offer, I think my soul is very safe. Just strike me down now, and stop wasting my time!'

'Strike you down? As you wish!'

Estebar stood up abruptly, unsheathing his sword and holding it high in one clean motion. Markus flinched involuntarily and shrank back from its glowing blade. The Chaos warrior appeared to be scowling and his dark eyes burned intensely.

'See, you still want life!' Estebar sighed as he lowered the sword slowly, then slid it back carefully into its black sheath. 'You have not the conviction you would like to believe you possess. I would not strike you down, you who I barely know and yet who intrigues me so much.' He shook his head and fixed Markus with a twisted grin. 'Your faith is uncertain, so what makes you think you really have Sigmar's protection?'

'My faith is certain; be sure of that, hellspawn!'

Markus surprised himself with the vehemence of his words. The priest wanted this strange conversation to end. This was not the threat of Chaos he had been brought up, and then taught, to fight. How could one fight an enemy who tried to defeat you with words alone, spoken by a voice which seemed to hover inside one's very mind. Markus did not want to answer Estebar's inquiry, but the warrior's voice seemed to reach into his head and pull the answers from his lips.

'Sigmar has saved me before,' Markus started before he knew what he was saying, his eyes glinting with defiance. Estebar looked at him quizzically, one eyebrow raised. That one simple gesture seemed to have a world of meaning and Markus felt a tug at his consciousness, pulling the story from the depths of his memory.

'I grew up in a small village near to the World's Edge Mountains. I was the son of a miller and fully believed that I would continue running the mill after he was dead or retired.' Markus's eyes were drawn to Estebar's. Those midnight orbs were like a bottomless gulf, pulling everything into them, sucking Markus ever deeper. The words came tumbling from the priest's mouth, despair overwhelming his heavy heart.

'Then one day, in the spring, the beastmen came. They attacked without warning: the militia had no time to assemble. I saw my father and younger brother cut down by their wicked blades, and I watched as they chased my mother and sister into the foothills. I had been delivering our monthly tithe of flour, four half-sacks of the finest, to the shrine of Sigmar when they stormed out of the dark forests. They did not enter the shrine – they couldn't, it was too holy a place for their kind – but they had other plans. They were clever; they brought torches and stole oil from the store house and set light to the chapel while we were still inside.'

Markus's voice cracked and tears welled up in his eyes at the memory. The other man's black orbs continued to stare intently, as if sucking the information out of Markus. Wiping the tears from his bloodstained cheeks, the priest felt compelled to continue.

'The old priest, Franko, soon fell to the smoke and fumes and I hid in the crypt. The smoke and flames followed me, though, and I thought I was trapped and would certainly die. Even if I could get past the flames the beastmen would cut me down as soon as they saw me. Then another's voice was in my head, talking to me. It was Sigmar, you see,' Markus insisted, 'guiding me, directing me, telling me an escape route. One of the tombs was false; pressing a hidden lever I opened the secret doorway within and stumbled down a long tunnel which took me away from the village.'

Estebar's face was a blank mask, but the priest pressed on in eager confession. 'When I hit the open air again I ran and ran, and almost died of exhaustion before I came to the count's castle. He sent an army of his men to harry the foul raiders while his daughter tended to my health. She was sweet and I would have loved her... had I not heard another's calling even stronger.'

Markus remembered that feeling, of salvation from the flames, and how his own faith had been fanned from a flickering spark into the raging fire of belief. Looking at Estebar he felt his fears subsiding.

'From that day on I swore I would return Sigmar's grace. I took up the robe and hammer in his name. That is the root of my faith and though I may flinch at your blows, it is still strong enough to thwart your masters.'

Markus stared at the dark warrior, the defiance rekindled in his eyes, expecting some petty retort that would seek to belittle his convictions again. None came. Estebar sat looking thoughtful for a moment, his hand toying absently with the sculpted pommel of his sword. The warrior looked around him again at the carnage, then cocked his head to one side a moment before the howl of wolves, closer this time, echoed through the heavy air. He looked to the west and frowned.

'Sundown is nearly upon us, and the time is fast approaching. Shall I tell you of saviours and debts? Of divine deliverance and holy missions?'

As he saw the longing in the Chaos warrior's eyes, Markus's lips formed a sneer. 'I do not need to hear your tale of treachery and weakness. You are less than nothing to me!'

Estebar waved dismissively, as if Markus was little more than an irritating insect, and sighed. 'Whatever.' He looked up at the rapidly darkening sky, his memory lost in a dim, distant time.

'My faith started much younger than yours, and I had not the choice you were offered. I was the eldest son of a wealthy merchant family in Nuln. I had a good education, lots of friends and powerful allies, and all this before I had seen fifteen summers! Life was good – probably too good, my later experiences have taught me. Chaos was the bane of my family too. I can see why you were brought to me now; we have at least that much in common. Behind the strong walls of Nuln we were safe from marauding beastmen, but another peril, one much more loathsome and insidious, awaited us.'

The warrior's dark eyes were sad, though a faint glimmer of a smile played about his lips for a moment and then faded. He sat down on Alayma again, more gently this time, and stared at the ground. Absentmindedly, he began to pull off his heavy gauntlets.

'A cult, dedicated to the Lord of Pleasure, enticed us into a trap. For all we knew, it was just another magnificent party, another event in a busy social calendar. However, they locked the doors after we had entered, and then the sacrifices began. I will not say what perverse fascinations went on there, for it would take too long and I have no wish to be found alone on this field when the stalkers of the night come running. However, let me say simply that one by one the guests were sacrificed to Slaanesh, until only a few of us, the youngest, remained. Obviously we were highly prized. Fate had other plans for me, though, and when the Reiksguard broke down the doors and smashed through the windows I thought I was saved. They slew the cultists and freed us, but I was never truly free again.'

The Chaos warrior fell silent for a moment, his gaze fixed on the withered, blood-soaked grass between his boots. Then he gave Markus a crooked smile.

'Slaanesh, Prince of Chaos, had already caught my soul without even asking for it! The warpstone incense burnt during the long ceremony took a grip on me. Slowly at first, I remember, my senses grew more powerful. I could see minute details on plants and animals, I could hear the whispers of my neighbours like the thunderclaps of a storm and the feel of the silken clothes in my wardrobe against my skin approached ecstasy.' Estebar stroked a hand through dead Alayma's flowing mane and shuddered, his lip quivering and his eyes rolled up for a moment. Then he snatched his hand back, as if taking control of himself, and his eyes narrowed dangerously.

Markus could see that the memories were not as pleasant as Estebar would like him to believe. Who could tell how much the young man had endured, half-possessed by an ancient, evil god, forced to follow the ways of darkness. Perhaps, Markus considered, Estebar was longing for an end to his curse. Mind whirling, the priest started formulating a plan that would save them both from damnation.

'There is no need for this agony to continue. Come with me and I will teach you the old path of Faith. You will learn again what it means to have your freedom,' he insisted.

Estebar did not seem to hear or want to listen; he was wholly wrapped up in his own past. Regaining his composure, he carried on with his tale.

'That was not all. My mind expanded also, giving me a pre-science, a foresight into the future. Combined with everything else, my life was full of pleasure. I endured the moment to every extent and could see the later pleasures that would follow at the same time. I wasted these skills at first, taking pleasure in women and feasting and drinking. I used my foresight to amass a fortune at the gambling tables.

'When the rich society had been exhausted, a conquest of perhaps seven or eight years, I looked to lower quarters for my entertainment. Slaanesh had me in its grip and every night for years I frequented the dockside taverns, challenging death with cut-throats and other scum for the sheer excitement and rush of blood.' The Chaos warrior sighed again.

'Then suddenly I was bored again. A wanderlust filled me, and I travelled wide, revelling in every new experience; a night under the stars, the feel of a hearty farmhouse daughter, the taste of exotic foods. Slowly, but with a subtle determination, I made my way northwards, through Kislev, and a few elegant dances at the Tzarina's court, up into the Troll country, ever onwards to the realm of the Lost and the Damned. I was Slaanesh's pawn and loved it. I travelled those nightmare regions until I stood before the Great Gate itself and begged Slaanesh to allow me to enter into the beautiful paradise that lies beyond.' Estebar looked up, his face made of steel. 'I was flung back far, scorned and ridiculed for my impudence. Entrance into that plane was not to be given lightly. I would have to buy my way in.'

Markus was shocked. The implication of the other's words were clear. 'You seek no redemption, you truly are happy in your chains. You are a greater fool than I realised to be held by such a weak lure. The only eternity worthwhile to strive for is in the embrace of Sigmar, not some unholy hell forged from a mad god's whims!' Then another realisation dawned on Markus and he eyed Estebar with renewed suspicion.

'Souls. You must pay a number of souls to the Ruinous Powers before they let you cross over, isn't that it?'

Estebar laughed loudly and for a long time. With an enthusiastic grin he nodded. 'Yes, yes! My dear Markus – but of course I know your name; how sharply your wits are honed!' The Chaos warrior smiled benevolently. 'But not any souls. Oh no, that would be far too easy. The souls I have claimed for Chaos, for I forswore Slaanesh as my sole patron, have been men of high standing, strong of courage and moral fibre like yourself.'

Markus was shocked. 'How can anybody willingly give themselves to Chaos? Even you are not guilty of that stupidity!'

Then another thought occurred to him: they hadn't gone willingly at all, they had been used and perverted by the same subtle power that Estebar was using on him right now. In the twilight, the Chaos lord seemed to swell. An aura played about his body, spilling through the air like a vapour. As Estebar spoke, Markus fancied he could feel the insubstantial tendrils of that vile aura reaching out to wrap around him too.

'Lord Sigmar, Father of the Empire, Shield of Mankind, protect me from evil…'

Estebar seemed to grow angry, his face twisted in a sneer, eyes boring deep into Markus's head. 'You will be my last soul! You will be mine! Guided by the Lord Tzeentch, I have slaughtered thousands just to bring you here. My precognition has waxed powerful over the years and I saw this day long ago. It is the day of my ultimate triumph. I could kill you now, swifter than a blink of your clouded eye, but only you can vouch your soul to my cause. Your soul will be given over to my lordly masters. As you take my place and serve them in this world, I, Estebar, the Master of Slaughter, bringer of despair to a hundred towns, will ascend to the glories of the Otherworld. It is written in my destiny. It will be so!'

ESTEBAR RELAXED his hands, which had been gripped in fists so tight a trickle of blood dripped from his palms where his nails had dug deep into the flesh. Taking a deep breath, he calmed himself.

'And yet, at the last, you still have a choice. Renounce your faith in Sigmar and I will depart to greater glories. Without me at its head, my army will fragment and scatter and the Empire will be safe. If you defy me, I will burn, torture and defile every man, woman and child between here and Altdorf searching for another who will fall before my grace.' He sighed. 'There is no point resisting, I will have another soul, so make it yours and you can save thousands of lives, end the torment and suffering and earn your own salvation. Just a simple nod or word is all I need.

'What does it feel like to be the saviour of the Empire, Markus?'

'Lord Sigmar, Father of the Empire, Shield of Mankind, protect me from evil...' the priest groaned.

Markus's prayers brought no solace. The fiend's subtle words were playing tricks with his mind. The bargain sounded so simple, and he did not doubt the truth of Estebar's pledge. Markus was confused, his mind travelling in circles. How could he tell if it was truly Sigmar who had saved him from the fire in the chapel? Could it have been the twisted Chaos Gods who had freed him so many years ago simply so that he would be here now? No doubt the plans of the Dark Powers were bold and only the test of time would see their fruition. Plans within plans, wheels within wheels spun in Markus's terrified mind. Summoning his mental strength he spat out his defiance, wrenching each word from the depths of his soul.

'I will... not... betray... my... lord!'

Estebar spoke again, his voice at its most subtle, sliding into Markus's consciousness and leaving its indelible mark. 'Thousands will live or die by your choice, yourself included. Whether you listen to your heart or your head, you have no real choice. Perhaps one day you will come to join me in Dark Paradise.'

Doubt crept into Markus's mind like an assassin. Perhaps he could claim his abandonment of Sigmar and thus save the Empire from the ravages of this madman, but in his heart remain true to his faith. Maybe Sigmar had been his saviour, for the very same reason that he alone could avert this catastrophe. Either way, the priest's past life took on a whole new meaning and many mysteries were now explained to him.

But what if that was but the first chink in the armour of his faith? Could he truly lie about what he believed? Was this the same path trodden by Estebar's past victims, believing themselves safe until they realised that they had lied one time too many and they were now damned? Could faith ever be feigned and would Estebar realise Markus's lack of sincerity?

As Markus wracked his brains for the right answer, the agonised yowling of some forest creature's final moments sounded across the darkness, followed by a series of monstrous roars. Estebar stood up and gazed towards the forest in the distance, pulling on his gloves.

'Make your choice quickly, priest. Other creatures more fell than wolves stalk this night. That is the cry of Khorne's hunters, the flesh hounds. I will make the choice simple for you. Even if you could free yourself you might not escape the swift chase of those daemon stalkers. You must have a symbol of your new allegiance to protect you from their ripping claws and savage jaws.'

Estebar stood and drew his sword from its scabbard once again. Startled, Markus was transfixed by the ill-forged blade. It was of the blackest metal, inscribed with golden runes that writhed under his gaze. For a brief moment, though, Markus could understand them; he could decipher the dire spells of cleaving and maiming that they embodied. The moment passed and they turned into evil but nonsensical sigils once again. Estebar thrust the sword blade down into the ground a foot to Markus's right, within easy reach. He plucked his cloak off the cold body of Markus's horse.

'Cut yourself free, priest, and you and thousands of your countrymen will live. Fulfil your destiny and take up the sword! Do not deny this; it has been written in fate since the stars were formed and the cursed sun first burned. Now I will leave you with your thoughts. Don't take too long or the choice will be made for you.'

With a bow of his head and one last regarding look, Estebar fastened his cloak again and strode away into the looming darkness of the early night.

For a long time Markus did not move, but lay with his eyes closed and listened to his own ragged breathing. There was no one else to convince but himself and he could not lie to his own heart, even if his head could be betrayed. Could he wield that twisted blade at all, even to cut himself free and still remain faithful to Sigmar? There was no guarantee that the sword would let him wield it without first swearing his allegiance to Chaos. There were tales of holy weapons that would burn the hands of the impure if they held them. Perhaps similar unholy weapons existed to test the faith of the impure. Markus was lost inside his own arguments.

A howl split the silence, and Markus imagined he could feel the padding of many huge clawed feet across the ground. The sound of bestial panting came out of the darkness. Markus opened his eyes.

The moon of Morrslieb, harbinger of Chaos, was rising over the night-shrouded forest. Silhouetted against that baneful orb was the grip of Estebar's sword. In the unearthly green glow of the Chaos moon, it looked to Markus for all the world like a hand reaching out to take him into the darkness.

Also from the Black Library

TROLLSLAYER
A Gotrek & Felix novel
by William King

HIGH ON THE HILL the scorched walled castle stood, a stone spider clutching the hilltop with blasted stone feet. Before the gaping maw of its broken gate hanged men dangled on gibbets, flies caught in its single-strand web.

'Time for some bloodletting,' Gotrek said. He ran his left hand through the massive red crest of hair that rose above his shaven tattooed skull. His nose chain tinkled gently, a strange counterpoint to his mad rumbling laughter.

'I am a slayer, manling. Born to die in battle. Fear has no place in my life.'

TROLLSLAYER IS THE first part of the death saga of Gotrek Gurnisson, as retold by his travelling companion Felix Jaeger. Set in the darkly gothic world of Warhammer, Trollslayer is an episodic novel featuring some of the most extraordinary adventures of this deadly pair of heroes. Monsters, daemons, sorcerers, mutants, orcs, beastmen and worse are to be found as Gotrek strives to achieve a noble death in battle. Felix, of course, only has to survive to tell the tale.

ISBN 0-671-78373-4 • March 2000

Also from the Black Library

SKAVENSLAYER
A Gotrek & Felix novel
by William King

'BEWARE! SKAVEN!' Felix shouted and saw them all reach for
their weapons. In moments, swords glittered in the half-
light of the burning city. From inside the tavern a number
of armoured figures spilled out into the gloom. Felix was
relieved to see the massive squat figure of Gotrek among
them. There was something enormously reassuring about
the immense axe clutched in the dwarf's hands.

'I see you found our scuttling little friends, manling,'
Gotrek said, running his thumb along the blade of his axe
until a bright red bead of blood appeared.

'Yes,' Felix gasped, struggling to get his breath back
before the combat began.

'Good. Let's get killing then!'

*SET IN THE MIGHTY city of Nuln, Gotrek and Felix are back in
SKAVENSLAYER, the second novel in this epic saga. Seeking
to undermine the very fabric of the Empire with their arcane
warp-sorcery, the skaven, twisted chaos rat-men, are at large
in the reeking sewers beneath the ancient city. Led by Grey
Seer Thanquol, the servants of the Horned Rat are
determined to overthrow this bastion of humanity. Against
such forces, what possible threat can just two hard-bitten
adventurers pose?*

ISBN 0-671-78385-8 • April 2000

Also from the Black Library

DAEMONSLAYER
A Gotrek & Felix novel
by William King

THE ROAR WAS so loud and so terrifying that Felix almost
dropped his blade. He looked up and fought the urge to
soil his britches. The most frightening thing he had ever
seen had entered the hall and behind it he could see the
leering heads of beastmen.

As he gazed on the creature in wonder and terror, Felix
thought: this is the incarnate nightmare which has
bedevilled my people since time began.

'Just remember,' Gotrek said from beside him, 'the
daemon is mine!'

*FRESH FROM THEIR adventures battling the foul servants of the
rat-god in Nuln, Gotrek and Felix are now ready to join an
expedition northwards in search of the long-lost dwarf hall of
Karag Dum. Setting forth for the hideous Realms of Chaos in
an experimental dwarf airship, Gotrek and Felix are sworn to
succeed or die in the attempt. But greater and more sinister
energies are coming into play, as a daemonic power is
awoken to fulfil its ancient, deadly promise.*

ISBN 0-671-78389-0 • May 2000

Also from the Black Library

INTO THE MAELSTROM

An anthology of Warhammer 40,000 stories, edited by Marc Gascoigne & Andy Jones

'THE CHAOS ARMY had travelled from every continent, every shattered city, every ruined sector of Illium to gather on this patch of desert that had once been the control centre of the Imperial Garrison. The sand beneath their feet had been scorched, melted and fused by a final, futile act of suicidal defiance: the detonation of the garrison's remaining nuclear stockpile.' – **Hell in a Bottle** *by Simon Jowett*

'HOARSE SCREAMS and the screech of tortured hot metal filled the air. Massive laser blasts were punching into the spaceship. They superheated the air that men breathed, set fire to everything that could burn and sent fireballs exploding through the crowded passageways.' – **Children of the Emperor** *by Barrington J. Bayley*

IN THE GRIM and gothic nightmare future of Warhammer 40,000, mankind teeters on the brink of extinction. INTO THE MAELSTROM is a storming collection of a dozen action-packed science fiction short stories set in this dark and brooding universe.

ISBN 0-671-78386-6 • April 2000

Also from the Black Library

FIRST & ONLY
A Gaunt's Ghosts novel
by Dan Abnett

'THE TANITH ARE strong fighters, general, so I have heard.'
The scar tissue of his cheek pinched and twitched slightly,
as it often did when he was tense. 'Gaunt is said to be a
resourceful leader.'

  'You know him?' The general looked up, questioningly
  'I know *of* him sir. In the main by reputation.'

GAUNT GOT TO his feet, wet with blood and Chaos pus. His
Ghosts were moving up the ramp to secure the position.
Above them, at the top of the elevator shaft, were over a
million Shriven, secure in their bunker batteries. Gaunt's
expeditionary force was inside, right at the heart of the
enemy stronghold. Commissar Ibram Gaunt smiled.

*IT IS THE nightmare future of Warhammer 40,000, and
mankind teeters on the brink of extinction. The galaxy-
spanning Imperium is riven with dangers, and in the Chaos-
infested Sabbat system, Imperial Commissar Gaunt must lead
his men through as much in-fighting amongst rival regiments
as against the forces of Chaos. FIRST AND ONLY is an
epic saga of planetary conquest, grand ambition,
treachery and honour.*

ISBN 0-671-78375-0 • March 2000

Also from the Black Library

EYE OF TERROR
A Warhammer 40,000 novel
by Barrington J. Bayley

Tell the truth only if a lie will not serve

'WHAT I HAVE to tell you,' Abaddas said, in slow measured tones, 'will be hard for you to accept or even comprehend. The rebellion led by Warmaster Horus succeeded. The Emperor is dead, killed by Horus himself in single combat, though Horus too died of his injuries.'

Magron groaned. He cursed himself for having gone into suspended animation. To be revived in a galaxy without the Emperor! Horrible! Unbelievable! Impossible to bear! Stricken, he looked into Abaddas's flinty grey eyes. 'Who is Emperor now?'

The first hint of an emotional reaction flickered on Abaddas's face. 'What need have we of an Emperor?' he roared. 'We have the Chaos gods!'

IN THE DARK and gothic future of Warhammer 40,000, mankind teeters on the brink of extinction. As the war-fleets of the Imperium prepare to launch themselves on a crusade into the very heart of Chaos, Rogue Trader Maynard Rugolo seeks power and riches on the fringe worlds of this insane and terrifying realm.

ISBN 0-671-78390-4 • June 2000

Also from the Black Library

SPACE WOLF
A Warhammer 40,000 novel
by William King

RAGNAR LEAPT UP from his hiding place, bolt pistol spitting death. The nightgangers could not help but notice where he was, and with a mighty roar of frenzied rage they raced towards him. Ragnar answered their war cry with a wolfish howl of his own, and was reassured to hear it echoed back from the throats of the surrounding Blood Claws. He pulled the trigger again and again as the frenzied mass of mutants approached, sending bolter shell after bolter shell rocketing into his targets. Ragnar laughed aloud, feeling the full battle rage come upon him. The beast roared within his soul, demanding to be unleashed.

IN THE GRIM future of Warhammer 40,000, the Space Marines of the Adeptus Astartes are humanity's last hope. On the planet Fenris, young Ragnar is chosen to be inducted into the noble yet savage Space Wolves chapter. But with his ancient primal instincts unleashed by the implanting of the sacred Canis Helix, Ragnar must learn to control the beast within and fight for the greater good of the wolf pack.

ISBN 0-671-78399-8 • July 2000